THE
ONLY GOOD
LAWYER

Other John Cuddy novels by Jeremiah Healy

Blunt Darts
The Staked Goat
So Like Sleep
Swan Dive
Yesterday's News
Right to Die
Shallow Graves
Foursome
Act of God
Rescue
Invasion of Privacy

Published by POCKET BOOKS

JEREMIAH HEALY

A JOHN FRANCIS CUDDY MYSTERY

THE ONLY GOOD LAWYER

POCKET BOOKS
New York   London   Toronto   Sydney   Tokyo   Singapore

POCKET BOOKS, a division of Simon & Schuster Inc.
1230 Avenue of the Americas, New York, NY 10020

ISBN: 0-671-00953-2

First Pocket Books hardcover printing March 1998

10 9 8 7 6 5 4 3 2 1

In memory of Dario J. Azzone and Howard E. Greene

Prologue

WOODROW WILSON GANT just loved the way his BMW 530i held the road.

And doing fifty on a dry, snaky pavement at night was better than hitting eighty on some straightaway Interstate in broad daylight. He especially enjoyed this little stretch as it wound through probably the longest section of tree-lined valley in the whole city of Boston. Woodrow'd say to his friends, black or white, "Hey, man, you close your fists on the wheel—that nice leather wrap like they put around a good tennis racket?—and you can feel the power, surging from the engine right into your body."

Feel the power. That was what Woodrow remembered after graduating law school and starting with the district attorney's office. No more living at home with his mother and brother, and the first African-American to prosecute a homicide case in that suburban county's old-timey courthouse. But as a city-boy at heart—funny, Woodrow didn't mind using "boy" in that context—he missed Boston. So, when the time came to move on from the D.A., Woodrow joined Mr. Neely's fine little downtown firm in its fine little office building close by the waterfront. And he felt the power again.

Different kind of power, though, because it was a different kind of practice. He'd had his fill of criminals and cops, sharing office space with an asshole and his bed with a wife didn't understand his needs. Now Woodrow Wilson Gant was single again and a divorce lawyer—what the bar association liked to call a "domestic relations attorney." And the power was the weight of money, not the threat of prison. Enough money for him to live in a fancy condo and wear fancy clothes, buy a fancy car and enjoy fancy ladies.

Just then the lady of the moment in the passenger bucket next to him snorted. Or snored, Woodrow wasn't exactly sure which. The big blond hair was all you could really see, what with the shades still on so nobody'd recognize her. One reason they'd gone back to that Vietnamese place Deborah first took him to. You're an assistant D.A. coordinating gang prosecutions, you realize pretty soon that witnesses of Color-A have a hell of a time identifying defendants of Color-B. Used to be a real problem for Woodrow back in the courtroom. Now he could use it to his advantage.

The woman made the noise again, head lolling on the whiplash protector, hand banging against his cellular phone in the console between them. Drunk as a skunk, and on chardonnay, yet. Woodrow knew it was the alcohol content and not the color of the liquid that mattered, but you still had to wonder why white women drink white wine if they can't hold the stuff.

The BMW entered one of the few straight portions of the road. Even with so many curves, though, it was the shortest distance between the restaurant and Woodrow's condo. All things considered, he'd rather take his pleasure at her place— so he could just leave when they were finished? But Woodrow understood better than most why her situation at home made that more than a bit dicey.

So, enjoy the ride in your fancy car before enjoying the ride in your fancy bed.

Woodrow had cracked the front windows a few inches because the lady said she was feeling a little woozy leaving the restaurant, and he didn't want her getting sick on the leather upholstery he'd just had cleaned at the car wash that day. Woodrow kind of liked the crisp October air flowing by his cheeks—not to mention that nice hum of the Beemer's tires over the macadam—only the breeze seemed to put the woman to sleep more than sober her up.

Probably best not to shoot for a doubleheader tonight. Just once over the moon and take her downstairs afterward, stick her ass in a cab. At least a thirty-dollar fare for the trip back to the lady's place, but that'd be better than having to drive her there yourself, listen to the complaining once her wine wore off.

And besides, it's only money, and once "Ms. Barber" gets back to you, Woodrow Wilson Gant, Esquire, will be keeping a lot more—

The sharp bang of the blowout made him jump, the shoulder strap of his seat belt yanking his torso short like a parachute harness. Through the open driver's window, Woodrow's left ear registered what seemed a crumping echo of his tire's sound coming off the hillside across the road. Wrestling the steering wheel against the skid, he was able to bring the BMW to a shuddering, humping stop against the grass sloping down at the right of the pavement.

Woodrow drew in a breath, realized he needed a couple more. Taking his hands off the wheel, he could see them shaking in silhouette against the dull glow from the dashboard gauges. Woodrow glanced past the woman and out her window.

Thanks be to God you weren't doing sixty. Even this fine machine would've sent your ass into the gully down there.

Woodrow nudged the woman's left arm. "Hey?" He nudged her again. "Hey, man, you awake?"

Just a ragged snore.

Under his breath, Woodrow said, "You got to wonder, is a little sexual healing worth all this?"

Then, remembering how her body accommodated him, he decided it was.

3

Woodrow opened the driver's side door, the BMW's courtesy lights wrecking his night vision. As he stepped onto the pavement, he could feel the twinge from his bad left knee and a breeze blowing across his face from the front of the car. Except for the courtesy and running lights, everything was midnight dark. Raising his head and blinking, Woodrow could make out stars and a little sliver of moon, like somebody had clipped a toenail and hung it up in the sky. Reflexively, he reached back into the Beemer and activated the emergency flashers, then tried to remember if he'd ever seen any other cars, all the times he'd driven this road at night.

No, too desolate. People'd be afraid of breaking down and getting stranded.

Slamming the driver's side door, Woodrow walked back to his left rear tire. The pulsating glow from the flank lights was enough to see the bad news. Flat as a pancake, must have gone over one motherfucking piece of rubber-tearing shit.

Across the dark road, he heard a rustling sound, some kind of creature working its way down the hillside through the brush. Woodrow looked to the left, blinking some more, but couldn't see anything beyond thirty feet from his lighted car. Probably just a raccoon. People wouldn't think you'd have raccoons in a city like Boston, but with the Charles River and other water running through it, they could survive, even thrive. In fact, Woodrow knew personally of a lady woke up during the night with a raccoon on her fire escape, those demon-red eyes staring in through the bedroom window, scaring the hell out of her.

The memory of that lady's experience made Woodrow laugh, and that calmed his mind some. Momma always counseled her sons to look on the bright side of things. Well, it wasn't a front tire, so he hadn't pivoted and maybe rolled into a vehicular homicide. And Woodrow knew the spare in the trunk was solid because he'd had the dealer check it the last time they'd rotated the tires.

Be good not to have anybody else see you with this woman, but you sure as shit are not about to get down on your hands and knees in this fancy suit to change a flat. And besides, what's a guy in a towtruck gonna know about who she is? *Nada*, right?

So, pick up your cell phone, and call the Triple-A.

The rustling sound from across the road was getting louder, which meant the raccoon or whatever was getting closer. Woodrow suddenly remembered another story, one he'd read in the newspaper. About how a lot of raccoons were carrying rabies.

Maybe it was time to get back in the Beemer, make your call from the safety of a strong metal box.

Woodrow turned to step toward the driver's side door. Then the breeze shifted from the front of the car to the rear, and he got his first whiff of gasoline.

Mother-*fuck*-er.

Forgetting about raccoons and rabies, Woodrow moved quickly around to the back bumper, the smell growing stronger. He bent down, his bad knee protesting, and looked through the strobing of his hazard lights. Something was dribbling out from near the right wheel.

Woodrow touched a finger to the pool of liquid on the ground, but his nose confirmed what it was before he'd brought the finger halfway to his face.

Which made no sense, none whatsoever. How the fuck do you get a leak in your gas tank from a flat tire? Even if whatever it was caused the puncture kicked up from the road, how could it be going fast enough to penetrate—

The sound of brush parting and crunching footsteps across the road made Woodrow stand up abruptly, the knee now screaming at him for it. His eyes must be going, too, because he surely couldn't understand what they were telling him.

A human figure, dressed in a bulky parka, was clumping toward Woodrow and his fine machine. Both hands were in the pockets of the coat, the hood up and tugged low enough that it shielded the face. But there was something familiar, too. About the walk or . . . something.

"Car trouble?" said the figure, still approaching.

The voice placed the walk for Woodrow, but that didn't help

him understand things any better. "What are you doing out here?"

For an answer, the figure stopped about ten feet away, a hand sliding from one of the pockets. The hand had a shiny leather glove on it, but in his car's flank lights, Woodrow caught a different kind of reflection.

The glint of blued metal.

"Hey, man?"

"You betrayed me, Woodrow."

"Wait, wait. We can—"

The first shot struck just above the belt, ratcheting Woodrow's rear end up in the air as it brought his shoulders folding downward. Both of Woodrow's hands clasped his stomach, the blood already running freely between the fingers and onto his pants.

Hunched, he looked up at the figure, some pain beginning to filter through the shock of the impact. "No, please—"

The second bullet hit Woodrow high on the left shoulder, turning him, almost spinning him, away from the hooded figure. Woodrow tried to make his legs work—like from the football drills back in high school? Drive and lift and stride, but between the bad knee and the wounds, all he could manage was a lurching shuffle toward the grass at the right-hand side of the road.

The third bullet punched Woodrow squarely in the back, shattering a vertebra and ripping through his heart. He dropped like a rag doll, face first and turned toward the BMW, the upper half of his body in the grass, the lower half still on the pavement.

A last thought crossed his brain. "My fancy car . . . What's gonna happen to . . . ?"

The hooded figure moved quickly to the fallen man, squatting down to watch the light of life fade from the eyes. Having Woodrow Wilson Gant die here was consistent with the plan, but being close enough to see that glazing effect in the pupils was also more . . . satisfying as well.

Standing again, the hooded figure breathed three times.

Deeply and slowly, in through the nose and out through the mouth, to regain complete control of all body parts after the adrenaline rush of taking another's life.

And, with luck, not even the last for this night, either.

The figure moved very steadily to the passenger side of the BMW. It was important that the woman not have heard the brief exchange with Gant, not be able to remember a voice or even a speech pattern.

If she did, the plan would have to be changed, and she would have to be killed, too.

But no, no worry of that. The woman was dead drunk, as she'd appeared when the vehicle's courtesy lights had come on a few minutes before, as she'd appeared those other times when—

The woman began to stir, though her eyes remained closed. The hooded figure hesitated only a moment, then decided to follow through on the original plan, just without using the car door.

After redundantly wiping the outside of the revolver against the parka's material, the figure slipped the weapon through the partially open side window, allowing the gun to drop so that it landed in the woman's lap.

At which point the hooded figure ducked down below window level and scuttled, crablike, to the rear of the BMW. Moving diagonally away from the woman in the passenger's seat, the figure recrossed the road and began climbing back up the hillside.

To retrieve the rifle used to shoot out the tire and return to the car hidden over the ridge.

Somewhere in the dream, the cute male flight attendant stumbled, dropping an anchor right into her lap.

An anchor. Just what she needed, after all the bumps and banging noises on this airplane already. Her first real vacation in years, all by herself to the Caribbean without any cares, any responsibilities. But despite paying for a first-class ticket, the flight was bumpy and the engines were making all these banging noises and then the attendant has to drop . . .

Wait a minute. I took an airplane, not a cruise ship. What's an anchor doing on a 747?

She opened her eyes then, and at first thought she'd somehow wandered into the cockpit of the airplane, because she was staring out a windshield. Like the pilot would, you know? There wasn't much light, and she couldn't see any clouds or anything, just some trees and a hood, some gauges and a door. . . .

A door? A car door. Woodrow's BMW.

Oh, shit. She shook her head, clearing it of the airplane dream. Right, right. Only . . . "Where the hell are we?"

She turned her face to the left. "I said, where are . . . ?" But Woodrow wasn't behind the wheel, and the action of swiveling her head triggered a wave of nausea, just like she felt after that goddamn Vietnamese meal. With the six-dollar chardonnay they marked up to twelve. And that gucky soup, the . . .

Now, thinking about all the disgusting food, she felt more sick.

Handkerchief. Handbag.

She dug into the main compartment of the bag till she found a hankie. Even before she held it up to her mouth, however, the gag reflex started.

Have to get out of here.

Yanking the door handle while holding the hankie, she realized her seat belt was still on. With the knuckles of her left hand, she struck the button that releases the metal tab, sensing the belt itself retract but without taking the strap of her handbag with it.

Aspirin in the bag, too. Make me feel better. After.

She bashed the door open with her shoulder and swung her legs out of the BMW, feeling something heavy slide off her lap and onto the ground. The anchor, of course.

Only it wasn't an anchor. In the light from the car's interior, she could see it was a gun, lying on the grass. A gun like . . .

God, no. "Woodrow?"

She struggled to a standing position, the ground under the

grass sloping down, giving her vertigo. Which made everything else so much worse, both in her stomach and in her head.

"Woodrow?" Oh, God, no. Please, no. "Woodrow, where are you?"

I'm going to be sick.

She took two steps down the slope and slid onto her rear end, expecting to throw up into the grass to her left. But all she could manage was the dry heaves.

The gun. He didn't . . . couldn't have. Even he's not that stupid.

Regaining some control, she called out again. "Woodrow?" Please, God, where is he? "Woodrow?"

She struggled to her feet again, turning toward the back of the car.

And saw Woodrow Wilson Gant's lifeless eyes staring at the right rear tire.

"Oh, God, no!"

He did it. He really did.

I have to . . . Have to get as far from here as . . .

She began running along the side of the road. Away from the BMW and the restaurant miles behind it.

Running into the night.

Stumbling to the ground.

Then staggering up and running some more.

And dropping down intentionally only when she'd see another car's headlights coming up the road toward her.

Chapter 1

IN MY OPINION, it had been a tough year for the neighborhood Boston calls "Back Bay." Our only family drugstore, a fixture opposite the Lenox Hotel for decades, closed after three discount giants bunched around it like Davy Crockett's shot pattern. A candy store on Newbury Street also left, thereby eliminating the irony of the diet center occupying the retail space directly beneath it. And the Exeter Street Theatre building had suffered a devastating fire, nearly destroying one of the city's most upscale landmarks.

Concepts like "upscale" and "landmark" struck me all the more that Tuesday morning as I climbed the stairs of Steven Rothenberg's building, the elevator broken again. You couldn't call the structure that contained his law office anything but a dump, especially with one of its neighbors already torn down, leaving a gap like a punched-out tooth in that block of Boylston Street.

I'd first met Rothenberg a few years back, when he represented an African-American college student named William Daniels. The student was accused of killing his white girlfriend, and I was helping out as a favor for a black lieutenant in the Boston Homicide Unit. Since then, Rothenberg had hired me to do the private investigator work on a number of criminal matters. This time around, he'd left a message with my answering service the afternoon before, asking me to drop by the next day.

I reached Rothenberg's floor and, after a turn, the office suite he shared with half a dozen other sole practitioners. The lawyers' names were done individually on horizontal slats of wood stacked vertically to the side of the doorjamb. Each slat had been lettered by a different engraver on differently grained wood, a xylophone designed by committee. I thought a few of the names might have changed since the last time I'd been there, but Steve's was still in the same place.

Inside the front door, a young female receptionist with orangeade hair cut in a shingled pattern typed on a desktop computer. Angled away from me, she wore little earphones, the wire running down out of sight. She might have been listening to an old dictation machine or a new Walkman. Given the way she was rocking her head, I put my money on the latter.

Coming up on her blind side, I said, "Excuse me?"

She twisted around and, in a practiced way, used her left index finger to flick the earphone behind her ear for a moment. Even from four feet away, I could hear techno-rock music.

"John Cuddy to see Steve Rothenberg."

She held up the index finger in a "Wait one" way and tapped a couple of buttons on the telephone console before saying, "Steve, a John . . ." She looked up at me.

"Cuddy."

"Right. A John . . . Oh, okay." She put the earphone back in place. "Third door."

"Thanks."

Steve Rothenberg appeared at his office threshold, which meant he was more anxious to see me than I was to begin running the meter. Inside, his furniture was still kind of shabby, the upholstered seats on the client chairs looking like somebody had shined them. Rothenberg let the coat-tree handle his suit jacket, the dress shirt he wore rolled twice to the elbows, the tie tugged down from an unbuttoned collar, even at nine-thirty on a cool October day. His beard looked trimmed, but what was left of the salt-and-pepper hair had grown a little shaggy.

"Your barber out of town, Steve?"

"Yeah."

"Maybe you should try somebody else."

"No." Rothenberg waved me to one of the client chairs before sinking into his own behind a cluttered desk, some veneer peeling at the corners. "No, I'd rather have it be long for a couple of weeks than wrong for a couple of months."

"Makes sense." Sitting down, though, I thought his hair-cutting schedule pretty much matched the office decor. "How can I help you?"

Rothenberg picked up a pencil, fiddling with it. "Are you still dating that A.D.A.?"

Nancy Meagher, an assistant district attorney for Suffolk County and the first woman I'd felt anything for since my wife, Beth, had died of cancer. "I'm still seeing Nancy, Steve. So if she's your direct opponent in whatever—"

"She's not, but . . ." Rothenberg looked at his window, a pie-wedge of the Boston Common showing through the pane. "You were out of town last week, right?"

"Out of state, actually." Rothenberg was being oblique, and oblique never made anything easier. "Steve, can we maybe cut to the car chase here?"

He tossed his pencil onto the desk. "John, I've got Alan Spaeth."

The name rang a bell. "Who is . . . ?"

"The defendant in the Woodrow Gant case."

I felt a tightening in my chest. Even from three hundred miles away, I knew that the shooting of the prosecutor-cum-divorce-attorney had rocked Boston the prior week. The police arrested the husband of a woman Gant had been representing. After returning to the city, I'd gently asked Nancy if she'd known Gant. She said that though he'd prosecuted for another county, she'd met him once, then changed the subject.

Understandably, I'd thought. Some things are harder to think about than others.

Rothenberg said, "John?"

I started to rise. "Good luck with Mr. Spaeth."

"Wait, please. Alan needs an investigator."

"Steve—"

"John, hear me out?"

I stayed standing. "The victim's a former A.D.A. and—what, the third divorce attorney in two years shot by—"

"—allegedly shot by—"

"—an enraged husband."

"You don't have to tell me." Rothenberg lowered his voice. "But please, John. Spot me ten minutes, then you can leave, you still want to."

Given Nancy's job, and sensibilities, I didn't see him convincing me. On the other hand, he'd sent a good deal of business my way over the years, and loyalty entitled Rothenberg to the chance.

I sat back down. "Ten minutes, and counting."

"You didn't recognize my client's name, you don't know that I was already representing him against his wife."

Rothenberg was right. "I thought you did strictly criminal?"

"Mostly, but I don't want to do it forever." A weak smile. "And besides, this economic climate, you have to diversify."

Under the circumstances, not funny. "Nine minutes, Steve."

The weak smile disappeared. "Okay. The bad news first. A couple of months ago, Gant was taking Alan's deposition in the divorce case when my client went ballistic. Screamed and yelled in Gant's conference room and all the way out the door."

"Did Spaeth threaten him?"

"Expressly. In the hearing of half a dozen witnesses and using the 'N'-word."

I remembered Gant had been African-American. "How about the murder weapon?"

"Left at the crime scene."

"Fingerprints?"

"Not on the revolver itself, but yes on the shells in the cylinder."

I felt like standing up again. "Spaeth's prints were on the shells?"

"Afraid so. Probably his gun, too."

"Probably?"

"Alan says he filed the serial numbers off one of his firearms, but it was stolen."

One of his firearms. "So, Spaeth stole the gun, then—"

"No, no. Alan claims he bought the thing years ago on a trip—to one of those states where you don't have to show much?—then he wiped the numbers, and thereafter it was stolen from his room."

"His room?"

"At the boardinghouse he'd been living in."

"Stolen how long ago?"

"Four weeks before the murder."

Convenient.

Rothenberg read something in my face. "John, Alan says that's the reason he moved out of the rooming house, because he thought the owner of the place had stolen his piece."

"Moved to where?"

"An apartment, three or four blocks away." Rothenberg paused. "Part of the good news is that Alan's alibi will also confirm the business about somebody stealing the gun."

"Spaeth has an alibi witness?"

"Yeah, one of the other men who lived in the boardinghouse."

"Steve, I don't remember hearing about that on the news."

Spreading his fingertips, Rothenberg combed the beard with his nails. "He hasn't come forward yet."

I closed my eyes. "Meaning neither you nor the police know where the guy is."

"John, I won't lie to you. Our alibi witness is a drinking buddy of Alan's. He could be anywhere, but we need to find him."

I opened my eyes. "You need to find him, Steve."

Rothenberg clasped his hands on the desk. "I said I wouldn't lie to you, John. I won't try to kid you, either. Alan Spaeth was a miserable son of a bitch through most of the divorce case. But we pretty much had it settled—house to the wife, my client to absorb their son's future college costs, if any. We even distributed some of the money from the marital estate to both spouses."

I thought about it. "Kind of reduces Spaeth's motive to kill Gant."

"Exactly. In fact, I thought Alan'd finally adjusted to the situation, had 'let go of his wife,' as I've heard the shrinks call it. He used some of the money to move to an apartment, start looking for a new job—"

"New job?"

"He'd been laid off, before the marriage broke up. One of the reasons it did." Rothenberg changed his tone. "John, my client's been made to look like a pariah, especially given our rash of divorce-attorney killings. And because this one was done execution-style, I have to show the jury a somebody else who might have wanted to shoot Gant. Now the man had an ex-wife himself, plus a real questionable brother. And he even prosecuted gang members once upon a time."

"Steve—"

Rothenberg raised his right hand, palm toward me. "All I'm saying is that if we can bring forward Alan's alibi witness, my version of the story becomes a lot more salable."

"Your version."

"It's my client's version, too."

"That a 'somebody else' set him up with his own gun?"

"Do me a favor, John?"

"What?"

"Talk to Alan before you make up your mind about taking the case."

I gave it a beat. "Why should I, Steve?"

Rothenberg stared down at his desk. "Because he's convinced me."

The old Suffolk County jail had been called simply "Charles Street," a brown-and-yellow stone monstrosity erected when

Americans wearing blue and gray uniforms were still killing each other. Inside, the architecture would have reminded you of a five-story birdcage with the decibel level of a nineteenth-century asylum.

The new jail—on Nashua Street—was a soaring seven stories of brick on about two acres of land, with razor wire around the parking lot. The sheriff who finally got the county to build it had to go through a couple of Supreme Court appeals before receiving permission to double-bunk the inmates, but he also included things like a weight room on the second floor and an open-air recreation deck for basketball on the fourth, with wire mesh enclosing the court to prevent the loss of both bouncing balls and footloose players.

Inside the main entrance, the lobby held three rows of black wire chairs for visitors and a bank of orange, hexagonal lockers for their belongings. Steve Rothenberg had called ahead, and after a deputy in a powder-blue shirt stamped the back of my hand with invisible ink, a sergeant took me up in the elevator, making small talk about the fine weather and the New England Patriots and how he wished the architect for Nashua Street hadn't included so many different colors for the building's walls because six years later it was a bitch to keep track of all the paints for touch-up work. No mention of any angry husbands killing their wives' divorce lawyers, which was fine with me.

Exiting the elevator, the sergeant led me along a corridor to an attorney-client consulting room. Its interior was maybe eight feet square, with a butcher-block table and caned chairs on each side, a distinct improvement over the wire jobs in the lobby downstairs.

"Your guy will come through the trap there," the sergeant said, gesturing toward the door on the other side of the desk. "I have to tell you not to pass him anything?"

"No."

The sergeant pointed to what looked like a light switch. "This here's a confidentiality switch. You push it over, our audio-surveillance of the room stops."

"Thanks."

He pointed again. "Panic button, in case the guy gives you any trouble."

"He been any trouble?"

The sergeant gave me a deadpan expression. "Not since he showered yesterday."

I sat down as the trap to the corridor closed behind me, wondering if I'd know what that was supposed to mean.

One look at Alan Spaeth, and I knew what it meant.

He said, "You're the investigator Steve Rothenberg called me about, right?"

"Right." We shook hands. "John Cuddy."

"And you're wondering where I got this, too."

Spaeth put an index finger to his left eye, the purple-and-ocher blotch of a shiner not quite closing it, the knuckles on both hands bruised and scabbed. Standing, Spaeth was about six feet in plastic shoes, maybe a hundred-ninety under the one-piece jumpsuit with no pockets. Only late thirties, his unshaven cheeks were already jowls and sagging a little loosely, as though jail chow wasn't agreeing with him. He had a wide, greedy mouth, and a nose that showed more nostrils than bridge. His hair was black and curly to the point of clotted, despite yesterday's "shower."

I said, "What happened?"

Spaeth grinned cruelly, though he must have hurt the eye area some to do it. "End of the housing unit, we got five showers. Five for all fifty of us in there. When it was my turn yesterday, one nigger thought he was tough decided to whale on me account of he heard I killed this nigger lawyer." A grunt. "He found out I was tougher."

"Three's the charm, Spaeth."

A confused expression. "What?"

"You've used the 'N'-word twice. I hear it a third time, and you'll be sitting by yourself."

"Hey, sport, who the fuck's paying the tab here?"

"Steve Rothenberg, if I decide to help him with this case."

Spaeth chewed on that. Literally, from the way his jowls worked. Then his chin dropped to his chest. "Look, this thing's got me all screwed up. I don't like what I'm learning about 'jailing' here, and so I'm showing off, trying not to act . . . scared. But I am." Spaeth's head came back up. "Christ, I'm scared shitless."

A little twinge in my gut. "Okay. Here's the deal. I'm talking to you because Steve asked me to. You tell me your side of things, and I go back to him with whether or not I'm on board. Clear?"

Alan Spaeth straightened some in his chair, the bruised hands folding themselves on the butcher block. "Clear."

"Where do we start?"

"How about with, I didn't kill the bastard."

"I heard you threatened to."

"What, at his law firm?"

"If that was the only time."

Spaeth raked a hand through his hair. "Look, you're talking August, all right? Over two months ago. I was going through a tough time. I mean, Gant's representing Nicole—my wife?"

I nodded.

"And he got this 'vacate the marital home' order against me. Well, the company had laid me off from my marketing job like three weeks before, so I had to go live in a boardinghouse. Try to imagine that, sport. One day I'm coming home to this nice place in West Roxbury I sweated blood to carry, and the next I'm sleeping with the fucking derelicts in Southie."

South Boston. "I grew up there."

Spaeth put the hand to his face this time. "Christ, I'm not doing such a good job of getting you on my side."

Truth to tell, he wasn't. And yet . . . "That day at his law firm, did you threaten to kill Woodrow Gant?"

A nod before letting his hand fall back to the table. "In front of like, I don't know, six, seven people. I really made my fucking point." Spaeth looked up at me. "But you gotta understand, he was fucking me over the coals, and he was fucking . . ." Spaeth trailed off, shaking his head. "Fucking me every way from Sunday. Poisoning Terry against me, too."

"Terry's your son?"

"Yeah, Terence, actually, after Nicole's father. She got custody—so Terry could stay in the house and keep with the same school. Not the school where she teaches, that's not . . . That's not important. What is important is that Gant tells Terry, 'Look, your father has visitation rights, but that doesn't mean you have to see him.' The kid's fourteen, so the judge leaves it up to him, but meanwhile Gant's poisoning my own son against me."

Sounded like more motive, not less. "Back to that day at the law firm. What exactly happened?"

Spaeth blew out a breath. "I go in, because Rothenberg tells me they can take my 'deposition,' ask me a lot of questions under oath. So we're sitting around this table in a conference room—like where we are here, only a lot bigger and nicer, view of the harbor and all. And Gant's needling me, really tucking it under the saddle with his questions."

"Like what?"

"Oh, I don't mean the words themselves. Hell, a couple weeks later, Steve gave me this copy of the thing—a 'transcript'?"

"Right."

"Okay, so I read the transcript, and from Gant's words, you don't get what he was doing. He was too fucking smooth. No, it was more his . . . like facial expressions, and—what's the word? 'Inflection,' yeah. The inflection of his voice. Gant was needling me, and I blew my stack. I said the only good lawyer, like the only good . . ." Spaeth stopped.

"That word I've heard enough of."

"Yeah." A sniff, almost a good-natured laugh. "Yeah, I called him that and more, storming out of the conference room yelling . . . yelling I don't remember exactly what. But I know I said if he kept it up, I was gonna kill him."

"Kept what up?"

Spaeth stopped. "Fucking me over."

Something didn't feel right. "But Steve told me things settled pretty soon after that."

"They did. That's what I mean about not killing the bastard. The divorce was basically over with. And lawyers are a dime a dozen. Even if I did shoot Gant, Nicole would've just gotten herself another one."

Thinking about what kind of witness this defendant would make, I shook my head.

"What's the matter?"

"Nothing," I said. "Let's go back to the murder weapon. Your gun?"

Spaeth started to say something, then just, "I don't know."

"You don't know?"

"Look, I haven't seen it, all right? The revolver the cops say got used. I do know I had one just like it, a Taurus 85. I bought the thing on a business trip in the South, filed the serial number off it."

"Why the hell did you do that?"

"I read in the paper about the 'Castle Law' we got here—where the state lets you off if you kill a guy coming into your house? Only the newspaper said the guy would have to be trying to kill you, so I figured, anybody ever broke in and I shot him with one of the guns I bought up here, it'd be nice to have a throwaway piece for the cops to find on the guy."

Alan Spaeth kept getting better and better. "How many other firearms do you have?"

"When I was living in the 'marital home,' three more hand-guns and two rifles. I used to take Terry deer hunting until all this shit hit the fan."

"Where are these other weapons now?"

"Locked away in storage, along with most of my stuff from the West Roxbury place."

"But you kept the throwaway piece?"

"Brought it to the boardinghouse, yeah. For protection, understand? Only the Taurus got stolen from my room. One of the reasons I moved out. Fucking owner of the place had a thing against guns, and I figured Dufresne was the one who took it."

"Dufresne being the owner."

"Yeah. 'Vincennes Dufresne,' the little frog fuck."

I let that one pass. "Whether it was your weapon or not, the shells in the cylinder had your prints on them."

2 1

"Steve told me my prints weren't on the Taurus itself, though. You think I'm stupid enough to wipe my prints off the gun and not off the bullets?"

"Happens all the time."

"And then leave the thing by Gant's car?"

Stupider still, granted. "How would somebody get shells with your prints on them if it wasn't your gun?"

Spaeth looked at me hard with the good eye. "That's why I think it was my Taurus, sport. And my shells in it. Somebody set me up."

"Dufresne?"

A stop. "No, that doesn't make sense."

I felt the twinge again. "Who, then?"

"If I knew that, I wouldn't need you, right?"

There was something about Spaeth, down past all the obnoxious bluff and bluster, that rang true. And it bothered me.

"Okay," I said. "Steve told me you had an alibi witness."

"Damn straight. Mickey, guy I met at Dufresne's."

"You know his last name?"

"Of course I do. We were drinking buddies the whole time I was staying there. Had to have something for social life, once Gant got me kicked out of my house."

"And Mickey's last name?"

Spaeth paused. "Actually, his real first name's 'Michael,' middle initial 'A.' "

"Michael A. what?"

Spaeth chewed a moment. "Mantle."

"Mickey . . . Mantle?"

"I saw his birth certificate, he carries it with him everywhere, win drinks off guys in the bars. He calls himself 'Mickey Mantle,' and he can prove he's entitled to it."

"Just like he can prove you're innocent."

"Damned right. We got shitfaced together in my apartment the night Gant was shot."

"Your apartment?"

"I used the money Steve sprung from the divorce to put a security deposit on a real place."

"Why?"

"Why what?"

"Why would you use some of your tight money to rent an apartment instead of staying at Dufresne's till you were employed again?"

"Hey, sport, you ever tried to get a job—a good job—with no private phone and a boardinghouse for an address? Plus, like I told you, the guy running the place probably stole my gun."

"So you move to an apartment, and this Mantle comes over to drink."

"Yeah."

"Why not go out drinking with him?"

"Cheaper this way."

Spaeth could tell I wasn't buying. "And besides, you live in a little room at a boardinghouse long enough, even a small apartment is a nice place to spend some time." Spaeth looked behind him, into the unit. "Believe me. Here I got a cell maybe half the size of my room at Dufresne's."

"Aside from Mantle, can anybody else vouch for where you were the night Woodrow Gant was killed?"

"No." Spaeth raked his hand through the hair again. "No, like I said, we got shitfaced together. The Mick must have left sometime after I fell asleep, because the first thing I remember is a couple of homicide cops banging on my door after they couldn't find me at the rooming house."

"And they can't find Mantle, either."

"Which just means they haven't really looked for him. I mean, he's this little, scraggly guy. Reddish hair, reddish beard. Probably hasn't gone more than five miles from Dufresne's in the last year without somebody to drive him."

"So he should have turned up by now."

"Unless he's in a drunk tank somewhere, or . . ." Spaeth ran out of gas. "Look, I'll level with you, sport. I listen to my story as I'm telling it to you, and I don't believe it myself. All I know is, I didn't kill that bastard lawyer Gant. It doesn't make any fucking sense to me, either, but somebody must have set me up to take the fall, and if you can't find Mickey, I'm gonna spend the rest of my fucking life with guys ten times worse than the one busted me in the shower. And I don't think I can . . . can take . . .''

At which point Alan Spaeth began to cry from both the good eye and the bad one, and I felt that twinge in my gut a third time.

When I walked through the door of Steve Rothenberg's office suite, he was just turning away from the disco receptionist and she was just readjusting her earphones. Rothenberg looked at my face, frowned, and beckoned me back to his own office.

Once inside, he moved around his desk and dropped into the chair while I took one of the worn seats in front of him. Then Rothenberg began combing his beard with his fingers again. "You saw Alan Spaeth?"

"I did."

"And?"

"Your client's a jerk."

For some reason, Rothenberg seemed to take heart from that. "Most of my clients are."

"A racist jerk, Steve."

The frown again. "I was afraid that might show through."

"It'll 'show through' wherever he happens to be, especially the witness stand."

Rothenberg swung in his chair a little. "There are three decisions I have to leave to the client in every case, John. The first is whether to plead out or go to trial."

"The D.A.'s office likely to offer much for a plea?"

"Zip, without that alibi witness."

"Named 'Mickey Mantle.' "

Rothenberg winced. "If it's to be a trial, then the second decision I leave to the client is whether to have the judge or a jury as the decider of fact."

"Won't matter here, will it?"

Rothenberg chose not to answer. "What I was building to is the third decision, whether the accused takes the stand in his own defense."

"Spaeth testifies, even a rookie prosecutor would draw him out on cross, and either a judge or a jury would crucify him."

"But . . . rightly?"

I watched Rothenberg as he watched me. "You mean for the murder of Woodrow Gant?"

"That's what I mean."

We watched each other some more.

"No," I said finally.

Rothenberg let out a breath I hadn't realized he was holding. The fingers went back to grooming his beard. "So, you joining the team?"

"Who's got the file at Homicide?"

"Robert Murphy."

The black lieutenant I'd helped on the William Daniels case. "And you're sure Nancy Meagher's not connected with this prosecution?"

Rothenberg reeled off the names of two A.D.A.'s. I'd never heard Nancy mention either one, not so surprising when you consider Suffolk County employs over a hundred of them.

Then Rothenberg came forward in his chair, palms flat on the desktop. "Look, John. For what it's worth, here's my view. Somebody killed one of my brothers at the bar in cold blood on a deserted road. Shot the poor devil three times from like ten feet away. I picture that, and I can't let the somebody get away with it, all right? But I'm not a cop or a prosecutor, so I can't go after the real killer. I'm just the lawyer who's trying to show the system that they need to keep looking because the defendant they've settled on is the wrong one. And with your help, I just might be able to do that. Now, what do you say?"

Rothenberg might have a shaky practice and a shabby office, but he had that guild loyalty I'd sensed in the people around me during my one year of law school many years ago. And he'd also been loyal to me.

I sat back and told Steve Rothenberg what I was going to do.

Chapter 2

LEAVING STEVE ROTHENBERG'S office for the second time that Tuesday, I bought a tuna pita from a deli in Boylston Alley. Eating the pocket sandwich on a bench along the border of Boston Common, I watched the flow of people past me. The homeless with their shopping bags drooping from hyperextended hands, stiff blankets around their shoulders like starched shawls. Day care workers pushing six-foot vegetable carts, filled not with cabbages and tomatoes but rather three-year-olds, twisting and squirming but mostly smiling and laughing as they got wheeled around the park. Beyond the curb, tourist trolleys—kind of vegetable carts for adults—motored by, their drivers echoing spiels about historical sights left and right.

Walking back to my own office on Tremont Street, I pretty much ratified the position I'd taken with Rothenberg. I spent most of the afternoon on paperwork in other cases. Then I tackled the utility and other bills from the condo I was renting, sorting them into piles mentally labeled "Due," "Past Due," and "Lights Out."

Suitably depressed, I decided to leave those problems at my locked office door and went downstairs for the walk to the courthouse.

From the last plaza step outside the main entrance, I noticed Nancy Meagher come through the revolving door. My heart did the little dance it learned the first time I'd ever seen her, presenting the Commonwealth's side in an arson/murder hearing. She was dressed the same way, too, in a skirt-and-jacket gray suit, white blouse, and modest heels that kicked her height up to five-nine and change. The autumn-length black hair just brushed her shoulders, framing a face of bright blue eyes over freckles and pearly teeth, an image on a postcard from County Kerry. Nancy had received a cancer scare of her own a month before, and our working through it had brought us closer together.

Shifting the strap of her bulging totebag onto a shoulder, she went up on tiptoes to peck the corner of my mouth. "If I'm not mistaken, it's your turn to pick drinks and dinner."

I gave her a one-armed hug. "It is indeed."

"We walking or driving?"

"Walking, unless the totebag's going to give you trouble."

"The weight won't, but what's inside it might."

I turned us toward Beacon Street. "Tough trial?"

Nancy shook her head. "The legislature's finally approved some new superior court judgeships for the governor to fill, and I'm supposed to help our administrative people decide if there's any current nominee we should be opposing."

"Based on trial attorneys like you litigating against the nominees as opponents?"

"You got it."

"Not much fun."

"No, but it's important to my boss, and he's been loyal to me, so . . ." Nancy shook her head again. "How about if we talk about something besides the court system for a while, okay?"

I'd wanted to bring up the Alan Spaeth case with her, get it over with, but right then didn't seem the time.

*   *   *

Twenty minutes later, Nancy said, "Don't tell me you've joined the Harvard Club?"

"I was Holy Cross, Nance," though we had reached the intersection of Massachusetts Avenue and Commonwealth. I gestured toward a doorway in the hotel on the corner.

She read the name over the threshold. "The Eliot Lounge?"

"This is drinks."

We stepped down into the dark, wood-paneled room, a bar in front of us with stools and taps, a raised platform area off to the right with tables.

Nancy looked around, allowing her eyes to adjust, I think. "I've never been here, but . . . ?"

"The Boston Marathon."

"Oh, right. The place that has a party afterwards."

"Not *a* party, *the* party."

She said, "Then how come we didn't come here when you ran?"

"Because after I finished the race, my legs were barely able to climb curbs, remember?"

"I remember how stupid it was for a man six-three—"

"—a little under, Nance—"

"—and almost two hundred pounds to run twenty-six miles without stopping when he didn't have to."

"And I remember you, waiting for me at the finish line."

"With my camera."

"It was the 'you' part that mattered."

A smile crossed her face, almost from ear to ear. "That was certainly the right thing to say. Where do we sit?"

I ordered a pint of draught ale for each of us and led her to a table under the "Wall of Memory." There were photos and testaments to Johnny Kelley, who ran more Bostons than any other human being, winning several times around 1940 before finally having to stop in the early nineties. I identified some candid shots of Joan Benoit Samuelson, the great women's and Olympic champion, and of course Boston's own Bill Rodgers, who finished first an incredible four times in six years.

Nancy looked up at the wall as our drinks arrived. "You really know who all these people are?"

Alberto Salazar, Greg Meyer, Cosmos Ndeti. "Most of them. But this was never just a runner's bar. Professors from Berklee College of Music played jazz. And reporters from the old Phoenix kibitzed with state senators ducking quorum calls. Even the great Bill Lee made an appearance."

"Bill Lee?"

"The Spaceman. He was pitching for the Red Sox one afternoon at Fenway when the game got delayed by rain. He came over to the bar in his uniform and cleats, drinking beer while monitoring the rain on television, running back to the park to retake the mound."

Nancy looked at me. "And when was all this?"

"The mid- to late-seventies."

"John?"

"What?"

"In the mid- to late-seventies, the only time I'd have seen any of those people would have been if they'd come to show-and-tell at my grammar school."

"Drink your ale."

As Nancy smiled at me over the top of her glass, I looked around the room, then noticed Nancy's expression change.

She said, "Something's wrong, isn't it?"

"How do you mean?"

"Your face just went sad."

"The reason I brought you here."

"Which is?"

"The owners of the hotel aren't renewing the bar's lease. They want to aim at a more upscale crowd."

"So, this is kind of last call at the Eliot Lounge?"

"Kind of."

Nancy reached her right hand across the table, closing on my left one. "Then I'm glad you cared enough to have me come with you."

"You and no other, kid."

"What a lovely evening," said Nancy.

We were walking east on Newbury Street, Boston's answer to Rodeo Drive. A little funkier on the Mass Ave end where we were, a little ritzier—appropriately—as you got closer to the Ritz Carlton Hotel overlooking the Public Garden. There were a few outdoor cafés, tables set but no diners seated.

"John?"

"Agreed," I said. "Lovely evening."

Nancy took my arm, giving me a sidelong glance. "You still down about the Eliot?"

"Yes, but I did what I could, which was to send the place off with as much good feeling as it gave me back when."

"Then there's nothing else you can do."

"Right."

Nancy tone changed. "You know the photos of the runners on the wall?"

"Yes?"

"I bet you'd look cute in one of those little running outfits, with the silk singlets and short shorts."

"You should catch me in the swim-suit competition."

Nancy drew my arm toward her more tightly. "I was kind of hoping for the birthday-suit competition."

"If you can curb your lust until after dinner."

"You're on."

Just past Dartmouth, we turned down a set of stairs to Thai Basil.

Nancy smiled. "My tummy's happy already."

The owner, a smiling man with full cheeks and a bustling manner, takes such pride in the place I've never eaten there when he hasn't been behind the cash register. He welcomed Nancy and me before leading us to a table separated from its neighbor by a clear glass panel. Though the restaurant isn't huge, there's always a sense of privacy accompanying the intimacy, and it's become my favorite place in Back Bay.

I ordered a Dry Creek Fumé Blanc from the ponytailed waitress, whose command of English still reflected the tinkling accent of her homeland. The mixed appetizer plate for two (shrimp toast, spring rolls, and five or six other delights) arrived so quickly you almost couldn't believe it was freshly prepared, though one taste convinced. And, as always, the entrée dishes of Tamarind duck and garlic pork and pad Thai noodles were truly to die for.

Nancy spooned a few more finger-sized slices of duck onto her plate. "So, you given any thought to what we'll do for the weekend?"

"No. You?"

"I was thinking of a road trip."

I had some wine. "To . . . ?"

"Mystic Seaport."

"In Connecticut?"

"It's only a hundred miles or so, John. We could stay at a bed-and-breakfast Saturday night."

I pictured the bills in piles back at my office.

Nancy warmed up to her subject. "One of the other prosecutors went last weekend, and she said it was neat. The seaport itself has all kinds of shops set up the way they were in the whaling days, with ships and demonstrations of sail rigging and anchoring and so on. Be a real nice break from the city, not to mention my judge-review homework."

As good an opening as I was likely to get. "I don't know, Nance. I might have a case I'm starting that would make it tough for me to take off like that."

She blinked. "You don't know whether you're starting the case or not?"

"I told the lawyer who wants to hire me that I needed to talk with you about it first."

"Me?" Nancy sipped some wine. "I don't understand. If it's a case I'm working on, you really shouldn't take it, but otherwise there's no conflict."

"Not directly, maybe. But . . . Nance, it's Alan Spaeth."

Her face lost all color, and I suddenly had the impression that if she hadn't set her glass down, she'd have dropped it. "You can't be serious."

"Steve Rothenberg asked—"

"I know who the defense attorney is, John. Everybody in the office is on eggshells about it."

"But Steve said you weren't one of the trial lawyers assigned."

"I'm . . . I'm not."

"Nancy, I met with Spaeth at Nashua Street."

She stared hard at me. "And?"

"I don't think he killed Woodrow Gant."

Nancy coughed out a breath. "I don't believe this."

"But you just said there's no conflict."

"I don't care what I just said."

"Nance, when we talked about this last week—"

"Last week you asked me about a news headline, John. Now you're talking about helping the man's killer."

Her voice was rising, so I thought I should lower mine. "Nancy, you mentioned loyalty to your boss before. Well, I have some loyalty to Steve Rothenberg, too. Besides, I'm really talking about trying to find out who shot Gant because I don't think Spaeth did."

Nancy's face seemed to close down. "You've already made up your mind, haven't you?"

"About Spaeth's innocence? Yes. But—"

Nancy reached for her totebag and started to stand. "Do what you feel is best, John."

"Wait a minute."

She stepped around the table. "I said, you should do what you feel is best, and it's obvious that means you should take on this case. But I can't . . . I have to get out of here. I'll call you."

I swiveled in my chair. "Nancy—"

"I'll call you," she repeated over her shoulder.

The owner was trying not to look from Nancy to me as she strode out of the restaurant. The waitress, who'd been in the kitchen, came through its door and glanced only at our table before asking brightly if she should bring a dessert menu.

I told her I didn't think so.

Chapter 3

THE NEXT MORNING, I woke up in the bedroom of my rented condo on Beacon Street. Woke up alone, and more than a little angry. The way I saw Nancy's blowup the prior night, she was upset at me for just doing my job.

After using the bathroom, I thought I'd try to burn off those feelings and clear the mind for business. I stuck my head out the kitchen window to gauge the temperature. Too warm for the new hooded sweatshirt I'd bought, a quarterback's hand muffler as front pockets against the coming arctic winds. Instead, I pulled on running shorts, a cotton turtleneck, and a T-shirt over the turtleneck. Before lacing up the Brooks HydroFlow running shoes, I reached for some tube socks and the knee brace I now have to wear on my left leg.

Downstairs, I crossed Beacon to the Fairfield Street pedestrian ramp over Storrow Drive. Heading upriver along the Charles, I used the macadam paths that had recently, and stupidly, been divided into "travel lanes" by a white, broken line painted down the center. There were a dozen guys in dark pants and yellow T-shirts, some picking up trash and bagging it, others cutting brush and piling the branches near a nondescript minivan. If you're not a river regular, you probably wouldn't notice that during summers, the landscapers are male and female teens wearing orange tops, while the fall and spring folks are all older men in yellow ones. Reason? The younger workers constitute summer help from the city schools, the older workers, trusted inmates from the county jail, with the guy who tries never to leave the driver's seat of the minivan a uniformed sheriff's officer there to guard them.

Our tax dollars at work.

Passing the Boston University railroad bridge a mile later, I thought I had the situation with Nancy under control. I'm dense about some things, and somehow I'd badly misjudged her reaction to my taking Alan Spaeth's case. She'd let me wonder about it for a day or two before calling to explain what I'd missed and then bury the hatchet. Seemed reasonable, if regrettable, and as I turned at Western Ave to head back downriver, I moved on to organizing my day.

I'd have to start in South Boston, either with Lieutenant Robert Murphy on the homicide itself, or with Vincennes Dufresne, the owner of the boardinghouse where Spaeth used to live and his alibi witness might still. Weighing things, it seemed to me that Murphy was less likely to be in, but easier to reach, and the earlier I visited the rooming house, the sooner I might find Michael Mantle.

I finished my run with a sprint of a hundred yards or so from the Mass Ave bridge back to the Fairfield ramp, feeling a lot better than I had starting out.

After one shower and two English muffins, I changed into a blue suit, white shirt, and quiet tie. Downstairs, I got behind the wheel of my silver Honda Prelude, the last year of the original model. Twenty minutes later, I found Vincennes Dufresne's boardinghouse in Southie, a few blocks from where East Broadway ends at Pleasure Bay. The neighborhood is mostly blue-collar and virtually all white, a questionable legacy of the desegregation crisis two decades earlier.

The rooming house itself was a wooden four-decker on a block of threes, so it stood out like the gawky kid in a class photo. At one time maybe a forest green, the paint on the clapboard had weathered from salt, sun, and snow to a streaked and peeling olive drab. The trim around the bay windows stacked on either side of the centered portico also needed painting, and the concrete steps leading up to the front door were crumbly at every trod edge. If you could read a book by its cover, the only thing holding the place up would be the party walls shared with its neighbors.

At the entrance, a sign block-printed on a pink five-by-eight note card was tacked above the bell. The sign read:

> THE CHATEAU
>
> NO TRESPASSING
>
> NO SOLICITING
>
> NO SHIT

My kind of place.

I pushed the button and heard a sound inside like a dentist's drill. I let up, waited a minute, and hit it again. Same noise.

I was an inch away from a third try at the button when something heavy bumped against the door from the inside. The wood creaked loudly on its hinges and opened.

The man in the doorway stood about five-six and blinked blearily. His black, curly hair was as long on his eyebrows as on his head, which hadn't seen a comb yet. The mustache had bars of red through it, hooking over and covering his upper and lower lips like hundreds of narrow, curved claws. He hadn't shaved yet, either, the black stubble on the pale cheeks, jaw, and neck as riddled with red as the mustache. The man wore a strappy T-shirt over brown pants cinched a little too high. Once the eyes stopped blinking, though, they were dark and full of fire, with enough crow's-feet at the corners to make me push his age up ten years from the thirty-five I'd originally thought.

He said, "You got a name?" a vestigial accent softening some of the consonants.

"John Cuddy."

"Let's see some ID, eh?"

I took out the leather folder with the laminated copy of my license in it. The man looked down through the plastic, cocking his head to squint, as though his eyes didn't focus straight-on.

Then he looked up at me. "Private means you're not a cop."

The accent now sounded French-Canadian. "Right."

"And not cop means you got no official business with my place, and I don't got to talk with you."

My place. "Vincennes Dufresne?"

His eyes didn't like that. "So?"

"It's just that you have a choice. You can talk to me here and now, or we can subpoena you in for a deposition, have you sit around a law office downtown for a day or two."

His eyes liked that even less. "Now you sound like a lawyer, eh?"

"I'm working for one."

"Lawyers. When they swim, you can see their fins breaking the surface."

"Meaning you think of them as sharks."

"Worse. You give a shark a hunk of meat, he eats it, maybe leaves you alone. A lawyer, you give him a hunk of meat, first he eats you, figuring he can always go back for the meat."

If we weren't on the Chateau's front steps, I thought the owner would have spit. "Tell you what, Mr. Dufresne. How about you ask me inside, and that way everybody saves some time with the lawyers?"

He cocked his head a different way, shifted his lips to the right, and turned without shutting the door on me. I followed him into a dimly lit foyer, then left through a freshly painted door.

And into a different world.

Framed movie posters from the forties were mounted on walls soaring ten feet to molded plaster fretwork around the perimeter of the room. A three-tiered chandelier anchored the middle of the space, with delicate, antique chairs and burled, carved tables straddling a tiled fireplace. The floor was hardwood, sanded and polyed to the point that it shone like the mirror over the mantel.

I thought, "time-warp," but kept it to myself.

Dufresne settled himself into a Louis-the-Someteenth chair and motioned me toward the more substantial couch. "Not what you'd expect from the street, eh?"

"Not exactly. Where'd you get all this?"

"My mother." Dufresne motioned to one of the posters behind him, showing a waist-up portrait of a man with slicked-back hair and a pencil-thin mustache leaning against a woman with high cheekbones and a hairdo that could have coined the term "wavy." From their expressions, they were facing the difficulties of a postwar world with desperate courage. "Best role she ever had, B-movie with Zachary Scott that went nowhere fast. The posters are hers, the furniture what she got from divorcing husband number three."

The name "Danielle Dufresne" appeared in lettering next to and the same size as "Zachary Scott" on the one poster, in the first or second line of supporting cast for the rest. "She was in a lot of films."

"Films." Dufresne looked at me a little more carefully. "That's what she called them. Not 'movies,' or 'flicks,' or 'bombs,' which half of them were. 'A movie, Vincennes, is what a salesman takes of his vacation so he can bore the neighbors; a film is a work of creative art.' And then more bullshit after that."

"Being in films make her happy?"

"No, but that don't make her different from anybody else on God's earth, eh? She didn't have the talent of an Ingrid Bergman, and she couldn't lose enough of her accent to be anything but the 'French girl.' " Then Dufresne seemed to remember he hadn't invited me over for a seminar on the cinema. "What's a lawyer interested in me for?"

"Not you. Alan Spaeth."

"I should have known." Dufresne dropped his head, making me notice he was wearing old-style bedroom slippers, those leather scuffies that sell well only before Father's Day. "What an asshole."

"You didn't care for him."

"I should have booted Spaeth out the first night he was here."

"Why?"

"You told me at the door, I let you in, we can save some time. It'd take days to give you everything on him."

"How about just the high points?"

"High points? There weren't any. Guy looked down on the Chateau like it was a flophouse, but I still had to chase him every Friday for the weekly." Dufresne waved, his hand seeming to take in everything outside his sitting room. "I grant you, most of the guys living here are down on their luck, one way or the other. Oh, a couple of them just got old, nursing pensions but without any family to give them something to do, something to live *for,* you know? The rest are like Spaeth, divorce squeeze. Or drunks trying to dry out, druggies trying to kick the monkey."

"How'd you get into the business to start with?"

Dufresne cocked his head a different way. He seemed to have a variety of positions to convey emotion without words. "Divorce myself. Why I feel sorry for guys like Spaeth, I suppose. The wife got everything but my mother's furniture, and I had to live somewhere. My divorce lawyer—may he burn in hell—had a friend who owned this place, was retiring to Florida. That sounded good to me, so I come see the Chateau—it wasn't called that then, 'the Chateau' is my name for it account of my mother, she always was talking about living in one instead of some third-floor walk-up."

Dufresne took a breath. "Well, this was twenty years ago, and I was thirty years young. Somebody else'd said, 'Go run a resort hotel, up in New Hampshire or Maine for the *Quebecois,* want to come down to the States on their vacation.' But I didn't have enough money from the divorce for a real 'resort,' and when I went to this talk some 'expert' was giving on bed and breakfasts, all he kept saying was the three gotta's."

" 'Gotta's'?"

"Yeah. He said, you wanna run a B&B, you gotta be clean, you gotta be friendly, and you gotta—I loved this—you gotta 'exceed the expectations of your guests.' Well, that sounded to me a lot like being married, which I already knew I wasn't crazy about, eh? So I said fuck it and bought this place with a mortgage like the White House oughta have and found out my own three gotta's."

"Which are?"

"Gotta pay me, gotta pay me, gotta pay me."

Dufresne laughed, a honking sound that contrasted with the way his accent smoothed over some of his consonants. "So here I am, a Frenchy in an Irish neighborhood, running a welfare hotel for deadbeats."

He seemed to run down, and I decided to build slowly toward Michael Mantle, the alibi witness. "About Spaeth?"

Dufresne seemed to look at me for the first time, a new angle for the cocked head. "What about him?"

"I'd like to see the man's room."

"It ain't his anymore."

"The one he used to rent, then."

"There's a viewing fee, eh?"

The fourth gotta. "How much?"

"I go by the amount of time I spend. So—"

"—Twenty bucks for twenty minutes, if that."

Dufresne said, "Let's see it."

I dug out my wallet, handed him the bill. He stood up and led me out of his sitting room to the corridor and a central staircase.

As we topped the first flight, I could see four room doors, all closed. Labored, wheezy coughing came from behind the one nearest the steps. "He all right in there?"

"No, he's dying in there." Dufresne glanced over his shoulder toward the door. "Hank's got emphysema. Some day he's gonna stop coughing, and I'll be cleaning his lungs off the floor along with everything else."

"Did Hank know Spaeth?"

"No."

"You sure?"

"Spaeth wouldn't go near him. Scared Hank had something contagious."

We climbed to the third floor, Dufresne stopping at the first door on the right of the staircase. "Your asshole used to be in here."

Dufresne didn't have to use a key because the old-fashioned glass knob twisted in his hand. Entering the room, I could see carved foot- and headboards, the same polished hardwood floors as downstairs, and wallpaper that was separating only a little in one corner from a water stain browning the ceiling plaster.

"Nice room," I said, meaning it.

"You rent from me, you get your money's worth." Dufresne gestured at the floor. "Every time somebody moved out, I'd do over his room. The floors, the walls. Bring up furniture from the basement, restore it with sand-paper and varnish. Got through twelve of the fourteen before I realized I'd never make my money back."

"Fourteen?"

"Right. Four per floor on two through four. Just a pair of roomers on the ground floor."

"Because you have the other half of it."

"Like you saw, eh? My bedroom's in the back of the parlor we were in."

Parlor. That's what it'd felt like, too.

I walked around the room Spaeth had told me about. However nice, it was only twelve-by-twelve, one window on the back wall and a simple overhead light. A nightstand with no drawers stood on one side of the bed, a bureau with no mirror on the other.

I pointed to the closed door on the window wall.

"Bathroom?"

"Closet. Bathroom on this floor's next to the kitchen."

"So, four renters share the hopper and shower?"

"And sink. Some of them'll try to brush their teeth in the kitchen, but I stop that pretty quick."

"Why?"

"You let them use the kitchen for bathroom stuff, pretty soon they're pissing in that sink, too."

I looked at Dufresne, then went to the closet. Empty, musty.

Turning back to the room door, I saw a dead bolt on it, an old keyhole lock under the knob. "You give the roomers keys to those?"

"The ones I got keys to."

"Including this room?"

"Yeah, but tell you the truth, the locks are so old, just about everybody's is like a master key for all of them."

Which meant that Spaeth's story about somebody stealing his gun wasn't so crazy. But given what Spaeth had said about Dufresne's attitude on firearms, I thought I ought to hold that until after I asked about the alibi witness.

"You said the man with emphysema didn't know Spaeth. Anybody else here friendly with him?"

"With Spaeth, eh?"

"Yes."

"Just the Mick."

Here we go. "Irish guy, you mean?"

"Hey, no offense. I mean, you're Irish, too, right?"

"Grew up about ten blocks from here."

"Ten blocks? You might know him, then. With his whole name and all."

"Who?" I said, innocent.

"This barfly named 'Mickey Mantle,' like the baseball player."

"Never had the pleasure."

"You ever go to the Quencher?"

God, that took me back, all the way to high school. The drinking age in Massachusetts was supposed to be twenty-one, and it was enforced everywhere except for private homes or college campuses. And at the Quencher, a dive with benches in the booths and the smell of stale smoke and fresh urine in the air. The owner was named Victor, an older guy from Poland, though there were photos around the bar of him as a younger man, in the circus and very muscular.

Dufresne said, "The Mick claims it was dimeys at the Quencher got him started on the brew."

It was possible. You could get served there if you had proof of being at least eighteen. Construction workers would mob the bar after they left the job sites, buying a round of "di-meys"—a six-ounce glass of beer that cost a dime—for any kids in the place.

Dufresne shook his head. "Only thing is, I know a lot of guys say they had their first beer at the Quencher, but not all of them became boozers."

"This Mantle really likes the stuff?"

"Likes it too much. Half-lit, funniest guy you ever been around. Anybody'll talk to him, even women. And the things he comes out with. You know there's this new Irish cable channel?"

"I've caught it a couple of times."

"Well, the Mick, he sees some kind of music show on the screen at a bar, then hears about this Portuguese guy over in Somerville who's on a hunger strike till they carry a Portu-guese channel, too. The Mick says to me, 'Hey, Vinnie, you got to have a rent strike till they give you a French channel.'" The honking laugh. "See what I mean?"

"Funny," I said, guessing you had to be there.

"Yeah, but that's only when he's half-lit." Dufresne shook his head again. "All the way drunk, the Mick's a fucking mess, days at a time."

"Could we check his room, too?"

A cocking of the head I thought I recognized. "Viewing fee's double when somebody's still living there."

I gave Dufresne the forty, and he moved diagonally across to the front room on the other side of the staircase. He fished around for a while in his side pocket, coming out with a key that turned in the lock right away.

I said, "Handy you had that with you."

"This?" He held it up. "This isn't the Mick's key. I had the locksmith come in, make me a real master." Dufresne twisted the glass knob, and we entered a bay-windowed front room that was bigger than Spaeth's, maybe fifteen feet square. The walls were painted instead of papered, but similar furniture and floor. However, the sheets on the bed lay filthy and un-made, the air smelling like the Quencher in high August. I wasn't surprised that nobody was there.

Dufresne frowned. "Fuck, it's no better than last week."

"Last week?"

"Yeah. I had to help him up the stairs one night. The Mick's a carpenter, makes good money when he works. But he's been on and off the benders for over a month."

The only towel I saw in the room was heaped on the floor by the bureau. I walked over to it and bent down. Bone dry. "You remember which day last week?"

Dufresne cocked his head a new way. "That I helped him? Monday or Tuesday, maybe?"

Woodrow Gant had been shot on Wednesday night. "Can't you just throw Mantle out?"

A confused look now. "I don't get you."

"He keeps his room like this, and him not working means he's not paying rent. Is the—"

"Oh, the Mick's all paid up."

I stopped. "What?"

"Yeah. A month ago maybe, I caught him coming in drunk again, only this time just the half-lit, eh?"

"Go on."

"Well, he wasn't working, like I told you, so I said to him, 'You've already missed two Fridays now. What's the story, you got money for the brew and not the weekly?' And the Mick says, 'Hey, Vinnie, I'm sorry, really.' And he reaches into his pants, pulls out this wad of cash, and pays the two Fridays he owes and the next four as well."

"Wait a minute. He paid you the whole arrearage—"

"Right."

"—and a month's advance?"

"Right, right."

"All at once?"

"Like I just said."

I thought about it. "Do you remember when this was, too?"

The same canting of the head. "A Monday. I remember thinking, 'He didn't have two weeklies three days ago, and he's got six for me now?'"

"So, a Monday, a month ago."

"Right."

4 3

About the time that . . . "Mr. Dufresne, was this before or after Alan Spaeth moved out?"

Dufresne got angry. "Right before. I remember thinking about what my mother used to say, eh?"

"Your mother?"

"Yeah, she'd tell me, 'Remember, Vincennes, God gives with one hand and takes away with the other.' "

"Meaning?"

Dufresne looked disappointed in me. "Meaning I get money I'm owed plus upfront from the Mick, but this asshole Spaeth is in my face about me stealing his gun and says he's leaving. Which also means I got five empty rooms, and the mortgage bank don't care about—"

"Please, Mr. Dufresne, this could be very important."

He stared at me.

I said, "A month ago, Mantle gives you six weeks' worth of rent, all in cash at the same time."

"Right. What he owed me, plus the advance."

"Just before Spaeth accuses you of stealing his revolver."

"I don't know what kind of gun it was."

"You don't?"

"Hell, no."

"You never saw it?"

A new cocking of the head. "I never even knew the fucking thing existed, eh? When Spaeth come to rent from me, I told him the house rule was 'no guns.' Then, after he's lived here for a while, the asshole claims I went into his room and stole the thing. Says he's moving out to an apartment three blocks over because of that."

The version Spaeth told me at the Nashua Street jail. Which might be just a good setup by him for why Woodrow Gant could have been killed by a gun with Spaeth's prints on its shells.

But then why wouldn't the guy just have taken the revolver with him from the crime scene and pitched the thing where it wouldn't be found and linked with the shooting?

Dufresne gave me a new angle of his head. "Eh, you okay?"

"Sorry." I moved around the room, more to think than to

look. "You said you helped Mantle up here last week on Monday or Tuesday."

"Right."

"When did you see him last?"

"Last?"

"Yes."

Dufresne stared at the hardwood floor. "I think that was it."

I stopped. "You haven't seen Mantle for a full week?"

"Yeah, but that's not so unusual, you know. I mean, the guy does his carpentry, he's got to be on the job by seven in the A.M. sometimes."

"I thought you said he hadn't been working for the last month?"

"Yeah, but I don't really know that. Besides, the guys here drift in and out at all hours. I try to get them to lock the front door, but they're not exactly the most responsible people on God's earth, eh?"

"How long has Mantle lived here?"

"Two, three years. More like three."

"He ever pay you in advance before?"

"Once. His uncle died, left him some kind of inheritance."

"But other than that . . ."

"The Mick's strictly hand-to-mouth."

Adding things up, I said, "You think he might have gotten the advance money this time by stealing Spaeth's gun and selling it?"

"No." Dufresne shook his head. "No, the Mick's got his faults, but he's no thief. And he's loyal, too."

"Loyal?"

"He wouldn't screw a friend, even just a drinking buddy like your Spaeth."

"They drink here?"

"Here and around here. Couple of bars up Broadway, and another on L Street toward the beach."

"These places have names?"

A shrug. "Not that matter."

Growing up in Southie, I knew what he meant. "Well, thanks for your help."

As I moved into the hall, Dufresne said, "It's a good rule, eh?"

I stopped and looked back at him. "What is?"

"My thing about guns. Can't have them in the house, not with these losers."

"Mr. Dufresne—"

"My mother, she was part Indian, where those cheekbones came from? She always said her grandma on the tribe side told her, 'Firewater and guns, they don't mix.' "

One of the honking laughs before Vincennes Dufresne took out his master key and locked Michael Mantle's door.

Chapter 4

THE BOSTON HOMICIDE Unit is on D Street in Southie, a block off West Broadway. It has the second floor of the old District 6 police station, a two-story building of bricks soot-darkened to that dingy brown of dried blood. The windows show boxy air conditioners and green trim around them. White stones embedded in the brick arc above the main entrance, like the doorway to a chapel. However, the Stars and Stripes flaps overhead, a separate black-and-white pennant remembering POW's and MIA's just below the flag they were lost fighting for.

I stopped at the battered counter on the first floor and asked a woman from Warrants for Lieutenant Robert Murphy.

Hiking a thumb over her shoulder, she said, "I think he's in the back, fuming some relic."

The department had let the Homicide Unit turn a portion of the old station's garage area into a fuming tent for spotting latents on vehicles suspected of being involved in homicides. Robert Murphy was standing safely away from two men working near the wooden frame covered with clear plastic, a low-slung Pontiac from the seventies getting the treatment inside.

About six feet and barrel-chested, Murphy was wearing a long-sleeved shirt and geometric tie, the gold wedding band on his left ring finger contrasting against his black skin as the hand did against the pale gray pants. There was a Glock 19 over his right hip because the commissioner doesn't want plainclothes officers wearing their weapon for a cross-draw that could spray bullets at a civilian before the muzzle comes to bear on the righteous target. Murphy held a clipboard in his left hand, frowning at something he saw on it.

"Lieutenant."

Murphy looked over. "Cuddy. Keep your distance, 'less you want a fine layer of Crazy Glue on that suit."

"Not exactly a dust-free environment."

A smile. "Commissioner's promising us this real fuming facility—bigger version of that room the M.E.'s got over at the new morgue? We just have to wait for 'Headquarters Building 2000' to go up." Murphy turned to the men near the tent. "How you doing?"

"Nothing yet, Lieutenant."

I looked toward them, too, but spoke quietly to Murphy. "That stuff really work?"

"If there's anything there to find. This particular vehicle, I'm not so sure we'll need it. Case it's from might be a real bunny."

"Meaning open-and-shut?"

A nod. "Three neighborhood civilians eyeballed a homeboy they knew from the time he was three empty his Tech-9 into two merry wanderers from a turf ten blocks away."

"A Tech-9? That's thirty-two bullets."

"If the clip was full. Homeboys don't always remember to reload, and the Crime Scene techs didn't hope to recover all the slugs."

"Motive?"

"Witnesses said it was because 'they be down with his lady.' He yelled it from the rear window as one of the other kids he hangs with obliged him as wheelman." Murphy stuck the clipboard under his arm like a drill sergeant on parade. "If only they weren't so stupid about it." Then he seemed to remember I'd come to see him. "So, what are you wanting?"

"I'm on the Alan Spaeth case."

Murphy's face turned toward me slowly, the eyes giving me nothing, but the lips pursing some. "Steven Rothenberg."

"He asked me to talk with his client over at Nashua Street. I did."

"Not gonna make you many friends."

"And I don't want to trade on the ones I've already got."

Murphy turned back to watch the progress on the Pontiac. "Meaning I should go over things for you without you asking right out."

"You once told me how you hated asking for favors."

Murphy nodded. "William Daniels."

The case I'd helped him with. "Which was why Rothenberg thought of me on this one."

The clipboard changed arms. "Funny how things come back around, isn't it?" A little pawing of the floor with his right shoe. "Cuddy, the Gant killing is as high-profile as a homicide can get."

"All the more reason to be sure that, pretrial, you've got the right guy for it."

Lieutenant Robert Murphy looked at me, then set the clipboard down on a table before calling over to the two men at the plastic tent. "I'll be out on the street a while."

The maroon Crown Victoria that Murphy had signed for back at the Homicide Unit turned left in front of me. I followed in the Prelude as the road became more rural and twisty. It's easy to forget there are still some sections of the city like this, a two-lane parkway through a forested valley.

Murphy slowed to maybe twenty miles an hour, eventually pulling onto the grassy shoulder near skid marks darker than their neighbors on the pavement. The Crown Vic trundled along the shoulder a while more, coming to a stop about fifty feet before a tree at the bottom of the slope. The tree had a strip of yellow plastic tape tied in a simple knot about eye-height on its trunk. I stopped behind Murphy's bumper, and we both waited for a break in the traffic before exiting our driver's side doors.

Shrugging into his suit jacket so the Glock on his belt wouldn't scare the people passing us on the roadway, he walked around the front of his vehicle to its righthand headlight, waiting for me.

"You notice the skids?" he said.

I glanced back toward where they started. "From the blown-out tire?"

"Shot-out tire." Murphy pointed ahead and toward the near treeline. "You see the tape?"

"Yes. Crime Scene stuff?"

"Right. Marked that trunk even with Gant's body, behind his car."

"What make?"

"BMW 530i." Murphy gestured. "Gant was lying half on the pavement, half on the shoulder."

"Can we walk over there?"

"Sure."

As Murphy moved ahead of me, a lot of traffic whizzed by in both directions. Above the noise, I said, "Busy road."

"This time of day, maybe."

"But not at night?"

"Gets kind of lonesome, account of folks don't want to take the chance of breaking down, middle of nowhere. We figure that's why your boy Spaeth picked this spot."

"Only how did the killer, Spaeth or otherwise, know to pick it?"

"Meaning how could he be sure Gant would come along here?"

"That's what I mean."

Murphy drew even with the taped tree and turned his head, back the way we'd come. "This parkway, maybe a mile beyond where we turned on it, gets pretty commercial. Auto parts, discount houses, restaurants. We know Gant and some woman had a late dinner at this place called 'Viet Mam.'"

"Viet *Mam?*"

"Right, two M's." Murphy swung his head back to the direction we'd been going. "Four, five miles up there, you've got Gant's condo building."

" 'Four, five miles'?"

Murphy almost smiled. "I clocked it at four-point-six on the odometer."

"And this parkway's a good route between the restaurant and Gant's place?"

"Most direct, anyway."

I thought about it. "I still don't see how the killer knows Gant will be coming by here."

"Well, we don't believe Spaeth staked out one restaurant out of a thousand, hoping Gant and this woman would eat there. But all your boy would have to do is be following Gant, watching for a chance to do him, and then figure after dinner, the man'll be coming back this way to go home."

"Or take the woman back to her place."

Murphy kicked at a stone. "We don't know whether they came to the restaurant together or in separate cars."

"You don't."

"Uh-unh. The parking lot's on the side of the restaurant building, no windows. All the Viet Mam people could tell us is that Gant and the woman walked in together and walked out together."

"How about a cab?"

"Checked with the companies. No pick-ups or drop-offs near the restaurant that we couldn't eliminate."

I shelved the car issue for a while. Looking down at the shoulder, I could see a patch of stones and grass that seemed almost bleached. "What caused this?"

"Gasoline."

"From the BMW's tank?"

"Right." Murphy pointed across the road to the other slope of the valley. "Ballistics figures it was a rifle of some kind. Bullet went through the left rear tire, ricocheted up, and punctured the gas tank."

"But without exploding it."

A real smile this time. "Cuddy, you watch too much TV."

I looked back over at the hillside where the shooter supposedly had been. "Any kind of make on the bullet or rifle?"

"No. Slug was too deformed by the things it hit. But from the composition of the metal, we know it wasn't the same as the ones found in Gant."

"Meaning two different guns."

"Right. A rifle and a revolver. M.E. dug two readable rounds out of Gant's soft tissue, and Ballistics matched them to Spaeth's Taurus Model 85 revolver."

"To the revolver found at the scene."

"With your boy's prints on the shell casings still in the cylinder. And he admits to owning a Taurus 85."

I didn't have a good answer to that one, other than Spaeth's believing somebody stole the weapon from his room at Dufresne's boardinghouse. "Lieutenant, you have anything on the woman with Gant that night?"

"No. Owner of Viet Mam says he never noticed her face. And the waitress there doesn't have great English, says just that the woman was blond and attractive, wore tinted glasses and drank chardonnay."

"Enough wine so she wouldn't be able to drive?"

Murphy looked at me. "Waitress said the bottle was empty, but she's not sure who drank how much."

"The lab do Woodrow Gant's blood alcohol level?"

"Point-oh-three."

"Pretty low."

"He was a biggish man, Cuddy."

Okay. "Let's go back to the woman. Height, weight?"

"Medium everything, according to the owner."

I looked down the road in the direction of the restaurant, then across, into the trees. "Lieutenant, can I work something through with you?"

"I'm listening."

"Either Gant and the woman that night were in separate cars or the same car, which would have been Gant's BMW."

"Go on."

"But either way, the killer has to take some time setting up across the road. And that means gambling that Gant is going

to drive back this way to his condo instead of taking or following the woman home."

"I suppose, but there's another reason to think Woodrow
Gant was alone when he got shot. We traced the man's movements that day. Found out he had the car washed and waxed
after lunch. Armor All on the dash and upholstery, whole nine
yards. There wasn't a readable latent on the BMW or in it that
didn't belong to Gant or one of the wash crew we took elimi-
nation prints from."

I looked at Murphy. "Which leads you to think no passenger
in the car."

He held my gaze. "Right."

"And Spaeth's threats at the law firm combined with his
prints on the shell casings found in the murder weapon lead
you to believe he did the killing."

"Right again."

"So this should be another . . . bunny, then."

Murphy looked away. "Just about."

"Only if it were," I said, "you wouldn't be out here with
me, going over things as much for your benefit as mine."

Abruptly, Murphy walked toward the ribboned tree. I followed him.

When we got there, he turned his back to the trunk, eyes
ranging around the valley. "You take away all the cars going
by, this is a real pretty spot."

"Lieutenant—"

"Shut up a minute, listen to what I'm saying."

I nodded.

Murphy spoke more quietly. "Nationwide, what percentage
of the population you think is African-American?"

I started to feel we were skating on different, and thinner,
ice. "Ten?"

"About twelve and a half, actually. How about folks on
death row or executed in the last twenty years?"

"No idea."

"About forty percent black."

"Jesus."

Murphy rolled his shoulders into the tree, like a bear

scratching an itch. "It gets worse. Nationwide, most of the ho-micides—eighty percent, in fact—involve victim and killer from the same race. Most of the other twenty percent is black doing white. But here, we've got white doing black."

Even with the traffic, the crisp October air seemed awfully quiet.

Murphy said, "There's not much doubt why this Gant killing landed on my desk. High profile, from a lot of different angles. Victim's black and a lawyer, plus a former A.D.A. and the third divorce attorney to be killed in the Commonwealth over the last few years. Lots of constituencies interested in this one. And who's our best suspect? A white opposing client, man who likes to own guns and shoot off his mouth as well. The depart-ment expects me to clear this case, get a conviction. But, if your boy walks, the brass wants to be able to sit down—with the bar association, the African-American interest groups, the media—and say, 'Hey, we put a senior homicide detective on it, and he's even black, too; no way Murphy'd let Spaeth walk, if the white guy was really guilty.' "

"Sounds like lots of pressure for you."

"Double-boiler." Murphy clucked his tongue off the roof of his mouth. "When I came on Homicide, though, a guy named Peter O'Malley broke me in right. He had over thirty years in the unit, and he told me there's really just one rule. You never lie anybody into jail."

I waited Murphy out.

He pushed off the tree. "Only thing is, there's no need to lie here, not even the temptation to do it. We got plenty enough evidence to convict. Motive, threat, means, opportu-nity. Shit, a third-grader with a Dick Tracy badge could submit this case to the D.A. and not look bad."

"Then what's the problem?"

A quick, "Experience."

"I don't get you."

"Too many things that add up right but feel wrong." Mur-phy raised his index finger. "One, we get a call to the local fire station saying there's a body on the road out here."

"The call went to the fire department, not nine-one-one?"

"Right."

"Male or female voice?"

"Male. Woman taking the call said the man 'sounded black.' "

I filed that away.

Murphy raised his middle finger. "Second thing, I was there when we arrested Spaeth the morning after. Brought an Entry Team with a fourteen-pound sledge to go through his door. But hell, your boy's just lying in that apartment's bedroom, still half-dressed and still half-crocked. When he asks us what the fuck is going on, I tell him flat out that Woodrow Gant's been killed. You know what the fucking idiot said?"

I got ready to cringe. "Do I want to?"

"Spaeth says, 'Well, you know what they say. The only good lawyer is a dead one.' And then he goes to roll over. And I roust him some more. Ask him where he was. He says, 'Here, drinking. Just ask the Mick.' And Spaeth tries to roll over again. Not like he's acting, either. I think he's too stupid for that. It was more like he really wasn't concerned."

"The way an innocent man might behave."

Murphy moved on to his ring finger. "Third thing doesn't feel right. Every other case I know of with a husband killing his wife's lawyer, the guy grandstands. Does some obvious, hot-dog thing, like shoot in broad daylight on a city street or a courtroom plaza to have an audience, be the center of attention. But this here was set up as though the guy wanted to get away with it."

I looked up at the hillside and nodded.

Murphy noticed me looking. "That's the fourth thing."

"What is?"

The pinkie now. "My way of seeing it, the killer has to be following Gant for a long time, figure out about the restaurant and this route. Granted your guy had plenty of opportunity to do that since his threat at the law office back in August. But I also see our shooter sitting up there on that hillside during a fairly chilly night for quite a while, watching for Gant's BMW. Then the killer lines up the rifle and pops off the tire. But after the car comes to a stop here, what doesn't the killer do?"

Murphy's face stayed on the hillside. "The killer doesn't use the rifle to take out Gant nice and safe from a distance. No, our shooter makes his way down here, maybe while the victim's walking around the back, checking his tire and the gas smell. The killer gets up close and personal, then drills the man three times. Why?"

I pictured it. "The shooter wanted Gant to know who killed him."

"Right. To look into Gant's eyes as the man recognizes who it is. Maybe say something, even." Murphy finally turned to me again. "That's cold, Cuddy. Very fucking cold. And it's also why I don't see the woman from the restaurant—whoever she is—still being in the car then. Somebody that stone-kills doesn't leave witnesses lying around."

"I like the 'somebody' part."

A sound between a sigh and a grunt. "I can prove Spaeth did it, but I don't *feel* he did. I wouldn't be lying your guy into jail, but I'd be doing the next thing, helping whoever set him up."

"Which is why we're out here."

"And why you're getting nothing more from me. Somebody hears I led you to this spot, I can always say I thought you might let something slip. After today, though, it's me working with my side's lawyer, and you working with yours."

Murphy began walking away from me.

"Lieutenant?"

He kept walking.

I said, "Granted you're in for the prosecution, but who are you rooting for?"

Murphy stopped, then turned around. "Woodrow Gant was a role model. The kind we need, especially for the work he did as an A.D.A. I were you, I'd talk to the Gang Unit sometime soon."

It took a minute more for the lieutenant to reach his maroon Crown Vic and start the engine. Then, like the careful man he is, Robert Murphy waited for a break in traffic before easing onto the pavement.

Chapter 5

I WAS A good deal closer to the restaurant than the Gang Unit. Back in the Prelude, I waited for another break in traffic to execute a U-turn and head toward the commercial strip Murphy had mentioned.

The countryside gave way to a self-only filling station, then a smattering of outlet stores that would have last year's styles in odd colors. After a food market and two hair salons, I saw a marquee for the "Viet Mam" restaurant on the right. It was in a stucco building shaped like a shoebox, the main entrance on one of the shorter ends of the box, parking to the side against a windowless wall. After leaving my car in an angled spot by the garbage dumpster near a back door, I stepped over a pyramid of dead cigarettes and walked to the front door. As Murphy had implied, from the entrance you couldn't see the parking area.

Opening the door and moving inside, I was struck by the salty smell of *nuoc mam*, a fish-based dipping sauce and probably the source of the play on "Viet Nam" in the place's name. The smell also carried me back several decades and thousands of miles, to the streets I'd patrolled as an M.P. lieutenant in Saigon. The scents of anise and cilantro and garlic spilling out from the open-air restaurants. The unfiltered exhausts of ancient Renaults and Citroens. The sweat of stringy men pedaling bicycles and rickshaws around me as I hoped nobody was going to greet my jeep with a grenade or—

"Just one?"

That nasal, slightly clucking accent that held me back there nearly as much as it snapped me forward. I turned to see a man about five-three in black pants and a white, buttoned-down dress shirt, collar open. Coming around the counter supporting the cash register, he was painfully thin, both the pants and shirt like hand-me-downs from a huskier older brother. Maybe forty-five himself, he wore his hair in a flyaway cut that looked as though one of his soup bowls could have been its inspiration. The horn-rimmed glasses were black, similar to the army-issue ones in the sixties, and they slid down his narrow nose toward a mustache with few enough strands in it that they could be individually counted.

I said, "One for lunch."

He nodded but seemed disappointed, as though hoping I might be the advance scout for a tour bus. Led by him toward the middle of the twenty tables, I could see why. Only three others were occupied, one by a young Asian couple wearing business suits and a second by two teenaged Asian women decked out in the sort of designer "active-wear" that never sees the inside of a gym. At the third table, an old man in a flannel shirt hunched over a large bowl of what looked like *pho*, a rich, traditional soup of meat served over noodles and other goodies. Everyone looked to have Vietnam somewhere in their heritage, though after a year in-country, I'd learned you could never judge ethnicity accurately by appearance alone.

My table was square and wooden, with a formica top and three violin-back chairs around it. As I sat down, my host laid the menu against a small lazy Susan in front of me, chopsticks in a ceramic mug like pencils in a holder. Plastic-scoop soupspoons lay stacked between the mug and some squeeze bottles containing what I'd bet would be sweet and chili sauces.

The man said, "I am Chan. Your waitress come quick."

Chan walked back toward the cash register, and I looked around the room. Widely spaced ceiling fans hung from the old, stamped tin above, wobbling as they turned to piped-in music that sounded an awful lot like Vic Damone. Thatched, manila wallpaper provided background for paintings of ducks, geese, and other waterfowl. Along one wall, the lighting dimmed, and there were four banquette booths of green and gold leatherette, white tablecloths under glass protectors for easier cleaning.

One of two swinging doors at the back opened, and a woman—dressed exactly like Chan—brought out a tray for the teens. Her right foot circled in a floppy but controlled limp as she balanced the tray and negotiated the spaces between the tables. The teens were closest to me, and before she set their meals in front of them, they asked for silverware in unaccented English, unless you count "Valley-Girl" as a dialect. While the waitress served them, they continued talking a blue-streak stream of consciousness about tennis camp and nail polish and handbags at the mall.

I turned to look instead at the old man in the flannel shirt. He used his chopsticks to sprinkle mint leaves and bean sprouts into the bowl and mix them into his soup. Satisfied with the blend, he then shoveled the noodles into his mouth with the scoop spoon, the chopsticks directing the long strands without either twirling or cutting them.

"Welcome to Viet Mam. I am Dinah, your waitress."

I turned back and looked up at Dinah as she emphasized the last syllable. Also about the same height and age as Chan, Dinah tried to be cheery despite the gaunt cheeks and dark, sad eyes. A whiff of stale smoke came off her, and I noticed amber nicotine stains on the knuckles of her right hand. The shortish black hair seemed professionally coiffed, as though that were the only feature worth enhancing. A scar beginning at her Adam's apple trailed down under the shirt collar, and she stood hip-cocked on her left leg, maybe to allow the right one a brief rest.

I said, "Is Dinah your real name?"

She paused, the cheeriness flickering a little. "No. Owner give me that."

"The man at the counter, you mean?"

Another pause. "Yes."

"Why?"

"My Vietnam name not good for work in restaurant."

"What is it?"

A hacking, smoker's cough. Then, "Dung."

Chan may have had a point. "Well, Dinah, this is my first time here."

"I think I never see you before." She gestured toward the tabletop. "You need help with menu?"

"Haven't looked at it yet. What do you recommend to drink?"

"I show you." Dinah reached down and flipped the menu over, drinks listed vertically and indexed by numbers the way you often see the entrees in a Chinese restaurant. "We got beer, we got wine, we got soda. We got limeade, we got pine-apple—"

"A pineapple shake would be good."

She smiled without showing teeth and began to move away. For each stride, the right foot circled like a plane before landing.

I scanned the menu, index numbers again next to each item, words like *bo* for beef, *heo* for pork, and *ga* for chicken coming back to me a little. I decided on fried spring rolls for an appetizer, chicken with lemon grass and ground peanuts as a rice dish.

Dinah brought my drink, a straw sticking straight up in the tall glass. She let me taste it—kind of a piña colada without the kick—before saying, "You need help with anything?"

Ignoring the index numbers, I said, "*Cha gio* and the *com ga xao xa ot.*"

Dinah looked at me. "You fight in Vietnam?"

"Yes."

Without writing down my order, she nodded. "My husband, too."

As Dinah limped back toward the kitchen, I had the distinct feeling that she hadn't meant Chan.

The singer on the music system changed over from what I'd thought was Damone to a piece I knew to be Sinatra's. I watched Chan sitting by the cash register reading a newspaper, his fingers tapping the counter in time to the beat. I cleared my throat, and he looked up at me. When I beckoned him over, his sigh was almost as loud as the music, but Chan put down the newspaper and came to my table.

"You got problem with waitress?"

"No."

"She slow with leg, but—"

"I don't have a problem with Dinah. You're the owner, right?"

He didn't like the twist this was taking. "Why you want to know?"

I took out my license holder, but just flashed it open and closed. "I'm investigating the death of Woodrow Gant."

Chan's lips were two thin lines. "I already talk to all police."

"Then why don't you sit down now, while I'm waiting for my meal, and talk with me?"

He was torn about something, but he took the violin-back chair next to me. "I don't see anything that night."

"Why don't we start with your name?"

A stare, but he said, "I told you already. Chan."

"Mr. Chan—"

"Just Chan. No 'Mr.' "

Okay. "What time did Mr. Gant arrive here?"

"I don't know."

I looked at him.

Chan said, "I don't care what time customer come. I care, do they pay before they leave."

"When Mr. Gant arrived that night, did you recognize him?"

Chan shifted in his chair, the eyes blinking behind the black-rimmed glasses. "I see him here before, yes."

"With anyone?"

"With woman."

"Same woman as that night?"

"Yes."

"How about any other women?"

Chan shifted and blinked some more. "One."

"Who?"

"Don't know."

"But did you recognize this other woman, too?"

A stop. "She say she lawyer-woman, like him."

"Like Mr. Gant, you mean."

"Yes."

"Was she black, also?"

"No. Chinese, maybe, but I don't know her name or nothing."

"All right," I said. "Let's go back to the night Mr. Gant was killed. Can you describe the woman he had dinner with?"

"White American."

"Color hair?"

"Blond."

"Eyes?"

"She have sunglasses."

"You think that was a little strange?"

A shrug.

I said, "For an October night?"

Another shrug.

"How tall was she, Chan?"

"Don't know."

"Was she taller than you, shorter?"

He looked at me steadily. "Shorter than lawyer-man."

"By how much?"

"Don't know."

"Was she heavy, thin?"

"No."

"No what?"

"No heavy, no thin. In middle."

"Medium."

A nod.

"You said you'd seen this woman here with Mr. Gant before."

More shifting in the chair. "Yes."

"And yet 'medium' is the best description you can give me?"

"They sit in booth, not so much light. Who woman is, that not my business."

"Would it be your business to let her drive after she drank too much wine?"

"No! Never I do this."

"Because you could lose your liquor license, right?"

"Have only wine-and-beer license."

"But you could lose that if you weren't sure somebody who drank too much wasn't driving, right?"

Chan didn't answer.

"So," I said, "if somebody had too much wine, maybe like the woman that night, you'd try to sneak a peek outside after they paid their bill, be sure the man was driving or that she took a cab."

"Woman drink wine, maybe. But she not drunk, no. So I not look out door."

I saw Dinah coming from the kitchen with a plate of spring rolls. Noticing Chan sitting at my table, she seemed to falter in a way I didn't think had anything to do with her bad leg. Then she continued in our direction.

I said, "Who was their waitress that night?"

Chan started to turn toward the swinging doors, then caught himself. "Dinah."

She was now at our table, asking her boss a short, swift question in Vietnamese. Chan shot something back.

I said, "I'd like to speak with Dinah myself."

"She my only waitress here." He waved a hand. "Must work other tables."

I was beginning to get tired of Chan. "You cover them for her."

"What?"

"Dinah sits with me, you work the tables. And if you say anything more to her, say it in English."

Chan didn't like that, but got up without another word in

either language and walked over to the young couple in business suits.

I looked at the chair he'd vacated, but Dinah went to the third instead. After setting down my spring rolls, she used her right hand to lower herself into the violin-back, as though the leg didn't work very well when bent.

"From the war?" I said.

The eyes grew sadder. "Yes."

"I'm sorry."

"War is over." And the eyes tried to come back, too.

"I'm investigating the—"

"Can I see ID, please?"

Interesting. "You asked Chan in Vietnamese if I was police, and he said that's what I told him."

She looked around, saw her boss go into the kitchen. "ID, please?"

I took out the leather case and handed it over. Reading, Dinah glanced twice to the swinging doors, being sure Chan was still out of sight before sending it back to me.

Very quietly, "You not police."

"No."

The hacking cough again. "You lie to Chan?"

"No."

A smile now, but still without showing any teeth.

I said, "Chan is not as smart as you are."

She stared at me. "Why should I talk to you?"

"To help someone."

"Who?"

"The man I'm representing. The police think he killed Woodrow Gant. I don't."

Dinah seemed troubled. "I cannot help."

"Why not?"

"I . . . it is danger for me."

"Danger from what?"

"Please. Mr. Gant and woman have dinner. That is all I know."

"Dinah, what are you afraid of?"

Chan came out of the kitchen glaring at us as he carried a tray for the young couple.

Dinah levered herself up from the chair, coughing once more. "Please," she said, and then limped back toward the swinging doors, never looking at Chan.

He walked over to me, his tray now empty. "Waitress bring rest of your food now. You eat, you pay, you leave."

As Chan went back toward his cash register, I tried the spring rolls. Kind of soggy. I also tried to figure out what was scaring Dinah, and probably Chan, too.

Giving up on that for the moment, I pushed the spring rolls aside just as Jerry Vale came over the stereo.

An hour later, I parked the Prelude as close as possible to Boston's Area B police station. Families and the elderly were taking the nice fall air within sight of it, like settlers staying around a cavalry fort when trouble was expected.

Which, for Area B, amounts to a twenty-four-hour-a-day proposition.

The station was home (in some sense of that word) to the department's Anti-Gang Violence Unit. The unit had been organized when Boston set its all-time record for homicides in 1990. I've always thought a better name would have been the "Gang Anti-Violence Unit," but nobody ever asked me.

As I went in the downstairs door, an African-American woman and two little girls I took to be her daughters were coming out. The woman had on a green, tailored suit, her hair pulled back into a bun. The girls, maybe a year apart, wore identical print dresses and cornrowed tresses. Some beads had been carefully worked into the braids, creating a dazzling, almost crystal-curtain effect every time either girl moved her head. Which they were doing a lot, as both they and the mother were crying their eyes out.

I was still shaking my own head as I asked the officer at the desk for Larry Cosentino or Yolanda King.

"Hey. Cuddy, right?"

Ilario "Larry" Cosentino stood near a tall window, his right foot up on the corner of a desk chair. He was tying the lace to a Turntec running shoe that hadn't gotten any cleaner since the last time I'd seen him, some months before when a gang of young girls thought their path to riches would be clearer without me in the middle of it.

About forty and stocky, Cosentino was wearing rumpled blue jeans and a rugby shirt, cuffs pushed halfway up his hairy forearms. There was a little less of the hair on his head than I remembered, but the wide mouth and plug-ugly face hadn't changed much, still belonging more to a bullfrog.

Cosentino turned to the woman sitting at the next desk. "Al, this is the guy I told you about, had that shoot-out with *Las Hermanas*."

The woman swung her chair around. Early twenties, she was petite and pretty, wearing a brown tweed skirt and a yellow blouse. Her eyeglasses rode up at her hairline, the hair itself a shade to the blond side of brunette and drawn into a ponytail above her left ear, trailing down onto the shoulder. "Alicia Velez."

"John Cuddy."

"Oh, sorry," said Cosentino, finishing with his shoe and getting both feet back on the floor. "I forgot, Yollie and me were still partnered up back then."

I said, "She's left the unit?"

Velez nodded. "Yolanda moved over to a district detective slot." The eyebrows went toward Cosentino. "Couldn't stand Larry's one-liners anymore."

Cosentino said, "The thanks I get, breaking her in. Sit down, sit down."

As I pulled over a straight-back chair, Velez said, "You went up against those BWA's, we're lucky to be seeing you."

"BWA's?"

" 'Bitches with an attitude.' Girl joined *Las Hermanas*, she got mean in a hurry and didn't go back."

Cosentino cracked his knuckles, grew serious. "You been visited by any of them, Cuddy?"

"Not so far."

"Well, then." He seemed to relax again. "What can we do you for?"

"I'm helping the defense in the Alan Spaeth case."

"Be seeing you," said Velez, standing.

Cosentino lowered his voice. "Al, just a second, okay?"

"Larry, this guy's—"

"A second, please?"

Velez sat back down.

Cosentino turned to me. "Cuddy, inside the department, an officer or an A.D.A.—even an ex-A.D.A.—gets killed, we still call it by the name of the victim, you know? To us, it's not the 'Alan Spaeth' case, it's the 'Woodrow Gant' case."

Velez stuck in, "The man's vocabulary isn't why I was leaving."

"I know that, Al." Cosentino never moved his eyes off me. "But Cuddy here took down some pretty bad kids we couldn't protect him from, and I heard he risked his fucking life when one of them had another citizen by the balls out in suburbia. So maybe we hear what he has to say."

Velez didn't like it, but she stayed seated as I tried to figure Cosentino out. He might be trying to help me, or he might be trying to get information on my client that he could feed to the prosecution, with Velez as a corroborating witness in case I tried to backpedal on anything. Either way, though, I needed Cosentino more than he needed me.

I said, "Somebody suggested I ought to come see you."

Velez asked, "Who?"

I glanced at her. "Whoever you guys tipped about something not being right in the Gant killing."

Cosentino said, "Al?"

Her eyes went to her partner.

He said, "I told Murphy over in Homicide what I told you."

"Great." Velez's eyes now went to her lap. "Just great."

I looked from one to the other. "There are some things about the murder that don't add up to Alan Spaeth as the shooter. Since Gant once prosecuted gang members, and the killing was done execution-style, I'm thinking maybe somebody decided to settle a past grudge."

Cosentino crossed his ankles, swinging his sneakers back and forth a little. "Eight, nine years ago, there was this task force set up, trying to deal with Asian gangs."

"I remember reading about the Chinatown prosecutions."

"Yeah. The triads started out from Hong Kong, then the tongs got organized here in the states by Chinese-Americans, then the young-punk street gangs arrived on the scene. But it wasn't just Chinese."

Velez put in, "Vietnamese, Cambodian, you name it. Very equal opportunity."

I looked at her. "But all that's Boston. Gant prosecuted in the suburbs."

"Right," said Cosentino, "but bear with me a minute, okay?"

"Okay."

He spoke more slowly. "Say you're an immigrant, but you've saved your money or somebody loaned you a grubstake, and you go into business for yourself. Restaurant, dry cleaners, convenience store. Only in your home country, the banks and all are kind of shaky, and the tax collectors are always shaking you down. Now, your business is mainly a cash-and-carry kind of operation that turns a nice profit. What do you do?"

I said, "You carry the cash home so it's safe and not reported as income."

Velez said, "Gold star. But, let's say word gets around among the workers at your restaurant or whatever that the boss is pretty flush and keeps the take at his house. What happens next?"

Pretty simple. "Home invasion."

"Exactly," said Cosentino. "The locals get wind of a bank without guards or vaults, and all they got to do is go into the boss's house with some guns and duct tape. Terrorize the guy's family, and he gives up his stash."

"And, because of the tax-dodge angle, the owner can't turn to the police about the robbery."

"Or won't, because back home, the cops were even worse than the banks or the revenue service." Cosentino opened his hands, a sermonizing priest asking the flock a question. "Result? People over here are still leery of getting involved with the authorities."

I stopped to think about it. "I'm guessing that a lot of the successful Asian immigrants move to the suburbs."

Velez said, "Soon as they can. Bigger house, better schools for the kids, a sense that all their hard work is paying off."

"So the crime against essentially a Boston business gets pulled in a suburb, and nobody tells the police anywhere about it."

Cosentino nodded. "Yeah, except some of the suburban immigrants now have real friends—their own kind or neighbors—who tell them they're better off going to the police, otherwise they'll just get ripped off again, over and over."

"Which is how Woodrow Gant came to be involved with the gang unit here in Boston."

"Right. The D.A.'s office he worked for didn't have an Asian-American prosecutor at the time, so Gant got assigned by his boss to this task force I mentioned to coordinate with us, try to nail some of these Boston guys before they hit another landscaped split-level out there."

"And the task force was successful?"

"Yeah," said Cosentino, "but mainly against the Vietnamese gangs."

"Why them?"

He moved off the desk, went around behind it to look out the window. "Bunch of reasons. Most of the Vietnamese gangs have only five, six kids in them, so they're manageable to prosecute. Also, they're pretty vicious. The kids in the Chinese gangs grew up in a real family system. You do things a certain way, rules and shit."

Velez said, "Many of the Vietnamese came to the States from refugee camps, got scattered all over the map without a family support system in place. They didn't know much English, had a lot of trouble in school. . . ."

Cosentino turned back to me. "Home invasion, a Chinese gang will say to the victim, 'Call the cops, we kill one of your daughters.' The Vietnamese will say, 'We're gonna take a finger off this daughter here right now, just so you know what'll happen to the rest of her, you report us.' "

"Also," said Velez, "the Vietnamese gangs are more mobile. They go state-to-state in cars, kind of roving bandits."

I thought about that. "But if the gang members aren't from the area, how do they know who to target?"

Cosentino and Velez exchanged looks. Then he said to me, "Traditionally, when you had a mixed neighborhood, you'd get some mixing in the gangs, too."

"Meaning?"

Velez said, "Meaning, you have Irish, Latinos, and blacks living in the same couple of blocks, maybe you have a rainbow-coalition gang, too."

Cosentino stayed by the window, cracked his knuckles again. "That never used to be true with the Asians, though. The Chinese hated the Vietnamese, the Cambodians hated the Koreans, and vice versa all over the fucking place."

"I follow you, but I don't see where you're going."

"Larry's point," said Velez, "is that now we're starting to notice some cooperation among the different Asian groups. Makes it even harder for us to trace who's doing what if a Vietnamese gang knocks over a business or home owned by a Chinese."

I shook my head. "Yeah, only what does this have to do with Woodrow Gant? He hadn't been prosecuting for years."

Cosentino came away from the window and sat on the desk again, but fidgety. "I heard some noise about one of the gangs Gant helped put away back then."

"Vietnamese?"

"Kind of."

"What does that mean?"

"It was an Amerasian gang, mostly teens whose mothers were Vietnamese women, fathers GI's during the war. You spent some time in Saigon, right?"

"Right."

"So you know what I mean. The kids were neither fish nor fowl to the purebred Vietnamese. And not just because of the mixed blood, either. It was more that the kids reminded the

THE ONLY GOOD LAWYER

rest of the people what the war had done to their country, which made any Amerasian a real outcast over there."

"And not much better treated over here," said Velez. "I remember in my school, nobody would hang with a mixed-race kid except the others."

Cosentino cracked another knuckle. "That task force I told you about set up kind of a sting, caught four Amerasian kids in a house out in Weston Hills, Gant's jurisdiction."

I'd had a case in the town a while ago.

Cosentino said, "Two of the kids got killed, the other two prosecuted and turned over to DYS."

Division of Youth Services, our Commonwealth's reformatory system. "And Gant was their prosecutor."

"Right. Only problem was, even with the killings that night—and maybe five others we could guess about—DYS couldn't hold them past their eighteenth birthdays."

"Wait a minute. How old were the kids when they pulled the home invasion?"

"The two survivors were fifteen and sixteen."

"How'd they get out there in the first place?"

"Stolen car." Cosentino shrugged. "You don't have to be old enough to get a driver's license in order to drive, Cuddy."

"Okay," I said. "So these—what were their names, anyway?"

"The muscle was Oscar Huong, a real Mr. five-by-five. Father supposedly a black Marine boxing champion. The brains was Nguyen Trinh—or 'Nugey,' for short. He had no idea who his daddy was."

"So Huong and Trinh were with DYS—"

"—until they turned eighteen. Then the system had to cut them loose. Only Nugey learned a few things while he was away. One, Oscar could protect him. Two, you get along by going along."

"Meaning?"

"Nugey started brokering deals inside DYS. One group of bad guys cooperates with another, everybody gets better treatment as a result."

"How about when he got out?"

"Went straight," said Cosentino, his face neutral.

"And that's the 'noise' you heard about him? That Trinh actually reformed?"

Cosentino looked at his partner. "You want to leave now?"

Velez reached her left hand up to the ponytail, curling an inch or two of hair around her index finger. "I've sat through this much, I'll stay for the punch line."

"Which is?" I said.

Cosentino came back to me. "When Nugey and Oscar graduated from DYS, they had a nest egg. They started loaning it out to people who got turned down by your normal kind of banks."

"Sharking."

"Yeah, but very quiet, very . . . progressive. Not the 'I-need-five-hundred-for-the-rent' types. More business investments where the ultimate payoff might be bigger."

"You make them sound like venture capitalists."

Velez laughed, nervously.

Cosentino didn't even grin. "When Woodrow Gant got killed, I asked around about Nugey. On instinct, you might say. I found out he has a half-assed office out in Brighton."

A western part of Boston. "Which led you to Trinh's loan-shark/investor profile."

"And led me to something else, too."

"What?"

"You know Woodrow Gant ate at a restaurant the night of the murder?"

"Place called Viet Mam."

"Right," said Cosentino. "Now, you want to guess who owns the building it's in?"

I looked from Larry Cosentino to Alicia Velez and back again, both of them nodding.

No wonder Chan and Dinah were so scared.

Chapter 6

BEFORE LEAVING THE gang unit, I got Nguyen Trinh's office address. I thought about paying Chan's landlord a visit, but my original trip to Viet Mam might itself trigger something, and given Cosentino's description of Oscar Huong, I'd want to meet the Amerasians on my ground rather than theirs. Also, Woodrow Gant's eating at a restaurant in a building owned by a prior defendant could have been just random chance. In fact, it was hard to see any reason why a former A.D.A. would ever intentionally patronize such a place. However, if Gant's meals there were more than coincidence, my best hope for learning what that reason might be would more likely come from the man's present circle.

And Steve Rothenberg had given me a wedge for penetrating that.

Commercial Street curves with the waterfront while providing land access to a dozen wharves jutting into the harbor between the Aquarium and the Charlestown Bridge. The wharves support substantial condominium complexes, both business and residential uses in the same buildings to retain that "quaint" look. Unfortunately, Boston's real estate recession had really whacked most properties east of Quincy Market's "ultimate shopping experience."

The address of Epstein & Neely, attorneys at law, turned out to be a five-story combination of red brick and weathered gray shingle. It stood across from Spaulding Wharf, facing southeast toward a hundred-slip marina, twenty or so sailboats-to-yachts still creaking against floating docks. The building's directory was displayed next to a set of buttons on the jamb of the downstairs entrance. The directory showed a travel agency on the ground floor, open slots for the second and third, and the law firm on four. Nothing for the fifth, which from the sidewalk seemed to be built across only half the roof.

I looked into the picture window next to the door. A bare counter, a single chair, and two posters of the Caribbean with water as natural-looking as a tinted contact lens. It seemed that our recession had caused even the travel agency to pull the rip cord.

Before pressing the button for the law firm, I tried the main entrance door. It opened onto a postage-stamp lobby with a staircase and a tiny elevator sporting one of those old-fashioned, diamond windows.

In the elevator—and out of curiosity—I pushed the button for "2." The little number outline didn't light up. Same for floor "3." The fourth button did make contact, and the door slid closed.

When the backlit "4" went dark, the cab opened onto a reception area with wine-and-gold swirled carpeting. I got another view of the marina through a glass-walled conference room that had a bigger picture window to the outside world than the departed travel agency downstairs. The higher perspective made the boats seem less impressive against the greater expanse of harbor.

A polished teak reception desk graced the carpeting between the elevator and the conference room. A woman in her thirties looked up at me from the telephone console as she massaged her left wrist with the other hand. Reddish hair was drawn back into a bun, and a pair of half-glasses perched halfway down her nose. If she wore any makeup, I couldn't see its effects. Her suit jacket was brown, the blouse under it maize.

A spindly pilot's mouthpiece angled toward thin lips and a narrow jaw. In a very controlled voice, the woman said, "I'm afraid Ms. Ling is out of the office right now." Stopping the massage, she reached for a pen, raising it to a hovering position over a spiral notebook with serrated, pink and yellow bi-part message slips in it. A plastic, compartmentalized holder contained the pink copies of other messages. "No, for some reason the system isn't accepting voice mail, but I can take a . . . Very well."

Her left hand moved subtly, and I had the feeling the connection had been broken, partly because the woman said to me, "May I help you?"

The controlled voice still. "Yes. John Cuddy here to see Mr. Epstein or Mr. Neely."

"I'm afraid that's not possible."

"I can wait."

A labored sigh. "Mr. Epstein passed away four years ago."

Not one of my better starts. "I'm sorry. I didn't—"

"Obviously not. And Mr. Neely is in conference."

"Then I'll wait for him."

"His schedule is rather full." She didn't need to consult anything to determine that. "Our telephone number is five-one-three, two-two-oh-oh. Perhaps if you called to make an appointment?"

"Perhaps if you told Mr. Neely I'm here investigating the death of Woodrow Gant?" I put one of my business cards on the desktop, but before the woman looked down, her whole face drooped.

"Please . . ." A more hushed voice now. "Please be seated for a moment."

Arranged in a corner were a love seat and two wing chairs, the same polished teak as the desk and upholstered in fabric that picked up more of the carpet's wine than its gold. I took one of the chairs as the receptionist touched something on her board. Before she could speak into the mouthpiece, a man in his thirties with a military walk and suspendered, pleated suit pants entered the reception area from a side corridor.

He said, "Imogene, I just got off a conference call, but there weren't any messages on my voice mail."

She pointed at the machine in front of her, then lowered her hand, palm down, toward it.

"Again?" said the man. "That's the third time this week, and it's only Wednesday."

Imogene just glared at him, now pointing to her mouthpiece. After taking two pink slips from a slot in the message holder, he turned. I could see for the first time a streak of white on the right side of his well-groomed hair, like a male Bride of Frankenstein. Without looking toward me, he strode away.

Then Imogene whispered something into her mouthpiece. I couldn't hear what she said, which, given her controlled attitude so far, didn't surprise me.

"Mr. Cuddy, Frank Neely."

He extended his hand to shake, the full name "Francis Xavier Neely" on calligraphed diplomas from Boston College High School, Boston College, and Boston College Law in ascending order on the wall behind his own teak desk. Around here we call that a "Triple Eagle," after the schools' shared mascot. At the side of the desk, there was even an old bookbag-style briefcase, the kind the nuns preferred you to carry in grammar school, the initials "FXN" in faded gold near the handles on top.

Neely next said, "Thank you, Imogene," and his office door closed behind me. "Mr. Cuddy, have a seat while I just enter something on my time sheet here."

Sitting down, Neely tapped at a computer as though he were afraid it might explode on him. Standing between the teak desk and matching credenza, Neely was a shade over six feet, maybe two hundred pounds. What looked like a closet door to the right wasn't open, and while he might have put on the windowpane suit jacket just to greet me, I somehow didn't think so. His eyes were blue—what an aunt of mine would have called "devilish"—in a ruddy face, the nose prominent.

His hair was that straw-blond that skips gray and goes straight to snow at the sideburns. A sepia photo on the wall showed a youthful Neely in World War II combat fatigues, a Ranger patch stitched to one shoulder, his arm a horse-collar around the neck of another soldier in the same uniform. The horse-collar appeared to be a favorite pose of Neely's, as he used it again in a color photo with a very slim, very distinguished, and very bald man, the neckties and hairstyles suggesting the shot went maybe ten years back. However, the Ranger one meant Neely would have to be pushing seventy, even if seemingly in better-than-fair shape doing it.

"Leonard Epstein."

I brought my eyes back to Neely. "Which photo?"

He actually turned to look. "Oh, the color shot there. Len and I founded this firm together seven—no, sweet Jesus, it's eight years now." A bittersweet smile with a head shake. "Heart attack took him early, never saw sixty-five. God wants the good ones sooner, I guess."

"I'm sorry for both your losses," I said.

Even the bittersweet smile disappeared now. "Imogene said you were here about Woodrow."

"That's right. And I really appreciate your seeing me without any notice."

"Which must be the way you thought best."

Direct. "When I call first, people usually manage to be away from their desk."

Something rumbled in Neely's chest, but he didn't laugh out loud. "I'm a trusts and estates man, Mr. Cuddy, so I'm almost always in. But I take your point." His left hand went up to scratch at his temple, the back of the hand matted enough with the snowy hair to cover any age spots. "Imogene said she'd seen a business card. How about a little more definite identification?"

I drew out the leather folder, and then my wallet, flipping to the driver's license photo before passing both across the desk. Neely compared them without reaching for any glasses, then passed both back.

"So," he said, "how about if it's 'John' and 'Frank' for now?"

"Fine with me."

"You're working for Mr. Alan Spaeth, then?"

The same inflection on "Mr." as on each syllable of the name. "I am."

"Figured as much. You were with one of the insurance companies, somebody *would* have called first."

I said, "One of the companies?"

"Woodrow had a couple of life policies, payable to family members. And of course we had firm insurance on him."

"As a key employee."

A nod. "Learned that lesson with Len. We didn't have but five hundred on each of us back then, and it was tough sledding for a while after he died."

"Five hundred thousand?"

Neely shifted in his chair. "Correct."

"And how much on Mr. Gant?"

Neely seemed to want to shift again, but didn't. "Straight million, same as each of us."

"You mean, on each partner?"

"On each attorney. Don't let Uta hear I said this, but the associates are worth at least as much as the partners in terms of time invested on cases."

But not, I'd have thought, rainmaking. "I'm sorry, Uta is . . . ?"

"Uta Radachowski. She's my third . . ." Neely closed his eyes briefly. "She's my other partner, now. Elliot Herman and Deborah Ling are the associates."

Which would probably make Herman the man I saw in the reception area. "So, not counting Mr. Gant, the firm has only four attorneys, total?"

Neely did shift again this time. "Yes, but what difference does that make to your work?"

"I don't follow you."

The man came forward in his chair, the hairy hands having a hard time nesting comfortably on his desktop. "John, I've shown you my cards so far, don't you be holding yours close to the vest, okay?"

"Frank, I honestly didn't get what you meant."

Neely sat back. "You're working for Mr. Spaeth, you'd be wanting to know about the blowup here when he threatened Woodrow."

Neely's cooperation was important to me, even if keeping it meant telling him I might have some cards in my hand. "Frank, there are enough things about Mr. Gant's death that bother me, I'm not sure what I want to know."

"The police seemed to think your Mr. Spaeth is their man."

"I don't."

The lawyer's eyebrows closed together, two caterpillars trying to pass on the same twig. "You genuinely believe somebody other than Mr. Spaeth might be responsible for Woodrow's death?"

"Yes."

Neely looked down at his hands a moment. "I'll not ask you who or why, because in your position, I wouldn't say. I'd ask only that you bear some things in mind." He looked back up at me, some of the combat stare in his eyes. "The people in this firm are like family to me, and, I believe, to each other as well. When Len died, Uta and I were the only attorneys here. The emotional impact was as though she'd lost an uncle and me a brother. But Woodrow's . . . death was worse. Far worse. Senseless, horrible, someone else's nightmare come home to roost. We all cried openly in the halls and offices for days, and it'll be years before we can think about it without pain."

Neely paused, I think to see if I'd say anything. I didn't.

He nodded once. "But, John, I'm a lawyer, too. And I believe every criminal defendant has a right to vigorous, zealous advocacy. Only way to keep our system honest. And I also call the shots around here. When the police first contacted me about Woodrow, I was in shock, but even then I realized that somebody from the defendant's side would be calling on us about the scene in the conference room, and I've been bracing myself for it ever since. I was prepared to let whoever that somebody might be talk to everyone who knew anything about it, air the incident out and be done with it. But now you're telling me you think that might not be all, correct?"

"Correct."

"Very well, John. You have carte blanche. Ask your questions of all of us, though I'll not order anyone to say something he or she wants to keep in confidence. And obviously I can't let you invade the privacy of our clients."

"Understood."

"Understand two more things, then. First, I want whoever killed Woodrow—Mr. Spaeth or otherwise—drawn and quartered. Second, if I find that you've put anyone in this firm to unnecessary grief because of questions that didn't need to be asked, I'll make you sorry you ever heard the name Frank Neely. Have I been clear enough?"

"Crystal."

We looked at each other the way I remembered from my war.

Then Neely said, "I'm not trying to dictate your program here, but I'd start with the lawyers. Probably Uta first, since she's been here the longest. Then I'd talk with Elliot and finally Deborah."

"I'd also like to see Mr. Gant's office and speak with his secretary."

"His . . . ? Oh, that's right. You've seen Imogene only at the reception desk. One of the secretaries covers it when the receptionist's on break or whatever."

"Imogene was Mr. Gant's secretary?"

"Shared secretary. Financial necessity, this day and age."

"Who did he share her with?"

"Me," said Frank Neely in a matter-of-fact voice before rising.

Sure enough, when Neely walked me to his door and opened it, Imogene was sitting at the kangaroo-pouch desk in front of his office that had been empty when she'd escorted me back there. Imogene turned from folding correspondence, the creases razor sharp, the edges perfectly aligned. Four of the pink message slips lay on her desktop. More toward the center, near a single rose in a clear vase, was a little brass pup tent with "IMOGENE BURBAGE" etched into the metal.

"Imogene," said Neely, "would you take Mr. Cuddy to Uta, then check back with me?"

"Certainly."

As she led the way around a corner, I said, "Ms. Burbage, I understand you worked with Mr. Gant as well?"

A little stiffening of the shoulders in front of me. "As his secretary for three and a half years."

"I'd appreciate being able to speak with you, too, before I leave."

"I'll ask Mr. Neely about that."

"He's already okayed it."

Burbage started to turn. "If you don't mind, I'll ask him anyway."

Another woman, in her twenties and seeming frazzled, came toward us. A bundle of manila files were clutched to her chest, both hands crossed over them, a couple more of the pink message slips between two of her fingers. She stopped and started to extend the folders toward Burbage.

"Oh, Imogene, these messages and files are for Mr. Neely, too."

"Patricia, can you please leave them on my desk."

There was no rising, question-tone at the end of Burbage's statement, and Patricia simply said, "Sorry."

I walked past four hung prints of the same lighthouse at different seasons of the year. Near the end of the hall, Burbage paused at an open doorway without saying anything. I heard a hearty female voice inside say, "She's here now," and then the plastic bonk of a phone receiver redocking. "Please, Imogene, show Mr. Cuddy in."

Burbage turned to me and nodded before going back up the hall.

Entering the office, I saw a broad-shouldered, stolid woman coming around the desk to meet me. Radachowski's brown hair, dull but full, was leavened with the silver of untended middle age and cut so that it didn't quite reach her shoulders. She wore silver aviator glasses over features that bordered on homely. Her suit was tweed, the salt-and-pepper material flecked with red nubs. The eyes behind the glasses were sharp, but slightly distorted by the prescription so they looked a third bigger than they were, kind of like viewing fish under water from the air above. A subdued smile showed long teeth that could use some whitening, but there was something about the way she engaged you with those oversized eyes that made you want to be her friend.

"Ms. Radachowski?"

"Uta, please."

"John."

We shook hands, hers nearly as large as mine. "John, I hear you might make me cry some more."

Quite an opening, I thought, as Radachowski released my right hand and waved me toward a chair.

The phone burred, and she apologized for needing to answer it, having just sent her secretary off on an errand. As Radachowski said something into the receiver about rescheduling a deposition, I took a seat and looked around her office. The desk and accompanying furniture were dark like Neely's, but I thought maybe cherry rather than the firm's signature teak. A computer squatted on the desk, and Radachowski cradled the phone on a shoulder as she began clacking away at the keyboard with the facility of a high-speed touch-typist. Her wall displayed photos showing Radachowski speaking from different podiums, the banners of various charitable organizations above and behind her. A different shot had Radachowski standing between Frank Neely and Leonard Epstein, the former with his horse-collar embrace of her, the latter looking sickly, even frail, Radachowski's arm around Epstein's waist seeming to be all that was holding him up. There were also plaques, the only one I recognized given by the Lambda Legal Defense Fund, its "Liberty Award."

Radachowski pressed another key and said, "Got it," into the telephone, followed by, "My direct dial? For the voice mail—if it's working—use five-one-three, two-two-oh-five. . . . Right, bye." She hung up. "Sorry, John."

"The wonders of modern technology."

"When they're not on the fritz."

I gestured toward the computer screen. "You have your calendar in there?"

"Yes, but more than that. The software I use for docket control lets me overlay projected court deadlines and appearances for any county I've got a case pending in. If a deadline changes, the program ripples the modification through like a dollar-item change on a spreadsheet. I want a printout of tomorrow's—or next month's—events, I just hit another button and carry that with me."

"And I remember being in an insurance office when the arrival of a mag-card typewriter was like splitting the atom."

A roar so loud and long it was literally a belly laugh. "I like that." Then Radachowski leaned back in her chair, elbows on its arms. Clasping her hands and steepling the index fingers, she tapped the nails against her chin. "But you aren't here for an update on office technology."

"No, I'm not."

"As Imogene brought you to my door, I was just finishing with Frank Neely. He said to tell you anything I wanted to about Woodrow."

Neely appeared to be a man of his word. "What do you want to tell me?"

"First, that I believe your client killed my friend and partner."

"I have reason to think maybe not."

"So Frank said. But you should know that I'm speaking to you only because I, too, believe in the concept of 'innocent till proven guilty,' however . . . statistically inaccurate it might be."

I wondered if Woodrow Gant, the former prosecutor, had convinced her of that last part.

Radachowski seemed to sense what I was thinking as she tapped her chin some more. "Woodrow was a fine lawyer, and we all miss him tremendously."

"Did you spend much time with Mr. Gant?"

"It's a small office, John, small enough that each person interacts with the others a great deal during the day. Staff meetings, lunches . . ." Her voice dropped. "In fact, I remember an informal brown-bagger all we lawyers had in the conference room a few weeks after the scene your client made there. Woodrow mentioned that he was glad the Spaeth case was going to settle, because Nicole had told him about her husband being 'fond of firearms.' "

Nicole. "You worked with Mr. Gant on the case, then?"

"No. No, because of Epstein & Neely's size, we often bill hours on each other's cases, but Woodrow and I less than most."

"Why was that?"

"He did mostly domestic," said Radachowski. "That's divorces, as you probably know. I'm more civil litigation, with a little charitable organizations work thrown in."

"Not so little, from the Wall of Fame."

The belly laugh again. "You get involved with one, you get asked to speak at another. I'm proud of all, though." Radachowski gestured toward the Lambda one. "Some more than others."

"I don't know much about the Liberty Award, but it's for legal work regarding the gay and lesbian community, right?"

"Regarding discrimination against us." Radachowski waited for a reaction from me, but I don't think she saw one. "I got that award the same night as a congressman and a literary agent. You have any idea what it was like to be a woman—much less a lesbian—graduating law school twenty years ago?"

"None."

Radachowski softened her eyes, bringing me into that cone of friendship I'd noticed before. Must work wonders with a jury.

"Today it's different, John. Many law schools are almost fifty-fifty male/female, with a number of female faculty. While women comprise only ten or fifteen percent of the partners in most large law firms, that will change as today's female graduates move in and up by sheer force of numbers and ability. Back in my time, though, there were literally more black males than women of any color in my graduating class, and only a handful of declared gays or lesbians." Radachowski seemed to go inside herself for a moment. "The fall of my senior year, all the big Boston firms interviewed me, mainly because, one, I had the grades and, two, my law school had a placement policy that forbade overt discrimination based on gender or sexual 'preference,' as they called sexual 'orientation' in those days." Then the eyes hardened a bit, like wary animals turning angry behind the curved walls of a glass cage. "However, there was some obvious discomfort about how I'd 'fit in' with the other lawyers already there."

"Christmas parties and firm outings—"

"—to concerns about loitering with innocent young secretaries in the ladies' room." Radachowski stopped. "But one interviewer was different. He looked down at my résumé, and instead of focusing on the gay/lesbian extracurricular stuff, he asked me what I wanted to do. And, given how little I knew then about how the legal system worked, I told him 'become a . . .'" For the first time, Radachowski seemed to grope for her words. "'A litigator, try jury cases.' Well, the man indicated he thought I'd be good at it. That interviewer was—"

"Uta," said the voice of Patricia from the door. "I left those files and messages—oh, sorry, I didn't know you . . ."

"That's all right," said Radachowski.

"Will you be needing me to do anything else?"

"Not just now, Patricia."

I heard shoes along the carpet outside.

Radachowski shook her head. "Temp," she said to me, lightly. "Trying to do a good job, but a wee bit dense on matters of protocol."

"Not to mention stepping on your line."

The big-toothed smile. "As you've probably guessed, that man at my interview was Frank Neely. He got Leonard Epstein to swing with him, and the firm's hiring committee made me an offer."

Hiring committee? "I thought they *were* the firm?"

"I'm talking two stops ago."

"Then I don't get what you mean."

Radachowski spread her large hands on the desk. "The old firm that hired me was . . . Well, never mind the name of the place. Let's just call it A, B & C."

"Okay."

"A, B & C thought it was quite something for them to have hired a lawyer named 'Epstein' or even 'Neely' thirty years before me, if you get my drift."

Meaning "restrictions" based on religion and ethnicity. "I understand."

"Well, A, B & C began to lose some of their best players as those attorneys realized they couldn't change a partnership structure embedded in the nineteenth century. A number of the lawyers—including Frank and Len—broke off to form a new firm."

"But since you said 'two stops ago,' I take it that 'new' firm wasn't this current one."

"Right."

I thought back to my one year of evening division law school. "Am I also right in thinking that A, B & C couldn't impose a covenant not to compete on its former lawyers?"

"You are. Violation of the Rules of Professional Responsibility, though I have to tell you, it's just a guild protection rule."

"How so?"

"If you're an engineer or a sales manager, your employer can get you to sign a covenant, then get it enforced—reasonably as to geography, duration, and scope of services—if you try to go work for a competitor. You're an attorney and your law firm tries that, it's against public policy."

"Putting lawyers kind of above the law applied to the rest of us."

"Kind of. Anyway, let's call the second firm D, E & F. Frank and Len insisted as a condition of forming that firm that I be allowed to join it as a partner. There was still some resistance—you ever hear the term 'CASP'?"

"Casp?"

"C-A-S-P."

"I don't think so."

"It stands for 'Catholic Anglo-Saxon Protestant.' "

The light dawned. "People who've been discriminated against themselves becoming—"

"—that which they profess to despise the most. There were

a few of them who wouldn't hesitate to use the words 'lezzie' and 'dyke'—or even 'Polack,' for that matter—when I wasn't around. But Frank and Len wouldn't stand for it."

"So?"

"So after some years there, we three decided to split off as a matter of principle and form our own firm. Only this time it looked as though D, E & F might go under first."

"Why?"

"Mostly mergers and acquisitions in the corporate world. Your client is the smaller fish, the law firm for the bigger fish eventually ends up handling all the combined fishes' legal matters. Also, there were a lot of clients simply getting more cost-conscious regarding the legal fees they were being asked to pay."

I considered that. "But Epstein and Neely thought they could take some of even those clients with them."

"Right."

"And again there was no covenant not to compete that could stop them."

Radachowski nodded. "We still had to be careful, though." Another belly laugh. "All the hush-hush steps we conspirators took at D, E & F. The ambiguous memos, the out-of-office meetings. We even had a code name for the real estate broker helping us shop for our new office space here."

"Code name?"

"To put on telephone messages or appointments calendars, so the other partners at D, E & F wouldn't tumble to what we were doing."

It was a nice education for me, and nostalgia trip for Radachowski, but I thought we should return to my case. "Woodrow Gant didn't join up until after you all were here, though, correct?"

She stopped, seeming to remember why I was sitting in front of her. "Correct. Three—no, three and a half—years ago. Woodrow wanted out of the D.A.'s office, and we were a good fit for him."

"How so?"

"We didn't have anybody doing divorce, and in a small firm,

it can be a profit center. Plus, Frank really believed in what he and Len did with me."

"Meaning hiring for . . . diversity?"

A little hardening again, more the cross-examination look than the jury one. "Meaning giving a person of talent a good base."

"So things worked out well."

"Very well. Woodrow thrived here, loved the open atmosphere."

I thought about Imogene Burbage calling her boss, "Mr. Neely," but skipped it. "How do you mean?"

"Woodrow was just . . . real loose. For example, he'd come up to me and say, 'Hey, man, this place is the ultimate comfort zone.' "

Sounded off to me. "He called you 'Hey, *man*'?"

Radachowski shrugged. "He called everybody that. Male, female, old, young, didn't matter. Universal greeting for Woodrow. Which was about the only formality he insisted on."

"Formality?"

"That we all use his full first name, 'Woodrow'—instead of 'Woody'? I think he didn't want anybody linking him even subliminally to that naive bartender on *Cheers*."

I could see Gant's point. "Were you here the day Mr. Spaeth appeared for his deposition?"

A sudden chill in the air. "No, but that doesn't mean I don't feel some responsibility for it."

"How do you mean?"

"I was the one who recommended Woodrow to Nicole in the first place."

Remembering that Radachowski had used Mrs. Spaeth's first name before, I leaned forward. "When was this?"

The eyes behind the thick lenses swam left-right-left for a moment. "I think I can tell you without violating any confidences. It was during the Boston Adult Literacy Fund benefit— at the Charles Hotel in Cambridge? I spoke there seven or eight months ago," a flourish toward the wall of photos behind her, "and of course they introduced me as a lawyer. After my talk, this woman came up to me from the audience, said she needed a divorce lawyer and could I recommend one. Naturally, I gave her my card and Woodrow's name."

"Didn't you say before that divorce work at a small firm can be a 'profit center'?"

"Yes."

"I might be missing something, but it's hard to see how Epstein & Neely could make any money on the Spaeth divorce, given that the husband was out of work."

Radachowski showed me the big teeth. "You might be surprised, John. But that's why I said 'can be' a profit center. The firm doesn't make much off my charitable work, either, but we still believe it important."

"Did you ever meet Alan Spaeth yourself?"

"No. Never even saw him until . . . until the television coverage." Radachowski's eyes began to fill.

I didn't want to lose her cooperation. "I'm sorry to put you through—"

"John," a little harshly, to cut me off while she swiped at the tears with the back of her hand. Then, in the softer tone, "Do you really think you have to apologize to a litigator for anything you ask her about?"

"I guess not."

"So, go ahead."

"There's no question Mr. Gant ate at a restaurant called Viet Mam with a woman that night. There's at least a possibility she also was present when the attack occurred."

A sober nod. "That woman wasn't me."

I said, "Do you have any idea who she might be?"

"No. Woodrow had an . . . active social life, I think, but while we were good friends here at work, we didn't go out much together afterwards, and I don't remember him mentioning anyone in particular as being a steady relationship."

A subtle way to suggest Gant played the field. But also a pretty elaborate answer to my pretty simple question.

I said, "Do you have any suggestions on who might know the woman's identity?"

"Sorry."

Last shot. "How about why Mr. Gant would have picked that particular restaurant?"

"Try Deborah Ling."

"One of the associates here, right?"

A nod. "It seems to me that she recommended the place—no, that's not right. Deborah took him there once."

"When?"

"Oh, months ago."

"How do you know?"

Uta Radachowski steepled the fingers again, tapping her chin in tune to a silent melody. "The name of the place was unusual enough that I remember Woodrow telling me he didn't enjoy the food very much."

Chapter 7

COMING OUT OF Uta Radachowski's office, I was wondering why Woodrow Gant would return, apparently with a date, to a restaurant where he supposedly didn't like the fare. Then I saw the man I believed to be Elliot Herman rushing back into an office. I went up to the doorway and watched him shoveling file folders into an attaché case opened like a clamshell.

Before knocking, I took in his workspace. It was spartan rather than barren, with just some diplomas on the wall, a mini-fridge against it, and two Marine Corps captain's chairs across from a cluttered desk. A paperweight in the shape of the Corps' globe and eagle held down a stack of correspondence next to his computer terminal. Standing on the corner of his desk was a Lucite frame holding a portrait photo of an attractive woman about Herman's age with long, honey-blond hair. The frame was angled so she could be seen from the captain's chairs, a conversation starter should the current visitor not be into the Halls of Montezuma or the Shores of Tripoli.

I rapped my knuckles lightly on the jamb.

Herman looked up, the streak of white hair seeming to ride his head like a racing stripe. "Who are you?"

"Mr. Herman?"

"Yes, but—look, go back to the receptionist, and maybe she can—"

"You're the one I want to see."

"Not a chance." He went back to filling his briefcase. "I've got a meeting outside the office in . . . ," a glance at his watch, ". . . fifteen minutes."

"I'm John Cuddy. Did Frank Neely mention me to you?"

Herman stopped with a file half on its way to joining the others. "Woodrow?"

"That's right."

He frowned. "Look, how about if we talk while I walk to my meeting?"

"Fine with me."

Herman crammed in two more folders, then closed the brief-case by leaning down on its corners with his palms before engaging the clasps with his thumbs. Viewed fully from the front, he had features matching the intense manner I'd seen in the reception area. His eyes were close-set around a strong nose and stronger jaw that looked like it enjoyed giving orders in the old days and chewing out anybody who didn't follow them to the letter.

Herman came toward me briskly with the attaché case, set-ting it down only long enough to grab the jacket of his suit off a hook behind the door and shrug into it.

As he reached again for the case, I said, "Your collar's up."

"What?"

"The collar of your jacket is turned up, as though you're cold."

"Oh. Thanks." Herman fixed it, then snapped his fingers, saying, "Cold, right," and went to the mini-fridge. He opened the door and took out a can of what looked like pineapple juice. Coming back, Herman grabbed his briefcase again and charged by me. As I caught up to him at the reception desk, he said to a woman I'd not seen before, "Out of the office. My wife calls, tell her I'll be back by five."

"Back here, Mr. Herman?"

"Yes," he said testily as he hit the elevator button and was saved a coronary by the door opening for him immediately. Once we started descending, Herman pulled a tab off the top of the can and began gulping.

I said, "Juicing it?"

"What?"

I pointed to his drink.

"Oh. Negative." Herman held the can so I could see the brand name on the label. "This is a liquid meal for people like me who don't have the time to eat."

I nodded, thinking that maybe the cuisine hadn't improved all that much since his days in the Marines. "How does it taste?"

"Like fast food from a can. But it keeps me going."

We reached the lobby, and he was out of the elevator and moving fast in two strides, today's lunch back to his lips. I matched his pace as we hit the street.

"All right," said Herman, throwing the already-empty can toward a trash receptacle screwed into a light pole. "So what are your questions?"

I decided to use what time I had with him on the big issues. "Do you know anybody who had a motive to kill Woodrow Gant?"

At the curb, Herman came to a full stop, apparently a rare enough occurrence for him that he teetered forward. "Yeah. Your client."

"And if Alan Spaeth didn't do it?"

"What are you talking about?"

"There's evidence to suggest that somebody else might have shot Mr. Gant."

Herman stepped into the street, his head bobbing to gauge other pedestrians and vehicular traffic. "I thought the police found Spaeth's prints on the gun?"

"The shells. But even if it was his gun, that doesn't mean he pulled the trigger."

Herman glanced away from his navigating long enough to show me what he thought of that idea. "I do corporate and tax, Mr. Cuddy, mostly for closely held businesses. The last time I read up on criminal law was when I studied for the bar exam. But I was a Marine, too. OCS during college, then active duty before law school."

Herman used his right hand to brush against the white streak in his hair. "In fact, I've got the Corps to thank for this."

"Combat?"

"What?"

"The hair turned white under fire?"

"Oh. Negative. I got hit by lightning."

"Really?"

"Really. Bolt struck a tree, and the shock jumped from it to the three of us nearby. Killed one, paralyzed the other. Me, all I remember is a flashbulb effect and a . . . tingling, spinning sensation, like I was drunk or dizzy. No pain, though, and the only physical vestige of the experience is this hank of hair. But that day next to the tree taught me something important."

"Which is?"

Herman glanced down at his watch. "Never waste any time, because you don't know how much of it you've got left."

I didn't want to lose him to the client clock. "You were saying about Alan Spaeth?"

"About . . . Oh. Right. Back in the Corps, I learned a lot about weapons, enough to sense that your client had something to do with Woodrow's murder, even if I hadn't seen the blowup at the firm."

We were walking parallel to City Hall now. "Can you describe it for me?"

"The blowup?"

"Yes."

"I was in my office that afternoon. When I went to get some coffee, I could see Woodrow seated with a bunch of people in our conference room. A deposition, given the stenographer. There was another woman and two other men, one with a beard, one without. Woodrow did mostly divorce, so I assumed one of the men was the husband, the other his lawyer."

"Wait a minute. Why couldn't one of the men have been Mr. Gant's client?"

Herman waited a beat too long before answering. "I suppose that's possible. But the woman was sitting next to Woodrow on the far side of the table, and maybe I recognized her from another time she was in the office. I don't know. What I do know is I'm pouring my coffee when all hell breaks loose."

"Meaning?"

"Meaning your client, Spaeth, jumps up from the table and starts yelling. That glass in the conference room wall is pretty thick, but you could hear him clearly. Curses, racial slurs, everything. And he comes backing out the door into the reception area, still yelling."

We reached State Street. "Do you remember what he said in particular?"

Another sidelong glance as Herman maneuvered past the rear bumper of a panel truck. "I do, but you don't want to hear it."

"Try me."

"Okay." Herman looked around, less for traffic and more to be sure no one was within earshot. Then he spoke softly. "Spaeth says—yells—'You fucking nigger, you're fucking me over. The only good lawyer is a fucking dead one, nigger.'" Herman looked at me. "And so on."

"But you never saw Spaeth approach Mr. Gant."

A darkening. "What is this, cross-examination?"

"I just mean, the way you described things, Spaeth was backing away from the conference room, not looking to confront or directly threaten Mr. Gant."

"You weren't there."

"Meaning?"

"Meaning I was." We dodged a UPS van. "Look, back in the Corps, I saw a lot of fights. Even had to break up a few. In my opinion, your client was berserk, but not crazy enough to take on Woodrow with only his bare hands."

"How did it end?"

"Frank came out of his office and bellowed at the guy to shut up. You ever hear Frank's voice when he's angry, 'bellow' doesn't quite describe it. More like a mortar round detonating. And it did shut Spaeth up."

"Then what happened?"

"Frank ordered Spaeth to leave, and he did. Good thing, too."

"Why?"

"I could barely hold Grover back."

"Grover?"

"Woodrow's brother."

I remembered Steve Rothenberg mentioning that Gant had "a real questionable" brother.

Herman said, "Grover was in the reception area when all this erupted. I don't think Spaeth could have seen him, backing out the conference room like he was. But I sure did."

"See the brother."

"Yeah. As soon as I heard the 'N'-word, I rushed up to Grover and put a bear hug around his arms, to keep him away. Not the easiest mission in the world, either."

"Because?"

"The brother isn't as strong-looking as Woodrow was, but he's big, too. And he was four-plus mad."

I turned it over. "Did Grover Gant threaten Alan Spaeth at all?"

A shrug. "He might have. I wasn't paying attention to what he said. I was just going, 'Hey, easy now. Take it easy.' "

"Was there anybody else there?"

"Just about everybody, I think. Deborah—Deborah Ling, another associate?—she was in the hall by her office. Stayed out of it, though. And poor Imogene was covering at the reception desk. Looked scared to death."

I tried to picture it. "Ms. Burbage was Woodrow Gant's secretary, right?"

"Right."

"And she kept her boss's brother waiting in the reception area?"

Herman seemed uncomfortable with the question. "I don't know for how long, though."

Meaning it seemed odd to Herman as well that Imogene Burbage wouldn't have Grover Gant wait for his brother in the lawyer's own office.

I said, "And from the conference room, Woodrow Gant at

the far side of the table could see through the glass to where his brother was waiting?"

Herman got very casual. "I suppose." He glanced across the next street, his voice changing back to curt. "My meeting's in that building."

"Just a few more questions, please."

Another check of his watch. "Hurry up and ask them."

"It seems Mr. Gant was having dinner at a Vietnamese restaurant the night he was killed. With a woman. Do you have any idea who she might be?"

"Negative."

"None at all?"

"Woodrow fancied himself a real stud. But whenever he'd say something about seeing a show or going to a restaurant, and you'd ask him with who, he'd always just say, 'Hey, man, a lady,' and smile. All right?"

"All right. Just—"

"Last question." More clock-watching. "I'm pitching a new client here, try to make up some of what we're going to lose by having to refer out a lot of Woodrow's cases. And my wife's coming all the way in from Weston Hills by train to meet me for dinner and *Phantom* over in the theater district."

Weston Hills, the town where Nguyen Trinh and Oscar Huong pulled the home invasion. But no time for that now. "How did Woodrow Gant react to the deposition incident with Mr. Spaeth?"

"React?"

"To what Mr. Spaeth was yelling at him."

"Woodrow just grinned."

"Just grinned?"

"Yeah. Why not?"

"I don't understand you."

Herman shook his head. "Woodrow knew he had him. Cold."

"Mr. Gant said that?"

"He didn't have to. As a lawyer, you drive an opposing client batshit-crazy, you've really done your job."

At which point Elliot Herman turned on his heel and went

through a revolving door hard enough to keep it turning after I'd lost sight of him.

"Ms. Ling?"

"Yes, Mr. Cuddy. Please, come in and sit down."

When I'd gotten back to the law firm, the new receptionist had told me that Deborah Ling also had returned and asked that I see her as soon as possible. By the time I reached Ling's office door, she was looking up at me from her high-backed judge's chair behind a black, lacquered desk, a nondescript credenza holding a computer behind her.

About five-three when she stood to shake hands, Ling had black hair that framed her face in what we once would have called a pixie cut. Her eyes were solemn over a businesslike smile, three diamond studs in the lobe of each ear. She wore a pale green suit with faint pinstriping and a birthday-gift bow under the collar of her white blouse. The desk was completely clean except for a legal pad and pencil.

"Beautiful piece of furniture," I said, taking a seat.

"Thank you." Sitting herself, Ling trailed the fingertips of her right hand lightly over the black surface. "My parents brought it from China, then gave it to me when I graduated law school." Ling looked up at me. "Reluctantly."

"I'm sorry?"

"The traditional Chinese family, Mr. Cuddy, wants its female children educated, but not too educated. The role of the daughter is to care for her parents when they grow older. In the United States, that requires some schooling, even college, but not a degree nearly so . . . portable as a J.D."

"So you traveled a ways to end up in Boston."

"About three thousand miles. There would have been opportunities for me on the West Coast, especially as Hong Kong investors take a closer look at what the mainland has in store for them. But there's also a lot of gender prejudice among the newer immigrants. When most Asian men think of Asian women outside the family circle, they picture Thai and Cambodian 'pleasure girls,' not real estate attorneys."

"Which is your specialty?"

"That's right. Mostly small projects, speculative ventures sometimes. However, enough of that expatriate money makes its way to Boston that I can still use my heritage to wheel and deal some of it. Which is good news, given the student loans I'm still carrying."

The way Ling moved around from topic to topic might be a help to me, so I went with it. "I've heard they can be a bear these days."

"The loans? More like Tyrannosaurus rex. My monthly debt service equals my rent, and I know a couple of people graduating this year who'll total a hundred thousand in principal, with no way of getting a job that will come close to letting them pay it off. You can't deduct the interest on your tax return, and even if you declare bankruptcy, the loans aren't dischargeable as debts."

"Which means it's a good thing you're here."

Ling stopped, suddenly cautious. "At Epstein & Neely, you mean?"

"Yes."

"You bet," she said, more at ease again. "Frank encourages all of us to bring in our own business. Some friends of mine from school, who went to the big firms? They're wearing golden handcuffs now."

"Golden handcuffs?"

"They took jobs that paid a lot, but with little hope for a piece of the pie. Less than twenty percent of male associates ever make partner. And that drops to five percent for females, which is worse than statistics I've seen from the seventies, despite what Uta's always saying. So my friends earning their big bucks are just carrying their loans while they service the clients of the firm and never build their own base."

"Like you are here."

"That's right, Mr. Cuddy. Working in a solid operation with fine people." Another stop. "Including the one your client killed."

"Frank Neely spoke to you about me."

"As soon as I got back from my closing." Ling looked at a

gilded clock on her wall. "And I have another in less than an hour. So, if you have any questions for me, let's get to them."

Ling folded her hands on the desktop, like a sharp third-grader slightly bored by the teacher.

I said, "For starters, I think there's a strong possibility someone other than Alan Spaeth murdered Woodrow Gant."

Ling's face showed no emotion. "I'd expect you to say something like that. Your questions?"

"Do you know of anyone who had a reason to kill Mr. Gant?"

"No."

"Threats or intimidation?"

"Just from your client."

"Let me hold that for a while, and—"

"Deborah, I'm real sorry."

From behind me, the voice of Patricia, the temp who'd also interrupted when I was with Uta Radachowski.

"What is it?" said Ling.

"An urgent call from Ms. Barber."

"Tell her I'll call her back."

"But she tried to reach Mr. Gant, and—"

"Take her number, Patricia," some juice behind it.

"Yes. Sorry."

Ling waited a moment, then looked at me. "Temp."

I nodded.

"I was helping Woodrow with a couple of his divorce clients—selling the marital home? They all need you yesterday."

I nodded again, though I wondered why Ling felt any explanation was necessary. "I'd like to start with the restaurant Mr. Gant ate at the night he was killed."

Except for her lips, Ling might have been a statue. "Why?"

"I understand you introduced him to the place."

"Oh." She shook her head, but it seemed unnatural, like a magician's gesture to an audience. "A friend of mine had tried it, so I took Woodrow there for lunch one day."

"Kind of far from the office for lunch."

"We both had to be in Dedham that morning, him for court, me at the registry of deeds. So we drove out in separate cars, but decided to have lunch together on the way back, and I remembered this restaurant my friend had mentioned. 'Viet Mam,' right?''

"Right," I said evenly.

More head-shake. "I guess I feel a little guilty about it."

"Because?"

"Well, it's probably silly, but if I don't take Woodrow there, he might never have found the place himself."

Five miles from where he lived? "Did Mr. Gant enjoy his lunch at Viet Mam?"

Ling looked at me strangely. "He must have. Otherwise, why go back there?"

"Any idea who the woman with him might have been?"

"No. No, Epstein & Neely is a friendly place, Mr. Cuddy, but Woodrow didn't talk much to me about his personal life."

"Did he talk about it with anyone at the firm?"

"Not that I know of."

"Could we turn to the incident with Mr. Spaeth here in the conference room?"

"If we must."

"You feel uncomfortable discussing it?"

"Mr. Cuddy, Woodrow Gant was a good friend and colleague. When I first came here a year and a half ago, he tried to help me learn the ropes he'd learned two years before that. Frank said we should tell you everything we know so the criminal justice system can function properly. Which to me means nailing your client to the cross he built for himself that afternoon."

"The afternoon of the shouting match."

"If you want to call it that. Your client was the one doing all the shouting."

"Could you describe things for me?"

Ling drew in a breath, then gave pretty much the same account as Herman had, finishing with, "And then Frank ordered your client out, like a father scolding a misbehaving child."

"So, Mr. Spaeth never physically approached either of the Gant brothers?"

Ling stopped a third time. "No, I saw your client only backing away, not actually fighting or even going up to either of them. But I did see his face."

"Mr. Spaeth's now?"

"Yes." Deborah Ling shook her head again, somewhere between natural and theatrical this time. "You ever heard the expression, 'if looks could kill'?"

Who hadn't.

"Mr. Neely said you wanted to see Mr. Gant's office, and he thought it might be more comfortable for you to have me here."

Glancing around the dead man's former space, I said, "But is it more comfortable for you?"

Imogene Burbage gave me one of her controlled smiles, no trace of humor. "Mr. Cuddy, circumstances require me to be in here more than half the day. Mr. Gant's cases have to be referred to other attorneys."

"Can't you just bring in another divorce lawyer to handle them?"

"*I* certainly can't. Perhaps you could ask Mr. Neely about that."

Burbage pointed toward one of two client chairs in front of a desk of iron trestles and smoked glass, the most modernistic furniture I'd seen in the firm. Sunlight from the windows behind Gant's desk refracted through the smoked glass, combining with some heat currents to make whorling patterns on the plain carpet. One long wall had a modular bookcase, complementary African masks mounted on either side of it. The other long wall had a lowboy filing cabinet, a seascape centered above the top. The short wall with the door had diplomas and a trio of football photographs. The first shot showed Gant kneeling on a helmet, and he was identifiable by the number on his jersey in the other, action ones. In effect, most visitors to the office—client, ally, or opponent—probably wouldn't see the sports photos until leaving, and you had to believe that was Gant's intention.

As Burbage took the other client's chair, she crossed her legs at the ankles, bringing both hands to her lap and massaging the right wrist this time. "Mr. Gant was proud of those days."

"Looks like high school."

"It was. He had a full scholarship to college," she gestured vaguely at one diploma, "but Mr. Gant injured his knee somehow in the first practice, and the school canceled his grant-in-aid the next year because he couldn't play anymore. So, after recuperating from the operation, Mr. Gant worked any jobs he could to pay his way through."

I nodded, thinking that Burbage had a better oral presentation style than any of the surviving lawyers. Then she shifted her massage back to the other wrist.

I said, "Arthritis?"

Burbage glanced down at her hands. "C-T-D."

"Which stands for?"

" 'Cumulative trauma disorder.' Comes from hunching over computer keyboards too many hours. The worse kind is carpal tunnel syndrome, but I'm still far from that."

"I hope it stays that way."

Burbage looked at me differently, changing her tone as well. "Does this really work?"

"Does what really work?"

"Appearing to sympathize with the problems of the person you're interrogating."

Quick study, Ms. Burbage. "It works sometimes, when I'm using it as a device. I wasn't just now."

Her expression told me she thought I'd just added another layer of . . . device.

Burbage said, "Perhaps if you'd just ask your real questions."

Okay. "You told me earlier that you'd been with Mr. Gant for over three years?"

"All the time he was here."

"And how long have you been with Epstein & Neely?"

"Since its third month of operation, eight years ago. Originally, Mr. Neely brought over his secretary from the prior firm, but she was pregnant and decided not to return after her maternity leave."

"How many other staffers are there?"

Burbage's expression now told me she thought that an odd question. "Why?"

"I'd like to get a handle on how many more people I might have to interview."

"I'm the only permanent 'staffer,' in the sense I think you mean. The receptionist and the other secretary are temps."

"Isn't that pretty thin on the clerical side?"

"Not at all. Things have changed quite a bit in the last ten years, Mr. Cuddy." Burbage began rubbing her right wrist with her left again. "Most lawyers are now not just computer literate, but computer comfortable. They do a lot of their preliminary drafting by calling up prototypes and altering the forms onscreen themselves."

"Even so, there must be bookkeeping—"

"Which is part of my job."

I turned that over. "In addition to being secretary for the senior partner and Mr. Gant?"

"Mr. Neely's work and Mr. Gant's are . . . were inverse to each other." A more explanatory tone to her voice. "Trust and estates documents tend to be long but not urgent, domestic relations ones shorter but more urgent. Plus, Mr. Neely wanted someone he could . . . someone he knew was familiar with the firm's operation to act as bookkeeper. And we have a computer program that does most of that for me, of course."

Of course. "But doesn't the temp-side kind of disrupt things from a continuity standpoint?"

"Again, not at all. Much of what they do is purely clerical—transcription typing, filing. Besides, it's less expensive to hire temporary help than to provide all the benefits the firm offers to full-time employees." The controlled voice replaced the explanatory one. "I hope that answers your question."

I got the impression that Burbage had felt the conversation was once more veering away from the mandate her boss had given her. "I understand you were at the reception desk when an incident with Mr. Spaeth occurred about two months ago."

"I was."

"Can you describe what you saw?"

Burbage switched the massage to her left wrist, then echoed the Herman/Ling version I'd already heard.

When she finished, I said, "Was there a reason you had Grover Gant wait out in the reception area rather than let him come back here?"

A little crack in her control. "I didn't want to . . . disturb Mr. Gant during the deposition, and, given the glass walls, I thought it best to ask his brother to wait so Mr. Gant could see him and come out at a good stopping point."

"In the deposition."

"Yes."

Plausible, but it wasn't delivered as well as her earlier efforts. "And am I right that you never saw Mr. Spaeth approach or swing on anyone?"

"No, I didn't. But what he *said* was a lot worse than what most people ever *do*."

I didn't envy Steve Rothenberg trying to keep Burbage reined in during cross before a jury. "There's reason to believe that all Mr. Spaeth did was talk."

Burbage stopped the massage to fold her arms across her chest. "You're saying you think someone else might have killed Mr. Gant?"

"Yes."

"But the police found his fingerprints."

"Bear with me a moment, please. You were Mr. Gant's secretary. Was there anyone else who ever threatened him?"

"No."

"You're sure."

"As you said, Mr. Cuddy, I was Mr. Gant's secretary. He would have confided in me."

I filed that away. "And he never mentioned any other problems?"

"Never."

"Not even about the people he used to prosecute?"

"That was all concluded years ago."

"Sometimes grudges die hard."

"Yes," said Burbage. "I know."

A hard person to read. "Witnesses at the restaurant say that a woman had dinner with Mr. Gant before he was killed."

"So I've heard."

"Do you have any idea who she might have been?"

"None."

"The woman was described as blond and attractive, wearing—"

"I don't know who Mr. Gant was seeing."

"He never . . . confided in you?"

Burbage's face lost its tension for just a moment, her composure fading into a checkerboard of paleness and color as she returned her hands to her lap. "That was . . . uncalled for, Mr. Cuddy."

"I'm sorry."

Burbage looked behind the desk, as though she were addressing someone sitting in the swivel chair. "Mr. Gant was very active socially. Women would call him here, but never meet him here."

"When they asked for Mr. Gant over the telephone, they didn't give you or the receptionist their names?"

"No. Mr. Gant didn't like us screening his calls that way. He said it might discourage a potential client who didn't want her name known as yet."

More plausible, given the divorce context. "Then how do you know these women reached him here?"

Burbage came back to me. "Mr. Gant would close his door." Abruptly, her tone shifted again. "Mr. Cuddy, I don't know who that woman in the restaurant was."

Those were Burbage's words. But I had the feeling that if she did know, Imogene Burbage wouldn't tell me anyway. At least out of loyalty to her dead boss, and maybe because of some other emotions kicking around inside her as well.

"Mr. Neely said he wanted to speak with you after you'd seen Mr. Gant's office."

Burbage announced that over her shoulder in a loudish voice when we were almost to the reception area. Aware of her, the temp behind the desk there said, "Imogene, could you please look at this?"

As Burbage walked toward her, I saw another woman sitting in the same wing chair I'd used. She looked a little older than in the photo on Elliot Herman's desk. Athletic legs were shown generously by a short evening dress, a coat lying across her lap. The hair was still honey-blond, but now clipped short in layers all around, like a furry hat the moths had found over the summer. Despite that, she remained attractive, a little mole just under the right eye accenting her face rather than de-tracting from it. Both eyes followed me as she nodded.

I nodded back.

The woman rose, making a production out of it in high heels that brought her to maybe five-eight. "I don't believe we've met. Karen Herman."

I took her hand. Warm and clutchy. "John Cuddy."

"I overheard what Imogene said to you." A conspiratorial tone as Herman released my hand. "You're going to be replac-ing Woodrow here at the firm?"

"No. I'm investigating Mr. Gant's death."

Her lower lip quivered.

"And by the way," I said, "if your husband's late for your date, it's my fault."

The lip quivered some more. "I don't care if Elliot's an hour late, so long as he was helping you put that murderer away."

Uh-oh. "Actually, he wasn't."

Herman's right index finger went to the mole under her eye, flicking at it. "I don't understand."

"I'm not a police officer, Mrs. Herman."

"You're not?"

"No. I work for the attorney representing Alan Spaeth."

The hand dropped to her side. Without another word, she turned and began walking toward the hall I'd used for Elliot Herman's office.

The temp glanced away from Imogene Burbage, then down to her board, then at Karen Herman's receding back. "But your husband's still on that conference call."

The busy associate's wife never even broke stride.

Chapter 8

IMOGENE BURBAGE LOOKED at me questioningly, but didn't say anything about Karen Herman. Instead, Burbage led me back to Frank Neely's office, and I followed her into it.

As Burbage moved toward the closed closet door, I could see Neely wasn't at his desk. "I can come back another day."

Burbage had her hand on the knob. "Mr. Neely's upstairs." She opened the door. "You first, please."

A wrought-iron, spiral staircase was spotlit from above like a piece of movable scenery on a stage.

As I walked up to Burbage, I got a closer look at a framed photograph next to the old one of the senior partner in his Army uniform. This shot was sepia, too, and showed Neely and a number of other GI's, wearing Ranger patches and ducking at the base of a cliff. Having seen a similar photo once, I thought I recognized the setting.

"Mr. Cuddy?" said Burbage.

I climbed the narrow, winding stairs. My shoes made the

iron steps clang hollowly in the closet shaft, Burbage coming behind me and creating echoes over echoes.

"I hope we're not trying to sneak up on him."

My guide didn't respond.

At the top of the single flight was another closed door, the spotlight now strong and warm on my head and shoulders.

"Open it, please," said Burbage behind me.

The door swung outward, and I had the sensation of being in one of those old horror movies, where the scene you see isn't what you'd expect.

In this case, a tropical garden.

"Come in, John, come in." Neely's voice carried through the foliage. "It's something of a jungle, but mercifully without the predators."

There was a walkway three feet wide, its base composed of square, inlaid tiles in burgundy. Stepping onto the path, I looked up. Greenhouse glass reflected that alien glow of grow lights, the glass set into an aluminum superstructure. The aluminum struts slanted down and away from the ridgepoled peak twelve feet above to a red-bricked knee wall rising maybe two feet off the floor. Around me were trees and bushes bearing blossoms of every color, some more typical, others more exotic. A thick, perfumed mugginess hung in the air, like the atmosphere at the prayer rail of a funeral home.

Burbage closed the door and edged past me on the walkway without brushing against my suit. "This way, Mr. Cuddy."

The path wound through the greenery to a seating area of wrought-iron patio furniture painted white and upholstered with cushions the color of the tiles. Frank Neely stood in front of one chair, a rolling, glass-topped liquor cart to his right, no drink poured as yet on the small cocktail table to his left. He'd changed clothes since I'd seen him downstairs, the lawyer uniform gone in favor of a long-sleeved chamois shirt, khaki pants, and boat mocs.

Burbage said, "Will you be needing me for anything else, Mr. Neely?"

"No, thank you, Imogene. Just make sure everything's

locked tight before you leave, and I'll let Mr. Cuddy out when he's ready to go."

"See you in the morning, then. Mr. Cuddy."

I turned, but Imogene Burbage was already walking away, her modest heels clicking back toward the staircase door.

Neely said, "I thought I'd give you a choice."

I turned back to him.

He tapped the round, marble top of the cocktail table. "We can have drinks here or on the terrace."

"Outside's fine with me."

"Yes. A little crisp, this time of year, but you look like the sort of man who doesn't bother with a topcoat till Thanksgiving. I love it inside among the flowers, but I've been told the air can be a bit close for others."

"Let's see the terrace."

Neely grinned, leading me along a different, curving path to the front of the building. French doors opened onto a twenty-by-fifteen area enclosed by an extension of the brick knee wall. The terrace was bordered on the right by the greenhouse and on the left by a sliding glass door to the living room of an apartment, the half-structure I'd seen from the sidewalk below. There was more of the wrought-iron furniture, but that wasn't what caught your eye.

Neely said, "Hell of a view, isn't it?"

No argument there. A hundred-twenty-degree slice of Boston Harbor shimmered beneath us under a veil of clouds like the trackmarks left by a bulldozer. Five stories up, Neely's roof was just far enough off the ground to muffle the unseen car traffic, just close enough to distinguish the people on the moored sailboats. Including one couple braving the wind off the water to neck on their quarterdeck, apparently oblivious to our being able to see them from above.

"Ah," said Neely. "Perhaps we should leave Romeo and Juliet to themselves."

Nodding, I turned, looking into the modest front room at the left decorated with couch and several easy chairs, louvered windows facing eastward as well.

I said, "How big is the greenhouse part?"

"Fifty by forty."

I did some quick arithmetic. "Doesn't leave you a lot of floorplan for apartment living space."

"That might depend on how you define 'living,' John. All I do in the penthouse there is sleep and read, and perhaps microwave leftovers from some take-out place or another. The terrace and the greenhouse are where I prefer to spend my time when—wait a minute."

I stopped, Neely looking back at the harbor. "Seems the lovebirds have repaired to a more comfortable billet below. Drinks on the terrace after all?"

"Fine."

"Ask for what you like. If it's not in stock, I won't be embarrassed."

"Vodka collins."

"Have a seat and enjoy the evening."

Neely was gone only about five minutes, but when he came back, the sky was nearly showing stars.

"The pity about this time of year," handing me my drink in a tall tumbler.

"Losing the light so early?"

"Exactly." Neely had about five fingers of what looked like scotch over ice in an Old-fashioned glass as he lowered himself into the chair next to me, sitting at an angle so we both could watch the harbor.

I said, "Is the view what sold you on this location for the firm?"

Neely sipped his scotch. "Before I bore you with that, did you speak to everyone you wanted?"

"Yes." I had the feeling each had reported to him after seeing me, but being polite wouldn't hurt. "Thanks again for being so cooperative and asking them to do the same."

Neely waved it off. "The right thing to do. But now for the boring part. At my first two firms, I was mainly a trial attorney. Both offices fronted the water, but prestige then meant the highest floors the firms could command, and in those buildings that was so far up, the views became . . . I don't know, 'sterile,' maybe? You'd see the planes taking off and landing at Logan, the yachts and the booze cruises and even some honest working folk when they could still commercially fish the harbor. But you couldn't see any faces or equipment, hear somebody's laughter or the wind whistling through the rigging. From here, you get it all, even some of the stink when summer heats up the pollution in the water."

"So you chose this building when you formed your own firm."

"I did. Or we did, Len Epstein and I."

"The partnership owns the building?"

"Ah, no. Actually Len and I bought it as real estate partners, not law partners. Tax reasons. When he passed on, the building passed to me."

"Along with its 'available space'?"

That bittersweet smile. "You'd be referring to the conspicuous absence of tenants on the floors below the firm."

"Must be one hell of a cash drain."

"It is, truth to tell. Len and I bought at the apex of the real estate frenzy, and after the market tanked, we were lucky to hold on." Neely seemed to look back in time. "When Len died, I sold a few things to sort of consolidate here. I built this little aerie and began living above the offices." A slow swinging of the head. "I like to tell people my commute's only fifteen vertical feet, which is about the height of that staircase you climbed with Imogene."

"So you traded prestige for convenience."

Neely seemed to stall a moment, like an airplane engine that hit a patch of turbulence it wasn't expecting. "Prestige isn't all it's cracked up to be, John. And besides, my client base now is trusts and estates. They're buying my capacity to do contingency planning for generations of beneficiaries."

"Contingency planning?"

"Yes. If X dies before Y, should everything go to Y? If Y dies, should the remainder go to Z? And so on." The rumbling from his chest. "An old trial lawyer's pension, John, is doing the probate of people who predecease him."

I thought of Steve Rothenberg, "diversifying" into divorce

work from criminal, which reminded me of why I'd come to Epstein & Neely in the first place. "Couple of questions?"

"About probating estates?"

"About Woodrow Gant."

Another, bigger bite of the scotch. "Ask."

"Do you know of anybody other than Alan Spaeth who could have a reason for wanting Mr. Gant dead?"

"No. Emphatically, no."

"Any ideas on the woman he was having dinner with that night?"

"As in who she could have been?"

"Yes."

"Afraid not, but I had the impression that Woodrow was what my generation would have called a 'ladies' man.' That woman you're asking about could have been any one of a number, none of them known to me."

"He never mentioned their names to you?"

"Never. In fact, it got so I'd listen for one, because he'd talk about taking a driving weekend to the Cape or the mountains. But Woodrow never used a name, just 'Hey, man, I was with a lady.' "

Neely put a lot of street-black into that last, but then he'd known Gant, and I hadn't. "How about what you remember from the day Alan Spaeth made the scene in your reception area?"

Neely's account was no different from the others, and he also conceded that he hadn't seen Spaeth move toward anyone. "But I'll tell you what I did see." Neely lifted the glass an inch. "I saw your client's eyes."

"His eyes."

"Yes, from less than ten feet away. The look in them, a willingness to . . . kill." Neely's drink rose another inch. "Something I hadn't seen up close for a long, long time."

I took a chance. "Not since climbing Pointe-du-Hoc?"

Neely stopped the scotch halfway to his mouth. "That is one hell of a guess."

"I saw the Ranger photos on your wall downstairs. And I had an uncle who landed with the Eighth Infantry on D-Day."

"The Eighth. They hit Utah Beach, correct?"

"Yes, the little he ever talked about it."

"It wasn't something we did talk about." Neely set his glass down. "I'm old enough to remember the Cocoanut Grove fire in 'forty-two, and I'll never forget the lines of people outside the old Southern Mortuary, praying and crying while they waited to identify their loved ones lost in the smoke and flames. But nothing else I ever saw compares to Omaha Beach that morning in June of 'forty-four. Nothing."

He seemed to address the harbor. "Our unit's mission was to knock out the one-five-five millimeter guns the Germans had mounted in concrete casemates at the top of the Pointe, six of them aimed at the Allied ships coming toward both Utah and Omaha. We were trained by British commandos, John, and they trained us well. Assaulting dress-rehearsal beaches and scaling cliffs in Scotland, double-timing everywhere we went, push-ups as a 'rest break.' But nothing prepared us for the Channel sea being choppy enough to swamp our landing craft if we didn't go slow, our coxswains having to fight the tidal current. All of which meant we hit Omaha more than half an hour late, way after the naval and air bombardment on the cliff was over, giving the Germans plenty of time to climb back out of their holes and open up on us. Devastating cannon and machine-gun fire, our boats exploding, corpses floating in the water, body parts . . . pinwheeling through the air. The noise, the . . . carnage. Unbelievable. And when we fired our rocket-guns to carry grappling hooks up to the cliff, the rope attached to our hooks was so wet it was too heavy. Which meant most of the hooks fell short while we were being cut to pieces crossing from the touchdown point through the shallow water and up to the base of the cliff. But a couple of the hooks made it, and we started climbing. Hand-over-hand, up the face of that rock, the Germans sawing away on our ropes and raining death down upon us. And finally, when we reached the top . . . ."

I'd read about it. "The guns weren't there."

Neely looked to me once before going back to the harbor. "That's right, John. Some telephone poles were sticking out of the bunkers, to fool the aerial reconnaissance. But our intelligence people had fouled up. They didn't know the Germans had moved the guns away from the shoreline, and they should have." Neely drummed his index finger against the arm of his chair by the scotch. "They should have known that, John."

"Maybe they knew it, but couldn't get word to you."

"They had radios. And even carrier pigeons that could cross the Channel with little rolled messages in metal quivers on their legs."

"The weather was pretty rough during the week before D-Day, wasn't it?"

"Awful."

"So, maybe they tried to send a message by radio or pigeon, but it didn't get through to England."

"No, John, no. They just didn't follow up on that casemate before we embarked. Oh, we found the guns eventually—inland a ways—and blew them to kingdom come with thermite grenades. But we wouldn't have had to climb that goddamn cliff and take more than fifty percent casualties doing it. We were . . . let down by our own people, John. And that's a pill too bitter to swallow."

I thought of Saigon during the Tet Offensive. "I know."

Neely suddenly leaned back. "Sorry. You've probably got your own memories like that."

My face may have shown him something. He said, "After we first spoke this afternoon, I made a few phone calls. You were Military Police in Vietnam."

"For a while."

Neely sipped some more of his scotch. "I learned one thing that day at Pointe-du-Hoc, John. You lose your innocence when somebody your own age dies in front of you."

That was the first thing Neely had said that sounded practiced, a line rolling a little too smoothly off the tongue.

He set his drink down again. "And I've learned maybe one thing since. Old age has no purpose, except to remind you of being young and to punish you for having pissed it away."

I gestured with my own glass. "I wouldn't exactly say all this came from 'pissing it away.' "

"No." Neely grinned sheepishly. "No, 'all this' is the product of a lot of hard work. When I first got started in practice, clients came to you because they trusted you, like the family doctor. And they took your advice, so you and the other lawyers could run the system, keep everything going for everybody. You decided to form a partnership, it was just a handshake among honorable men. And documents were typed up by secretaries you worked with forever. Now, nobody trusts lawyers, and the clients have taken over the system. Getting a big case is like a beauty contest, where you have to show up in a corporation's conference room and actually 'bid' on representing the company in a lawsuit. Attorneys spend more time in front of a computer 'on-line' than they do in a courtroom 'on-trial,' and with so many younger ones out there, the competition for even the smaller cases is fierce. Clericals of both genders are suing their firms for sexual harassment, and nobody's civil to anybody anymore. It's all cutthroat, John, just another business instead of an honored profession. Things have gotten to the point that lawyers are even hiring themselves out as temps."

"Is that what you'll do?"

Neely seemed thrown by the question. "What?"

"Is that how you'll deal with the loss of Woodrow Gant, bring in some temporary attorneys to replace him?"

"No. No, for a couple of reasons. First, I don't believe in hiring attorneys except for the long haul."

"As opposed to clerical staff?"

Neely picked up his glass, tilting it toward me. "*Touché*, if that doesn't date me even more than the war stories. You're right, we hire temps for support purposes because it's cost effective. But the kind of practice Woodrow had, the clients are hiring the lawyer, not the firm. I couldn't just bring in a 'substitute teacher' to cover his divorce cases, even if I wanted to. And it'll take a while to find someone who's good enough to join us. You see, Woodrow had a way about him that inspired confidence, and we'll just have to let his clients find other counsel. With our help, if needed."

"Which means you'll lose the fees from those cases."

"The unearned portions. But Imogene is going through the files and billing records, and we'll resolve that." Neely looked over at me. "I will have to replace Woodrow with someone soon, though, and so I'm going to ask you one question that I'd like a straight answer to."

I set down my drink. "Go ahead."

"A little while ago, I said there was no real purpose to getting old. But it does help with reading people. I'm reading you now, and I don't think you're just going through the motions."

"Regarding Alan Spaeth, you mean?"

"That's what I mean."

"You said as much in your office earlier."

Neely fixed me with the same look he used down there. "I know I did, John, but I have a firm to run here."

"I don't think I've heard your 'one question' yet."

Neely eased off the look. "It's because I need the answer but don't really want to hear it." His eyes moved to the scotch, then back to me. "Did you find out anything from us that suggests your client *didn't* kill Woodrow?"

The man had been straight with me, allowing me access he didn't have to, and I wanted to be straight with him. "Just what you told me about the insurance."

"The insurance?"

"Yes. You said Mr. Gant's 'family members' were the beneficiaries on his life policies."

Neely raised his drink. "Mother Helen and brother Grover— 'Grover Cleveland Gant.' I checked the paperwork after we spoke down in my office, but I'd written the company myself on their behalf, so I was pretty sure of the proceeds."

"Which were?"

"One hundred thousand each."

"How about the balance of Mr. Gant's estate?"

Neely took some more scotch, nearly finishing it. "His will became public record once it was filed, so I guess there's no harm in telling you what it says. Everything to the mother, with Grover as contingent beneficiary."

I nodded.

Neely said, "You're thinking the brother?"

"I've been wondering why Ms. Burbage would keep him waiting in the reception area rather than let him go to Mr. Gant's office."

Neely considered something. "That was Woodrow's instruction, actually."

"His instruction?"

"Yes." Neely rolled the cubes in his glass. "It seems that once—when Imogene did have Grover wait in Woodrow's office—there was something . . . missing afterward."

"What was it?"

"Cash, a couple hundred that Woodrow kept as an emergency fund in his desk."

I had the same habit, though my stash was tucked halfway through an old photo album in one of my desk's lower drawers.

Neely drained the last of the scotch. "Woodrow told me his brother has a problem with gambling."

"Thanks for the information."

"One other thing, John?"

"Yes?"

"It wasn't part of the firm coverage, but something Woodrow took out on his own."

"What was?"

"You knew he'd gotten divorced himself?"

"Just that, no details."

"Around the time he came with us. His ex-wife lives out in Brookline." The town just west of Boston's Brighton neighborhood. "Pollard's last name. Jenifer—with only one 'n.' "

Taking that in, I said, "And he had a policy on himself payable to her, too?"

"Part of the divorce settlement, Woodrow once told me."

"Face amount?"

"The same as the others, a straight hundred thousand."

I watched Neely for a moment. "Not that I don't appreciate the information, but why so helpful?"

He rolled the cubes some more, almost like dice in a cup. "I want to get to the bottom of this as much as anyone, John, and more than most. I recruited Woodrow for the firm, and now I need to replace him. The sooner we have closure on his death, the better for everyone."

Neely fixed me again. "Don't get me wrong. I believe your client did this terrible thing. I watched him downstairs that day, and I know what I saw in his eyes. But I also know what I see in yours, and that's a man who won't let go until he's convinced. So the sooner you check out these other possibilities, the sooner my job gets easier."

Frank Neely looked away then, giving me one more chance to appreciate the view from his terrace before he led me downstairs and out of the building.

Chapter 9

AFTER LEAVING THE law firm building, I stopped at a pay phone to check my answering service. A nice woman with a silky voice gave me several messages, but nothing from Nancy. Then I dialed my home phone, using the remote code to trigger the telephone tape machine. No messages, period. It had been less than twenty-four hours since Nancy had walked out on me at Thai Basil, but I tried her apartment in South Boston anyway. When her own answering machine engaged, I waited for the beep, then left a very neutral "I'll be out myself tonight, so I'll try you tomorrow at work."

No sense in pushing it, whatever "it" was for Nancy.

Then I walked uphill to Tremont Street to get my car.

Dorchester is a section of Boston most people think of as infrequently as possible. In much of it, the storefronts tend to plywood windowpanes and gang insignia, the housing to rundown triple-deckers with blistered paint and rotting porches. But there are pocket neighborhoods that could be models for a magazine, and Helen Gant lived in one of these. Her home was a single-family, gingerbread-and-yellow Tudor, centered on a quarter-acre lot with a small lawn and tended shrubbery. A Mitsubishi compact stood in the narrow driveway, its grille snubbed up close to the house, as though making parking room behind it for a second car expected to arrive later.

I left the Prelude at the curb and used the cement path to approach the front door. Light shone through curtains, and when I pressed the doorbell, a hand was opening locks before the chimes had died away.

"Why you can't keep your house keys with—uh-uh?"

The African-American woman in front of me ended her sentence with a hiccuping sound as she saw who I was. Or wasn't. In her early fifties, with hair fashioned into silver-and-black kinks half an inch long, she wore a robin's-egg blue blouse over a plaid skirt and opaque hosiery, a commuter's tennis sneakers on her feet. The woman was only about five-two, but the set of both her eyes and her lips suggested she'd recovered enough to take charge of the situation.

"Who are you?"

"John Cuddy. Helen Gant?"

A cautious, "Yes?"

"Mrs. Gant, I'm a private investigator." I took out my ID and held it to her.

She read the printing quickly. "What's this about?"

"I'm looking into your son's death, and I was hoping you could spare a little time."

Hiccup. "Your company called me today, said they'd send somebody by my office tomorrow morning."

"I'm not here about the insurance, Mrs. Gant. I was hired by Alan Spaeth's attorney."

Her eyes went cold. "Then why should I talk to you?"

"Because from some things I've found out so far, I think the police might have arrested the wrong man."

Gant blinked twice, then put a hand to her eyes, more to cover them than to block tears, I thought. Then she took the hand away. "Those same police said I don't have to talk with anybody from that . . . man's side of the case."

"No, ma'am, you don't. But you should."

Gant moved her tongue against the inside of her cheek, then opened the door wider. "Fifteen minutes."

"Thank you."

I passed her, and she locked the door behind us. In front of me was a staircase with natural-oak balustrades just different enough that they had to have been hand-carved. Similar spokes rose vertically between the sills and tops of false windows on either side of the double-wide, interior doorway to the right. Beyond the doorway was a living room furnished with leather sofa, oak coffee table, and two barrel chairs arranged on an oriental rug.

The fireplace—also oak—dominated one wall, some family portrait photos on the mantel. I tried not to look at them, but Helen Gant must have caught me.

"I have a friend at the office who told me in her religion, when somebody dies, they lie the photos of that person face-down for a year. I couldn't bear to do that." The hiccuping noise again. "Please, take one of the chairs."

I did, and Gant sat at the end of the couch closest to me, leaving about five feet between us.

I said, "Where do you work?"

She composed herself with knees together, hands clasped on top of them. "Social welfare, Mr. Cuddy. I do mostly outreach and tracking programs."

"Meaning visiting recipients in their homes?"

"Some days. I'm a 'mandated reporter' under the state statute, so if I see evidence of abuse during my visit, I have to file a 51A with the DSS—the Department of Social Services? Then the department investigates, either to screen the incident out or . . ."

The hiccup again, but now a different look. "You're doing what I do."

"I'm sorry?"

"You're using the same technique I use for interviewing a family. Get them talking about themselves to see how they're functioning as a unit."

"Mrs. Gant—"

"By the way, it's Ms. Gant."

"Sorry again."

A level stare. "No need to be. I dropped out of high school to have Woodrow when I was fifteen, and stayed out for Grover two years later. Thought giving them the names of presidents might help them get past their fathers, neither of which being what you'd call a prizewinner." Another hiccup, and Helen Gant lifted her chin. "I lived with my mother, went to work as a housekeeper in a hotel downtown. Started at six A.M. in the laundry, washing and folding, then on to the rooms, scrubbing on my hands and knees in bathrooms, keep the mildew from getting a foothold. I'd be finished by four in the afternoon, five pounds lighter than I was getting there in the morning." Hiccup. "But I went right from work to school for my G.E.D., and then on to UMass/Boston for college. Got the degree, got the job at Welfare, got this house. And never looked back until your client killed my Woodrow. Now, what more do you want from me?"

Gant was impressive, containing her emotion rather than displaying it.

I said, "Witnesses agree your son had dinner with a woman at a nearby restaurant before he was killed."

"The police told me."

"Do you have any idea who she could have been?"

"No. Why?"

"The woman may have been with your son when he was shot. She might have seen something that would tell me who the killer really was."

Gant watched me carefully. "Or she might give that lawyer you're working for some kind of ammunition for reasonable doubt."

"That's part of my job, too."

Gant looked down at her hands. "Woodrow hated that O.J. Simpson business."

Until she said that, it hadn't struck me that Spaeth's wife was also named "Nicole."

"My son felt the way that trial was televised destroyed people's faith in the system." Raising her eyes, Gant hiccuped again. "Well, Mr. Cuddy, I've seen the system. Seen kids beaten by their parents, and beaten by their stepparents, and beaten by any somebody who just happened to be dropping by that night for a couple of rocks in the crack pipe." Hiccup. "Those are the kids end up getting beaten by the police, too, or shot by each other. It's not cases like O.J.'s that destroy people's faith in the system. It's the people themselves and the system itself."

"Yet you're still working within it."

"You have to do something to try and help people." Gant relented a little. "People helped me when I needed it."

"And I need your help now."

She moved her tongue around again. "We back to who that woman might be?"

"Yes."

"Mr. Cuddy, I truly don't know." Hiccup. "When Woodrow was in college and law school, he went out a lot, but I never met any of them. Then he got married, and I thought he'd finished up with sowing his wild oats. But after the divorce, Woodrow went right back to them. Don't get me wrong, he was a good son. Come by on Sundays for dinner, always remembered birthdays and holidays." Hiccup. "But his social life was his own, and I never met anybody after Jenifer."

"His ex-wife."

"Yes."

"I plan to talk with her, too."

Gant hesitated. "Why?"

"See if she can help."

A skeptical look. "You think a man would tell his ex-wife about a new girlfriend?"

"It's possible that Ms. Pollard would know someone who had a reason to kill your son."

Hiccuping, Gant closed her eyes once, then opened them slowly. "That system we were talking about me working in? Well, Woodrow worked in it, too, Mr. Cuddy. Did everything he was supposed to, and it got him killed. When he was with the district attorney's office, I worried for him, on account of I knew the children I'd seen at age five he'd be seeing at fifteen. A lot of them don't have any feeling except hate, and that they keep burning in a special place deep inside them, a place nobody can touch." Hiccup. "And they don't forget. But the police say your client killed my son, and so far I haven't heard anything from you that tells me different."

A car with a Gatling gun for a muffler pulled up near her house. "Ms. Gant—"

"You asked for me to talk with you, and I did. I didn't have to, but I did, and I'll even tell you why. It's because talking about Woodrow is better than thinking about him. Talking about him makes it seem like maybe there's still something there, a part of my son still with me." Hiccup. "When I'm just thinking about him, all I can see is his body, lying in the coffin at the wake that night or being lowered into the ground that next morning. Which is a hell I wouldn't want even Mr. Alan Spaeth to share."

As Helen Gant rose, I heard a key in the front door. She turned that way and spoke to someone I couldn't yet see.

"Grover?"

"Yeah, yeah, yeah."

"This man is here about Woodrow." Hiccup. "You can talk to him or not. I'm going upstairs."

"I was just at this TV thing?"

Grover Cleveland Gant sat on the couch as his mother had, but he leaned back into the cushions. About six-two, Gant hid his weight beneath a bulky, crewneck sweater and shapeless pants. The hair ran almost long enough—and tall enough—to be an Afro from the seventies. His face was puffy, like a prize-fighter who'd been not so much hammered as jabbed, lightly but constantly, over the last couple of days, his lips closed into a dazed, somehow satisfied smile. His fingers were puffy, too, and if what I could see was any indication, he wasn't in great shape under the clothes.

"TV thing?" I said.

"Yeah, man. Weird, we-*ird*, *we*-ird. I got this invitation card in the mail, come down to a hotel on Tremont by the old Combat Zone. Well, I didn't have nothing better to do with my time, so I went. There's about a hundred of us—white, Chinese, wheelchairs, you name it. At the door to a ballroom, these two foxy ladies in dressy outfits, they taking down names and jobs you did and such, then they have us sit around these four TV sets raised up high in the center of the room and pointed every which way. The foxy ladies tell us we got to sit through these two pilot shows, give them our views on what we like and don't like. Only thing is, there's more commercials than show, and they ask us lots of questions about those, too. More, in fact, like they really interested in whether we go out and buy the things than watch the programs. Which was just as well, account of the shows really sucked. I walked out, halfway through the second one, and don't nobody try to stop me."

I thought Gant might have stopped off himself somewhere for a couple of pops on the way home, but as long as he was talkative, I was happy to let him go on. "You watch a lot of television?"

He squinted at me. "No way, no *way*, *no* way. I got better things to do with my time, usually."

"Like what?"

A sly smile replaced the dazed one. "Track."

"Horseracing?"

"Not 'less I can help it. I'm a greyhound man, myself. With the ponies, you got what I call the human factor working against you."

"The human factor?"

"Yeah. You got the jockey on your horse, the jockeys on the other ones. You don't know who wants it more or who got paid to hold back this race, let somebody else finish in the money."

"But with the greyhounds, it just the animals themselves."

"Right, right, right. You can trust a puppy, man. Can't trust people."

As good an opening as any. "Mr. Gant, you understand I'm here to talk with you about who killed your brother."

"Police got who killed my brother. White mother—no offense."

"None taken." I adjusted my voice. "It may be they have the wrong guy."

The features closed down some. "Uh-unh. I seen him, man."

"Who?"

"That Spaeth dude. At Woodrow's lawyer office. He was screaming, 'Nigger, nig-*ger*, *nig*-ger,' and like that. I come close to killing him myself." A pause. "Wish I had. Then Woodrow be alive now."

"Did you see Mr. Spaeth approach your brother at all?"

" 'Approach' him? Man, what you talking about? The dude was ranting and raving. About how Woodrow fucked him over, how lawyers ought to die. I mean, what more you got to know?"

"You were close to your brother then?"

A cloud came over the eyes. "Say what?"

"You said you wished you'd killed Mr. Spaeth to save your brother, so I assume the two of you got along."

"Yeah, yeah, yeah. We got along just fine. Momma had us from different men, but she raised us together." The sly smile again. "Wasn't Woodrow's fault he got the brains and I got the good looks."

"Then your brother would have confided in you if something was bothering him?"

The cloud again. "What you trying to put in my mouth here? Woodrow was a good brother. Loan me money when I needed it, let me drive that fancy BMW car of his."

For a moment, I wondered if somebody could have mistaken Woodrow Gant for Grover behind the wheel that night, then discounted the thought based on body type and dress code. "Lent you money when you needed it for the track?"

"Man, I already told you, I like to gamble some. They pass a new law I never heard about?"

"Most people gamble with their own money."

"Yeah, well, I'm like between jobs right now."

"What do you do when you're working?"

"Restaurants."

"Waiter?"

"That's right." The sly smile made another appearance. "And none of them cheap places, neither. Expensive restaurant, you do a halfway decent job, they gonna tip you fifteen percent minimum, maybe even eighteen, twenty on a hundred-dollar tab. Even at the low end, though, that's fifteen dollars in your pocket. Cheap place, the bill's gonna be more like forty, say, but you still got to make the same number of trips to the kitchen or the bar. In fact, any time I'm looking for work, I walk into a restaurant like I'm a customer first, ask to see the menu. That way, I can tell does the place have cheap stuff."

"What if there're no prices on the menu?"

The smile got slyer. "I like those kinds of restaurants the best. Ritzy, not glitzy, and you can get humongous tips from guys bringing the old lady out for their twenty-fifth. He's gonna go overboard on the wine, maybe even some brandy. Don't want to look like a tightwad on her one big night on the town, and he'll tip the way them Rockefellers ought to."

"But you're not working in a place like that now."

"No, man. Like I said, I'm between jobs at the moment. Woodrow, he was the one always trying to get ahead. And look where it got him."

"The night your brother was killed, he ate at a Vietnamese restaurant."

"So?"

"He was with a woman, Mr. Gant. Do you have any idea who she might have been?"

"Uh-unh, uh-*unh*, *uh*-unh. Woodrow and me, we mostly see each other at dinner over here. He don't talk about his ladies in front of Momma."

"And he never mentioned anybody to you?"

"Not since he got divorced from that English bitch. She made him real careful about lady kind of things."

"Did you know his former wife well?"

"Ain't nobody knows that Jenifer 'well.' You know her at all, though, you watch out for her."

"How do you mean?"

"Body armor, man." Grover Gant ran both hands from shoulders to knees. "You going anywhere near that bitch, you got to wear it." Then he hitched the right hand at his crotch. "At least a cup, you hear what I'm saying?"

"Why don't you spell it out for me?"

A snort. "Bitch is a ball-buster. Eats 'em for breakfast, man, you let her."

I stood up. "Well, Mr. Gant, thanks for your time."

He stayed seated, the sly look back. "So, when am I gonna see my check?"

"Your check?"

"For the insurance, man. The money I got coming to me on Woodrow's policy."

"I don't have anything to do with that."

"What're you talking about?" Sly turned sour. "I call the company, they say they be sending somebody out to talk to us, Momma and me. That ain't you?"

"No."

Gant rose, needing to use both palms on the arm of the sofa to do it. "Then what the fuck you doing here?"

"I'm working for Alan Spaeth's lawyer."

Gant leaned toward me with his chest, but bumped me with his stomach. "The fuck you shucking, man? Momma said—"

"—that I was here about your brother."

Sour turned mean. "You lie to my Momma?"

"No. Before I started with your mother, I told her what I'm telling you now."

Gant bumped me again. "Motherfucker, mother-*fucker*, *mother*-fucker! What am I supposed to do? I got obligations, you hear what I'm saying?"

I moved back. "Mr. Gant—"

He took another step toward me, clenching his fists. "I'm gonna throw you the fuck out of this house."

"Mr. Gant?"

"What?"

"I'm not Alan Spaeth, and there's nobody here to hold you back."

Gant stopped talking for a moment, but he also stopped moving.

I said, "I'm leaving now. Thanks again for your time."

Figuring to keep an eye on things, I backed toward the ornate entryway that led to the front door. Gant trailed, but kept his distance.

He said, "What about the car, at least?"

"The car?"

"Woodrow's BMW car. When can I get that?"

A great guy and loving brother, Grover. "Up to the police, and then Frank Neely, I'd guess."

"The lawyer-man at Woodrow's company?"

"Yes. He's handling your brother's estate."

"Bullshit, bull-*shit, bull*-shit! One more way I'm fucked over in this thing."

Letting myself out, I saw a junker Chevy parked behind the Mitsubishi, but I was thinking that Grover Cleveland Gant sounded a lot like Alan Spaeth supposedly did, that day at the law firm.

Chapter 10

JENIFER POLLARD'S ADDRESS turned out to be a high-rise tower on a rolling hill just over the Brookline border. Given the size of her building, I expected at least a doorman in the lobby, but instead there was only an intercom system outside a security door. Five seconds after pushing the button for her unit, I heard a tinny, female "Hello?"

"Ms. Pollard?"

"Get on with it."

A trace of English accent came through the speaker. "My name's John Cuddy. I'm a private investigator."

"I never saw any auto accident."

"It's about the death of Woodrow Gant."

A pause—long enough that I almost asked if Pollard was still there—before the tinny voice returned with, "Are you good-looking?"

What do you say? "Moderately."

"Even if you're lying, a sense of humor might be refreshing, mightn't it? Twelfth floor, and I'll meet you at the lift."

A buzzing noise came from the security door, and I went through into the lobby. There were only three elevators, the middle one standing open. When I reached twelve, the door slid back to show a woman leaning against the opposite wall of the corridor, fists on hips.

Pollard was about thirty and tall, at least five-nine in flat sandals. Clothes consisted of a floppy green sweater over those long, black shorts that I think were developed originally for biking but now qualify as walk-around casual. The Spandex in the shorts might have had a girding effect, because while her legs were long, the thighs seemed barely thicker than her calves. The effect, however, was not so much anorexic as athletic. Add straight, auburn hair that draped down on either side of a bony face more striking than pretty, and I had the feeling I'd seen Pollard somewhere before. Of more immediate concern, though, was the fact that her right hand wasn't quite big enough to hide the bottom of a small can.

"Pepper spray?" I said.

The eyes went down to her right side, then came back up at me, almost sleepily. "Just in case you really were lying."

"I can show you some identification?"

She shook her head. "No, you look the part. Come on."

Pollard walked with a loose-jointed elegance. Trailing behind her down the corridor, I said, "Are you an actress?"

"No," over the shoulder. "Model, though. Why?"

"I thought your face was familiar."

"Just my . . . face?"

A saucy smile as we reached her door, a book between it and the jamb, apparently to keep the door open against a spring of some kind. Pollard put her shoulder just below the peephole and waved me into an apartment that had a galley kitchen to the right and a living room dead ahead. The couch was a day-bed covered with throw pillows against one wall. An entertainment center and some bookcases filled the second wall, and windows looking downhill toward Boston comprised the third. The only other furniture was a rocking chair and coffee table, and given the open door showing a shower curtain, there was no bedroom.

I said, "Quite a view."

"It's just a studio, but those windows make the space seem bigger, don't they? Couch or chair?"

"Chair's fine."

"Coffee or something stronger?"

I sat down. "Nothing, thanks."

Pollard moved to the daybed, lowering herself into it so that her right leg was bent with the ankle curled under the knee of the other, left foot dangling like a silent wind chime. She seemed very aware of herself, as though trotting out a stock pose for approval.

Pollard set the can of pepper spray on the coffee table. "Probably a Filene's ad."

"I'm sorry?"

"Where you saw me. I did a couple of Sunday supplement things last year, modeling corporate wear." She vamped a little. "Chin down to illuminate the features, eyes wide open for that assertive, gal-in-charge look."

"Have you been modeling long?"

"Too long. And too late for the coming thing."

"Which is?"

"Unionization."

I thought back to a case I worked a while ago. "Don't models usually go through agencies?"

"Yes. But we're independent contractors, not employees, so no health insurance or pension. Or even credit unions for borrowing money. Some girls in New York got started organizing, but, as I said, it's a little late for me."

"Why?"

"My best earning years are behind me, Mr.—is John all right?"

"Sure."

"And I'm Jenifer, with one 'n.' Know why?"

"Why your best years are—"

"No." A strident laugh. "No, I meant why only the one 'n' in 'Jenifer.' "

"Got me there."

"It's because the name's derived from 'Guinevere,' as in King Arthur and Lancelot."

"Learn something new every day."

Disappointment crossed Pollard's perfect bone structure. "You're not going to turn banal on me, are you?"

"I'll try harder."

"Do. We were off to such a good start, weren't we?"

I didn't answer that.

"Anyway," said Pollard, "I never did make more than thirty thousand in my best year as a runway model, and I generally strike advert' execs as too glamorous for Mummy-shepherding-the-kids stuff, so my current options are a bit limited. Hence this miniature apartment, and Woodrow."

"Mr. Gant?"

"Why I married him, John. He provided total benefits while we were together, and enough alimony to see me through after we split. Good thing, too, since I couldn't very well rely on my family."

"Your family."

"Right." Pollard raked her left hand through the hair on that side before tucking it back behind her ear. "Mum grew up in London, and Dad was a Yank pilot over from Chicago. Met during the Blitz, so you'd think they'd be open-minded about relationships, wouldn't you? But no, neither of them was exactly thrilled when I decided to marry a 'black-a-moor,' which was Mum's way of showing off her Shakespeare and chiding me in the bargain. They disowned me, and frankly never have forgiven me."

"I'm sorry."

"Hey, man—whoops, that's Woodrow talking now. But truly, John, don't be sorry. Life with barrister Gant was good while it lasted."

"How did you meet?"

"I let him pick me up in a bar, one of the model hangouts on Boylston Street across from the Pru. He was lounging on a stool, I came up to order a drink from the bartender. Woodrow said, 'Let me get that for you,' and I asked him—because I'm five-ten and he was sitting down?—'Just how big are you?'

And he smiled that wide smile of his, and said, 'Can you be more specific?' And then—oh." Pollard's eyes glittered. "I've shocked you, haven't I?"

"Not so far."

"Well, then, this might. Woodrow had one you could slam a door on without hurting it much. A genuine Merlin."

"Merlin?"

"Camelot again. A 'Merlin' is a burning wizard in bed."

"Jenifer, I'm—"

"Oh, please don't be 'sorry' again, John." A wave of melancholy suddenly washed across Pollard's features. "It's not your fault that what started out with Woodrow as 'bewitched, bothered, and bewildered,' degenerated into 'repelled, repulsed, and revolted.' "

The first evidence of sincerity I'd seen from her. "What I was going to say is, I'm working for Alan Spaeth, trying to—"

"Spaeth? The irate hubby the police think did it?"

"I think differently."

"Well, then." Pollard seemed to brighten a little. "I have a bit of advice for you, John."

"Which is?"

"Focus on whomever Woodrow was sleeping with. God knows he made me want to kill him often enough."

I watched her a moment before saying, "A woman was seen with him at a restaurant before he got shot that night."

"There you are."

"But I can't find anybody who seems to know who she was."

"Well, Woodrow certainly stopped confiding in me long ago. But I can tell you this. He was into sex, very heavily."

"So I gathered."

"No, John. If what I said before shocked you, prepare for electrocution." Pollard leaned forward, as though she were posing again. "Woodrow liked me to dress up. Fishnet body stockings, lavish wigs, grotesque makeup, you name it. Frankly, I found it to be fun at first, but then that was all he wanted to do." The melancholy again. "Eventually there came a point when he must have asked himself, 'Why stick with a one-woman show when you can have the whole repertory company?' "

I stopped. "Meaning he might be seeing more than one woman at a time?"

"It wouldn't surprise me."

I thought about Imogene Burbage and Deborah Ling. "How about people at work?"

"Never really met his law firm chums, though I did get a letter from the one handling Woodrow's estate."

"Any women from his job in the D.A.'s office?"

A stagey shrug. "I'm not sure any of them would still be there. Rather a transitional environment, I always thought, and it was over three years ago that he left."

"Any names you recall?"

"No," she said a bit quickly, then saddened again. "I guess I'm not technically Woodrow's 'widow,' but his murder reminded me of being the wife of a prosecutor, and I suppose it surprises me that I still can . . ." She looked out her wall of windows. "Miss him."

A second slip into sincerity, and I found myself wondering just how attractive Pollard would be if she could just stay there. "How about any males?"

She turned back to me, confused. "John, I can assure you that Woodrow was heterosexual."

"Not what I meant. Were there any men from his time in the D.A.'s office who might have known him well?"

"Oh. Let me see. . . ." Back to posing, a finger to her chin. "Woodrow did have an office-mate. Now, what was—yes. Yes, a Tom someone or other. Spelled it queerly, though."

"How do you mean?"

"T-H-O-M, if I'm remembering correctly."

"Last name?"

"Oh, no hope there, John. It began with an 'A,' though. Arthur, Arnold?"

Another stagey shrug, and I got up from the chair. "Well, Jenifer, thanks for your time."

She leaned back into the throw pillows, yet another pose. "I'm not at all like Woodrow, by the by."

"You lost me."

"I find a man I like, I stick with him."

"Good trait."

The glitter came back into her eyes. "I was hoping you'd think so."

Ah. "Unfortunately, I'm already spoken for."

"We wouldn't have to spend all that much time 'speaking.' "

"Thanks again, but no."

"Pity," said Jenifer Pollard, finally breaking the pillow pose. "You seemed about the right . . . size, too."

I drove slowly down V.F.W. Parkway in West Roxbury, the section of Boston that lies farthest from downtown. The houses in West Rox are mostly modest single-family homes, the demographics heavily white. I found the Spaeths' street and turned onto it, both sides lined with small ranches.

The address I had was 396. In front of 388, four early-teen kids were playing in the street under the lights. Wearing baggy shorts, sleeveless sweatshirts, and backward baseball caps, they'd arranged themselves in a rough rectangle, tossing what looked like an orange toy football in a diagonal pattern, corner-to-corner among them. Rather than break up their game, I parked and began moving down the sidewalk toward the Spaeths' house.

As I drew even with the closest boy, a throw to him went a little awry, the football spiraling down near me. That was when I heard the whistling howl of incoming artillery and almost hit the deck before the thing landed six feet away.

"Sorry," said the kid, wearing a San Diego Padres cap and a little silver ring through his left eyebrow. "But it wasn't, like, going to *hit* you or anything."

I watched as the boy came over and picked up his "toy." It was football-shaped upfront, all right, though plastic fletching—like a giant throwing dart—stuck out from the back.

When the Padres kid tossed it to his friend, I could hear the artillery whistle again. "What is that?"

The boy said, "A Howla."

" 'Howla'?"

"Yeah. Sounds just like a cannonball coming at you. Cool, huh?" The word "cool" came out in two syllables, "koo-uhl." The kid then said, "You want to know where you can buy one?"

I thought back to a time before the lads were born, when I wasn't that much older than them, and the other side's "how-las" were for real. I said, "Thanks, anyway," and walked on.

When I reached 396, there was a Mazda hatchback in the driveway and lights coming through the windows. As I went up the path, a dried yellow leaf, shell-shaped, skittered across the flagstones like a crab scrabbling over a dock.

Shortly after I rang the bell, the door was opened by a woman in her mid-thirties, with sandy-brown hair clipped like a helmet that stopped at the tops of her ears. Nudging five-five in sneakers, she also wore a lemon-colored sweater and blue jeans. I'd have called her attractive, with haunting hazel eyes and full lips, but right then she looked more tired than fetching. There was a hardcover book with a clear plastic cover in her right hand, the index finger marking her place.

"Nicole Spaeth?"

"Kind of late to be selling something, don't you think?"

A tired voice, too. "My name's John Cuddy. I'm investigating the killing of Woodrow Gant."

Her eyes narrowed, her tone deepened. "I've already talked to the other police officers."

"I'm not the police, either."

Spaeth moved her left hand, as if to close the door. "No reporters, no interviews."

"I'm working for the attorney representing your husband."

She hesitated, her eyes suggesting she was trying to work something through.

"Mrs. Spaeth, please. I won't take very long, and you might be able to help me help him."

"That's pretty funny," she said, as though it were anything but. "Okay, I'll talk to you."

I followed her into a living room with wall-to-wall carpeting, that sculpted style popular fifteen years back. There was matching but also aging furniture, all the wooden surfaces shining as though freshly polished. Spaeth laid the book on an end table and waved me toward a chair while she took the sofa, sitting straight up rather than leaning back into the cushion.

A lot like Helen Gant, once you noticed it.

From the chair, I said, "Just so you know where I'm heading, I think there's some possibility your husband didn't shoot Woodrow Gant."

"I don't," she said, stonily. "But ask your questions."

I thought back to my talk with Alan Spaeth at Nashua Street. "You're a teacher, correct?"

"Sixth grade." She named a district three towns away. "Not exactly a great job, either."

"How do you mean?"

"All I do is try to keep track of the students, not really teach them anything that might be considered academic. The courses are supposed to get them 'in touch with their feelings' so they can 'develop to their fullest potential.' "

"Glorified day care."

"More like horrified night-*mare*. But, it pays the mortgage and gives us medical coverage, thank God. And Terry's old enough that I don't have to worry too much about him when I have parent-teacher meetings at night."

I remembered her husband telling me that Terry was the son. "So, your job provided the bulk of the family income?"

"All of it." Spaeth seemed to hesitate again. "No, that's not really fair. Before he got laid off, Alan was a good provider. I must even have loved him, once upon a time." She sounded as tired as she looked. "But since Alan lost his job and started drinking, Terry and I have been on our own in more ways than one."

"Mrs. Spaeth, other people described the way your husband behaved at Mr. Gant's law firm the day of the deposition."

"I hope that means you don't have to ask me."

"It'd be a help to hear your version."

"My version." She closed her eyes. "My version is that Alan was—and is—crazy. Maybe not legally, technically crazy, but functionally. He imagines things, then blows even the things he imagines way out of proportion."

"Could you give me some examples?"

"You name it, Alan overdid it. The drinking, the hunting stuff with Terry."

Her husband had told me that, too. "He took your son hunting?"

"After deer, without discussing it first. No, that's not fair to my side of things. Terry was excited about going, but I said no, and Alan took him anyway."

"How old was your son at the time?"

"It was last year, so only thirteen. Can you believe it?"

Didn't seem completely "crazy" to me, but then I'm neither for nor against the sport. "Mrs. Spaeth, witnesses at a restaurant say a woman was with Mr. Gant the night he was killed."

Her eyes narrowed again. "So?"

"So I was wondering if maybe he mentioned something to you about who he was seeing."

The eyes now became slits. "Why in the world would Woodrow do that?"

"As a matter of small talk. You were a client, he would have spent time with you."

"No. No, Woodrow never said anything about his personal life to me. All we ever talked about was my divorce. Which is another headache."

"Headache?"

"Now I need to find somebody else to finish the case."

Frank Neely and Imogene Burbage had said they were referring Gant's clients to other attorneys. "Can't the law firm help you with that?"

Spaeth drew herself up a little straighter on the couch. "Mr. Cuddy, Woodrow was a fine man." Her voice began to crack. "He helped me through the hardest time of my life, divorcing a husband who flew off the handle over every little thing. And I don't think it's fair to make his firm relive its own loss by trying to help me anymore."

"Especially since it was a member of the firm who put you in touch with Mr. Gant in the first place."

Spaeth grew stiff this time, reaching up a finger to wipe away a sudden tear. "That's right. Now, if there's nothing else?"

"Hey, like, what were you doing in my house?"

It was the kid with the Padres hat and eyebrow ring. He stood on the sidewalk at the end of the flagstone path, his friends nowhere to be seen.

I finished coming down the path. "Terry, right?"

A jaundiced look. "Who are you?"

I showed him my identification, which he had to angle up to the streetlight to read. "A private detective?"

"Investigator. Detectives are on police forces."

"But this is so cool," the two-syllable variety again. "What're you trying to find out?"

"Let's start with the eyebrow ring. Doesn't it hurt?"

A laugh. "Everybody asks me that. No, it didn't hurt to have my eyebrow pierced, account of it's only skin there. You don't have any, like, nerve endings or stuff. And it doesn't hurt to keep the ring in, either. Only real pain was when . . ."

"When what, Terry?"

"I got into a fight at school. Over what my dad . . ." Then he seemed to remember why he stopped me. "So, what were you talking to my mom about?"

"I'm trying to help your father."

It was like a curtain came down, ending the first act abruptly. "Because he killed Mom's lawyer."

"That's what the police think, and why your father's in jail. But I think maybe he didn't do it."

"Hey, that's pretty lame, you know? I can read. The police have his fingerprints."

"Which is just evidence."

"Yeah, well, I was staying over at my friends for Bachelor Pad that night, so what can I tell you?"

"Bachelor pad?"

"Space Age pop music. You gotta be old enough to remember that instrumental stuff from the fifties and sixties. Neal Hefti, Quincy Jones, all those dudes."

I was having trouble with this. "You and your friends listen to that music?"

"Yeah. It's major cool. You can go to the old shops that sell used vinyls, or there's some fresh tracks coming out on CD. They even have fan mags and a website you can browse."

I shook my head. "Look, Terry, I'm trying to help your father with—"

"Yeah, well, I'm not gonna help *you*."

"Why not?"

"My dad's been a shit from day one in this whole thing, and my mind's, like, on overload just thinking about it."

"But what if he didn't kill Mr. Gant?"

"He did, dude." Terry compressed his lips, having trouble himself with what he was about to say. "You heard about my dad going, like, nuts at the law firm, right?"

"Right, but—"

"No but's, just listen, okay?"

"Okay."

"Just before that, he calls me when Mom's not home. Says he thinks her lawyer's been hitting on her."

"Hitting . . . you mean, sexually?"

An exasperated huff. "Of course, 'sexually.' My dad claimed that wasn't right, that he was gonna report the guy to the lawyers' thing."

Uh-oh. "The Board of Bar Overseers?"

"I don't know the name of it, okay? But what got me is, my dad wanted me to spy on Mom for him. Like, can you imagine that? The guy turns into a drunk, leaves us with zero money, and he expects me to . . ." Terry shook his head.

"Did your mother and Mr.—"

"I don't know that either, okay? I just know what my dad wanted me to do, and I wouldn't do it. Now, I've told you, so be prepared, okay?"

Absently, I said, "The Boy Scout motto."

Terry looked at me, confused now. "Boy Scout . . . ?"

"Motto. 'Always be prepared.' "

A smirk. "I was thinking more, like, condoms against AIDS, dude."

As Terry Spaeth walked up the path, I had to keep reminding myself: A different world, they're growing up in a different world.

Since Nicole Spaeth had stressed that her relationship with Woodrow Gant had been strictly professional, I decided to talk with Steve Rothenberg and his client before pushing her. But that could wait till the morning. Another stop shouldn't.

After pressing the bell button and hearing the dentist's drill noise, I waited under the center portico of the Chateau. A few minutes passed, but I didn't want to tick off Vincennes Dufresne by ringing again if I could help it.

The big door took a hit from the interior side before creaking open. Dufresne peered out at me, the head cocked and a half-glass of red wine in his right hand. "You again, eh?"

"John Cuddy, Mr. Dufresne."

"I'da remembered that."

"I was wondering if you'd seen Michael Mantle."

"Not since the last time you was here."

"Mind if I check his room, anyway?"

"I don't exactly feel like hiking up two flights with you."

"A good chance I can find it myself."

"I'll have to give you the master key." Digging around in his pocket, Dufresne lowered his eyelids and recocked the head. "And then there's another viewing fee, of course."

"Of course," I said, reaching for my wallet.

Once on the third floor, I went directly to Mantle's door. Nobody else was in sight, though more wheezing came from the room on the landing below where Dufresne had said a man with emphysema was living. Or dying.

After knocking twice, I used the master key to open Mantle's door. The place still looked like it had been shot at and hit. Hard to say for sure, but nothing seemed to have been moved, and the towel at the foot of the bureau remained dry to the touch.

*　　*　　*

As I went back downstairs, I heard another wheezing cough from the second-floor room. I thought, Nothing ventured.

Pocketing Dufresne's master key, I knocked on the door. If I hadn't been listening for the response, I'm not sure I'd have recognized it as a word. Or even a human voice.

"Come."

I turned the knob and pushed, the smell inside yanking me back to grade school, when I had bronchitis and my mother had plastered facecloths slathered in Vicks VapoRub to my chest. The room appeared to be a duplicate of Alan Spaeth's former one overhead, but it contained the clutter of a man who'd minimized the number of steps required for basic existence. Next to a red, seam-burst easy chair were stacks of newspapers and magazines. In front of the chair stood two TV trays, one holding envelopes and papers, a mate with plate, fork, and coffee mug.

The boarder himself was propped up in bed, three pillows behind his back. An old western movie rolled and flickered on the screen of a dinosaur black-and-white threatening to collapse its rickety stand. The man's face was round and flushed, the gray hair on his head two inches long and bristling in the spikes of a man long between the sheets and short of shampoo. His chest seemed nearly concave under an old robe, the nose running freely from one nostril and not at all from the other.

"Name?" in the croaking, almost-voice.

"John Cuddy. I'm a private investigator."

"Remember your . . . tread."

"My tread?"

A jerking nod. "Tread on . . . the stairs." The old man's throat contorted, as though he were swallowing something. "From this morning. . . . Like a signature."

"I understand." Dufresne had mentioned his name, but I couldn't remember it. "And you are?"

"Hank."

I didn't have the heart to prompt him for a last name. "Hank, you might be able to help me, but I want to make this as easy for you as possible."

The jerking nod.

144

After closing his door behind me, I moved deeper into the room. "Can I get you anything?"

One shake of his head as the index finger of a veined, liver-spotted hand pointed toward a full water glass and half-full pitcher on a nightstand.

I stopped next to the bed. "Let me ask you mostly yes or no questions, then. Nod or shake, okay?"

The nod.

"Did you ever meet Alan Spaeth?"

Pointing to the ceiling, Hank nevertheless gave a shake.

"You knew he lived on the next floor, but you never met him?"

Nod.

"How about Michael Mantle?"

Another nod, the pointing finger now aimed diagonally up and toward the front of the building. "The Mick."

"Right." I looked at the door. "When's the last time you saw Mantle?"

A shrug of the face, but something like a twinkle in his eye, too.

"You haven't seen him for a while, but you have heard his . . . tread?"

The twinkle and a nod, plus a smile that showed two separated canine teeth on top, three others bunched on the bottom.

"When's the last time you heard Mantle walking?"

"A week . . . at least." Swallow. "Went down."

"Meaning down the stairs?"

Nod.

"And out of the house?"

Shrug.

"How sure are you that he hasn't been back for a week?"

"Pretty sure. . . . Can't sleep . . ." Swallow. "Much anymore."

"Was anybody with Mantle when he left?"

Shake.

"Have you heard anyone else walk to his room?"

"Vincennes. . . . You."

I couldn't see what more the man could tell me. "Thanks for the help, Hank. Anything I can do for you before I leave?"

The jerking nod.

"What?"

He raised his right hand, pointing the index finger now at his temple. Using the thumb, Hank pantomimed the cocking and fall of a pistol hammer.

I looked into the face of old age and illness.

Shrug. Twinkle. Smile.

Back downstairs, I knocked on Dufresne's "parlor" door. He opened it, wineglass still in hand, but now full, a woman singing a French ballad on the stereo.

"The hell took you so long?"

I gave him back the master key. "Have to be thorough."

"Thorough."

"Speaking of which, it seems to me you haven't seen Mantle now for a solid week."

"About right."

"You said he had money a month ago. Could he have gone on a trip?"

Dufresne's honking laugh. "No way. The Mick wasn't a traveling kind of guy. And besides, he'd paid up in advance. Who's he to waste that kind of money by not living here, eh?"

It was a good question, I thought.

After telling Vincennes Dufresne that I'd still make it worth his while to let me know if he saw Michael Mantle, I decided to visit the bars within walking distance of the Chateau.

Just off Broadway near Flanagan's Market, the closest was a tavern in the same sense that a mud hut is a house. If the air at the threshold made you gag, the atmosphere inside urged you to follow through. I managed ten minutes of putting questions to the night bartender (who didn't know who the real "Mickey Mantle" was) and two patrons (each of whom was contributing his own special something to the environment).

The next place was called "O'B's," a little farther west on Broadway, and evidently part of the area's recent renaissance.

The air was clean, the bar top cleaner. The keep behind the taps nodded to me in a "take-any-stool" way as he drew two pints of Harp. The pints were destined for a couple in their fifties at the end of the bar who couldn't have looked more married to each other if they'd been yoked at the necks. I sat down, and after the keep finished with the newlyweds he came over to me.

"Haven't seen you before, have I?"

A thick brogue that matched the red, curly hair and the muzzy freckles across his thirtyish cheeks.

I said, "First time. How's the Harp?"

"Fresh as a morning's dew."

"One, please."

He drew the pint, poured off, and topped it with a quarter-inch of head. Setting the glass on a shamrock coaster, he said, "You've the sound of the neighborhood in your voice."

"Grew up within blocks of here."

A hammy hand was extended across the bar. "Paul O'Brien."

I shook with him. "Paul, John Cuddy. You the proprietor?"

"I am. Tended bar till I had the hang of it and enough money to open a pub of my own. 'O'B's' for 'O'Brien's.' " He rested both palms on the bar, gave me a measured look. "You'd be police, then?"

"Not for a long time." I took out my ID. "I'm in business for myself now. Like you."

O'Brien read the holder's laminated card and nodded in an "I've-seen-enough" way. Expressive nodder, Mr. O'Brien.

He said, "Which means you're here for something more than a pint from the *auld sod*."

"I'm looking for a man named Michael Mantle."

"The Mick, you say?" O'Brien turned toward the couple. "Leo, this fella's after the Mick."

"Good," said Leo. "You find the little weasel, remind him he owes me a round from last Monday."

I looked over at the husband as his wife said, "Tuesday, Leo. It was Tuesday last."

The man didn't have the brogue, but the woman did. I said, "You haven't seen him since?"

Leo closed his eyes briefly. "Moira?"

She said, "Not since, no. Maybe he's gone down."

I looked from one to the other. "Down?"

O'Brien interpreted. "As in 'down the line,' John. To one of the less . . . pricey establishments on the avenue."

"Mantle drink here often?"

"Never," said Leo, "at least not until maybe a month ago. Then he'd be in here with a bunch of other guys, buying them rounds."

Moira put in, "Or them buying him."

O'Brien waved his hand at the taps. "Guinness, mainly. A black-and-tan upon occasion."

I went back to the couple. "Any idea where he might be now?"

Moira said, "Drinking or sleeping, that one."

"He's not at his rooming house, and probably hasn't been there for a full week."

"Since last Monday?" said Leo.

Moira cleared her throat. "Tuesday last. Have you gone deaf on me as well as senile?"

"Tuesday," Leo agreed.

O'Brien shook his head. "The Mick, he went through money like a hot knife. Could fool the drop-ins with his birth-certificate routine, but the regulars wised up to his tricks pretty quick."

"All except my Leo," said Moira.

Her husband didn't look at his wife. "An act of charity, and she'll never let me forget it."

I tried to take in all three of them at once. "So, no sign of him here since Tuesday of last week."

Consensus, but consistency is not always a virtue.

I said, "Any other ideas?"

"Try the drunk tank," offered Leo.

Moira grunted a small laugh. "And you with the word 'charity' falling from your lips not a minute past."

I didn't have any more luck at the other watering holes, so I walked to Alan Spaeth's new apartment building. The address was a three-decker, his name on a yellow Post-it over the second-floor button, no names identifying the other two. I tried the first and third anyway, getting no response for my trouble.

Then I thought of something. According to Spaeth, he and Mantle had been drinking together upstairs. If Mantle were hiding from something—or someone—maybe he'd use his friend's empty apartment. I pushed the middle button, but got nothing again.

I was about to leave when the front door opened on a chain and yanked taut, a dour woman in her forties looking out tentatively through the four-inch gap.

"What do you want?"

"The name's John Cuddy." I held up my license folder. "I wonder if I could ask you a few questions."

"It's about that horrible man on the second floor, isn't it?"

"Maybe if I could come in—"

"Not a chance. I can tell you all I want to through this chain." She glanced behind her. "I live on the first floor here. I was coming in from a shift at the hospital, dog-tired and dirty, when that man tried to proposition me."

Alan Spaeth, making friends wherever he goes. "Look—"

"He wouldn't take no for an answer, either."

"I'm sorry. Truly, Ms. . . . ?"

"No. No, I'm not giving you my name. He's a horrible man, and I'm glad he's in jail."

"Did you hear anything upstairs last Wednesday evening? It's very important."

She chose her words carefully. "I was on the four-to-midnight, but we had a carryover case, so I didn't get home until almost one A.M. Then all the commotion with the police woke me up at five." Careful yielded to petulant. "Only four hours of sleep after the night I had at the hospital. Now, I ask you, is that fair?"

"It sure isn't. You know of anyone else here I could talk with?"

"There was a nice old lady—Mrs. Crawford—who lived on the third floor, but she died two months back, and nobody's moved in yet."

Last hope. "You said you live on the first floor and Mr. Spaeth on the second?"

"That's right. Had to keep my door to the back stairs locked because of him trying to proposition me. Never needed to do that before."

I waited until she finished. "Since Mr. Spaeth was arrested, have you heard anyone moving around up there?"

Her features scrunched together. "That . . . really . . . sucks."

"I'm sorry?"

"Scaring me with 'Is anybody living up there in secret?' That really sucks, you know?"

"Look—"

"I mean, this is my home you're talking about. My life, even, and you have to ask me that?"

"But have you heard—"

"No. No!"

The door slammed hard enough in my face that I felt the vibration through my shoes.

After walking back to the Prelude, I drove past another three-decker. There were no lights burning in Nancy's third-floor apartment. Given my luck so far that night, I didn't stop.

Reaching Back Bay, I left the car in its slot behind the corner brownstone and went around to the Beacon Street entrance. Upstairs in the living room, the fuzzy glow from the street lamp outside seeped through the stained-glass windows. The polished, oak-front fireplace hadn't been used since early spring, but it was comforting to think of Nancy and me, curled up on the rug with a couple of birch logs crackling and snapping.

What wasn't comforting was to look at the answering machine. The "0" in the message window meant none from her.

Two hours later, I went to bed with the telephone squared toward me on the night table. Figuring, Nancy might still call.

Might, but didn't.

Chapter 11

"STEVEN ROTHENBERG."

"John Cuddy," I said into the phone Thursday morning, trying to keep my irritation at Nancy out of my voice while balancing a bowl of cornflakes on my lap.

"Can I get back to you, John?"

"Probably not."

A sigh combined with the rustling of paper. "Okay, shoot."

"I'm calling from my apartment because I want to drive out to Woodrow Gant's old prosecutor's office, maybe talk to some people who knew him when."

"When he was prosecuting?" said Rothenberg.

"Yes."

"What do you have so far?"

"You're pressed for time, right?"

"Right."

I gave Rothenberg a summary of what little I'd developed, leaving the Gang Unit out of it except to say, "I also have a lead on the restaurant I want to follow up."

"What lead?" he said.

"I'd rather get more information first. But there's something we need to talk about with your client."

"Our client, John."

"Barely."

Rothenberg paused. "I'm not liking the sound of that."

"You'll come to like it even less, I think. Can we see Spaeth at the jail today?"

"Is that necessary?"

"Maybe vital."

Another pause. "I could make it by, say . . . eleven-thirty?"

"Good for me," I said.

"John, basically what's the matter?"

"Spaeth told his son that Daddy thought Mommy's lawyer was hitting on her."

"Is that all?"

I nearly took the phone away from my ear to stare at it. "Isn't that enough?"

"John, you don't work a lot of divorce cases, do you?"

"Not if I can help it."

"Well, when the wife's lawyer is a male, the husband tends to see him as a competitor for the position the husband used to occupy with her. It's a psychological thing."

"Is it a 'psychological thing' for that husband to report the wife's lawyer to the Board of Bar Overseers?"

A dead silence this time on the other end of the line. "Say it ain't so."

"I thought I'd stop at the Board, too. See if I can find out whether there was a formal complaint filed."

"I doubt they'd tell you," said Rothenberg. "But, shit, if there was . . ."

". . . then whether or not Woodrow Gant and you negotiated a settlement in the divorce case, Spaeth believing strongly that Gant was involved with his wife would enhance your guy's motive for killing the man."

" 'Enhance' doesn't quite capture it, John."

I was just getting into my suit jacket when the phone rang back. The bedroom extension was closest.

"John, it's me."

Somehow, despite being disappointed over no contact since Tuesday night at Thai Basil, I wasn't prepared for the sound of her voice. "Nance, I'm glad you called."

"Don't be so sure. We need to meet, talk this through."

"How about dinner tonight?"

"No. No, I was thinking lunch, today. Can you make it?"

I wouldn't not make it. "Where?"

"Cricket's by Quincy Market."

Tourist Central. "Not very . . . private, Nance."

"I know."

Okay. "When?"

She said, "It would have to be at one o'clock."

"Cricket's at one," I said, trying to keep my temper while taking her dictation.

"See you then, John."

Nancy hung up before I could say anything more. After a few moments of squeezing the receiver so hard my hand cramped, I did the opposite of what I wanted to and set the plastic instrument gently back in its cradle.

The drive to Gant's former county almost let me push Nancy out of my mind. The purple flower that blooms in late summer still covered the marshland bordering the Charles River, contrasting with the red, gold, and orange leaves of October. After some suburban twists and turns, I found the building with the district attorney's office and parked in the rear.

At the reception counter upstairs, a male security guard in a blue blazer sat next to a female in a polka-dot dress, an elaborate console of buttons and lights in front of her.

The guard was already sizing up whoever had come in behind me when the woman said, "Can I help you, sir?"

"Hope so. I'd like to see a prosecutor who spells his first name 'T-H-O-M.' The last name might begin—"

"That's Thom Arneson. And you are?"

"John Cuddy."

"Is he expecting you?"

"I doubt it."

Both the security guard and the woman looked at me then, but she punched a button, anyway.

My identification holder came sliding back across the desk. "So, you're 'John Cuddy, Private Investigator.' Why are you darkening *my* door?"

I started to answer when Arneson's phone jingled and he held up his hand. As he took the call, I looked around the small, shared office. There was another, identical desk against a second wall, no one sitting at it and no windows for either prosecutor. Arneson had stacks of red manila case files on two corners of his desk, a computer on a third, the telephone on the fourth. Talking in staccato jargon, he swung through a twenty-degree arc in his chair under a poster entitled "THINGS INVENTED IN NORWAY," the list below the title including skis, paper clips, and fishnet underwear.

Arneson himself was at least thirty-five, with a widow's peak of nearly platinum hair and fainter eyebrows. I pegged his height at six feet and change, weight about two hundred if he maintained the sort of shape all over that the rolled-up sleeves revealed. His jawline was strong, and the cleft in his chin approached Kirk Douglas proportions. The general impression leaned toward ruggedly handsome, but a "me-first" glint playing around Arneson's eyes also suggested you might not want him covering your back in an alley.

Saying, "Then he does the max, Don baby, and you don't make a dime more on it." Arneson hung up the phone and returned to me. "Sorry, but I hate it when defense lawyers whine."

"Any lawyer."

Arneson nodded, like he agreed. "So, what's going on, Cuddy?"

"I'm working with Steven Rothenberg."

"Let me guess. The Gant case."

"Yes. I understand you and Mr. Gant were office-mates here."

Arneson leaned back into his chair, doing the little swing routine again. "Why should I talk with you?"

"I'd think you'd want the right person sent away for the crime."

"We're the representatives of the people, Cuddy. Ordinarily, that's exactly what I'd want. Only thing is, our office isn't the one trying the case."

"I know, but you might be able to give me some information on some people your office did try."

Arneson nodded again. "Really meaning, people Woodrow tried."

"A good starting point."

A third nod, and Arneson came forward in the chair. "I believe in presenting a charge fairly in the courtroom, Cuddy. In fact, I make an effort to conduct myself at all times as though a jury was watching me."

I'd heard Nancy and other prosecutors say something similar. The difference was, I'd thought they'd been sincere, while Arneson's little speech sounded more like the party line.

He went on. "However, I'm leery of maybe fouling up Suffolk's case on your guy."

"Could telling me about Nguyen Trinh foul up their case?"

"Nugey?" Arneson looked away for a moment, then came back, grinning. "You meet him?"

"Not so far."

"Give me a call if you do. I'd like to know how that baby's faring." Arneson dropped the grin. "Look, Cuddy, Woodrow prosecuted Trinh and his buddy Oscar-somebody at least eight or nine years ago. If you're thinking some kind of revenge, they've been out plenty long enough to have done something about it before now."

"Your office caught that case because the home invasion happened in Weston Hills?"

"Right. Trinh and—Huong, that was the buddy's name. Oscar Huong. Anyway, Trinh and Huong were from Vietnam, then probably a dozen other places before they ended up on our doorstep. We coordinated with the Boston force and together nailed the punks. End of story."

Not exactly, but I didn't want Arneson knowing about

Trinh's restaurant connection before Rothenberg did. "Gant was a good prosecutor?"

"What are you doing now? Trying to blame the victim?"

"Trying to get a handle on the victim from somebody who knew him well."

Arneson leaned back again, but didn't swing the chair. "I'm not sure anybody knew Woodrow well."

"How do you mean?"

"He was a loner, Cuddy. Don't get me wrong. Everybody has to be by themselves some in this job, just like any other. But Woodrow wasn't one to go out for drinks after work or play on the office softball team, you know?"

"Somebody told me he had a bad leg."

"Knee problem. Football, I think. Bottom line is, Woodrow didn't socialize much. I think I met his wife—sorry, ex-wife—maybe once. Jessica?"

"Jenifer," I said.

"Right, Jenifer. English girl. Anyway, like I was saying, Woodrow didn't pal around much, but he did his job well. And he was the best I ever saw at the prosecutor point."

"The 'prosecutor point'?"

"Yeah. You know, the way an A.D.A. can point to the defense table when a witness is identifying the accused as the robber or a crime scene tech is testifying about his fingerprints. Woodrow had refined the gesture to a stylized art. He pointed at you three times, and, baby, you were gone in the eyes of that jury."

"Other than Trinh and Huong, anybody else who might have a reason to kill Mr. Gant?"

"Like I said before, even they didn't have much of a motive after so much lapse of time." Arneson went from merely careful to completely serious. "Look, Cuddy, I'll grant you that Woodrow was a hard charger, all right? He had a pair of stones on him so big, they'd brush the ground between his feet. But Woodrow'd been out of here for what, three years now? He stayed a while, then went private, like most of us."

"But not like you."

The chair swing again. "Yeah, I've stayed. I don't blame the ones who haven't. They got big dreams like Woodrow, or maybe kids to educate. But I'm still here because I like the work, being on the moral side of issues. Also, you stay long enough, you get to be the smartest fish in a dumb pond, everybody else being so junior by comparison. And the secret to being smart as a prosecutor is simple: attention to detail." Thom Arneson laughed. "Ten years ago, I was a breast man. Now I'm a detail man. Kind of like I'm losing ground, huh?"

Actually I was wondering why the supposedly smartest fish still had only a shared office in the pond.

The Board of Bar Overseers is located at 75 Federal Street in Boston's financial district. The building, nestled between a couple of banks, was constructed of sturdy gray granite with Art Deco touches of chrome. Despite the nice facade, I'm told that lawyers summoned there view it as a cross between a police department's Internal Affairs Division and the old K.G.B.'s torture chamber at Lubyanka prison.

When I got off the elevator, the Board seemed to occupy the entire seventh floor. I followed speckled, marble tiles to the front counter. A young blond woman sat behind greenish security glass, overlapped so that papers (but nothing more dangerous) could be pushed under and up to her. An opaque vase holding an arrangement of Japanese dried flowers stood serenely in a niche on the left, solid oak doors closed at both edges of the reception area.

As I reached the counter, the young woman was speaking into her telephone. "My name? Heather. . . . Yes, ma'am. . . . We have a computer directory here, if you could give me his . . . Is that with an 'M' or an 'N'?. . . . Just one second . . . yes. Yes, we have him in Wellfleet. Here's his address and telephone."

After Heather finished with that last, she paused, then said, "You too, ma'am. Bye now." The receptionist looked up at me. "Sorry, sir. How can I help you?"

"I'd like to find out if a lawyer had any complaints lodged against him."

A rueful smile. "I'm afraid that's not public information."

"But the lawyer involved is dead."

"Sorry," said Heather. "Unless there's been a public discipline, all those records have to remain confidential."

I took out my identification. "I'm investigating a murder where any complaint here might be important."

A polite head shake. "Again, I'm afraid—"

"It's the murder of Woodrow Gant."

Heather's face creased. "Just one moment."

"Mr. Cuddy?" the man rising behind his desk in a nonshared office.

"Yes."

"Parris Jeppers." We shook as he said, "Thank you, Heather."

The receptionist who had led me to him closed the door on her way out. Jeppers was about five-ten and slim, his forty or so years showing themselves by sprinkled gray in the short, brown hair, both his carefully trimmed mustache and goatee a shade darker. He wore tortoiseshell glasses, one of those neon surfer cords attached to the templates so he could drop the specs in front of him like a bib. Jeppers' suit was a faint herringbone, his dress shirt blue, but with white collar and cuffs. The paisley bow under his Adam's apple looked more tied than clipped on.

Despite the Yankee clothes, he had a Rebel accent. "Heather told me over the telephone that you wished to see any complaints about a given attorney?"

"I'm thinking, Mr. Jeppers, that she also told you that attorney's name, or I wouldn't have gotten an audience with—what are you, anyway?"

A tight smile. "If you mean title, 'assistant bar counsel.' "

"What else would I mean?"

The smile grew tighter. "Sexual orientation, perhaps? If you were guessing I'm gay, you're right."

I didn't think I'd been guessing at all. "That's coming on a little strong, isn't it?"

"Sometimes strong is a better gambit than courteous. Sorry if I offended you."

"Only by assuming that your orientation might affect my view of your professionalism."

Jeppers's expression changed. "Then I'm truly sorry for my assumption." He used his right index finger to push the glasses higher on the bridge of his nose. "So, you're here about Woodrow Gant?"

"Yes. I'm working with Alan Spaeth's defense attorney, and it occurred to me that it'd be helpful to know whether there might be someone in your files who had a motive to kill Mr. Gant."

"A disgruntled client of his?"

"Or an angry opponent."

"Most lawyers settle any differences between them with paperwork, Mr. Cuddy."

"I meant to include opposing clients."

Jeppers adjusted his glasses again. "As Heather must have told you, those records are confidential."

"I can appreciate that. But Alan Spaeth is going to be on trial for murder, and I've found other information that suggests he may not have done it."

"Still . . ."

"Meaning I need a court order to see if there are any potential suspects in your files."

"That would be up to you. Or to Mr. Spaeth's attorney and the presiding judge involved. However, given my . . . breach of good manners at the beginning of our conversation, perhaps I can save both of us some time. And embarrassment as well."

"Thank you."

Jeppers's hand went to his bow tie for a moment. "Mr. Spaeth himself came here to file a complaint against Mr. Gant regarding Mr. Spaeth's wife."

Half-expecting that, I tried not to let my face show Jeppers anything. "What kind of complaint?"

"Mr. Spaeth behaved in a belligerent manner out front, so Heather referred him to me. It seems your client believed Mr. Gant was having an affair with Mrs. Spaeth. The man was rather insistent about it, too, though long on belief and short on details."

"What did you do about his complaint?"

"Told him it had no foundation."

I stopped for a second. "How could you know that?"

"Don't misunderstand, Mr. Cuddy. I'm not talking about factual foundation. I mean legal foundation."

"Legally, it's all right for a lawyer to have sex with his divorce client?"

"The Commonwealth's attorneys have long been governed by the Code of Professional Responsibility, which for our purposes is divided into aspirational ethical considerations and stricter disciplinary rules. Is it ethical for a lawyer to engage in such an affair? No. Is it a direct violation of a disciplinary rule? No again. Hence, there was no legal foundation upon which we could proceed, even if Mr. Spaeth's version of the situation was true."

"Which it might not have been."

The tight smile again, and another adjustment of the glasses. "That's almost immaterial, don't you think? Mr. Spaeth's belief that it was true is the damage I'd bring to his defense counsel's attention."

I thanked Parris Jeppers for his advice, and he called Heather to escort me back out to the elevators.

"Shit," said Steve Rothenberg. "You're sure?"

"There a reason why this Jeppers at the Overseers would lie to me?"

The lawyer shook his head. We were sitting inside the client interview room at the Nashua Street jail, waiting for the guard to bring Alan Spaeth to us.

I'd started Steve off with my last stop, and now I went back to the beginning. "I hit Michael Mantle's place at the rooming house twice. No sign of him there since late Tuesday of last week."

"The night before Gant was shot."

"Right. And Mantle hasn't visited his usual watering holes, either."

"Also since that Tuesday?"

I nodded. "Plus, everybody at the law firm confirms that Spaeth went nuts that day at his deposition."

"Ah, yes," said Rothenberg, a dollop of sarcasm in his voice. "I remember it well."

"However, I also got everyone there to admit that Spaeth just yelled, that he never approached anybody physically. And that Woodrow Gant's brother was the one who had to be restrained."

"That's 'Grover,' right?"

"Grover Cleveland Gant. Though if I'm the prosecution, I think I'd bypass him and put the mother on the stand. She'll have the jurors standing in line during recess to learn the hangman's knot."

Another shake of the head.

"On top of that," I said, "almost nobody has a bad word about the deceased. Good partner as well as good son and brother. His ex-wife says he played around during their marriage, but once Gant's single, that's a risk I think the jury would let him run."

"Besides, it never looks good to paint the victim bl . . . in a bad light on sex stuff. Unless you've come up with a connection to the woman he was with that night?"

"Nobody seems to have any ideas about that."

Rothenberg looked skeptical. "None at all?"

"I don't buy it either, even though everyone took great pains in telling me Woodrow Gant kept his personal life to himself."

"Well, keep trying. If the woman was with him when the shooter opened up, she may have seen something."

"In which case," I said, echoing Lieutenant Murphy, "why didn't our killer get her, too?"

"Maybe that's exactly what happened."

"Steve."

"What?"

"No other body was found."

"So, the killer took the woman away."

"Why?"

"Maybe for just the reason we're having trouble finding out who she was."

"The killer wanted to hide her identity?"

"Look, this woman tried to disguise herself, right? I mean, dark glasses in a restaurant at night?"

Rothenberg had a point.

He waited a moment, then said, "Anything from Gant's time as a prosecutor?"

"I drove out there, talked with a current A.D.A. named Arneson, who was Gant's office-mate. Arneson says Gant was aggressive and effective but fair."

Rothenberg said, "Gang members who get sent away aren't usually consoled much by 'fair.' "

"Which brings us to the only piece of good news."

"Anything at this point."

I lowered my voice. "One of the bad guys Woodrow Gant put away was a home-invader named Nguyen Trinh. But Trinh was only a juvenile at the time, and after paying his debt to society, he expanded into other lines of work."

"What other lines?"

"Loan-sharking, but bordering on venture capital."

"Venture capital? Bankrolling what?"

"A certain Vietnamese restaurant."

"No," said Rothenberg, brightening visibly.

"Yes. It's probably just a coincidence that Woodrow Gant ever ate at Viet Mam—one of the other attorneys in the firm had it recommended to her by a friend and took him there once. But maybe Trinh happened to see him at the restaurant."

"And got the idea to take his revenge by following Gant the next time the man came by."

"Except that A.D.A. Arneson thinks it's pretty unlikely Trinh would wait so many years before getting even."

"John, let's not taketh away with the other hand, okay?"

"Meaning this is the best evidence we've got so far."

"By a mile. You're sure about this former gang guy's connection to the restaurant?"

"That's what a pretty reliable source told me, but I think one of us should hit the Registry of Deeds, link the property to Trinh through documentation."

"I can have somebody there run the title and fax the papers to you."

"The Suffolk registry's not that far from my office. Have your searcher drop an envelope through the mail slot in my door."

Rothenberg stared at me. "You still don't have a fax machine, do you?"

"Steve, I never even learned how to type."

Rothenberg was giving me a "that-doesn't-compute" look when we heard a perfunctory rap/rap on the other side of the interior trap.

In a petulant voice, Alan Spaeth said, "I did tell you."

Rothenberg shook his head. "Alan, what do you take me for, an idiot? I'd have remembered."

"Our first meeting, Steve. About the divorce thing. I remember it clear as a fucking bell. You asked me if my wife had a lawyer yet, and I told you, yeah, this colored guy, and you asked me for his name. And as you were writing it down, I said, 'The way he looks at her, I think he's getting some on the side.' "

It sounded too "Spaeth-like" to be a lie, so I broke in. "You met Woodrow Gant before you retained Steve on the divorce?"

"Sure," a little defiance now from across the desk, the heel of his left hand rubbing the slowly healing "shower" eye. "Hey, sport, I was a pretty good marketing executive, and I handled dozens of negotiations where I sure as shit knew a lot less about the landscape than I did in my own fucking marriage. I figured I'd be able to handle things, no sweat. Only this Gant brings down a mountain of shit on my head, papers on 'Vacating the Marital Home,' and 'No Impositions on Wife's Personal Liberty.' Well, what about my 'personal liberty,' huh? Who was supposed to look after that, I didn't hire a lawyer, too?"

It wasn't Spaeth's decision to hire Rothenberg that bothered me. It was that I didn't think I'd asked Nicole Spaeth if there'd been any other incidents where her husband had threatened her lawyer.

Rothenberg focused on his client. "I'm not talking about what you said to me about your wife and Gant. I want to know why you never told me about your visit to the Board of Bar Overseers."

"Those fuckers." The petulant voice again. "This faggot there said—"

I interrupted him. "That's one, Spaeth."

"One what?"

"Once more with the slurs, and I walk."

Spaeth stared at me, then went to Rothenberg with, "I'm looking at prison for the rest of my life, and I can't call a spade a spade?"

Rothenberg cringed hearing one more reason not to put his client on the stand come trial. "Alan, just use names, not labels. Okay?"

"Okay, okay. This—" Spaeth looked up at me. "I don't remember his fucking name."

"Jeppers," I said.

"Yeah, 'Jeffers' except with 'P's,' I remember now. This Jeppers guy said what I told him would be confidential."

Rothenberg shook his head. "But why did you go there in the first place?"

"I thought it could help." Spaeth grew earnest now, trying to sell us on the package. "Look, I thought Gant was fucking Nicole—I heard plenty of guys say their wife's lawyer did the same thing in their cases."

Rothenberg said, "She was separated from you."

"I don't care. We're still married, it's adultery in my book, a fucking betrayal of loyalty. But I figured I told you about her and him when you started representing me—and you didn't do anything about it—then maybe some kind of . . . independent investigation would help."

"Independent investigation," I said.

"Yeah, like the lawyers' board there. I figured maybe they'd be more . . . believable, they found out I was right."

"More believable where?"

"With the judge in my divorce case, of course. Why else would I do it?"

"Then why didn't you ever mention it to me?" said his divorce lawyer.

Spaeth ran a hand through the black clots of hair on his head. "I don't know. That Jeppers, he didn't seem to think much of it, either. And, remember, I was doing a lot of drinking around then. I must've just . . . forgot."

"Forgot to tell me," said Rothenberg.

"Yeah."

I watched Spaeth. "But you didn't forget to tell your son."

The man flared. "The fuck does Terry have to do with this?"

I said, "He told me his father shared those suspicions about his mother."

"The fuck was I supposed to do? All the judge's orders against me—that 'personal liberty' shit Steve here said I had to obey—I couldn't go near Nicole myself."

I could see by Rothenberg's expression that he didn't get what Spaeth meant. "Steve, your client asked Terry to spy on his mother."

Rothenberg's voice dropped. "Alan, you haven't made this any easier."

"Easier?" Spaeth began to boil over. "You try living with a woman for sixteen fucking years, loving her and having a son by her, then getting ordered out of your own fucking house. And ordered to keep paying the fucking mortgage and every other fucking thing anyway. When you don't have a job anymore, and nobody wants to hire you for another one. See what you'd do, with the booze and all."

I said, "One thing I wouldn't do is ask my son to spy on his mother."

A sneer. "You married, Cuddy?"

A memory of Beth in her hospital bed flashed back on me. "Widowed."

Didn't slow Alan Spaeth down. "Yeah, well, think about it anyway, sport. How would you feel, you thought a lawyer was fucking you over the coals in a divorce and punching the wife you still loved to boot?"

I got out of there before I decked him.

*   *   *

"You okay?" asked Steve Rothenberg, genuine concern in his tone.

"No," I said, leaning against the corridor wall outside the client interview room, staring down at the floor.

Rothenberg leaned with me. "Alan Spaeth's a bigoted, insensitive lout."

"He's all that, and more."

"But you still think my client didn't shoot Woodrow Gant, don't you?"

I glanced at Rothenberg, then away again. "That may not be enough, Steve."

"It has to be, John. I need you to follow up on the alibi witness, the gang aspect, the restaurant—"

Restaurant? "Christ." I checked my watch. Almost 12:45, and Nancy had said 1:00. "Steve, I'm sorry, I've got to go."

"John—"

"I'm not quitting. At least, not yet."

There was a sigh of relief as I made my way back down the corridor, but it didn't come from me.

Cricket's is located in the South Market building, catercorner from Fanueil Hall itself. The hall is where great debates have been held since the American Revolution. You can see the red-bricked structure from the greenhouse dining area, though the only debate you're likely to hear in Cricket's is whether to go with the club sandwich or the daily catch.

I walked into the main entrance of the restaurant proper, the woman in a print dress at the hostess stand watching me, probably because I looked as nervous as I felt.

She said, "Mr. Cuddy?"

"Yes."

"Your party's already here. This way, please."

I followed her into the greenhouse extension, spotting Nancy as soon as I cleared a potted tree. She sat at a table for two, the sunlight slanting through the glass making her features glow, like something you'd see in paintings or films of the Tuscan hills. Two menus lay in front of her, but Nancy's attention was directed to a touristy couple outside on the cobblestones. The couple talked to a man in a business suit and gestured with their camera in a sign-language way, implying that they didn't speak English very well but wanted him to take their picture.

When the hostess delivered me to the table, Nancy and I both said "thank you" to her simultaneously. Everybody laughed, the hostess a little more naturally than either of us.

I sat down, extending my right hand across the table. Nancy took it, gave me a quick squeeze, and then let go. "Right on time."

I made a pretense of looking at my watch. "I was tied up, afraid I might be late."

"No, I was early."

We received a reprieve from that soul-numbing exchange thanks to the waiter coming by for our drink orders.

"Wine?" I said to her.

Nancy spoke to the waiter. "Just iced tea for me, please."

I wanted something stronger, but said, "Same."

After the waiter over-described a couple of lunch specials, we both watched him walk away.

I took a deep breath. "When he's out of sight, we have to start talking again."

A pause before, "I know."

I looked back at Nancy. "What is it?"

Her chin was down, like she was reading the menu instead of me. "I'm beginning to think this wasn't such a good idea."

"What wasn't?"

"Meeting for lunch like this. I thought we'd be able to talk first, build up to it."

"Nance, I'm afraid that until I hear what the 'it' is, I don't know what we should be talking about."

The waiter was brutally efficient, our drinks arriving in tall glasses with twists of lemon still circling the straws like milk-maids around a maypole. I think he could sense something was wrong between us, though, and he left the table without asking for our food orders.

Nancy put some sugar into her tea. Stirring it, she said,

"When you got back from out-of-state last week, and we first talked about Woodrow Gant, you asked me if I knew him."

"I remember."

"Do you remember what I said?"

"Something like, 'I'd met the man, but I never worked with him.'"

"Close enough." Nancy drew some tea through her straw. "Years before we . . . before you and I got together, there was a continuing legal education conference for prosecutors, a long weekend down on Nantucket. A.D.A.'s from all over the state attended."

I nodded.

"That's where I met Woodrow Gant."

I nodded some more.

"And that's where I . . . slept with him."

I tried to nod, but couldn't.

Nancy closed her eyes. "This is what I was afraid of."

"What?" It didn't sound like my voice.

She opened her eyes. "Your reaction, John."

"What reaction? I haven't said—"

"The way you're looking at me."

I could feel my blood rising. "Nance, at least give me a chance to say something?"

She watched me, but wary, like a cat that's been yelled at. "Go ahead."

I lowered my voice. "Why didn't you tell me this at Thai Basil?"

A hardening. "Rather than walk out on you?"

I kept my voice low. "Why didn't you tell me then?"

"Because you're such a . . . such an 'innocent' about sexual things."

"Nancy—"

"Put yourself in my shoes, okay? When we met, I fell in love with you—almost at first sight—but you put me off because you were still mourning Beth. I could handle that, I even respected you more for it. And then last month, when you helped me through the cancer scare, I felt so close to you I almost couldn't stand it."

I wasn't following her. "Stand what, the feeling?"

"Yes, but more the worry. I'd always been so independent, but the cancer scare made me realize how much I needed people, how much I needed you, above all. And what I couldn't stand was the thought of losing you."

"Nancy, you're not losing me."

She closed her eyes again. "When I just told you I slept with Woodrow Gant, your expression told me I might."

"Nance . . ." I tried to measure out the words. "I don't know how to describe what was on my face, because I can't see it the way you do, even if I were staring into a mirror. But I know what's in my heart, and what you did or didn't do before we met is your past, not our present."

Her eyes opened, welling with tears. "That's what I wanted to hear, John."

I reached across the table for her hand. "Great."

Nancy let me take the hand, but when I squeezed, she didn't squeeze back. "Only we still have a problem."

"Now what?" I said.

"Until the Gant case is resolved, we can't see each other."

I felt the blood rising again. "Nance, that's—"

She wriggled her hand free. "Please, John, let me finish?"

I withdrew my hand, too. In the low voice, I said, "All right."

"I'm not working the Gant case as a prosecutor. As soon as it came in, I told my boss I couldn't. So there's no technical conflict of interest in your helping the defendant. But I didn't give my boss the whole story."

"I can understand that."

"Then I hope you can understand what I'm about to say, too. It would tear me up to be seeing you, eating across from you, especially . . . making love with you while I knew you were still working the case. I couldn't be myself, and it would be miserable for you as well."

"Why, Nance? Because you once had an affair with the man?"

"It was just that one weekend, but if you need a label, call it loyalty to an ex-lover."

"Loyalty misplaced."

"John, a minute ago, you told me what was in your heart. Trust me now on what's in mine. It may not be rational, or even wise, but my heart tells me I can't be with you until the Gant case is resolved."

"Nancy . . ." I cleared my throat. "Nance, I trust you. That's not the problem."

"Then what is?"

"The case. It could drag on for months."

Her tone changed. "Does it have to drag on with you still in it?"

That stopped me. "You mean, quit the case?"

"Can you?"

I wanted to. Nancy's feelings, Spaeth's attitudes and actions, the evidence already piled up on the prosecution's side of the scales. Against all that, there was just one—

"John?"

"No," I said. "I can't. The guy's an asshole, but I still think he's innocent. And I have loyalties as well, to my profession, to Rothenberg. . . ."

I stopped again as Nancy swiped at a tear with an index finger, then reached her other hand across the table to close on mine.

She said, "You know, almost all of me wanted to hear a different answer. But I think—for our future—that's the best answer you could give."

"Our future, not our present."

Letting go of my hand, Nancy stood up. "Good-bye, John. Call me when . . . whenever."

I watched her walk away, taking what appetite I might have had with her. Our waiter caught my eye, and I made a tab-signing gesture to him. When I turned back for some iced tea to deal with the taste in my mouth, I saw the touristy couple walking hand-in-hand, the camera swinging at his side, her going up on tiptoes to peck him on the cheek.

I looked down into the glass. My job for Rothenberg was to find enough reasonable doubt to get Spaeth off come trial, months away. If I couldn't quit the Gant case, maybe I could accelerate things by going a step further and finding out who really killed him.

As the check arrived, though, Alan Spaeth's voice kept going around inside my head. The conversation with him at the jail less than an hour before.

Specifically, the part about what I'd do if I found someone else had been sleeping with the woman I loved.

Chapter 12

I WALKED BACK up State Street to Tremont. Inside the entrance of my office building, I chose the stairs instead of the elevator to help clear my head. Coming down the second-floor hall, though, I still must have been a little dazed from Nancy, because my key was almost in the lock before I noticed my door was already ajar.

I pushed it halfway open.

"About time, Mr. Private Eye," said an accented voice from behind my desk.

A slim man sat in my chair, his feet in cowboy boots and resting on the secretarial pull-tray. He had a clean-shaven face, with sallow skin and blurry Asian features, as though the angles of eye sockets and cheekbones had been arrested in early development. His hair was black, combed back along his head in a moussed wave. He wore a double-breasted jacket with lapels wide enough to challenge a zoot suit, just a yellow T-shirt underneath. The eyes were somewhere between blue and green, focusing on me the way a lizard does watching a bug it hasn't yet decided is worth the effort. His right hand held some of my opened mail up to the light from the window behind him.

Staying on the corridor side of the threshold—and relieved not to see my photo album with the twenties tucked in it—I said, "Anything interesting come for me today?"

"Just bills." He fanned himself with them. "You ought to pay these, man, you don't want a bad credit report on your ass."

A little more Boston flavor in his voice with more words in the air.

He laid the papers on my desk. "What's the matter, you don't want to come in your own office?"

"Not until I see who's behind my door."

A small smile, the tip of his tongue just peeking out between the lips. "Oscar?"

I heard shoes shushing on my carpet, and another man came into view, backing up toward my desk with his hands behind his spine like a soldier moving at parade rest. Oscar was only about five-ten, but well over two hundred, his shoulders and bent arms seriously straining a single-breasted, camel-hair sports coat that probably measured a size fifty-four to start with. His skin tone went a shade lighter than mocha, the hair harder to judge since it was shaved like a recruit's in boot camp. I thought Oscar's nose had been broken twice to the right and thrice to the left, though the sloping eyes above the broad cheeks blazed in a way that made me seriously doubt he'd even noticed the pain involved. His ears were barely bigger than the buttons on his coat, the right one cauliflowered.

I said, "If he's Oscar Huong, that would make you Nguyen Trinh."

A broader smile from the man behind the desk. "Call me 'Nugey,' everybody else does."

"Let me guess. The first time you got busted, the booking officer didn't know which was your family name and which was your given name."

"That's pretty good, Mr. Private Eye." He looked to his friend. "Oscar's momma, now, she give him a real American name, easy to spot over here. Mine, she more . . . traditional.

But I use 'Mr. Trinh' now, anyway. Gonna be in America, you gotta adapt to the culture, huh?'' Trinh stood up, at almost six feet a little taller than he appeared sitting down. His hand made a Macarena motion toward my desk chair. "Make yourself comfortable.''

As I moved into the office, Huong backed up farther, keeping himself between me and his boss. We all then did a slow-mo minuet, rotating so that I ended up at my desk chair and they one each behind my client chairs. Trinh and I sat down, but Huong remained standing.

I looked at them. "How badly did you hurt my door?''

A shrug from Trinh. "We didn't have no tools. I figured, man's in business, he gonna have his office open, you know?''

"So, Oscar put his shoulder to it.''

"Didn't have to,'' said Huong, speaking for the first time. Not exactly easy listening, either. His voice sounded as though whoever rearranged the nose had gone after the throat, too. Then he brought his hands out from behind his back, raising them as he said, "These were good enough.''

Usually when you look at hands, they seem in rough proportion to the rest of the body. But Huong's were huge, and there were bumps and callouses on the knuckles in places you don't usually see them.

I said, "Okinawan karate?''

Huong just grinned at me.

Nguyen Trinh said, "Oscar, he learn lots of shit back when we juvies in DYS. You do the bare-knuckle push-ups on those hard floors, man, you get like him, too. Don't nobody mess with us, they see Oscar's hands.''

"How about before Oscar's hands got like that?''

Any humor faded from the sallow face. Trinh said, "You were over there, right?''

"Vietnam?''

"No. Waikiki fucking Beach.''

I tried to relax in my chair. "You do some research on me?''

Trinh almost smiled again. "Don't have to, Mr. Private Eye. You got the look. I was five years old when my momma put me on that plane. But I remember the look.''

"What plane?"

Trinh seemed a little surprised, but he said, "The do-gooders, they called it 'Operation Babylift.' Back in 'seventy-five, just when the Commies was coming over the walls. The do-gooders, they figured the Cong gonna kill us, cause we got the American devil-blood inside. Color of my eyes, color of Oscar's skin. So we get loaded on these planes—didn't have seats or nothing, just mattresses and that net stuff, hold down cargo. And that's all we was, too, cargo they sending to the place our poppas come from. Only thing is, we land in Boston, and guess what? Ain't no poppas waiting at the gate with cameras and teddy bears. Lots of the kids, they was just babies, but Oscar and me, we old enough to see what's going on, know what's happening to us."

"And what did happen?"

Trinh swallowed, kind of hard. "We ain't cute like the little babies, everybody want to adopt. We don't got no English, either, except a couple words our mommas remember. Oscar and me, we get put in this orphan place, and then foster homes, but there was nobody really wanted us. Even in school, man, you sit down for lunch, all of a sudden you hear this noise. You don't got much English, first time you don't know what it is. Then you do. All the kids at your lunch table, they saying it under their breath, chanting like they monks or some shit."

"Chanting what?"

" 'Gook, gook, gook.' "

Huong broke in. "Or 'Nigger gook, nigger gook.' "

I wished I couldn't picture it. "Kind of a jump to doing home invasions in the suburbs."

Trinh did smile this time. "You the one doing research on us, Mr. Private Eye."

"Some."

"Yeah, well, we didn't go right to the big stuff, you know. We start small, pay our dues. Oscar beat up the kids said things to us, and that got us into DYS the first time. Once we there, we learn pretty quick what's what. You got to fight, or you get turned out."

Meaning raped. "But—"

Huong said, "Once you a punk, them booty bandits, they don't leave you alone."

Trinh waited till his friend was finished. "Oscar and me, we never do that kind of shit to nobody, man. Even back then, AIDS was everywhere, these junky kids been sharing needles 'in the ghetto.' But nobody never turned us out, either. Thanks to Oscar."

I wanted to aim Trinh more toward what I was investigating. "And after that, you graduated to terrorizing families for money."

"Hey, man, you do what you know. Secret of success in these United States." Trinh looked around the room. "I gotta tell you, though, I don't know where your clients come from, you in this shitty little building with no parking out front, that slower than shit elevator, and then a locked-up door to your office."

"Tell me something else, Nugey. You use Oscar for anything other than a human master key?"

The tip-of-the-tongue smile. "I got my hand in lots of things."

"Like loan-sharking."

"Helping people who need cash, can't get it from the bank without a mask and a gun."

"Before you went into the lending business, though, you and Oscar both knew Woodrow Gant?"

Trinh dropped the smile. "How come you asking around about him and us?"

"He had dinner at a restaurant you have a piece of."

Trinh paused for a moment, glancing up at Huong before coming back to me. "You know how come I rent to that little shit Chan?"

"No."

Trinh released a breath. "I find out, he want to open a restaurant. Only thing, he have one before, but he couldn't make it go. It close, Chan owe people, even went bankrupt. So now he want to try again, I give him a chance."

"You're a real soft touch, Nugey."

The loan shark smiled again. I decided I liked him better serious.

He said, "That Chan, he one pure-blood Vietnamese. We still over in Saigon, he look down on Oscar and me like we dogshit somebody track into his house." Trinh leaned forward, putting his hand on my desk, grinding a little with the thumb. "So now he like this under me. Chan need my money, he got to respect me."

"You set him up in the restaurant so he'd be in your control."

"You got it." Trinh leaned back again. "I even call him 'Charlie,' like the fat detective guy in the old movies. And his woman, I call her 'Dinah,' get it?"

I thought I did. "Dinah like 'diner.' "

"Right. And they got to take it because they got to respect me."

Something was off. Huong remained stoic, but Trinh seemed relieved and kind of pleased with himself, like he'd just put something over on me.

"So," I said, "your owning the restaurant building had nothing to do with Woodrow Gant eating there the night he was killed."

"Zip, zero. Mr. Private Eye, I never even know the lawyer-man liked Vietnamese food. He sure never mentioned it when he was working on sending Oscar and me away."

Trinh rolled out the half-tongue smile, then checked his watch before looking up at his friend. "Oscar, how about you bring the car around, we get out of here?"

That seemed more off to me. Why wouldn't they want to leave together?

Huong just nodded, though, watching me carefully as he backed out my door, closing it behind him.

I waited for Trinh to turn back to me. "And I thought we'd never be alone."

He smiled, but just the little one. "I don't like to say everything in front of Oscar. Sometimes he think I'm telling him to do stuff when I ain't."

"Meaning?"

"Meaning Oscar think you like a real threat or something to me, to my business, he maybe just decide to take you apart right here."

"Might be easier said than done."

Trinh looked me over, appraising something. "You one of those exercise geeks, go to the health club, jog by the river?"

"Every morning, and twice on Sundays."

A better smile. "Don't matter, Mr. Private Eye. You never seen Oscar do his thing. He into that extreme-fighting shit."

" 'Extreme fighting'?"

"You know, where these two guys get in a pit—with a fence like a schoolyard has around it?—and just beat the shit out of each other. No gloves, no rules except the eyes and biting."

I'd heard of it as "ultimate fighting" a few years before. "I thought that got outlawed?"

"They trying, man. But you got to go with the will of the people, and the people, they want to see blood. First one was in Denver. Oscar the shortest guy climb in the pit, but he still come out fourth."

"What's your point, Nugey?"

Trinh nodded. "My point is, I want to whack that lawyer-man Gant, I ain't gonna have him eat at Chan's restaurant, then shoot him on a road. We just catch him in an alley some-time, like when he getting his car, maybe. Then I tell Oscar to beat that Uncle Tom to death."

Trinh stood up. "Like I'm gonna have Oscar do to you, you don't stay the fuck out of my business."

As Nguyen Trinh walked into the corridor, I began to register why he'd have wanted Huong to bring their car around. As soon as I heard him push the button for the elevator, I went into my desk drawer for the old photo album.

I was already at my office door, making a mental note to call our superintendent and get it fixed, when I heard the elevator door close. Trinh had been right: The elevator was slow, slow enough that I could be downstairs and hidden by the time he was getting off and going out the main entrance. I watched him at the curb, folding into the backseat of a green, four-door Mercedes, which pulled away heading south toward the theater district.

I gave it a count of five, then slipped out the door, hailing a cab from the cover of the next building. When the driver slewed over to me, I said into his open window, "This is your lucky day."

"For Yuri, lucky already fifteen dollars."

The driver looked over his shoulder and through the Plexiglas, his accent Russian, the meter running. My visitors' green Mercedes was three vehicles ahead of us and showing no sign of reaching its destination.

Back in my office, I couldn't see any reason for Nguyen Trinh to have Oscar Huong bring their car around unless they didn't want me following them somewhere. Which meant I wanted to. But I'd never have time to get the Prelude, and besides, Chan or Dinah at the restaurant might have seen me driving away and described it to them. A cab would be a little less obvious.

If a lot more expensive.

Yuri pushed back the Kangol cap on his head and picked up the mike to his radio, saying something in terse Russian before replacing it. "You think this close enough, three cars?"

"Given the volume of traffic, yes."

He shook his head, waving a hand at the side streets. "A truck comes out, boom, we lose them."

"We get closer, they'll know I'm back here."

A shrug, then something to himself in Russian.

Another five dollars on the meter, and we were in Dorchester, skirting the edges of Mattapan. Yuri twisted halfway in the driver's seat. "I do not like these streets so much."

Hard to blame him. We were in a part of town you wouldn't mistake for Helen Gant's neighborhood. Building walls tagged with graffiti crumbled into trash-filled vacant lots. Kids in clumps wore Oakland Raiders and Philadelphia Eagles colors, watching the Mercedes glide by, then eyeing us.

"Pretty soon," said Yuri, "I do not want anymore to follow."

His last word still hung in the air when the Mercedes pulled to a stop in front of a coffee shop.

I said, "Go past them to the next street and turn left." Ducking down, I could see only the taped posters near the top of the shop's windows, advertising "OPEN AT FIVE" and "TWO EGGS AND TOAST $1.50, COFFEE EXTRA."

After Yuri turned, I told him to stop, too. Getting out of the cab, I gave him a twenty as good-faith money, then walked back to the corner building, a failed hardware store from the empty fixtures still inside. Looking at a slight diagonal across the street, I couldn't see Nguyen Trinh at first, but Oscar Huong was just going in the front door of the coffee shop, aiming his keyring at the Mercedes, which gave that little security-system chirp. Then I could see Trinh inside the shop, moving to a windowed booth. He slid onto the bench seat and stretched out, checking his watch again. Huong eased down opposite him, and I could see their pantomime conversation through the glass as a waitress brought them both cups and saucers, pouring from a Pyrex pot.

None of us had to wait very long.

About five minutes after the waitress left the booth, a junker Chevy came down the street and parked in front of the Mercedes. I'd seen the car only in bad light, but its muffler noise was an aural signature, and I wasn't very surprised when the driver's side door opened to show Grover Cleveland Gant derricking himself with difficulty out from behind the wheel.

Quietly and to my back, Yuri said, "Soon we must leave."

"Soon we will."

"Those kids in the next block, I do not like the way they look at my cab."

"Stand next to it and flex."

Yuri muttered something in Russian, but moved away from me.

I was watching the scene in the coffee shop. Oscar Huong had stood to let Grover Gant slide into the booth on his side, which put some serious tonnage on that particular bench. After Huong sat back down and the waitress poured a third cup,

Gant watched her walk away before reaching his right hand, holding an envelope, across the table. Nguyen Trinh took the envelope and opened just the flap, looking inside and thumbing the contents. Then he may or may not have said something to Huong, but the Ultimate Fighter's right hand disappeared under the table for a moment, and the shoulders of Grover Gant doubled over toward his coffee, the head bobbing in what didn't look like pleasure from my angle.

Yuri called out to me, "Two minutes more, then my cab and me go."

Now Trinh definitely was talking, aiming his comments at Gant's bobbing head. I thought Gant's lips were moving, but given the distance, it might just have been from pain. Trinh slipped out of the booth and Huong stood, then leaned over to Gant, whose head now snapped up, his upper body beginning to rise, nearly taking the table with him, coffee cups jumping and spilling. The two Amerasians moved off, through the door of the shop and toward the Mercedes, the chirp noise preceding them.

From behind me, "One minute."

I waited until Trinh and Huong were back in their car, doors closed, before turning away. "Yuri, start your engine."

"You know, my cab must be back by three o'clock to garage."

The Mercedes cruised fairly leisurely along the city streets, the meter on Yuri's dashboard in the mid-four-figures. I figured I could always find Grover Gant if need be, but I was curious where Trinh and Huong might go next, and I had only the office address the gang unit had given me for them.

Holding up his left wrist, Yuri twisted in his seat to say, "And is already two-twenty."

"Just hang in there a little—watch it!"

He swung his head forward, stomping the brakes just as a moving van pulled out from a righthand side street. The van didn't have the turning radius to clear the parked cars the first time, requiring a leviathan three-pointer to get squared away.

By the time Yuri was able to pass, the Mercedes was nowhere in sight.

"What do I tell you? A truck comes out, and boom, we lose them." He looked down at the meter. "Now?"

"Back downtown, Tremont Street."

"Where I pick you up?"

"Yes."

"This time of day, we will not until after three get there. Way—"

"Twenty-dollar tip, or no tip. Your choice."

A moment's hesitation, then Yuri picked up his radio mike and spoke some Russian into it before glancing at the inside mirror. "Again the address, please?"

Back in my office, I got our superintendent working on my door lock as I flipped through the mail Nguyen Trinh had opened. Nothing seemed to be missing among the flyers, insurance advice, and utility bills on the condo.

When I called my answering service, the woman with the silky voice gave me one message on the Gant case. Steve Rothenberg's title searcher at the Registry of Deeds would be dropping off a package of recorded documents on the Viet Mam property late that afternoon. There'd been no unstamped envelope on the floor under the mail slot, but I decided not to wait for it before driving out to the restaurant, since I thought a bluff would work, and I wanted to catch Dinah before she'd be involved in the preparations for their dinner crowd.

Frankly, I wasn't sorry there was no green Mercedes in the parking lot next to Viet Mam. I stopped the Prelude across the street, so that I could get a good view of the dumpster and the pyramid of cigarette butts next to it.

About fifteen minutes later, the outside door to what I took to be the kitchen opened, and Dinah stepped onto the black-top. Her right leg looped behind the left as she walked to the corner of the dumpster, her hair still perfect but slightly different, I thought. A cigarette was already in her mouth, a lighter coming up from an apron pocket.

I left the car and moved toward her. Dinah was just blowing out the first big plume of smoke with something approaching pleasure on her face when I must have appeared in her peripheral vision.

Standing hip-cocked, weight on the good left leg, her pleasure waned as she waited for me to reach her.

"Dinah, I need to talk with you."

She took another drag on the cigarette. "This my break." A hacking cough. "Chan give me five minute only."

"I know why you were so scared the last time I was here."

Dinah looked away, taking a deeper drag. "I not scared. I not know—"

"Nguyen Trinh and Oscar Huong?"

She winced, the way I suspected she'd learned not to with her leg. "I have nothing to tell you."

"I'm trying to help a man I think is innocent."

Dinah looked at me.

I said, "Please?"

She glanced once toward the kitchen door before refocusing on her cigarette. "When I in Vietnam, many 'innocents' die. My husband, too."

"I'm sorry." The first time I saw Dinah, she'd mentioned that he'd fought. "Was your husband ARVN?" meaning Army of the Republic of Vietnam, our southern allies.

"No. He from north, a Catholic." Dinah fixed me with her eyes. "One of the commandos in newspaper stories."

Jesus. Before I got to Saigon in the late sixties, about three hundred men who'd fled from the communist North had been recruited by our C.I.A. to parachute back up there because they knew the terrain and the dialects. Thanks to a North Vietnamese mole in the ARVN, they were captured, tortured, and often killed. Recently declassified American military records confirmed that our government had written off all of them.

Whether dead or alive.

I said, "There's supposed to be a payment from our Congress for survivors like you."

Dinah coughed out a laugh. "No. When my husband killed, American officer come to our village. With money, four thousand dollar. Family of my husband say he never marry me, and I have no record to show, so his family take all the money."

"But maybe you can get more now."

She looked at me with contempt. "No money then, no money now." Then she sucked in more smoke. "When Communists win war, they come find me. *They* believe I wife of my husband. They torture him, they torture me. My leg, my br . . . my chest." A hand fluttered helplessly to her neckline, the scar diving under her collar more livid in the late afternoon light. "And so now I am with Chan, and no money can pay for these things."

"Dinah, I'm truly sorry, but your husband tried to help people who needed it. Can you help me?"

She drew again on the cigarette, her eyes working hard on something. "What you want to know?"

A window, but one I didn't think would stay open very long. "The woman with Woodrow Gant that night. You'd seen her before?"

"Yes."

"With Mr. Gant?"

"Yes. Only."

"Only what?"

"Only with him."

"Do you know if they left in the same car?"

Dinah glanced to an empty parking slot. "I know they come in same car."

Bingo. Maybe. "You saw them arrive?"

A look over her shoulder. "I am walking out door for cigarette break. Chan always want me in restaurant to help when new customers come. I watch them get out of car, walk to front door. Same car, he drive."

"When they were leaving, did they call a cab?"

Genuine confusion. "Taxi?"

"Right."

"Why they call, they have car?"

One more. "The woman, was she a little drunk when they left?"

"She drink most of wine bottle."

Only a quick puff now, Dinah's cigarette almost gone, and I sensed my window closing.

I said, "Is there anything else you can tell me about the woman that night?"

"She always with sunglasses, always with same big hair."

"Same hairstyle, you mean?"

Dinah took a last drag. "I save my tips here, study for beautician school." The free hand went to her own head.

"Yes?"

Dinah dropped the stub on the ground near the pile of dead ones and crushed it out with the toe of the good foot. "I don't look at her face so much, but I look at the hair, like I look at everybody's." Another smoky, hacking cough. "Same hair mean not her hair."

Jenifer Pollard had said that Woodrow Gant liked her to dress in costume and . . . "The woman in the restaurant that night was wearing a wig?"

"Yes. That is all I know."

"Dinah—"

"I must go." She was already turned to move as she coughed a final time. "Chan give me five minute only, and too many cigarette bad for you."

By the time Dinah reached the kitchen door, I was halfway to my car. After what she'd been through, I thought lung cancer probably held precious little terror for the waitress of Viet Mam.

Back at my office by half-past four, I pushed open the door to find the package from Steve Rothenberg's badger at the Registry. It was a manila envelope, nine-by-twelve, folded over to fit through the mail slot in my now fixed door.

Opening the envelope, I found photocopies of the seller-to-buyer conveyance documents on the Viet Mam restaurant building, the book-and-page references in stencil-like letters and numbers at the top. Each page of the printed documents contained a number of typographical errors, all corrected by hand, as though someone hadn't proofread the ribbon originals until the closing itself.

I didn't find much to help the cause, the seller and his attorney—whose letterhead was on the deed—having Hispanic names that meant nothing to me. Nguyen Trinh apparently purchased the property through a straw, the "NT Realty Trust," probably to conceal his identity as buyer. No surprise there.

In fact, the only real surprise came at the very end of that document. It was the part where a notary public signs and presses a notarial seal in taking the seller's oath that "the above-entitled conveyance is my free act and deed."

The seller's name conformed to the typing at the beginning of the document, but the notary line wasn't signed by his attorney. You had to read the signature carefully, and without the seal's printing coming through in photocopy like a bad dot-matrix, I might not have taken the time to read it carefully enough. After three go-overs, though, I was pretty certain I'd gotten it right the first time.

The deed conveying the Viet Mam building to Nguyen Trinh had been notarized by one "Deborah M. Ling."

Chapter 13

ON THE WALK over to Epstein & Neely's offices, I thought about how to handle Deborah Ling. Riding to the fourth floor in that small elevator, I settled on an indirect approach.

When the door opened onto the reception area, Imogene Burbage was picking up a Federal Express packet from the desk staffed by a different woman than I'd seen only the day before. Burbage wore a gray suit, the style still conservative, the reddish hair still pulled into a tight bun.

Turning around, she seemed taken aback. "Mr. Cuddy?"

"Ms. Burbage. I'm glad to see you."

A troubled expression as she came toward me, massaging the left wrist with her free hand. "Why?"

I lowered my voice. "I'd hate having to explain myself to a new receptionist."

Burbage frowned. "Well, you should have called first, given how late it is. Mr. Neely's attending a bar association event, Mr. Herman's away on a trip till tomorrow, and Ms. Ling's at a closing."

Being able to account for all her charges. Control, *über alles.*
"How about Ms. Radachowski then?"

"John Cuddy."

I said, "Working late?"

With one big hand, Uta Radachowski pushed back a hank
of the brown-and-silver hair, using the other to close the file
on her cherry-wood desk and tap a key on her computer. "Not
really. I'm afraid the days of nine-to-five are but a distant and
fading memory." The magnified eyes looked at me from behind her pop-bottle lenses. "What brings you back here?"

Time for the indirect approach. "I've been trying to come
up with possible suspects, and it occurred to me that Woodrow
Gant might have had some clients who weren't part of the
firm roster."

Radachowski blinked once. "I'm not sure I follow you."

"Everybody here told me Mr. Gant didn't have any other
opposing clients who had threatened him. What I'm wondering is, could Mr. Gant have had some cases he was working
on outside the firm structure?"

Another blink. "You mean, that he was litigating on his
own somehow?"

"Yes, where he might have made enemies you all wouldn't
know about."

Radachowski shook her head. "No. No, I don't see that happening. Woodrow did divorce work, and he used a software
program for tracking them." She placed her right hand on the
computer monitor. "Like the one in here I told you about last
time. If he had 'outside' cases, as you've called them, he'd
have been crazy to enter them on the 'inside' program."

"Why?"

"His secretary, Imogene, is also our bookkeeper. If she were
to go into Woodrow's computer as his secretary, Imogene
might see a file she didn't recognize from her billing software.
And if he'd tried to litigate a case off the tracking program, he'd
have had a hell of job keeping all the commitments straight."

"Couldn't Mr. Gant just have kept his own, separate calendar for the outside matters?"

Radachowski paused a moment. "John, why is it you even think Woodrow might have done all this in the first place?"

"How about to make money he didn't have to share with the rest of you?"

She paused again. "No. No, it's just too big a risk. Even if Woodrow kept a separate calendar, he'd still have to be in court for hearings on your 'outside' cases when his docket program said he shouldn't be, and he'd have to double-bill some 'inside' client to 'hide' that time for bookkeeping purposes. Plus, there'd be disbursements, like discovery costs for depositions or fees for expert witnesses. And, secretarily, he'd still need pleadings and other documents generated at the firm for those cases, because Woodrow wasn't terribly talented at formatting formal paperwork on his computer. Not to mention all kinds of countering documents from the other side arriving here that Imogene might open first."

I thought about the typos in the deed I'd seen for the Viet Mam building. "How about if Mr. Gant had the opposing attorney draw up all the paperwork?"

"All of it? In a business deal, I suppose that might fly, assuming no long-distance calls from here that our billing program wouldn't find any 'inside' client to charge. But on a litigated case? No, the opponent would have to be crazy. Or Woodrow would have had to—"

Radachowski stopped short.

I said, "What is it?"

"Nothing. It makes even less sense than what you asked about."

I gave her a minute, because something had crossed my mind, too, as Radachowski was giving me what I needed for confronting Deborah Ling. "Were you about to say, 'Or Woodrow would have had to get Imogene to go along with the plan?'"

No blinking at all from behind the thick lenses now. "John, you'll have to excuse me. I really have a lot of work to do before I can go home tonight."

*　　*　　*

I asked the new receptionist if Ms. Ling was expected to return to the office from her closing. Given that Imogene Burbage had immediately ushered "Mr. Cuddy" in to see Uta Radachowski, the temp behind the desk probably thought it was okay to tell me that the real-estate associate had said she'd be back by six.

I sat down on the love seat to wait. About 5:50, I heard the elevator moving up its shaft, the doors opening to spill Deborah Ling into the reception area. She'd traded the pinstriped suit for a fawn-colored dress today, accessorized by a matching briefcase and handbag.

Race-walking to the desk, Ling never even glanced my way. "Any calls?"

"Three," said the temp, reaching into the plastic holder. "And Mr. Cuddy to see you."

"Mr. . . . ?" Ling turned, her pixie-cut hair quivering a bit as I thought she tried to maintain a poker face. "Again?"

"It'll just take a minute."

A sigh as Ling accepted her pink message slips from the receptionist. "Come into my office."

Circling around the black, lacquered desk, Deborah Ling sank into her swivel chair. "I've had a long, hard day, Mr. Cuddy."

"That makes two of us."

"Can we get on with it, then?"

"Sure. The last time I was here, you told me you introduced Woodrow Gant to the restaurant where he ate dinner the night of his death."

Very casual, but impatient. "That's right."

"Coming back from Dedham. On a friend's recommendation, I think you said."

Now just impatient. "Mr. Cuddy, we've already spoken about—"

"But I'm afraid you forgot to mention something else."

"What?" said Ling, impatience verging on exasperation.

"That you handled the purchase of the building Viet Mam is in."

For a moment, she didn't reply. Then, in a voice without inflection, "What are you talking about?"

"The property is leased to a man named Chan, who's trying to make a go of the restaurant. But you represented Nguyen Trinh when he bought the building."

A laugh that didn't quite come off. "Who?"

"Nguyen Trinh, though he told me he prefers 'Nugey.' Woodrow Gant prosecuted Trinh and a buddy of his named Oscar Huong for home invasion some years back."

Ling made no attempt to laugh now. "What in the world makes you think I'm involved in any of this?"

"You mean, because there wouldn't be any billing records here at the firm showing you ever worked on the transaction?"

Now she didn't even reply.

"Ms. Ling, your notary public seal and signature are on the deed to Trinh."

She tried to recover. "Oh, that? I was at the Registry one day, and another lawyer had forgotten his seal, so he asked me to just—"

"Do you really think the lawyer who represented the seller of the building is going to back you on that? Especially after you had him prepare all the conveyancing documents so there wouldn't be any embarrassing paper trail for Frank Neely or Imogene Burbage to stumble on here at the firm?"

Ling closed down, eyes, face, even torso. Then she looked up at me. "Are you trying to ruin my career?"

"No, but I would like the truth."

"The truth." Ling bit her lower lip. "All right. The truth is that I met Nugey Trinh over the summer at one of the dance clubs in the theater district. We started talking, about me being a real estate attorney and him wanting to buy a building. Nugey asked me to represent him on the purchase, but he wanted it 'off the books.'"

"Why?"

"Nugey said that since he met me at the club instead of through the firm, and if I was going to do all the work, why should Epstein & Neely get the fee? Then he—"

"Wait a minute. Trinh knew where you worked?"

Ling hesitated. "Yes. When we first started talking—about me doing real estate law—he asked where, and I told him."

So if Trinh had known Gant was at Epstein & Neely, Trinh also would know that Ling worked with him there. "Go on."

"Well, I told Nugey I'd have to think about it."

"Why did you even consider it?"

"Mr. Cuddy, Nugey Trinh is an attractive man. Exotic, with his racial background. And I'd broken away from my family, anyway, so I didn't have them to 'embarrass' by seeing someone who wasn't Chinese."

"Which might explain why you'd want to date Trinh, but not why you'd represent him 'off the books.' "

Ling looked away, out her window. "The first time you were here, we talked about student loans." She patted the lacquered wood in front of her. "Well, this desk was the last tangible help I got from my parents. They won't contribute to the loan payments, and the obligation isn't dischargeable in bankruptcy, even if I were willing to commit 'career-icide' by filing for it." Ling looked back at me. "Nugey's deal seemed so neat and clean. I'm in and out of the transaction with a few thousand in cash that neither the firm nor the IRS has to know about."

"How did you handle things with the seller's attorney?"

"I told him I was practicing out of my apartment. Enough recent law grads have to do that, it doesn't seem odd anymore. Only he forgot to send a draft of the deed to my home address for me to review, so the first time I saw it was at the closing, where I picked up on all the typos. I corrected them by hand, and then the incompetent fool didn't even have his notarial seal with him, meaning I had to take the seller's oath myself."

"Which shouldn't have been a problem, except for somebody like me having the building's title traced at the Registry."

"Yes. Why did you do that?"

The Gang Unit, but I wasn't about to reveal my source to her. "I thought Chan and the waitress at Viet Mam were awfully nervous, and I wanted to see if the records gave them some reason to be."

Ling sagged back into her chair, the eyes solemn. "So, what are you going to do now?"

"Before we get to that, why did you really take Woodrow Gant to the restaurant for lunch that first time?"

She straightened a little. "Just because I knew it was there. I wanted to try it, too."

"Doesn't wash, counselor. The last thing you'd ever do would be to bring a partner from the firm you'd shorted to the building you'd shorted it on."

Ling seemed to go inside herself for a minute. "Nugey and I had become . . . intimate. He's a very exciting man, Mr. Cuddy. Very different from the ones I meet through my work." She came out of her trance. "He wanted me to bring Woodrow there."

"To Viet Mam?"

"Yes."

"Why?"

"Nugey is . . ." Ling stopped, then started over. "Nugey had a very difficult life, one where because of his . . . heritage he was rarely in control of anything. I think the main reason he bought that particular building was so that he could exercise some control over a 'purebred' Vietnamese man, the kind who would have abused him back in Saigon."

Trinh had told me basically the same thing. "Go ahead."

"Well, I think there was some of that about having Woodrow and me in the restaurant, too. Nugey had been prosecuted by him, sentenced to a juvenile detention center for a long time. Now Nugey wanted to watch Woodrow eating in a building he controlled."

"Watch him?"

"Yes. When Woodrow and I ate lunch there, Nugey was kind of hiding in the kitchen, watching us through the swinging doors."

Christ. "That was all Trinh did, watch?"

Ling seemed confused. "Yes. I mean, Woodrow might have recognized him. What else could Nugey do?"

I was thinking of the way Trinh and Huong dealt with Grover Gant at the coffee shop, but I said, "Have you had any more ideas about who the woman might have been with Woodrow Gant in Viet Mam the night he was killed?"

"No. I don't even know why he'd go back there."

"Because?"

"In the parking lot that day after lunch, Woodrow mentioned he hadn't particularly enjoyed the food."

Not what Ling had told me the first time I met her, but consistent with what Uta Radachowski had said.

When I kept silent, Deborah Ling changed the tone of her voice. "I have a question for you, Mr. Cuddy."

"Go ahead."

She seemed to choose her words carefully. "Are you going to tell Frank Neely about all this?"

"I don't see a reason to."

Ling was visibly relieved.

"However," I said, "there's a life sentence of reasons why I have to tell Alan Spaeth's attorney about it."

Ling shook her head. "Nugey owns that building as a matter of public record."

"Only as the 'NT Realty Trust.' "

"But he could testify he's the one behind the trust."

I thought I could see where Ling was going. "Without involving you as the one who handled the transaction."

A very steady, "Yes."

"Ms. Ling, Steve Rothenberg hired me to find evidence establishing a reasonable doubt that his client killed Woodrow Gant. You're not a criminal lawyer—and I'm not a lawyer, period—but it seems to me that 'reasonable doubt' is kind of cumulative. And the facts that ex-gang-member Trinh was tied to the decedent as prosecutor and to the decedent's current law firm through you add up pretty persuasively."

"Mr. Cuddy, please? It would be crazy for Nugey to kill Woodrow like a gang execution just minutes after Woodrow left a building Nugey owns."

Trinh himself had made that argument to me. And it was a good one, unless Chan's landlord really was nuts.

An imploring look in her eyes. "At least think about it for a while before ruining me?"

I was tempted to tell Deborah Ling that was exactly what she should have done when Nguyen Trinh first made his "off the books" suggestion, but I couldn't see how it would do her any good now.

Precisely creasing correspondence toward insertion into envelopes, Imogene Burbage looked up at me from behind her desk outside Frank Neely's office. "You were talking to Ms. Radachowski for quite a while."

"Only part of the time since I left you. The rest was with Deborah Ling."

Burbage went back to her letters. "Well, I hope that you've now found out everything you need."

"Not quite."

When I didn't continue, she looked back up at me, a sheaf of unfolded papers spread before her like a giant game of solitaire. "Meaning what?"

"Meaning I still don't know the name of the woman having dinner with Woodrow Gant the night he was killed."

"We already discussed that."

I took a chance. "It's possible she was wearing sort of a disguise."

"Disguise?"

"Big blond wig, sunglasses."

Burbage made no reply.

I said, "Probably something that would be completely out of character for the woman, to throw people off on identifying her."

"Mr. Cuddy," said Burbage very slowly, "I have no idea who your 'mystery date' could be."

Five seconds went by, neither of us looking away. I leaned forward just a little, placing my palms on her desktop. "Could she have been you?"

Burbage obviously didn't like me invading her space. "You're being rude, as well as redundant. I've told you I wasn't that woman." Then a softening I didn't expect. "From the way

I behaved the last time you were here, I'm sure you can tell that I cared for Mr. Gant. Cared for him very much. But I didn't go out with him socially."

"Never?"

"Never. I don't behave like that."

"Always in control, Ms. Burbage?"

"Always," said a deep voice behind me.

I turned to see Frank Neely standing squarely. I hadn't heard him approaching down the hall from the reception area.

He said, "Weren't we helpful enough yesterday?"

"A few more things have come up."

Neely seemed to consider that. "Imogene, any fires that need putting out?"

"They can wait till morning."

He turned back to me. "John, I just left a bar reception because it was boring me to tears. As long as you promise not to do the same, we can talk in my office."

"So, what are the 'few more things'?"

Neely was seated behind his desk, me in front of it. No offer of drinks or view from upstairs this visit.

I said, "Let's start with the public record part. When Woodrow Gant was with the D.A.'s office, he prosecuted a young hood named Nguyen Trinh."

"Nguyen . . . Is that Vietnamese?"

"Amerasian, but he spent his formative years over here, learning extortion and home invasion before turning to loan-sharking."

The rumbling sound from Neely's chest. "Sounds like a prince. But Woodrow left that job over three years ago."

"Right. Only Trinh stayed interested in him."

Neely frowned with every feature on his face. "How do you mean?"

"Trinh owns the building that houses Viet Mam."

A widening of the eyes. "The restaurant where Woodrow ate that night?"

"Yes."

"Sweet Jesus." Either Frank Neely was one hell of an actor,

or the news really shocked him. Which probably meant he truly had no idea that Deborah Ling represented Trinh on the deal.

Neely's look became analytical. "So you think that this Nguyen Trinh set Woodrow up to be shot?"

"I'm not sure of that part."

"What?"

"It's possible that Trinh killed Mr. Gant, or even had him killed. But I've met Trinh, and he doesn't seem to me stupid enough to create a clear connection between a business he's part of and a murder he committed or ordered."

Neely shook his head. "Then I don't take your point."

"My point," I explained for the second person in an hour, "is reasonable doubt. Gathering evidence that somebody other than Alan Spaeth had a motive and the means to go after Mr. Gant."

"But you just said this . . . this loan shark wasn't stupid enough—"

"—to connect himself to an intentional shooting. That doesn't mean a jury would agree with me."

Neely stared across his desk, then nodded, slowly. "Of course. You're just doing your job, and I'm too close to the situation to appreciate that."

"Speaking of doing my job, any further thoughts on who the woman with Mr. Gant might have been?"

"The woman . . . Oh, in that restaurant, you mean?"

"Yes."

"No. As I said the last time you were here, Woodrow wasn't a braggart about his conquests."

Conquests. "Would it help if I said the woman in question might have been wearing a blond wig?"

Neely frowned again. "A wig?"

"Yes."

A moment as he looked down at his desk. "No." Two moments more. "No, I can't think of anyone I knew in his life who wore a wig or talked about one."

I stood up. "Well, thanks again for your time."

Frank Neely stayed seated. "I wish I could say I've enjoyed

spending it with you." His eyebrows knit together. "But as I told you once, John, it's to the firm's advantage to see this matter concluded as soon as possible. So, if need be, our doors are always open to you."

I wasn't sure anyone else at Epstein & Neely would agree with him.

Chapter 14

ANOTHER HUMP UP State Street, grabbing a
sandwich as a late substitute for the lunch I'd
never had. Back in my office, I called the answering service. No
messages with the silky-voiced woman this time, and, remotely
beeping my home tape machine, none there, either. After the
way Nancy had left things at Cricket's, I didn't really expect
to hear from her, but there was always hope.

However, hope couldn't fill an empty evening. And something that Imogene Burbage had mentioned about one of her
charges gave me a possible start on it.

They were in a suburban telephone book under Weston
Hills, and I'd been in the town often enough to find their
address without much trouble. It was an older garrison colo-
nial, white with green shutters and standing at attention on
about an acre. A Toyota Camry took up most of the driveway,
so I left the Prelude at the curb, my car the only one on the
street for blocks. Walking toward the house, I felt the hood of
the Toyota. Still warm on a chilly October night.

When I pushed the doorbell, I could hear a muted, four-toned chime sound inside. Then a whoosh as the heavy, raised-panel door broke its seal with the jamb.

Karen Herman looked at me strangely from across the threshold. Same honey-colored, patchy hair, but the wardrobe was jeans and an Yves St. Laurent sweatshirt rather than evening wear. In preppy loafers instead of high heels, she stood only about five-six. Fairly "medium," and a pair of sunglasses would just cover that mole under her right eye.

She said, "We've met, but where?"

It happens, when people see you out of context. "At your husband's law firm."

"Oh." The look went from strange to wary. "The . . . detective."

"Private investigator. John Cuddy."

"But Elliot's not here."

"I know. That's why I thought this might be a convenient time for us to talk."

"About what?"

More wary, and with a little edge in her voice, the kind attractive women develop to ward off jerks in bars. I said, "Woodrow Gant."

Herman's hand went to her face, the index finger flicking at the mole the way it did in the reception area the day before. "I have nothing to tell you."

"Mrs.—"

"Do I have to call the police?"

Despite not holding the right cards, I said, "Try nine-one-one for a uniform, but probably the detective division would make more sense. Or even the chief, since—"

"What do you want?" with a sharper edge to it.

"I want to talk with you. We can do it now in your living room, privately, or you can answer a defense attorney's questions in a courtroom, publicly. Your choice."

Only a minor hesitation before a reluctant, "Come in."

I went past her into the foyer, which led to a sunken living room on the left. The sofa and chairs were covered in cobalt-blue leather, their arrangement designed to make a slate-hearth fireplace on the long wall the focal point of the room. A wedding portrait occupied a miniature easel on the mantel, Karen and Elliot Herman with faces perhaps five years younger.

"Very nice house," I said as Herman pointed me toward one of the chairs. "Must be tough to maintain, though, with both you and your husband working."

"I don't work." She took the other chair, the length of the couch between us.

I smiled at her until Herman said, "I'm waiting."

"I need some help with a problem I'm having."

She flicked at the mole again. "What problem?"

"Woodrow Gant once prosecuted a couple of Amerasian gangsters who committed a home invasion."

A look of confusion. "I don't know anything about that."

"It happened here in Weston Hills, about eight or nine years ago."

Relief flooded Herman's features. "We only moved here three years ago, when Elliot began working at the firm." A different tone. "Now that I've answered your—"

"There's another problem, I'm afraid."

The relief washed back out like a sudden tide. "What?"

"The night Mr. Gant was killed, he had dinner with a woman in a Vietnamese restaurant."

Just a slight nod.

I said, "I'm hoping you can tell me who she was."

"How . . . how would I know that?"

I stopped smiling. "Mrs. Herman, Mr. Gant was very active socially. He rarely bragged about it, but 'rarely' doesn't mean 'never.'"

"You bastard."

She said the words flatly, no anger or other emotion driving them.

"Mrs. Herman—"

"You absolute, son-of-a-bitch bastard."

Still no emotion. I waited her out.

She hung her head. "Once."

"I'm sorry?"

Karen Herman lifted her chin. "I had sex with Woodrow Gant once, and it was nothing for him to 'brag' about."

Slowly, I said, "If we talk it over now, there's a chance nothing has to come out at Mr. Spaeth's trial."

"But only a chance."

"Yes."

Herman seemed to settle into herself, taking a few breaths before saying, "Elliot and I wanted to have a baby. We tried very hard, but nothing seemed to . . . happen. I was about to consult a fertility expert, to see if that was the problem, when Elliot stood me up one day for lunch downtown because some client meeting was running over."

"About when was this?"

"When? Last April."

Six months before Gant's death. "You're sure?"

A lifeless expression on her face. "I have reason to be. That same day—the lunch date—I saw Woodrow in the lobby of the firm's building as I was stepping off the elevator. He asked what brought me into the city, and I told him about Elliot not being able to keep our date. Woodrow said he'd just settled a custody case during trial, so he was unexpectedly free. Before I could reply, Woodrow suggested *we* have lunch instead. I didn't know him that well, but he was kind of Elliot's boss, so I didn't want to offend him, either. And besides, he—you never met Woodrow, right?"

"Right."

"Well, he was . . ." Herman's right index finger went to the mole under her eye again. "Engaging. A very engaging man. And I was a little ticked off at Elliot—no, a lot ticked off. I'd gotten all dressed up, and gone all the way into Boston, and we were so frustrated over . . ."

Herman ran down, then looked down, wringing her hands. "I had some wine while Woodrow got us a table, and more at lunch, and then some more still, until I was in no condition to drive home. So Woodrow said, 'Let's walk a little, huh?' And it seemed like a good idea. Only somehow we ended up . . . in a hotel room."

Herman now looked away. I felt badly.

202

"Anyway," she said, "it turned out that . . . that I wasn't the infertile one."

I felt worse, a lot worse.

Herman came back to me. "I hadn't taken any precautions, of course. Not for months. And Woodrow should have used a condom—no. No, I shouldn't have been there in the first place. But I'd had too much to drink and too much to deal with, and it just happened. Not rape or anything. I was just so . . . stupid."

Quietly, I said, "You became pregnant."

She looked away again. "Briefly."

"Did your husband know?"

Her head snapped back. "About the abortion? Of course not. I borrowed the money for the clinic from a girlfriend, and—"

"Mrs. Herman, did your husband know about you and Mr. Gant at all?"

"No. No, I wasn't that—wait a minute. You said Woodrow bragged about me."

"I did, but—"

"Who?"

"Mrs.—"

"Goddamnit! I need to know who told you, if Elliot could somehow find out the way you did."

"Nobody told me."

Her features seemed to empty. "Nobody?"

"I was going on your reaction to me at the law firm, and here at the front door, plus the fact that you match the description of the woman Mr. Gant had dinner with the night he was killed."

Herman watched me, something like comprehension seeping into her eyes. "You lied to me."

"Not exactly, but in effect."

"All of this . . ." Propping an elbow on each knee, she lowered her face into her hands, speaking through the fingers. "You put me through all of this to find out if I was the woman in that restaurant?"

"Yes."

"I wasn't."

"Mrs. Herman, I had to know."

She raised her face. "Know something else, then, all right? You know what the hardest part was?"

After what I'd just done to her, Karen Herman was entitled to have me play along. "No."

"It was waking up in the clinic's recovery room, after the abortion. Waking up to find myself crying. I knew it was Woodrow's baby, I knew it. But I wanted a child so badly, I couldn't stop crying. And then I looked around at the women on the other beds, and they were all crying, too. A room full of almost-mothers, crying our eyes out."

I didn't say anything.

"Well, Mr. Cuddy, I don't have any more tears. But if I did, I'd be crying them now. For what I went through then, and what you just put me through again."

"I'm—"

"When you asked me, I said I don't work. My parents paid for four years of college, so I probably should, but I don't. And the closest I've ever come to being a mother myself was in that clinic. But I'd rather wake up in its recovery room a dozen times than lie to people for a living the way you do."

I kept quiet.

"I've told you what you wanted to know." Karen Herman folded her arms across her chest. "Now get out of our home."

Driving toward the Brookline/Boston border, I tried not to think about the hurt I'd just resurrected, but it was hard. Especially because I expected to be following roughly the same course twice more that night.

I parked downslope of the highrise tower, arriving at the buzzer system and security door just behind a teenaged kid wearing a red paper hat and carrying a brown, leatherette case shaped slightly bigger than a large pizza. Over his shoulder, I could see him press the button for "POLLARD, J."

The tinny voice with that trace of Olde England came over the intercom. "Pizza?"

"You got it," said the delivery boy.

"I'm letting you in. Twelve-oh-seven."

"Hey, the van's double-parked." But he was talking into dead space as the door buzzer sounded.

Stepping in front of the kid and grabbing the handle of the door, I said, "Tell you what."

He half-turned to me. "What?"

"I'm going to twelve, anyway. How about if I pay you, and she pays me?"

The delivery boy squinted. "Yeah, and where's my ass if she calls the boss ten minutes from now with 'The fuck is my pizza?' "

For some reason, the kid's suspicious nature lifted my spirits. "I don't know what's on the pizza. Inside the case like that, I can't even smell the toppings. Figure the chances I'm going to keep it."

The kid looked toward the curb, then started to slide the pizza box out of his case. "Fifteen-fifty."

I gave him a twenty. "Keep it, ease your mind."

He left without a proper thank you.

Jenifer Pollard wasn't waiting at the elevator, with or without a can of pepper spray. But I remembered which way to turn, and after a few seconds was knocking on 1207.

"Get that, can you?" I heard Pollard say inside the apartment, dishes clattering.

A male voice answered. "Yeah."

The door swung open, and Thom Arneson, ADA, stared out at me, holding his wallet in one hand.

"Whoops," said I.

Arneson had on a dress shirt—unbuttoned twice down the chest—and the pants to a gray houndstooth suit. No tie. Or shoes. "What the hell is this?"

I stepped by him into the apartment, Pollard turning to look at her front door. She wore tennis shorts tonight, with a gauzy singlet top that would qualify as a mite racy for entertaining polite company.

Setting the box on the kitchen counter, I said to Arneson, "Put your wallet away. The pizza's my treat."

Pollard looked from him to me and back again. "He followed you?"

Arneson still held his wallet, but more like he wanted to brain me with it. "I don't see how. Or why."

"I wasn't following anybody. Just decided to stop by for a little visit, ran into the delivery boy downstairs, and—"

Arneson said, "How about if I tell you to go the hell back downstairs?"

"Then you'd be out of line, counselor. It's Ms. Pollard's apartment."

He took a step toward me, still hefting the wallet. "How about if I just throw you down the stairs?"

I said, "Then you'd be out of your depth as well."

Pollard didn't like the turn things were taking. "Perhaps instead we could all just sit down for a few minutes like civilized beings and find out what's going on?"

Arneson gave her a glare, but backed up and took the daybed as she followed him, perching on a corner of it, close enough to touch the man. Which left the rocking chair for me.

Looking out through the big windows, I said, "The view's even more impressive at night."

Arneson didn't react, so Pollard must have told him about my earlier visit. Probably before I'd seen him at the D.A.'s office.

Pollard said, "Mr. Cuddy, I thought you got everything you needed the last time you were here?"

It had been "John" back then, but her double meaning was still firmly in place. "A few new facts have surfaced."

"What facts?" said Arneson.

"Let's start with the current situation and work backwards. How long have you two been seeing each other?"

Arneson didn't surprise me when he said, "None of your fucking business."

"Thom." Pollard laid her left palm on his shoulder, symbolically holding him back, I thought. "Mr. Cuddy, I really don't understand how any relationship I have now could possibly relate to your problem."

"Even a relationship with your dead husband's former office-mate?"

"My dead *ex*-husband, to be precise. And given how long it's been since I had any connection to Woodrow, I really do think Thom is right."

More of the old country was creeping into her voice and phrasing. "I take it you're not counting the insurance proceeds as a 'connection.' "

Arneson gritted his teeth. "I don't like what you're implying, Cuddy."

"A hundred thousand up-front looks pretty attractive for a woman living in a studio apartment, even with this kind of view."

Arneson got more angry. "That was part of Jen's divorce settlement, years ago."

Pollard said, "And it was a hundred only at the beginning."

I looked to her. "What?"

She took her hand off Arneson's shoulder, using her fingers to tuck a hank of the auburn hair behind her left ear. "The policy amount was to be a hundred the first year, eighty the next, then sixty, and so on. Just enough to cover an annual twenty thousand dollars of—what did the judge call it? Oh, yes. 'Rehabilitative alimony.' " A smile and the vamping pose. "To get me back on my feet after the crushing blow of losing Woodrow." Pollard eased off the pose. "So, I'd be down to only forty thousand by now, wouldn't I?"

I shook my head. "One of the attorneys at Mr. Gant's firm told me the face amount of the policy was still a hundred."

Arneson and Pollard exchanged glances. She said, "I didn't know that." No posing at all now. "Why would Woodrow have kept up a larger policy than required?"

Arneson put into words what I was thinking. "Less trouble, Jen. He probably just bought a five-year term policy, and it was easier to keep that than go back for renewals and maybe new physicals. Might even have been cheaper, too."

"Well," Pollard said, clearly pleased, "I certainly don't intend to argue the point." She looked at me. "But given this good news you've brought us, I must insist on covering the pizza."

I watched the two of them. They couldn't have known I'd be coming over, and unless they'd rehearsed awfully thoroughly, this felt too natural to be anything but spontaneous. And therefore honest.

Arneson said, "Cuddy, what Jen means is that you can leave now."

"Just a couple more questions. Ms. Pollard, you told me Mr. Gant liked . . . wigs and things."

Arneson looked down at the floor rather pointedly, but Pollard's eyes glittered a little as she said, "Especially the . . . things."

"There's some reason to believe that the woman with him the night he was killed was wearing a wig—and sunglasses—as some kind of disguise."

"Disguise?"

"I think so. Can you think of any reason why a woman would want to do that with Mr. Gant?"

The glitter again. "In public, do you mean?"

"Yes," I said.

Pollard returned her hand to Arneson's shoulder, but now not like she was holding him back. More as though her mood had changed suddenly. "Thom?"

"I'm not going to tell him," said Arneson. "Hell, I shouldn't have told you."

Pollard looked at me, that ray of sincerity finally shining through. "I think you'd want to know this, but I need a promise back from you first."

"What's the promise?"

"That you won't tell anyone about Thom and me."

Arneson turned to her. "Jen, you actually think you can trust this guy?"

"From the way he behaved the last time he was here, yes." Pollard came back to me, still sincere. "I think Mr. Cuddy is a man who keeps his promises."

I said, "Odds are it would be more than a little embarrassing for a career prosecutor to be having an affair—"

"Relationship," said both of them, almost in unison.

"—a 'relationship' with the ex-wife of a former colleague."

Arneson seemed to choose his words carefully. "It wouldn't help anything."

Pollard gave him a moment to continue. When he didn't, she said, "Mr. Cuddy?"

"I'll do my best to keep things confidential, but only if your relationship doesn't impact Mr. Gant's death any more than the way I see it now."

Arneson grunted. "Hell of a promise."

"The best I can do."

The two of them exchanged glances again.

Pollard sighed and turned back to me. "During one of Woodrow's cases at the District Attorney's office, he became attracted to the victim. But we were still married, and so was she."

I was beginning to picture it.

Pollard said, "Woodrow had the poor judgment to go out with her to a bar, and Thom happened to see them together."

I looked at Arneson. "And recognized the woman."

"Yes," he said, biting off the word.

I finished the memory for him. "Even though she was wearing a wig."

He nodded, not liking it.

But if I had to guess, I'd say Thom Arneson liked it at least five times as much as I did.

The street in West Roxbury was dark, nobody playing "Howla." The Mazda stood in the driveway of number 396, though.

Moving up the path, I realized how much slower than usual I was walking. Tired, yes, but more than that.

I knocked, and ten seconds later, young Terry Spaeth opened the door, sans both baseball cap and eyebrow ring. He stared at me. "What do you want?"

"I'd like to speak to your mother."

"Yeah, right. After the extreme trouble you already got me into?"

From another room, Nicole Spaeth's voice called out, "Terry, who is it?"

He didn't answer her. To me, he said, "Look, just go hassle somebody else, okay?"

Terry started to push the door closed. I would have lodged my foot against it, but his mother's voice stopped him. "Couldn't you hear . . ."

Her face fell when she saw me, those haunting hazel eyes windows on her emotions.

I said, "Mrs. Spaeth, we need to talk."

Terry turned to her. "Mom, this dude's got no—"

"Go to your room, Terry."

"But, Mom—"

"Now. Or we extend the grounding another week."

Terry muttered something that sounded like, "Thanks a lot, asshole," but he moved off and out of view.

When her son was gone, Nicole Spaeth said, "I suppose you'll be wanting to sit down."

"I think we'd both better."

She considered that, my tone maybe more than my words, then led me into the living room, lowering herself onto the aging sofa while I took my third chair in the last three hours.

Spaeth waited until I was settled before saying in a tired way, "All right, what is it now?"

"You grounded Terry because he talked with me outside last night."

"How I discipline my son is no—"

"Because he told me about the Board of Bar Overseers complaint?"

She didn't say anything.

I said, "And because it's true."

An attempt at a laugh. "Alan was dreaming, Mr. Cuddy. His jealousy was . . . warping him."

"It goes further than that, though."

"I don't know—"

"I do know, Mrs. Spaeth. But I wish I didn't."

She managed a "Know what?"

"Who the woman was with Woodrow Gant that night at the restaurant."

"Then you know more than—"

"Since I saw you yesterday, I've spoken to a lot of people about Mr. Gant. One called him a 'ladies' man,' another said he would go out with 'inappropriate' women as well, including the victim in a case he prosecuted."

"I told you the last time, Woodrow and I—"

"Just the blond wig, Mrs. Spaeth?"

Her mouth stayed open, but nothing came out.

I said, "Just that one, or others as well?"

Nicole Spaeth dropped her eyes to the sculpted carpet, as though scanning the pattern from above for something she'd dropped. "I think you'd better leave."

"I have to hear what happened that night."

"Well, I don't want to hear it." She closed her eyes now. "Out loud, I mean. Bad enough to have what happened inside me without having to . . . relive it."

Mindful of not pushing her too much, I said, "Can it get any worse?"

Spaeth rose from the sofa. "I'll be just a minute."

"Mrs.—"

"I'm not going to run away or anything stupid like that. I just need to check, make sure Terry's in his room."

I nodded.

She was gone only long enough for me to send my eyes around the room, thinking this might have been a happy home once, in the long, long ago.

When Nicole Spaeth sat back down, she was stiff and, if possible, even more tired. "I couldn't hear Terry, you see, so I wanted to be sure he couldn't hear us. He's watching TV, with that little earplug attachment so the set doesn't blare. Terry likes it loud, but he also knows how much that bothers me."

I nodded again, not rushing her.

Spaeth brought both hands to her knees, maybe like the sixth-graders I remembered her saying she taught. "That last year with Alan here was a nightmare, and when I met Uta Radachowski at the Literacy Fund benefit, I was so glad she could recommend a divorce lawyer for me. Even gladder when I actually met Woodrow."

"Why?"

"I realized immediately that Alan couldn't intimidate him. My husband's bark has always been worse than his bite, but he can be pretty scary sometimes. Believe me." Spaeth stared into space. "As a prosecutor, though, Woodrow had seen the worst the world can offer—gang kids, rapists, murderers—and he handled Alan beautifully, just tied him in knots over everything. I began looking to Woodrow on every problem, and he'd solve it. Oh, I took psychology courses in college, and I knew that I was just transferring onto him as kind of a surrogate spouse, to help me through the real-spouse divorce, but . . . Well, it went further than that."

"Sexually?"

"Yes. Not at first. We'd just go out. But Woodrow said it would be bad to be seen together. Lunch wouldn't matter, but drinks and dinner? Not exactly within the attorney-client relationship. So he asked if I could kind of . . ."

"Disguise yourself."

The hazel eyes came back to me, a thumbnail picking at the cuticles on her fingers. "Yes. Frankly, I didn't mind at first. The kids I teach at school have parents, and if somebody's mother or father happened to see me 'stepping out,' things wouldn't get better in the classroom."

"At first."

"I'm sorry?"

"You said you didn't mind the disguise stuff 'at first.' What about later?"

"Woodrow started to get weird about it. He liked me to . . . stay in costume, so to speak." Spaeth seemed uncertain now. "You understand what I mean?"

"In the bedroom."

"Yes." She looked away. "Not just in the . . . bedroom, either. Woodrow was a very . . . imaginative man. One of the reasons I continued seeing him. He made me feel desirable again."

I didn't want to say anything to ruin that for Spaeth, but she looked back at me, suddenly energized. "Oh, I know I wasn't the only one. And I also know I was crazy in these plague-ridden times to be seeing a man who wasn't monogamous, even if I did insist on a condom. But I didn't have other options, and frankly, except for the guilt of 'sneaking around,' I liked the option he provided me just fine."

Now Nicole Spaeth dwindled a little. "At least until that night."

Quietly, I said, "Tell me about it."

She worried her fingers some more. "We picked evenings when Terry had something to do. That night, he was staying over at a friend's house to hear what they call 'Bachelor Pad' music." A weak smile. "Ironic, huh?" Even the weak smile faded. "Well, Woodrow and I had been to the Viet Mam restaurant before. The food wasn't great, but it wasn't crowded, either, and neither of us had ever seen anybody there we knew."

I thought about Nguyen Trinh, hiding in the kitchen during Gant's lunch with Deborah Ling.

Spaeth said, "So we ate, and since I wasn't driving, I drank a little too much wine—partly to cover the food, partly to cover the residual guilt, I suppose. I was aware we were back in the BMW, heading . . . I think about it now, we must have been heading to his place, but it was a school night, and getting late enough, Woodrow should have been taking me home. Anyway, I guess I passed out in the car, because after asking Woodrow to roll down the windows, I don't remember him stopping on that road."

"What do you remember?"

Spaeth sat back in the couch, hugging herself. "I was having a dream. About being seated on a plane, going to the Caribbean for a vacation. My first real vacation in a long time. And then I must have heard the shots or something, because the dream went screwy and somebody dropped an anchor in my lap."

"An anchor?"

"In the dream. But I stumbled out of the car because I was feeling sick and didn't see Woodrow. Well, the 'anchor' fell on the ground, and I could see it was a gun."

"Somebody had dropped a gun into your lap?"

"Through the part of my window that was open, I think, because the door was still closed."

"And this was the gun that killed Mr. Gant."

"I didn't know that—never even touched it—but Woodrow was lying on the ground, with his eyes . . ." Spaeth rubbed her forehead, trying to erase the image, I thought. "Then I just started running, and the few times I saw headlights, I'd hide."

"Hide?"

"Get down on the ground or behind a tree, so the drivers couldn't see me. The way I looked by the end of that road, I was surprised a cab would even stop for—"

"But why hide at all? Why not flag somebody down to help you and Mr. Gant?"

Spaeth gave me a withering look. "Because Woodrow was dead, Mr. Cuddy. And it was pretty obvious who'd done it."

"Meaning your husband?"

"Of course my husband. Alan was ripshit at Woodrow, suspected he and I were lovers. And on top of that, the gun looked like one of the two Alan kept in our nightstand here before we separated." Spaeth shook her head. "I knew it was Alan, but I also didn't want him convicted of murder."

"Why not?"

Another withering look. "Terry deserves a college education, Mr. Cuddy, and Alan promised in the settlement agreement that he'd pay the freight. How's he going to do that from a prison cell?"

I tried not to shake my head. "Mrs. Spaeth, you said a minute ago that the gun looked like one your husband had."

A sigh. "Right."

"But you didn't examine it to be sure?"

"No. I didn't have to." Spaeth leaned forward. "Look, I was obviously there when Woodrow was shot. Unconscious, maybe, but right in his passenger seat. And the killer knew I was there, because he dropped the gun in my lap. Now tell me something, Mr. Cuddy. I could have been a witness to Woodrow's murder, right?"

"Right."

"Okay. Then who else other than my loving, cloying husband would let me live?"

I tried very hard to come up with someone, but Nicole Spaeth had stumped the band.

Driving back from West Roxbury, I thought of the hurt I'd caused Karen Herman, the cynicism I'd seen in Jenifer Pollard, the fear I'd found in Nicole Spaeth. And then I thought of Nancy, and how much I'd have liked to get her take on those things.

But, if I couldn't talk about them with Nancy, there was still someone I could talk with about her.

The people who run the cemetery on the hillside overlooking the harbor are pretty good. About leaving the gate open for people who visit at night, that is. There's always the risk of vandalism to a headstone, but in a neighborhood as tightly knit as Southie, somebody would know whoever did it. And that somebody would tip a relative of the decedent involved, which would end that vandal's career.

And maybe even the vandal's own life as well.

I shook that off as I reached her grave. The lettering chiseled into the marble was beginning to show the harsh frost of winters and the acid rain of springs.

"Beth," I said, a hitch in my voice.

John. A pause. *You sound . . . cold.*

"More tired than cold."

And more depressed than tired?

"With some reason, I think."

Tell me?

I did.

Another pause. *And this . . . "fling" of Nancy's with Woodrow Gant was before she met you.*

"Years before."

A third pause, then, *I wish I knew what Nancy's feeling toward you was right now, but I never experienced it. You were my one and only, John.*

"I know." Below us, a barge was moving northeast past the

harbor's mouth, the hull and deck lights on her the only indication of her existence or direction, and even those telltales were distributed haphazardly, like a Christmas tree decorated by a drunk.

John?

"Sorry, kid. I'm winking out on you."

Or on yourself.

"What do you mean?"

John Francis Cuddy, you've always been a good man, but more than a bit dense when it comes to some aspects of the human condition.

"Thanks. That sure clears everything up."

I don't . . . She started over. *I think you have to let Nancy call the tune here, because neither you nor me knows better than she how to handle her feelings.*

I took a breath of the crisp, salt-laden air. "You're right, Beth. As usual."

As always, a hint of smile coming up from the ground that held her, I hoped more comfortably than I ever really believed.

Chapter 15

BY THE TIME I got back to my condo from the cemetery that Thursday night, it was pretty late. Rather than ruin Steve Rothenberg's dreams, I decided to sleep on the information about Nicole Spaeth and Woodrow Gant until the next morning.

I didn't get to sleep on it very long.

The clock radio read 4:50 A.M. when I picked up the phone by my bed on what I think was the second ring. "Yeah?"

"Cuddy, Murphy."

"Lieutenant, what—"

"Get your ass over here. Now."

I sat up. "Where's 'here'?"

It turned out to be a derelict, aluminum-sided two-decker in South Boston abutting several warehouses with chain-link fences and concertina wire festively enclosing their parking lots. The two-decker itself was probably white once, but the skin of paint had peeled off the siding, and the windows and doors I could see were all boarded up.

I parked the Prelude as close as a uniformed officer would allow, then asked for Murphy. The uniform led me on a wending route around early-bird rubberneckers held back by yellow plastic tape strung from telephone poles and the antennae of bubble-topped cruisers, the tape reading "POLICE LINE DO NOT CROSS." Inside the perimeter of cruisers were two unmarked sedans sandwiched around the Medical Examiner's white-and-blue minivan.

When we reached the back of the building, I could see that the rear door was open—forced open, judging by the way it hung from only its bottom hinge. The uniform told me to wait outside while he went into the house.

Pretty quickly the officer returned and walked past me, Murphy now beckoning from the threshold. As I moved toward him, he said, "You stop for breakfast along the way?"

"At five in the morning?"

Murphy nodded. "Best figure on a light lunch, then."

"It's that bad in there?"

"Let you decide for yourself."

I trailed behind him into what would have been the kitchen, now a wreck of torn-up linoleum whose age and color could be anybody's guess. All the appliances were gone, with open-faced, rusty pipes or just gaping holes in the cabinetry marking where they'd stood. The clittering of little clawed feet came through the walls, and a haze of dust motes danced in front of me. The air itself carried a strong smell of oil and a stronger smell of urine, but the strongest was that high, sickly-sweet stench which, once you've known it, can never be mistaken for anything else.

Murphy held a handkerchief in front of him, squirting a dose of some liquid onto it from a small squeeze bottle he took from a jacket pocket. "You want some of this?"

"Gasoline?"

"Yeah."

"No, thanks. I'll be all right."

Murphy raised the hankie to his nose. "Let's go, then."

At the corner of the kitchen was an open door, stairs to a cellar behind it. Bright lights flared below but not in that strobing way camera flashes will. As we descended the steps, both the oil smell and the sickly-sweet one grew powerfully.

When I reached the point that my head cleared the ceiling, I could see an old oil burner too big or too broken to move from the dirt-floored basement. A couple of men in business suits holding six-volt lanterns stood around an assistant M.E. in her white coat and surgical mask. She was kneeling beside a body in dirty, tattered clothes curled into the fetal position. The woman blocked most of my view, but I could see the corpse's face well enough. An older man with wasted features and reddish hair, the eyes bugging out as though he'd been pressurized from within. My bet would be that someone had strangled him, but the other characteristics of bulging tongue and blue lips weren't there.

Literally not there.

Murphy spoke through his handkerchief. "Rats been at him a while."

"Do we know who he is?" I said, though I had a pretty good idea.

Murphy hooded his eyes, giving me a sideways hint of them. "Why do you think I called you out?"

"Mantle, Michael A.?"

Murphy motioned to one of the other suits, who brought over a plastic evidence baggie with some kind of paper inside it. The lieutenant took the baggie and held it up for me to see. The paper lay open but heavily and dirtily creased in a cross pattern, as though it had been carried folded in fours for a long time.

"No wallet," said Murphy, "but this was in his pant pocket."

The lanterns threw just enough ambient light for me to read the printing on Mantle's birth certificate. "I'm told he used it for winning drinks at bars."

"Winning drinks?"

"As 'Mickey Mantle.' "

Murphy huffed out a "just-what-I-needed" laugh, then returned the baggie to the other detective. "Doc, can you give me an estimate on time of death?"

She didn't bother to look up. "Weather like we've had?

More than a few days, less than a few weeks. Lab results ought to narrow the bracket."

The shooting of Woodrow Gant occurred a week ago Wednesday. "You figure this man was strangled?"

In a sarcastic voice, the M.E. replied, "Unless he pictured me naked, and his eyes just popped out."

The top half of Murphy's face lilted toward the stairs. "Come on."

When we reached the kitchen, he said, "Breathing's better outside."

What passed for the backyard was strewn with broken beer bottles and busted toys, used condoms and torn shingles. We both stood for a minute as Murphy put away his handkerchief.

Then he said, "You never met this Mantle, right?"

"You're talking for positive ID now?"

"I am."

"We can try Vincennes Dufresne."

"The one I had to roust at Spaeth's rooming house?"

"Right."

Murphy nodded. "In due time." He gestured behind us. "Unless Dufresne surprises me, I figure you can forget about your alibi witness."

"How did you know the corpse was down there?"

"Got a call. Somebody said they went in the house to take a leak, saw the body."

"You have this tip on tape, then."

"Uh-unh. Man called Boston City."

"The hospital?"

"Our one and only."

"Not nine-one-one?"

"I talked to the hospital woman who caught the call, around three-thirty in the A.M. She said the man 'sounded black.'"

"Like the call on Woodrow Gant that night."

"Right. Though she's from the Dominican herself, so what does that tell you?"

"It tells me you've gotten two tips involving this case from somebody who sounded—"

"It happens, Cuddy."

"The one about Gant's body on the road, yeah. But let's face it, Lieutenant. Not many blacks tend to just wander into Southie."

"Only takes one."

"Did this morning's caller give the hospital an address?"

Murphy looked at me. "What do you mean?"

"Did the woman have the exact address of this place when she telephoned you guys?"

He thought about it. "Must have. Message slip had the number and street before we ever got a unit over here."

"Don't you think it's kind of odd a black guy strolling around this part of town at that time of the morning goes into an abandoned building to take a leak and then decides to do his business in the cellar?"

"If he was polite about it."

"And then, after seeing a body, the guy's also attentive enough to note the right address before he calls a number that by chance doesn't automatically tape the incomings?"

Murphy said, "What I think is kind of odd, your man's alibi witness is found dead four blocks from your man's apartment. And I'm betting the lab's going to establish that this Mantle got dead right around the time last week that Woodrow Gant was killed."

"Lieutenant, Spaeth is going to tell you the next morning when you arrest him that he has an alibi witness he strangled the night before?"

"Maybe he hopes we don't find the body."

"Seems to me that the cellar here is a pretty good spot for the body not to be found for a while, but certainly found after a while."

Murphy chewed on that. "So you're saying what?"

"I talked to a lot of people the last two days. One of them could have made this morning's call to the hospital."

"To tip us about Mantle's body, you mean?"

"And wipe out Spaeth's alibi after I rattled some cages on his behalf."

Murphy chewed on it some more, his eyes saying what he felt before the words got to his lips. "No. No, I'll tell you what

I think. My instincts fooled me on this one, Cuddy. When I went to arrest him, Spaeth had everything all worked out. He put on a great act, and I bought it. But no more."

"Just a—"

"Your man tapped Mantle as an alibi witness to drum up some reasonable doubt when he'd already killed him. The same night Spaeth did Woodrow Gant, so Mantle can't ever set things straight. It fits."

"It stinks."

Robert Murphy hooded his eyes again. "All depends on your point of view, I suppose."

"Why the hell does he call this place 'the Chateau'?"

"It's a long story, Lieutenant."

Murphy and I waited under the portico. The bump on the other side of the door made Murphy look up but not jump, and when the door itself creaked open, Vincennes Dufresne blinked out at both of us, the strap of a T-shirt-as-nightie slipping off his shoulder.

"Eh, you got any idea what time it is?"

Murphy said, "Mr. Dufresne, we're going to be needing you for a while."

The boarding house owner looked at me. "After all the help I been, you bring a cop to my place?"

"Always nice to be remembered," said the lieutenant.

Dufresne turned back to him. "What do you got to see?"

"Other way around," said Murphy. "First you have to see somebody, then probably we have to look at Michael Mantle's room."

"The Mick?" Dufresne blinked some more. "Aw, no. He's dead?"

Murphy glanced at me before saying to Dufresne. "Pretty good guess."

The head hung down toward the T-shirt. "Well, maybe he was right after all, eh?"

I said, "Don't get you."

"The Mick." Dufresne looked up. "One day, I say to him, 'Mick, the way you spend your money on the brew, you don't believe you can take it with you.' And the Mick, he says, 'Vinny, let me put it to you this way: You never saw no U-Haul behind a hearse, did you?' "

Forgoing his honking laugh, Vincennes Dufresne left us to get a coat against the stark chill of dawn.

Three hours later, I was sitting in Steve Rothenberg's reception area, watching the young woman with the headphones select the first of today's listening program from a drawerful of CD's in her desk. When Rothenberg came through the door, suit coat flapping and tie askew, he saw me and dropped his eyes dramatically.

"John, I'm already going to be late for a motion hearing."

"You catch the local news on TV this morning?"

"If I'm late as it is, I wouldn't have had time to—"

"Make time, Steve."

Rothenberg looked at me differently, then asked the receptionist to call a court clerk and say he'd be fifteen minutes late.

In his office, Steve Rothenberg sat behind the desk without shedding his jacket. "Speak."

I told him what I'd found out from Nicole Spaeth the prior night, and he shrunk down into his chair. I told him what I'd seen with Robert Murphy earlier that morning, and Rothenberg nearly disappeared from view.

To the desktop, he said, "My client's wife is the mystery woman."

"That's right, Steve."

"And his alibi witness is dead."

"Probably from the night Woodrow Gant himself was killed."

Rothenberg looked at me with the brown eyes of a dejected puppy. "Now what do we do?"

"My mind's a blank, Steve. How about you take that one?"

Walking back toward my office building on Tremont, I tried to use the bright fall colors on the Boston Common to help me think. While I'd agreed with Murphy's initial reaction at the Gant crime scene—that Alan Spaeth was innocent—I also couldn't fault this morning's turn of heart. For me to be right about Spaeth being framed, someone had to know about the revolver he kept at Vincennes Dufresne's boardinghouse in Southie. That someone then had to steal the gun and use it to kill Woodrow Gant. Dufresne had access to Spaeth's room, but no reason to want Gant dead. Michael Mantle had access, too, but also no reason to kill Gant, or to frame his drinking buddy, Spaeth. And besides, both Spaeth and Dufresne said Mantle wasn't the kind of guy to betray a friend.

Assuming I could get over that hurdle, who besides Spaeth would want to kill Woodrow Gant (and probably Michael Mantle, tipping the location of each body as a bonus)? Everybody at Epstein & Neely seemed to love Gant, or at least value his economic contribution to the firm, though the million-dollar policy on his life would go a long way toward salving that loss. And speaking of policies, Grover Gant needed money enough to talk with me when he thought I might be the paymaster on his insurance, and Jenifer Pollard (however well she acted with friend Thom Arneson) could also use some cash. The heat was probably higher under brother Grover, given the scene I witnessed at the coffee shop with Nguyen Trinh and Oscar Huong. And then you still had the connection between Trinh and Chan's Viet Mam restaurant, extending to Deborah Ling both professionally and romantically.

"Romance" reminded me, however perversely, of Karen Herman's afternoon with Woodrow Gant. Plenty of motive for husband Elliot, but she claims he didn't know about it. As a former marine, Elliot Herman had the weaponry know-how to pull off the ambush and killing, but for that matter so did Frank Neely, the ex-Ranger. Which brought me back to everybody at the firm liking Gant.

And, whoever did it, why let Nicole Spaeth live? After all, as Woodrow Gant's passenger in the car that night, she could have heard or seen something incriminating. And why drop the murder weapon in her lap? Because the killer hoped Spaeth's wife would be found in the car and blamed for the shooting?

None of it made any sense, but at least I realized I was about to pass my building, so I crossed the street.

"John Cuddy."

"Nancy Meagher."

My heart did a sit-up in my chest as I leaned forward in the desk chair. "Your voice sounds good, even just over the telephone."

"Yours, too." A pause. "I heard about the scene in Southie with Michael Mantle's body."

"Better to hear about some things than see them."

"No argument there." Another pause. "Does this mean Rothenberg's going to plead Spaeth out?"

My turn to pause. "I guess that's their decision more than mine, Nance."

"Sorry, of course it is," she said, quickly. "I just thought . . . maybe you'd already spoken with them, and they'd already decided."

"So that we could get back together without you feeling . . . conflicted?"

In a lower tone, Nancy said, "I miss you."

"Same. So much that it hurts."

"Then let's hope we won't be limited to the phone for much longer."

"Amen."

"However," she said, "I think our next call is yours to make."

"I'll try you at home, tomorrow night."

"I love you, John Cuddy."

"I'll save mine for a later time."

"Strike my last comment," said Nancy, but in a bantering way, before hanging up.

I sat in the office, breathing deeper and feeling better now that Nancy was genuinely communicating with me again. But talking together and being together were two different things, and the Spaeth case still stood between us.

I decided to reduce to paper my mental list of the people

who had the means of killing Woodrow Gant, with motive if I could see one. The list read:

Grover Gant: *money pressure*
Jenifer Pollard/Thom Arneson: *greed*
Vincennes Dufresne/Michael Mantle: *motive?*
Nguyen Trinh/Oscar Huong: *revenge*
Elliot Herman: *jealousy/rage?*
Frank Neely: *motive?*

Writing down Neely's name made me think of the other people in the law firm. I couldn't see means, but I added Deborah Ling (motive: Trinh?) and Imogene Burbage (motive: unrequited love?) to the list, anyway. There was no reason to add Uta Radachowski—or for that matter, Helen Gant—on any theory.

I looked back over the list, trying to decide what to do. Rattling cages was how I'd flushed out the identity of the woman in Woodrow Gant's car that night. It didn't make me happier, but that's how it came about. And maybe rattling cages would work again.

For this round, though, I opened the locked, bottom drawer of my desk and took out my five-shot Smith & Wesson Chief's Special.

Chapter 16

A FRIEND OF mine in the state administration building was able to access the personnel databank for our welfare bureaucracy, but even he couldn't penetrate the busy signal on the telephone number listed for Helen Gant. Getting out of the Prelude half an hour later, I looked at the exterior of the branch office where Grover's mother spent her days.

The bricks probably were all orange once, judging from the ones under the metal awning and therefore protected from the effects of weather and soot. Everywhere else the brickwork was dingy, and the people walking in the wide entry doors with me drab, from their shabby clothes to their resigned expressions. The only exception were the children, some smiling and even laughing, often holding each other's hands because mom had only the two God gave her to manage the four or five little blessings He'd given her in another sense.

Inside the doors was a seating area swelled to standing room only. It looked as though the younger folks had all given up their chairs, but there were still more senior citizens than places to seat them. A woman with three kids who had been just ahead of me marched directly to the reception desk, an old steel monster like a battleship guarding the entrance to the wallboarded harbor behind.

A young African-American man with processed hair staffed the desk. When the woman and her brood moved away, I walked up to him. Coming to a stop, I could hear the whitewater noise from dozens of voices talking at conversational level behind the wallboard.

He looked up at me skeptically. "Yes?"

"John Cuddy to see Helen Gant."

He reached a hand toward a stack of forms. "Have you filled out one of our—"

"I'm not a client of hers."

His hand stopped. "Doesn't matter. She won't get to you before lunchtime."

I took out my identification. "Maybe we should let Ms. Gant be the judge of that."

"Mr. Cuddy, do you have any idea how many people need to see me—uh-uh—today?"

The hiccuping sound. "I'm guessing I up the count to a hundred and one."

Helen Gant glared at me from behind a desk with twin towers of manila file folders stacked high enough to reach her elbows if she'd stood when I'd reached her cubicle. Which she hadn't.

Gant pointed to the client chair at the side of her desk. "Two minutes."

I stayed on my feet. "It may not take that long."

She leaned back into her chair. Not relaxing, more buying distance and maybe even some of her own valuable time. "What is it, then?"

"I need to find your son."

"He's still where we buried him."

The voice as hard as the look that came with it.

"I meant your other son."

"Grover?" Hiccup. "You already talked to him. In fact, he was so upset that—"

"I have to talk to him again."

"About what?"

"Do you really want to know?"

I could tell by a different look in Helen Gant's eyes that she didn't.

After leaving the welfare office, I drove north through the city, weaving my way to Route 1A. At the rotary beyond the dog track, I came back south and pulled into the lot. There was free parking to the right, "Preferred & Handicapped" to the left. "Preferred" turned out to cost a buck in order to avoid a two-block hike around rows of concrete Jersey barriers. Walking toward the main entrance, I passed hundreds of already-parked cars, which surprised me. Most of them were four-door, American sedans, which didn't surprise me.

Above the customer gate someone had carefully drawn a greyhound with a red blanket, "Wonderland Park" printed beneath it. The rest of the facade sported flagpoles and the word "Clubhouse" in white letters.

Admission proved to be all of fifty cents, and just past the turnstiles was a raised and railed seating area, bright and clean, with tables where you could eat or study a racing program in relative peace. Most of the people in the black resin chairs seemed retirement age, glancing up from food or form to the overhead television monitors touting the odds.

"Post time for the seventh race in six minutes," boomed the public address system. "Just six."

I didn't see Grover Gant in the seating area, so I moved around it to the right. A couple of men in conservative business suits passed me before taking an escalator to shielded box seating somewhere above us hoi polloi. After sixty feet more of tiled floor, I came to a larger, glass-walled viewing area.

"Paging the Rowley Kennel to the paddock. Report to the paddock, please."

To fit in a little more, I picked up a program and skimmed it. There were eight races yet to be run, the greyhounds bearing the screwy names you usually associate with thoroughbred horses and European aristocrats. If I was reading the stats correctly, the dogs ranged in weight by five pounds to either side of seventy, which seemed heavy to me, given how emaciated they looked.

"Under two minutes to post time. Under two for the seventh."

The crowd in the viewing area watched the oval track, even though I didn't see anything going on out there. Mainly male and mostly white, there was a smattering of black and Asian faces, usually in small groups. None of the African-Americans was Grover Gant, though.

I drifted to the betting counter, overhearing the short, one-sided conversations.

"Two dollars to win on number Four."

"Gimme a ten-dollar Quiniela on Two and Seven."

"Five bucks to show on the Six dog."

As I stood near the counter, one of the employees behind it, wearing a white, placket-collared shirt, said, "You want to place a wager?"

"No, thanks."

"Good," he replied. "Don't get in the habit, believe me. Look around the room, see what you're in for, you do."

I did look around the room, but still no Grover Gant. People smoking like chimneys mingled with others slumping in chairs or shuffling on canes, crutches, and even a few four-footed walkers. Behind me, a guy named "Richie" and a woman named "Jayme" discovered they owned houses just blocks from each other.

I saw three middle-aged black men, standing near a pillar. Two wore Houston Rockets ball caps, all looked to be in good shape.

The P.A. announced, "The greyhounds are entering the starting box. It's post time."

As I approached the black guys, one said to the other, "That's what I heard."

"It all come back on Rashid, playing in that thirty-five-and-over league like he was."

"I know, man, but you ain't that bad yourself."

"The hell I ain't. Doctor says I got to have his operation, too."

"What operation is that?"

"The one like Rashid have in his knee."

To the closest guy, I said, "Excuse me," just as the P.A. chimed in with, "There goes Swifty!"

The black guy held up his hand. "After the race run out, man."

I watched with him as eight or ten dogs tried in vain to catch a white, mechanical rabbit on a horizontal bar. The bar was attached to a motorized cart that rolled on narrow-gauge metal rails around the inside edge of the track itself. The race was all over in thirty seconds or so.

"Damn that number Five," said the man I'd spoken to. "You could time that pig with a sundial." Turning to me, "Now, what you be wanting?"

"I was wondering if you'd seen Grover Gant."

"Grover?" said the other.

"His mother told me he'd be here."

"Oh, he here, all right," the first guy gesturing with a pari-mutuel ticket toward the track. "It ain't snowing or shit, Grover like to stand by the puppies at the rail, talk to them."

"Dummy-ass think it help him," said the other.

As the people standing outside made their way toward us, I could spot Gant near the fence. "Appreciate it."

The first man let the ticket flutter from his hand to the floor. "While you out there, ask Grover will he tell that Five dog to please take himself a dump before the next time he racing."

"I'll do that," I said, moving against the crowd and toward the track.

Outside, the sun shone brightly from the west as a commuter train lumbered north on the far side of the grounds. Grover Gant was doodling with a red Flair pen on his racing form as a white guy spoke to him.

The P.A. voice said, "We have a field of juveniles for the next race. Open the floodgates for the first pup, a clear favorite in the eighth. Post time in eleven minutes."

As I drew close enough to hear the white guy, he was saying, "Fuck, that's four races in a row without a payoff."

Gant never looked up from his program. "So, what are you gonna do?"

"I don't know, Grover, but I'm sick of these goddamn skinny greyhounds. You ever hear of any place races dalmatians?"

"Dalmatians?" Now Gant did look up. "Why the fuck would anybody race dalmatians?"

"I don't know. They just look . . . healthier, I guess."

When Gant shook his head and went back to his form, the white guy moved off. I waited until he was thirty feet away before saying, "Nice day to be out in the air."

"Hey, man." Gant shifted his feet to face me. "Taking my advice, right?"

"Your advice."

"Yeah, yeah, yeah." Gant swept his hand toward the track. "Doggies over horses. Cheaper to get in, not so much hoopla between the races, so the action comes faster. And there ain't no human factor, remember?"

"I remember. In fact, I'd like to talk with you about the 'human factor.' "

Gant checked his watch. A big, bright one, with lots of bells and whistles on the face of it. "I got time before I have to lay my bet down on the next race."

"New watch?"

He looked at it again. "Kind of."

"Your ship came in."

"Say what?"

"The insurance on your brother's life."

"Oh, yeah. That." Gant made his tone even more casual. "Guess I got kind of mad at you over to the house."

"Kind of. The insurance must let you clear up a lot of debts."

The P.A. announcer said, "Post time in just under eight minutes," as a cloud came over Gant's eyes. "Meaning like what?"

I decided not to mention the scene I'd witnessed with Trinh and Huong at the coffee shop. "You said you'd borrowed from your brother. Now you can repay the estate."

"Oh, right, right, right." The sly smile. "So, what you want to know about the 'human factor'?"

"I'm still trying to figure out who shot your brother."

A shrug that settled into a laugh. "Man, I told you last time. The police, they got the mother'."

"Except they have the wrong one."

No more laugh. "Now what you mean?"

"Just what I said. Alan Spaeth didn't do it."

"Aw, man. Come on, come *on, come* on. You didn't see that dude in Woodrow's office there the way I did. He was like a maniac. Ranting and raving."

"Everybody gets mad. You got mad at me in your mother's house. Does that mean you'd kill me?"

The sly smile again. "Got no reason to kill you. I'm what they call 'a man of wealth and taste' now."

Somehow it sounded better when Mick Jagger used to sing it.

Just then, men and boys wearing red windbreakers began walking leashed and muzzled greyhounds toward the starting gate at the far left end of the track. As the dog wearing number "7" came even with us, he stopped and lifted a leg.

Grover Gant smiled wider. "Seven, you get all that out of your system, now."

I said, "Your brother wasn't the only one killed."

The wider smile froze. "Hey, man, you keep confusing me."

"Confusion isn't the half of it, my friend. The guy Spaeth says would be his alibi was found dead this morning."

"Alibi?"

I thought that was an odd part of my statement for Gant to home in on. "Spaeth claims he spent the night your brother was shot getting drunk with a man named Michael Mantle. This morning the police found Mantle dead in an abandoned building."

"I don't go into no abandoned buildings, man." Gant glanced left, right, and behind him. "Life's dangerous enough when there's people around you."

Which made me wonder who Gant might worry would spot him, provided Grover in Wonderland had used part of the insurance proceeds to pay off the balance of his "coffee shop" debt to Nguyen Trinh.

I heard a lot of yowling and barking from the starting gate. The handlers in the red windbreakers were all jogging up the track toward us.

Grover Gant said, "I got to put my bet down."

As he turned, I stepped in front of him.

"Hey, man, it's almost post time."

I said, "Missing one race won't kill you."

"Shit, shit, shit," but he stayed with me.

"So, to sum up, you don't know a thing about the departed Mr. Mantle."

"Don't know," said Gant, "and don't want to know."

"The police got a tip, telephoned into a hospital."

"Last I heard, hospital can't help no dead man."

"Clever thing, though. You kill somebody and want him found at the right time, you call a number that doesn't tape-record your voice as it comes in over the telephone."

"Yeah, well, that leaves me off whatever hook you trying to put me on, man."

"How do you mean?"

"One thing I ain't—and ain't never *been*—is clever. Otherwise, I wouldn't be needing Woodrow to die, put me on Easy Street, you hear what I'm saying?"

Unfortunately I did. And worse, as the fat man hustled toward the betting counter, I believed him. Setting up what had to be an elaborate frame of Alan Spaeth—down to the indirect reporting of one body on that road and another in that cellar—required brains, and Grover Gant didn't seem nearly clever enough to pull it off.

However, we both knew somebody who was.

I waited in the parking lot until the crowd began streaming out and back to their cars. As the lot emptied, I spotted Gant's rust-bucket Chevy three rows down and as many over, in the same "Preferred" section I was in. Finally, Gant himself made his way through the gate, shimmering like the proverbial bowl-ful of jelly as he waddled to his car. Once there, Gant opened the driver's door and climbed in. After some blue smoke belched from the exhaust pipe, the old Chevy joined the line of cars turning right, back toward the city.

I started up and followed.

We went down 1A, negotiating the traffic rotaries and driving almost sedately. I expected Gant to take the Sumner Tunnel, which would lead him to the Central Artery and the most direct path home to his mother's house. Instead he took the Tobin Bridge, then Storrow Drive along the Charles River. We went past Harvard University and the turn for Harvard Square, eventually getting off Soldiers Field Road in Brighton. Gant cruised through half of a warehouse district near St. Elizabeth's Hospital before pulling into a narrow parking area with angled white lines. There was only one other vehicle in the lot.

A Mercedes sedan, green in color.

I couldn't make out the license plate, so as Grover Gant left his car and walked in a side door, I checked the address Larry Cosentino had given me back at the Gang Unit. I was indeed sitting outside the offices of Nugey Trinh and Associate, Limited.

But not limited by much. I'd have bet even my own money on that.

Chapter 17

THE SIDE DOOR opened silently for me, but the hinge complained a little as it closed. I got some sounds of forklifts and hand dollies from behind an interior door on the first floor, but there were also heavy footfalls at the top of the shrouded staircase to my left. I waited and heard a metallic knock, Grover Gant saying, "It's me." Then a swishing noise before the sound of a door clicking shut.

I took the first half-flight to a landing and, seeing no one above me, climbed the rest of the stairs to the second floor. There was a heavy steel door for what seemed an office, so I walked up to it. Putting my ear against the jamb, I recognized Nguyen Trinh's voice saying, "Not enough, Grover."

I drew my Chief's Special before trying the knob. Unlocked. As I pushed hard, the door flung open, banging violently against the wall. I leveled the snubbed barrel of the revolver about heart high on Trinh.

Seated behind a desk, he stared at my gun. Grover Gant, in a chair across the desk from Trinh, twisted around to look at me, too. For just a micro-second, I registered Oscar Huong looming over Gant from behind before Huong literally sprung vertically three feet off the floor, spinning in the air to face me.

Huong's feet hadn't yet hit the ground again when Trinh snapped off, "Oscar, no!"

Huong landed in a martial arts stance, his body—shaved head on down—vibrating like a tuning fork from the strain of obeying Trinh against his apparent urge to feed the Smith to me an inch at a time.

Keeping the muzzle on his boss, I said, "Listen to the man, Oscar."

Trinh picked up. "Mr. Private Eye here, he ain't gonna shoot me, long as you don't do nothing."

Oscar's words came out like they were being dragged across a gravel driveway. "He does, he's dead."

I said, "Without this gun, Oscar, you'd have maimed me by now. I just want us to have a nice little talk."

Trinh nodded very slightly. "You followed Grover."

"Yes, but I had the address here anyway."

"How you get it?"

"Connections."

Another slight nod. "Oscar?"

Huong didn't move.

Trinh said, "Oscar, ease off. Let Cuddy come in, sit a while, we find out what he want."

This time Huong seemed to calm down. I realized that in the stance, his sports coat had been bulging here, there, and everywhere, like the old *Incredible Hulk* television show, Lou Ferrigno bursting out of the late Bill Bixby's clothes. Now Huong just looked normal.

Meaning homicidal.

But he shook down his sleeves above the huge hands before standing back against the wall.

Trinh did that wristy Macarena flourish toward the other empty chair across from his desk. "And you can put the gun away, too."

Sitting down, I kept the barrel on target. "I don't think so."

Gant spoke to me for the first time. "Mother-fucker, mother-

fuck-er, *mother*-fucker, I thought you was going to get my ass killed."

"Be patient, Grover," said Trinh. "It could still happen." Then, in my direction, "So what you come here for, Mr. Private Eye?"

"I thought maybe we'd go over all the ways you were involved in Woodrow Gant's life. And death."

The smile that showed just the tip of his tongue before Trinh laced his fingers and brought them over and behind his carefully moussed head. Reclining in the desk chair, he said, "You like a hungry dog, got a stick he want to be a bone."

"Meaning you had nothing to do with Gant's being killed."

Grover became agitated. "Say what?"

Trinh didn't bother to look at him. "Shut up, deadbeat." To me, "Like I told you before. I'm gonna kill the man, I don't shoot him."

"You'd just have Oscar beat him to death."

"Been a pleasure," said Huong from the wall.

His boss gave him a look that I thought meant, "That's enough." Then Trinh returned to me. "But it didn't happen that way."

"You've got a grudge against Gant. Makes you a prime suspect if he goes down, especially from a beating administered by somebody like Hands of Stone over there. Plus, you've been kind of dipping into his life, like getting him to eat in a restaurant you're bankrolling."

More agitation from Grover. "What you saying?"

"Nugey here isn't just your banker, my friend. He fronted the money for the restaurant your brother ate in the night he was killed. Owns the building, in fact."

Gant seemed like he wanted to say something more. But Oscar Huong came half a step off the wall, and the sentence died in Grover's throat.

Trinh rocked his chair a little. "So the man eats at a restaurant maybe five mile from his condo."

I thought, Nugey knows where Woodrow Gant lived, down to the distance.

Trinh kept rocking. "Shit like that happens."

"Only this time it didn't just 'happen.' You set it up, Nugey."

The tongue licked out and back once. "You wanna tell me how?"

"By having your girlfriend take him there for lunch the first time."

Now Gant turned in his chair toward me. "Girlfriend?"

Trinh said, "Grover, I tell you once already, shut up. Not gonna say it again."

I kept my gun on the man behind the desk. "Then let me explain things so your favorite customer here doesn't have to talk. Woodrow Gant put you and Oscar away for that home invasion. After getting out, you expand your horizons, eventually meet a lawyer in his firm. Which gives you an idea. You start threading your way back into Woodrow Gant's life. Loaning money to his brother who likes to gamble, moving—"

Grover Gant finally added things up and rose from his chair, rage in his voice. "You yellow mother'—"

Thanks to peripheral vision, I was aware of Oscar Huong moving, but I couldn't have told you what part of him struck Grover. I could see what part of Gant hit the floor, though. All of him, a cracking sound still dying away in the air as he writhed, hugging his right arm with his left hand and moaning. Huong's face said he wasn't finished.

I kept the gun on Trinh. "Call him off, or I put a round in you."

Just a tip-of-the-tongue smile from across the desk. "You lose your license."

"It's that, or lose Grover, right?"

Trinh stopped smiling. "Oscar?"

This time Huong needed more prodding.

"Oscar, enough, okay? Man's not gonna try anything more."

Reluctantly, Huong backed up to the wall again, Gant moaning louder.

I said, "Grover, you all right?"

Trinh shook his head. "Somebody come after me like that, Oscar usually break something."

"Just one bone," said Huong. "So far."

I watched Trinh. "You started dating Deborah Ling to get your hooks further into Woodrow Gant. But why?"

"She a good-looking chick."

"There's got to be more to it than that."

Trinh blinked twice, pursing his lips, then moved his eyes off to the right, where nobody could see them. In a smaller voice, he said, "I fell for her, all right?"

Grover Gant began to moan even louder, now sprinkling in a few words.

I said to Trinh, "Fell in love?"

"Yeah. Her, too. With me, I mean."

I tried not to shake my head. "Okay, let's say I believe that. I still don't see why you were stalking Woodrow Gant."

"You said it before."

"Said what?"

Trinh swung his head back to me, the eyes as involved as his mouth in what he was saying. "The 'grudge' thing. Gant put me away, Mr. Private Eye. Me and Oscar, for a long time. What happened to us back in Vietnam wasn't enough. No, you guys have to get us over here, too. So, yeah, I was 'stalking' the lawyer-man, but not to kill him. Just to . . . get him."

"Get him how?"

"Like I got Chan there with his restaurant. Make that pure-blood respect me."

"Only Chan knew he was dealing with you, and Woodrow Gant didn't, right?"

Trinh shrugged. "Best I could do. When the lawyer-man put us away, I couldn't do nothing. When I got out, I make enough money, I could. So I start in with his law-woman. And then I loan some money to his brother. Grover couldn't come up with enough to cover things, and so it was like old Woodrow was paying me direct, for all the time I was in the slam. And after that, I—"

Grover Gant began to cry. Deep, blubbering sobs.

I said, "You what?"

Trinh changed gears. "Nothing, that was it. Only way I could get the lawyer-man was without him knowing anything. In fact, it was almost better that way. I'm getting him, and he don't even know shit's happening."

"But Grover's into you for a goodly sum of money."

Trinh seemed thrown. "So?"

"So maybe you want to send a message to the deadbeat who owes you."

A squint. "You saying I kill old Woodrow because I want to put pressure on Grover?"

"It fits."

"Mr. Private Eye, what kinda shit you smoking, huh? I gonna shoot a lawyer-man put me away after he eats at a place I own? Not to mention old Woodrow's covering Grover's bad bets. How am I gonna get paid, I kill the goose laying the golden eggs for this deadbeat crying all over my floor right now?"

"Because Grover is the beneficiary on a policy covering his brother's life."

Trinh's nostrils flared, the vein at his temple pulsing under the skin. "Life insurance?"

"That's what we call it."

"This piece of shit here got money because the lawyer-man died?"

"One hundred thousand. You see the . . ." Looking down at Grover, I realized he wasn't wearing the watch anymore.

"See the what?" said Trinh.

"Never mind. Just take my word for it. The company paid Grover off."

Trinh stood up, Huong tensing at the wall.

I said, "Easy does it, everybody."

His palms on the desktop, Trinh craned forward far enough to see Gant. "You fucking piece of shit, Grover! You come in here and hand me three hundred you say you got at the track today, and your deadbeat ass is sitting on one hundred large at your momma's house?"

I said, "At least he was telling you the truth about the track part."

Trinh looked at me, then laughed. Only a titter at first, almost girlish, then heartier. Huong didn't see the humor in the situation, or at least, he didn't show it. Grover began moaning louder, the tears flowing freely.

Trinh sat back down, still laughing, but quieter now. "Mr. Private Eye, you just made my day."

"Mind letting me in on it?"

The middle finger of his right hand whisked under each eye, smearing a couple of tears. "You just tell me I don't got a thing to worry about. Lawyer-man's dead, I figure I got to wait till his nice car get sold, get my money from Grover's in-*heri*-tance. Now you telling me, my money's coming tomorrow, soon as that piece of shit get a cast on his one arm, count me out the bills with the other."

I waited a moment, but what Trinh said sounded right. And unless he was up there with Olivier and De Niro, it seemed to me that the insurance policy on Woodrow Gant was major-league news to him.

"So," said Trinh, "you got any more questions?"

"Not just now."

"Then do me a favor, Mr. Private Eye. You put your gun away and you take this piece of shit on my floor to a hospital."

"I don't know if he has insurance."

"You just told me his brother's policy—"

"I mean medical insurance, for the doctors and all."

"Oh." Trinh thought about it, then opened a desk drawer and took out some bills. Tossing them at me, he said, "Here's the three hundred from the track. I wait for it this long, I can wait some more."

Then Nguyen Trinh raised his voice, aiming it over the desk and down. "But, Grover, only till tomorrow, right?"

Chapter 18

TWENTY MINUTES AFTER dropping Grover Gant at St. Elizabeth's emergency room, I said, "No rest for the weary."

Imogene Burbage looked up from behind the reception desk at Epstein & Neely as I came off the elevator. She wore a conservative blue suit and a determined gray frown.

"Mr. Cuddy, we are a law firm—one which had a temp call in sick this morning—and I think we've already granted you more than enough of our time."

"Maybe Frank Neely would give me an extension?"

Frown to sneer. "Mr. Neely isn't in."

"How about—"

I stopped, cold, because I heard a familiar voice accompany footsteps from the direction of Uta Radachowski's office. A voice with a little of the South in it, but also one a little out of context.

"... and so I really don't see any problem."

"Good," said Radachowski as she and Parris Jeppers came into view around the corner.

Both of them seemed surprised to see me.

"Mr. Jeppers," I said, nodding neutrally.

The lawyer from the Board of Bar Overseers backpedaled. Verbally, if not physically, his hand coming up to the bow tie du jour and then his goatee. "Ah, yes. Mr. . . . ?"

"John Cuddy," said Radachowski, staring daggers through her thick lenses at me. "He's a detective representing Alan Spaeth."

"Of course." Jeppers extended his hand. "Sorry not to have remembered."

I shook with him. "Mine's an easy name to forget."

"Well," he said, "I must be off. Have a nice day, now."

Radachowski and I stayed silent until the elevator door closed and the light through the diamond window dropped away. I let her speak next.

"Mr. Cuddy—"

"I thought it was 'John' and 'Uta'?"

Radachowski bit back something before saying, "I'm afraid we can't give you any more of our time."

From the desk, Burbage said, "I told him the same thing."

I stayed with Radachowski. "This might be my last visit, and after all the cooperation Frank Neely's provided me, I'd hate to have to tell Steve Rothenberg that it's subpoena time."

"I don't like threats, Mr. Cuddy."

"And I'm not making one. But you're still a partner here, and therefore—"

This time I stopped because of the look on Radachowski's face, as though she'd just heard me use a four-letter word over Thanksgiving dinner.

I said, "Is something wrong?"

"No." Radachowski waved at the air. "No, you're right. I can order you out, and call the police if that doesn't work, but I'd rather everything remained on professional, if not friendly, terms, too. What do you want to see me about?"

First Jeppers's overly casual reaction to me, now Radachowski assuming I'd come to see her. Instinct said to go with it. "Just a few minutes' worth, maybe in your office."

*　　*　　*

244

Even sitting behind her desk, Radachowski looked ill-at-ease for the first time. "Your questions, please."

"Alan Spaeth's alibi witness was found dead this morning."

She seemed to relax a bit, like the worst was over. "I'm sorry to hear that."

" 'Any man's death.' "

"What?"

"It's a quote, I'm not sure from where. 'Any man's death makes us all the poorer,' or something like that."

Radachowski looked down at her desk for a moment, then back up at me. "Are you making jokes now?"

"No, I'm definitely not doing that. Two men are dead. One was your partner, and the other was a hard-luck guy whose major flaw seems to have been loyalty to a friend, though he can't testify to that anymore."

A shake of the head. "Mr. Cuddy, I don't see how I fit into this line of questioning."

"Would Mr. Jeppers fit into it any better?"

"Parris?" A grunted laugh, that patronizing sound lawyers make in court when a witness's answer hits them like an arrow through the heart. "What in the world could he have to do with your dead witness?"

"I'm not sure. I visit Jeppers yesterday morning at the Board of Bar Overseers, and we talk some about Woodrow Gant and Alan Spaeth. Then I come over here again, and he's visiting with you, a partner of the victim. I guess I have to wonder why."

Radachowski closed her eyes briefly, then pointed to one of the plaques on the wall above her head. "Parris and I are both trustees for a charitable organization. We confer from time to time on matters of policy regarding it."

When you ask a lawyer a question, you also have to listen carefully to the answer, sometimes as much for what's not said as for what is. "And that's why he was here today, to talk about 'policy'?"

A very measured stare this time. "I'm afraid that's confidential."

"As in referring a potential client to a colleague?"

Radachowski's face became a mask. "Now what are you asking me?"

"You met Nicole Spaeth at another charity event. She was in need of a divorce lawyer, and you recommended your partner."

"Whom I knew to be a fine domestic relations attorney."

"With maybe a disproportionate appreciation of the women he represented?"

Radachowski said, "I think that will be all, Mr. Cuddy."

"Before I go, could you try Elliot Herman for me?"

"Elliot?"

"I'd go back out to reception, but I hate to bother Ms. Burbage again, given all she has to do."

Packing papers into his briefcase, Elliot Herman said, "I have to be out of here in ten—no, five minutes."

"Won't take three."

"All right." Wearing pleated pants held up by whale-pattern suspenders today, he looked around the office instead of at me. "Sit."

Without closing his office door behind me, I took a chair. "I need to ask you an awkward question."

"Ask it." Herman slipped a file from the middle of a stack on his desk. "Concisely."

"I've heard rumors about Woodrow Gant."

The file wouldn't quite wedge between the others in the case. "What kind of rumors?" Herman asked, almost absently, as he tugged on the handle to a desk drawer.

"About Mr. Gant and some of his female clients."

Herman stopped with the drawer open. Rather than close it, he crossed the room and closed his door instead, beginning to speak again while he was still behind me. "Mr. Cuddy, I don't understand."

I waited until Herman returned to his desk, though he stayed standing, the pleats of his pants quivering as if the leg muscles were tensing underneath.

I said, "There's some talk that Mr. Gant used to see his clients . . . socially."

Herman's right hand smoothed the hair by his white, lightning streak. "I don't see how that—even if it were true—could matter to you."

"Alan Spaeth is accused of killing his wife's lawyer. I'd like to know if other opposing husbands might have had a motive to go after Mr. Gant as well."

I phrased my answer that way to see if it got a rise out of Herman, as a way of determining whether he knew of his own wife and Gant. But Herman's expression never changed.

He looked just as worried.

"Mr. Cuddy, you realize what this could do to the firm?"

"The rumors?"

"The discussion of them in open court."

"Maybe it doesn't have to get that far."

Herman thought for about three breaths. "Okay, there was some noise about Woodrow."

"Noise."

"Frank got a few calls, I think. He had a talk with Woodrow, stressing things like the firm's image and general appearances. That's all I know, okay?"

"Frank Neely just talked with Mr. Gant?"

Now a confused look. "What do you mean?"

"There was no 'Listen, once more and you're out of here' kind of warning?"

Herman watched me. "I couldn't tell you that. I just know what I've already told you."

"And how do you know even that?"

"How?"

"Yes."

Herman shrugged. "Woodrow and I had drinks once."

"Mr. Gant talked with you about this?"

"Yes."

"When was this?"

"I don't know. Five, six months ago, maybe."

Around the time of Gant being with his wife. But Herman wasn't showing anything to me except that constant concern about the firm's future.

I said, "Were any . . . names brought up?"

"Of the women clients? Negative. Woodrow wasn't like that, the kind to brag, I mean. But even if he had mentioned names, I couldn't tell you. Client confidentiality."

I asked my next question slowly. "And what did Mr. Gant say to you about Frank Neely's 'talk' with him?"

Herman closed his eyes, as though trying to envision something, then opened them again. "Woodrow said he wasn't sweating it too much."

"Why not?"

Elliot Herman glanced at his watch and nearly jumped for his briefcase. "Woodrow said the fees he brought in, Frank wouldn't dare call for a partnership vote with Uta, and if he did, Woodrow would bail out himself."

Imogene Burbage was on the phone, so I waited patiently in front of the reception desk.

"No, Ms. Barber, Ms. Ling had a meeting after lunch, and she isn't back yet."

The name was familiar. That divorce client of Gant's who wanted to sell her house.

Burbage said, "Yes, I left your earlier message on her desk. . . . Certainly, and the number? . . . Five-one-three, one-nine-four-four. . . . Thank you."

When Burbage hung up, I said, "Voice mail on the fritz again?"

She seemed exasperated more by me than the machine. "Yes."

"Well, I think you've already answered the question I was going to ask about Ms. Ling. Is Mr. Neely still gone, too?"

"He is."

"Do you know when either of them will be back?"

"No."

Burbage gave the impression that she was sorry the English language didn't have a shorter term for the concept.

I said, "Can I leave word for both to call me?"

"Yes."

But instead of putting pen to paper, Imogene Burbage swung the spiral message pad around so I could write out my own number for each of them.

Chapter 19

FROM THE OTHER end of the line, Steve Rothenberg said, "Anything, John?"

"Not that helps us. I can't come up with an identifiable motive, much less a plausible theory, why somebody would kill both Woodrow Gant and Michael Mantle."

Nothing for a moment. Then, "The sooner I plead Spaeth out, the better the deal's likely to be."

Rothenberg's words, but his tone of voice, too: tossing in the towel. "I thought you told me when we got started that the D.A. wasn't offering any kind of plea bargain?"

"John, what we'd be talking about is less 'how long' and more 'where.'"

"Meaning which prison."

"And cell block. How would you like to be a white-collar white guy like our boy consigned to general population after killing a black role model?"

"Steve, do me a favor?"

"What?"

"Don't call the prosecution for a day or two."

"A day or . . . ? Why not?"

"Because neither of us thinks Spaeth did it."

Another moment, then a sigh. "John, you remember that line from *Love Story* about not having to say you're sorry?"

"I remember the movie version."

"Yeah, well, the Alan Spaeth version is, 'We did our best, but there's only so much you can do without any evidence.' "

"Meaning we don't have to say we're sorry."

"Right."

"Steve?"

"What?"

"You contact the D.A. before I get back to you, I think we'll both be sorry. For as long as Spaeth sits in a cell anywhere."

I'd called Steve Rothenberg when I'd gotten back to my office from Epstein & Neely. After hanging up on him, I checked in with my answering service. The nice woman with the silky voice relayed a one-line message from Lieutenant Robert Murphy. "Cuddy, I want your ass at the South Market building, NOW."

The woman told me she wrote that last word in caps because that was the way Murphy said it. She was pretty sure of his feelings, too, because he'd called only ten minutes before.

The South and North Market buildings are the twin, Federalist-period shoe boxes flanking the better-known Quincy Market. Each has countless boutiques and several anchoring restaurants—including Cricket's, where I'd last seen Nancy. However, from all the commotion at the harbor end of the building, it wasn't hard to know where Murphy wanted me to be.

I'd walked down State Street from my office on Tremont, so I didn't have to find a parking place. That was the only fortunate part, given the sickening similarity the cruisers and unmarkeds and Medical Examiner's van carried with them from the scene in Southie earlier that day.

A different uniformed officer met me at the yellow-tape barrier. She led me under the "POLICE LINE DO NOT CROSS" lettering and around the corner to the alley behind the building. I saw a dumpster with some trash overflowing, unusual because the city was adamant about the restaurants and stores maintaining a neat appearance for our tourist showcase. When you got closer to the dumpster, though, you could see the thing wasn't really full. More like somebody had intentionally strewn garbage on the side of it.

And over what lay on the ground next to it.

"Cuddy," said Murphy, standing near the trash pile, "just what the fuck is going on here?"

I was close enough to see the shapely legs sticking out from under a flattened cardboard box. The pantyhose were torn up the right calf, that two-inch heel on, the other off so the left foot was visible, pointing toward the sky at a forty-five-degree angle. For just a second, my heart said it was Nancy, but my head kicked in quickly, because while the shoes were right, what I could see of the legs belonged to a shorter woman. Besides, Murphy wouldn't have sprung something involving Nancy on me, no matter what his mood might be.

I drew even with him and looked down at the other end of the trash pile. The orange rinds and banana peels had been brushed away from the face staring up at us. The eyes were bulging, the tongue gorged and turned that grotesque shade of blue.

The way Michael Mantle would have been if the rats hadn't been at him first.

"You recognize her," said Murphy, but not as a question.

I did, though what I saw on the ground made no sense. "Deborah Ling."

He nodded. "I met her when we did the Q&A over at Woodrow Gant's law firm, day after he was killed on the road."

"I was there a little while ago."

"The road?"

"No, at Epstein & Neely. The head secretary, Imogene Burbage, said Ling hadn't gotten back from a meeting after lunch."

Now Murphy was staring at me. "My question still stands."

"Why is this woman dead?"

"That's the question. What's your answer?"

"I don't know."

"Not good enough."

"Lieutenant—"

"No 'Lieutenant' bullshit, Cuddy." Murphy was getting hot, and tough to blame him. "I want the straight skinny, and I want it now."

I glanced around the trash pile. "I don't see her handbag anywhere."

"Neither did the poor son of a bitch taking out the trash, and I believe him."

"Which means, it could have been an unrelated mugging."

"That's how we'll carry it for now, media-wise." Murphy turned away from me and spoke in a softer voice. "But everybody who thinks that's likely, raise his hand."

Neither of us did.

I said, "Besides the torn pantyhose, any indication of sexual assault?"

"No," from Murphy, over the shoulder, "but we have to wait on the M.E. and lab tests to be sure."

"Speaking of which, you get any better time of death for Michael Mantle?"

He turned back to me. "We're not talking about Mantle. We're talking about Ling." Murphy took a breath. "Account of your client Spaeth being a guest of the county, he's in the clear on this one. So, who might've killed her?"

I couldn't see how keeping my promise to Deborah Ling would help the woman now.

"Cuddy, I'm—"

"She had a boyfriend," I said.

After giving Robert Murphy the information about Nguyen Trinh and his enforcer, I went back to my office and called Nancy. The person picking up her phone said Ms. Meagher was on trial for the afternoon. I left a simple, "If you see the news, I'm okay," and hung up on him.

Then I called Steve Rothenberg. The dippy receptionist connected me, and he answered after one ring.

"Hello?"

"Steve, John Cuddy."

"I've been thinking about what you said earlier, about me not calling the D.A. on—"

"He may be calling you."

Rothenberg coughed. "What happened?"

"I don't know. And that's not an evasive answer."

"All right, tell me what you do know."

When I'd finished about Deborah Ling, Rothenberg whistled. Then he said, "Forgive me if I say this sounds like good news for a change."

"Sorry, Steve, I can't."

"Can't what?"

"Forgive you for saying that."

"John, come on—"

"No, Steve. We missed something, and since you know pretty much only what I've been telling you, that means I missed something. And now there's a woman dead, maybe because of it."

"You can't blame yourself for Ling. Or for this Mantle guy, either."

"Mantle, no, because probably he died the same night Woodrow Gant did. And by the same hand. But I've been rattling cages for the last few days, and something I said or did set somebody off without me seeing it coming."

"Fine, John. You want the guilt of God on your shoulders, that's okay by me. I've got enough of my own to carry, thank you very much." A stop, and a different emotion came over the wire. "Seriously, John, I do thank you. Spaeth's case has been keeping me up nights, which never happens when the guy I've got is deadbang dirty and I'm just forcing the Commonwealth's side to be honest. Whatever you did, it may have somehow cost Ling her life, but I think it's going to give Spaeth back his."

From what I'd seen of both people, I didn't think it an even trade.

The phone seemed to ring differently than usual. Louder, somehow.

"John Cuddy."

"Murphy. We can't find Trinh or his muscle."

"Where are you, Lieutenant?"

"Their office in Brighton. It's not cleaned out, but there's not much to look at, either. At least, without a warrant."

"You try that coffee shop?"

"Yeah. The owner claims she never heard of them."

"How about the restaurant?"

"Viet Mam? The owner's story is that Trinh just helped him get started. Doesn't know shit from Shinola about Trinh spying on Woodrow Gant or dating Deborah Ling."

"Chan knows, Lieutenant. He's just scared."

"Well, maybe you ought to join him."

"What do you mean?"

"While I've been chasing after Trinh and Huong, one of my other detectives was at the law firm. Seems both that secretary Burbage and the head guy Neely thought Ling was upset about something ever since you saw her yesterday afternoon."

Her work on the Viet Mam building deal. "Meaning Trinh might be targeting me, too."

"That's what I'm thinking."

"How about Uta Radachowski and Elliot Herman?"

"What about them?"

"Did they have any contact with Ling last night or today?"

"My detective asked, and both said no, except that around lunchtime Herman saw a woman in Quincy Market who might have been her."

" 'Might have been'?"

"He was a ways away, and behind her."

"Well, you already know everything Ling and I talked about."

"This Imogene Burbage told my detective that a man with an 'Asian' accent tried to reach Ling by telephone all this morning, but she—Ling, now—wouldn't take his calls."

"You're thinking Trinh might have decided on a personal appearance?"

"You met the scumbag. He strike you as the type that's satisfied with 'no' for an answer?"

I thought about it. And about missing something that might

have gotten Deborah Ling killed. "Lieutenant, can you put somebody on Grover Gant?"

"The brother? Why would we want to watch him?"

"Not so much watch as baby-sit. Grover owed Trinh, and if Trinh and Huong did Ling, they probably did Mantle and therefore Woodrow Gant as well."

A pause. "Meaning Grover might be next on Trinh's list?"

"I don't know."

"That's not much reason for me to authorize a bodyguard, Cuddy."

"It's all I've got right now. But I'd hate to see another member of the Gant family added to the body count."

A shorter pause. "I hear you. Only thing is, we start putting people on Gant—or you and the other people at the law firm, for that matter—I'm going to be doing a lot of baby-sitting and not much investigating."

"Take it from me, Lieutenant. Investigating's vastly overrated."

Lieutenant Robert Murphy might actually have been laughing as he hung up his end of the line.

My phone was barely back in its cradle when it rang again. Somehow it seemed louder still, which I wouldn't have thought possible.

"Cuddy, this is Frank Neely."

"Frank—"

"I want you over here, and I mean now, mister."

I didn't say anything.

"Cuddy? If you aren't—"

"I don't work for you, Frank."

"Goddamnit, we tried to do the right thing! Cooperate with the defendant's side. And now Deborah's dead, too."

"I didn't say I wouldn't come over. I just don't like the 'command performance' attitude."

I thought I could hear the sound of teeth grinding, but in a different tone, Neely said, "As soon as possible, then. Please."

* * *

It was maybe fifteen minutes more than that, because I waited inside my office door for a while to listen for movement or breathing in the corridor outside it. And on the stairs, for the same. At the front entrance to my building, I looked across the street and both ways on Tremont itself before taking a zigzag route to the waterfront.

From Spaulding Wharf, I watched the old red-bricked and weathered shingle structure for a while more before walking over to it. Nobody in the lobby, and the elevator worked fine as it brought me to the fourth floor.

I guess I would have expected everybody to be in the glass-walled conference room, but they weren't. Uta Radachowski filled one of the reception area chairs, a bunch of Kleenex wadded in one of her big hands. Elliot Herman risked his suit pants by sitting on the wine-and-gold carpeting, back against a wall, heels at his butt and wrists resting on his knees. Imogene Burbage was behind the reception desk, the tears trickling down her cheeks not smearing her makeup because she didn't wear any.

And Frank Neely? He stood off to the side, by the conference room but not quite in its doorway, holding a Colt forty-five semiautomatic handgun the way they taught us back in Officer Basic, feet spread shoulder width apart, the muzzle steady and aimed at my chest.

Neely closed his eyes, but lowered the Colt. "I'm glad it's you."

He looked a little more comfortable at one end of the teak conference table, the forty-five on the wood in front of him, encircled by his forearms. Uta Radachowski sat to Neely's right, back to the exterior window, Elliot Herman next to her. Imogene Burbage was at Neely's left, pencil hovering over a steno pad, which I found quaintly affecting. It had seemed sensible for me to take the other end of the table, facing the senior partner across its long axis, and so I had.

Neely said, "We've been grieving so much lately, it almost seems like what we do."

"I'm sorry about Ms. Ling."

Radachowski leaned forward, looking at me. "What did you do that got Deborah killed?"

"I don't know that I did anything."

Herman said, "No more rations of shit, Cuddy. Two of us are dead, and you're saying you don't think they're connected?"

"I think they're connected. I just don't know what, if anything, I did to close the circuit."

Neely held up a hand. "This isn't the time to be extending metaphors, John. Elliot's right. We want to know why two attorneys from this firm are dead, but we also want to know whether the rest of us are in any kind of jeopardy."

I let my eyes go around the table. Everybody was looking at me except for Burbage, who seemed to concentrate on her steno pad.

I said, "Woodrow Gant was killed a week ago Wednesday night. Alan Spaeth claimed he had an alibi witness named Michael Mantle. Predawn today, this Mantle was found dead, probably a good week after the fact. Which means Spaeth's alibi witness died about the same time as your Mr. Gant. Then this afternoon, Deborah Ling is found dead, too, apparently killed by the same method as Mr. Mantle, but now while Spaeth is locked away in a cell. That's pretty much all I know. Any ideas?"

Herman kept looking at me, Radachowski switched to the table, and Neely to Burbage. "Imogene, when did you last see Deborah?"

Burbage wrote as she spoke. "Eleven-forty-seven, exactly. Ms. Ling said she had an early afternoon meeting, and therefore needed to eat a quick lunch first."

I said, "Ms. Ling's body was behind the South Market building. Anybody see her after she left here?"

Herman worked his jaw, and Neely caught it. "Elliot?"

"As I told the police detective, I went to one of the counter places in Quincy Market on the way to my own meeting. About a block away, I saw this woman who could have been Deborah, but her back was toward me as she walked, so I'm going mainly by that."

I said, "By the way the woman walked, you mean?"

"Yes. But her hair was right, too."

"How about clothes?"

Herman shook his head. "Didn't notice."

Burbage said, "Deborah was wearing a—"

Herman snapped. "I said I didn't notice, Imogene."

She bit at her lower lip, but kept writing on the pad.

Uta Radachowski turned toward me. "I never saw Deborah at all this morning."

I said, "Frank?"

Neely seemed uncomfortable. "What you're about to hear is . . . confidential information."

I looked at him. "The police aren't likely to respect that very much."

"I've already told them, John. I meant more that it was given to me in confidence by Deborah, and so I'd appreciate the rest of you keeping it that way as much as possible, too."

Neely waited until we all nodded back at him, then spoke toward his pistol. "Deborah came to see me early this morning, in my office. She said she had a problem of a . . . romantic nature. It required her to take at least a few days off, and maybe to request a . . . leave of absence."

Not what I expected. Nor what anyone else did, apparently. Herman closed his eyes, Radachowski shook her head, and Burbage raised her chin to stare very, very hard at her boss.

Neely looked at me instead of his secretary. "When I asked Deborah how long a leave she was talking about, she said she wasn't sure."

I watched the others. "I take it this is the first time the rest of you have heard of Ms. Ling's intentions?"

Nods all around.

Neely waited a beat, then said, "John, I'd still like your best analysis. Do we have anything to fear individually from whoever killed Deborah? Or Woodrow?"

I tried to engage each person at the table except for Burbage, who'd gone back to communing with her steno pad. "Ms. Ling was involved in a relationship with a pretty vicious man, an Amerasian named Nguyen Trinh. I'm guessing that's who was calling her this morning here at the firm."

Burbage started to look up at me, then broke it off and just kept writing.

I said, "Trinh and his henchman, another Amerasian named Oscar Huong, had a strong motive to kill Woodrow Gant, though for a whole host of reasons, I don't see them actually having done it."

Both Herman and Neely seemed about to say something, but each held back.

"However, I'm going to describe Trinh and Huong for you, and I'll ask the police to send over photos of both. If you see either man—or even if you've *ever* seen them—call Lieutenant Robert Murphy at Boston Homicide or ask to speak to someone from his squad."

Neely said, "I remember Murphy. And that other detective who was here earlier today left me his card."

Radachowski cleared her throat. "Mr. Cuddy, what you're saying is that each of us could in fact be in some danger."

"Honestly, I don't know."

Herman slammed his palm on the teak surface. "Which is exactly where we were twenty fucking minutes ago." He stood up and strode for the doorway.

"Elliot?" said Neely.

"I'm calling Karen at home, Frank. Warn her not to answer the phone or the door till I get there."

As Elliot Herman reached the reception area, he said, "What a fucking nightmare."

The atmosphere in the room felt like he was speaking for everybody.

Chapter 20

DOWNSTAIRS, I WAITED inside the lobby doors, watching Commercial Street to make sure I couldn't see the green Mercedes or its usual occupants. Outside, I hailed a taxi and told the driver to take me to the intersection of Beacon Street and Gloucester, a block past my condo building at Fairfield. I didn't see anything threatening as we drove by. The cabbie probably thought I was crazy, but he followed my instructions to functionally circle the block before dropping me off at the corner of Marlborough and Fairfield. I stood for a while, eyes now on the parking lot behind my building. Still nothing.

I can't say, though, that the two minutes it took me to walk around to the stoop outside the front door were the shortest in memory.

When I got upstairs to the condo, Nancy was on my telephone machine, with a "Call me at home" message. After dialing her number, I got the outgoing tape, but as I started to talk after the beep, she picked up.

"John?"

"Screening your calls?"

"Yes, but you're the one crank I wanted to hear from."

The bantering tone again. "That sounds hopeful."

"Thanks for letting me know you were all right."

"I wasn't sure what you'd think was going on."

"It sounds pretty . . . bizarre?"

I didn't want to worry her with the Trinh/Huong factor. "What's beyond 'bizarre'?"

Nancy's tone changed. "John, for obvious reasons, I can't ask at the office how the case against Spaeth is going, but I thought maybe you'd have heard."

"Nothing definite."

"Oh." A little breath over the phone. "That's too bad."

I took a chance. "What's beyond 'too bad'?"

Her throaty laugh. "I had some white wine chilled."

"And a fire stoked?"

"My apartment doesn't have a fireplace."

"I know."

Another laugh. "We'll just have to wait on that, too."

"Nance, this is torture."

"Then just think how good you'll feel when it stops."

I heard the click before my next line occurred to me.

The ten o'clock television news covered Deborah Ling's killing in the usual, tasteful manner.

Video captured the removal via gurney of the bagged body from the dumpster area to the M.E.'s van. A solemn voiceover by the reporter at the scene lamented another "murder by mugging" and the "tragic irony" of a second attorney from the same small firm meeting a "violent death" in two weeks. All of Ling's coworkers were "deep in their own grieving" and therefore "unavailable for comment."

I watched a different station at eleven, but the news didn't get any better. I went to bed right after that, laying my gun on the night table next to the telephone.

*　　*　　*

I woke up Saturday morning without the clock radio. When I turned on the all-news station, the weather forecaster said the temperature had plummeted to thirty overnight. An October taste of the December to come.

I was feeling tight and edgy, as much from not seeing Nancy as thinking about Murphy not finding our Amerasian mafia. A good run along the Charles might burn off the excess anxiety.

I pulled on my running shorts and the leg brace, then a pair of sweatpants. On top I wore a cotton turtleneck and the hooded sweatshirt with the quarterback hand muffler in front. I debated whether or not to put the Chief's Special in the muffler part, because then I'd have to run with both hands in there, my right to hold the handle, my left so I wouldn't look even odder.

Before leaving the apartment, I sat by the kitchen window for a while, watching Beacon Street. No sign of Trinh, Huong, or their car. Same from the foyer downstairs, so I opened the brownstone's front door and went outside.

The cold air was bracing under a painfully blue sky, the absence of clouds probably contributing to the radiational cooling that had sent the mercury dropping. The wind blew a good twenty miles an hour in the block between the buildings as I jogged from Beacon toward the pedestrian ramp over Storrow Drive. Once on the macadam path, I turned upriver first, the Charles to my right showing boulder-sized whitecaps against its basically black water. The now northwest gale had jumped up a notch to twenty-five or so, the windchill down around zero.

I remember thinking, That which does not kill us makes us stronger.

Usually the running paths are crowded on Saturdays, the yuppies realizing they've been drinking the micro-brewed beer and eating the high-test food all week, neither counting the calories nor countering them with a little exercise. But the cold snap probably encouraged most sane people to hit the snooze button and roll over till the next morning. Except for a man in a ski mask bicycling, a woman in a Gore-Tex suit Rollerblading with her malamute, and two jail trustees in yellow parkas bundling cut branches, I was the only fool out there.

In fact, the weather must have been affecting my brain as well. Because after the bicyclist and the Rollerblader went by, it took a full minute for me to register that the jail van was nowhere in sight.

Too slow by too many seconds.

The bulkier of the men in yellow was already running toward me from the water's edge, covering ground obliquely a lot faster than I was jogging straight ahead. My head was barely turning toward him when one of his feet, lashing up in a wicked arc, caught me on the right cheekbone, and I started going down face first. As I got my left hand out of the muffler to break my fall, another kick was delivered to my upper right arm and a third to my lower right torso. I felt a couple of ribs cave from that last one, the cold air burning when I exhaled, scalding when I tried to breathe again. And I didn't like the noise I made trying.

It sounded like a child, whimpering.

Above me, Oscar Huong's gravelly voice called out, "He's down."

From a distance, but closing at the rate a person strolls, Nguyen Trinh said, "Get comfortable, Mr. Private Eye. This gonna take a while."

Lying on my stomach and facing left, I tried to make the fingers of my right hand work inside the muffler. However, the kick to that arm had made me feel like I was wearing a boxing glove.

The toes of Trinh's cowboy boots stopped two feet from my face. "You come on like a real knight on the white horse, man." He kicked me in the left shoulder, the pointed toe piercing the muscles, making them spasm.

But I could feel my right pinky and ring finger wiggling a little inside the muffler beneath me.

"Only thing is," continued Trinh, "you just a piece of shit like everybody else." He moved around to my right side, out of sight. Then another kick, a little more juice behind it, to the ribcage where Huong had already done some damage.

I must have blacked out, because the next thing I remember is Huong saying, ". . . coming around."

Now Trinh again. "What's the matter, Mr. Private Eye? A little tender down there? How you think Deborah feel when you choking her out, huh?"

I got as far as "Trinh, that wasn't—" before another boot to the ribs made me feel like I'd been kicked by a horse.

But now I had all the fingers on my right hand flexing except for the thumb.

"You don't talk to me, you piece of shit. You listen." Trinh walked back around to my left side. "Roll him over."

Huong kicked me once in the right hip, the blow vibrating all the way through my body. Then he planted a heel on the hip, and pushed hard.

As I flopped over, I had to hold onto the inside fleece of the sweatshirt to keep my right arm from sliding my hand and gun out of the muffler pocket. But now my thumb was working, and I could feel it close around the butt of the revolver.

Trinh's face loomed into view from standing height above mine, the blue sky as backdrop giving the eerie sensation of being in a domed chapel, staring up at one of Lucifer's failed angels.

He said, "You don't like me calling you 'Mr. Private Eye,' right? I can tell that, the first day Oscar and me in your office, the address where you live on the fucking bills I'm reading, waiting for you. Then you shining on about 'jogging the river every morning,' tell me where we can find you. Well, Mr. Private Eye, I want you looking at me when we take your fucking 'private eyes,' man. I'm the last thing you gonna see, just like you the last thing my Deborah see."

Trinh's face swung toward Huong, and I let my head loll that way, too. Huong grinned at me as he stepped hard on my left elbow, pinning that arm to the ground. When I felt Trinh's cowboy boot begin to come down on my right elbow, I bent my right wrist inside the muffler to bring the muzzle up against the cloth. As Huong came down with his thumbs set for gouging out eyes, I shot him twice in the chest, little puffs of fleece wafting into the air as my ears rang from the reports.

Huong rocked back and over, and Trinh jumped back, too. I rolled away from Trinh as I cleared my gun hand from the sweatshirt, probably bellowing from the pain I caused myself in the ribs. Trinh had a nine-millimeter just about coming to bear on me when I pulled the trigger three times more, two slugs lifting his feet off the ground like somebody had lassoed him from behind, the semiautomatic clattering to the macadam as his back hit the path. There was no third shot because I'd had only four bullets in the five-shot cylinder.

I turned, looking back at Huong. No movement I could see or noises I could hear.

Trinh began wheezing. On hands and knees, I crawled over to him.

"You . . . fucking . . . white . . ."

"Nugey?"

"You piece . . . of fucking—"

"Nugey! Can you hear me?"

More wheezing on the way in, but a burbling sound on the way out, the blood at the bullet hole in his parka frothing pink from underneath. In the Army we were taught to call that a "sucking chest wound."

Which meant no hope.

Trinh's eyes rolled a little before focusing on me.

For a third time, I said, "Nugey?"

"Hear . . . you. . . ."

"I didn't kill Deborah Ling."

A smile, almost, blood at first trickling, then running down from the left, and lower, corner of his mouth. "Tell it . . . to a priest . . . you piece—"

"I didn't kill her, Nugey. Why do you think I did?"

"Call . . ." A cough that sounded like something a plumber does to a clogged pipe.

"Call who?" I said quickly, feeling him going.

The head rolled left-right-left in slow motion, like Trinh wanted to shake it. "No . . . call me. . . ."

"Who called you?"

"Gro . . . ver. . . ."

"Grover Gant?"

"Try . . . to make . . . his voice . . . all funny." The eyes started to rotate back into the skull.

"Nugey, what did he say?"

The eyes came down again, but the left one wouldn't focus on me. "Said . . . 'Cuddy . . . done . . . your lady.' "

"I didn't."

"Fuck you . . . white. . . . Fuck . . . you . . . all. . . ."

Then Nguyen Trinh made a gurgling sound like the plumbing pipe had broken, and he was gone.

As I used my left thumb and index finger to close Trinh's eyes, I heard a scuffling noise behind me. I was turning back when something like a battering ram hit my right cheekbone again, and the running path opened up into a long, deep tunnel that swallowed me whole before closing in over my head.

Once, after I'd been shot, my first conscious impression was that polar bears were pawing and poking at me while I lay helpless on my back. For a minute, I thought I'd been dreaming about that scene, then I realized my left eye was open, and the man and woman in white were pretty clearly defined.

"What time . . . is it?" my lips not working quite right.

The woman said, "Maybe we should start with what day it is."

Great. "You first."

The man didn't see the heroic humor in that. To me, he said, "Don't move." To the woman, "You can call them in."

Nancy Meagher was frowning. Robert Murphy, just behind her, was grinning, his eyes hooded into slits.

She said, "The doctor didn't tell you?"

"No."

I was looking up at her, but I didn't move. And not just because the doctor said so. Every time I breathed, it felt like hot knives were twisting inside my right side, scraping against the cartilage.

Nancy shook her head. "It's Sunday night."

"Sunday?"

"Yes. And if a woman hadn't called it in yesterday morning,

you would have frozen to death out there and joined the other two in the morgue.''

Other two. "Trinh and . . . Huong?''

Murphy said, "Both dead. Staties responding from the old MDC station by the Science Museum said Huong was on top of you.'' A broader grin. "Like you were Jack London, and he was your sled dog.''

Over her shoulder, Nancy said, "Lieutenant, please?''

Sled dog. "I want to . . . thank the lady . . . with the malamute.''

Murphy said, "Who?''

"Rollerblader . . . with her malamute or husky. . . . She must be . . . the one who phoned . . . the State Police, right?''

A shrug. "Beats me. Headquarters just got an anonymous tip from some woman on the nine-one-one tape. We called the Staties, then got over there ourselves.''

Well, Thank you, anyway, I thought.

Nancy said, "Even without the arctic temperature, you're lucky to be alive.''

"What's the . . . damage?''

"Two ribs, cracked but not broken.'' She pointed toward my face. "A shot you took to the right cheekbone closed your eye pretty well, but thank God didn't shatter the bone or get the pupil. I won't even ask how you feel because the doctor said the rest of your body looks like it went tumbling down a staircase.''

"Close enough.''

Murphy was grinning broader behind her. "Let me get this straight, Cuddy. You had a gun, and they still beat you up?''

Nancy said, "Lieutenant?'' again, but never stopped watching my one good eye. "John, is it over now?''

I didn't even think about shaking my head. "Not quite.''

"Meaning?''

My tongue was doing a lousy job of wetting my lips, not to mention stringing together words. "Trinh told me . . . Grover Gant called him . . . saying I was the one . . . who killed Deborah Ling.''

Murphy stopped grinning. "Nugey tried to take you out for that?"

"In his office . . . Trinh said he loved her. . . . But before Trinh died . . . he also said Grover . . . talked 'funny' on the phone."

Murphy gave me a hard look. " 'Funny'?"

"Yeah."

"So?"

"So maybe it . . . wasn't Grover . . . who called him."

Nancy canted her head at me. "But who else would have?"

"I'd count it a real favor . . . if one of you could find out."

Murphy laughed, Nancy muttering something under her breath.

"Sorry," she said, wrestling with the steering wheel of her Civic hatchback after hitting a pothole neither of us spotted.

"It . . . happens."

Nancy glanced toward me. "You okay?"

"Breathing just takes . . . a little concentration, that's all."

I'd cracked a rib during the last week of ROTC Basic Training the summer after my junior year at Holy Cross. In those days, you had to complete a Physical Combat Proficiency Test that final weekend, or else effectively "flunk" and have to be "left back" in boot camp. The PCPT included among its six "events" a fifty-yard low crawl, a hundred-and-fifty-yard fireman's carry of another cadet, and a mile run in combat boots. I wasn't about to repeat Basic, thank you very much, so I did the test with the rib screaming at me. But I passed.

Of course, I was also twenty-one at the time.

"John?"

"Believe me . . . it's okay."

Nancy went back to watching the light Sunday night traffic in front of us. "I didn't mean so much being in pain as . . . zoning out on me?"

"Don't worry, no . . . concussion. I was just . . . thinking back to the . . . last time I took a hit to the ribcage."

She nodded.

I said, "I'll be fine."

Nancy nodded again. "The Staties making you come down to sign a statement?"

"Tomorrow."

Since the scene with Nguyen Trinh and Oscar Huong had taken place on Metropolitan District Commission land along the river, technically the State Police had jurisdiction. A plain-clothes investigator and one of the troopers responding to the emergency call talked with me back at the hospital, Murphy shortening the interrogation to half an hour by saying he thought the incident might be tied into one of his homicides. The Staties happily ceded me over to him as a connected case, but they still wanted a formal statement to cover themselves. And they also confiscated my Smith & Wesson as a weapon involved in a shooting, allowing as how I wouldn't be seeing it for a while.

Nancy changed her tone. "I can't believe nobody at the hospital even taped your ribs."

"They used to."

I thought back to the Basic Training incident. After the PCPT, I finally went to the Infirmary, where two reservist medics wanted to wrap Ace bandages around me. When they were a little awkward doing it, I asked them what hospital they worked at in civilian life. One said, "Actually, I'm a social worker," and the other chimed in with "hearing aid sales-man." I told them if they tried to touch me again, I'd knock their teeth out.

Nancy said, "But they don't anymore?"

"What?"

She spoke more slowly. "The hospital doesn't tape cracked ribs anymore?"

"Oh." Maybe Oscar Huong did leave me with a concussion. "No. No, the doctor . . . said today that studies . . . showed it didn't help the healing."

A coy smile as she glanced at me again. "So you'll have trouble with any . . . vigorous movements?"

It took me a moment to realize what she meant. "Well, maybe not . . . if I was less the mover and . . . more the movee."

"I think waiting until after the Spaeth case is resolved still makes sense. Did Steve Rothenberg ever call you?"

"No, but then he might not have . . . heard about it yet."

"John?"

"Yes?"

"For most of the last thirty-six hours, you were probably in no condition to notice, but what happened was all over the news, especially TV and radio."

"Then there'll probably be a message . . . for me with the answering service."

Nancy dropped me at the curb outside my condo building on Beacon Street. Before closing the Civic's door, I assured her I'd be all right and would call as soon as anything changed officially in the Spaeth case. Until she pulled away, I walked steadily up the front stoop, but I took the interior stairs a lot slower. Once in the apartment, I popped a couple of aspirin and telephoned my service. The nice woman with the silky voice wasn't working Sunday nights, but a guy covering the line said there'd been two calls from a Mr. Rothenberg, who'd left his home number and would appreciate hearing from me at my earliest convenience.

After dialing, I got a little girl's tentative, "Hello?"

"Hi. Can I speak with . . . Steve Rothenberg, please?"

"Just a second." There was a dull, thudding noise, as though she'd dropped the phone, followed by a "Daddy, daddy, daddy," mantra that faded more with each repetition.

Then I heard what sounded like adult shoes on a noncarpeted floor. "Yes?"

"Steve, John Cuddy."

"John! Great to hear from you."

"I just picked up . . . your messages."

A hesitation. "Your voice is—are you okay?"

"A little worse than black and blue . . . , but I'm functioning. Any news about . . . Spaeth?"

"From the D.A., you mean?"

"Yes."

"I tried calling him, too. Gone for the weekend, with instruc-

271

tions for no forwarded messages. So I'm going to try again in the morning. But I can't see you doing anything else for Alan until I get the new lay of the land."

"Good."

"Will you be in the office tomorrow or at home?"

"I'll see how I feel, but I have . . . to visit the State Police, so I may as well . . . go into downtown from there."

"How about if I try you after two?"

"Fine, Steve."

"And John, thanks for everything you've done. It's all been in a good cause."

I was having a hard time still believing that, but I told Steve Rothenberg his sentiment was appreciated.

Chapter 21

SUNDAY INTO MONDAY, I got at most three hours of sleep. Partly that was because my brain had been turned off for so long in the hospital, even though my body probably thought a little more rest might help the cause. But I don't tend to lie on my back in bed, so the main problem was that throughout the night I'd awaken in breathtaking pain whenever some reflex in the subconscious made my legs roll me over onto the ribcage.

The next morning, my right cheekbone was pretty tender, and the face in my mirror looked a lot like Alan Spaeth's after his adventure in the Nashua Street shower. Breakfast tasted awfully good, even if the entire meal consisted of ice water and the softest bread in the fridge for toast.

My landlord has cable TV, and I watched the repeat of a local college football game, thinking it seemed more like a high school event, including the apparent age of the players when they took off their helmets. At noontime, I risked some tuna fish on more of the soft bread, and after lunch I felt recovered enough to call a cab and visit the State Police near the Museum of Science.

They were pretty gentle with me, so I decided to walk to my office. The half a mile took half an hour, but the body parts other than my ribcage started to loosen up and let me feel human again, at least until I stepped down off a curb or got jostled by another citizen in a hurry to make that next appointment.

Inside the lobby of my building, I treated myself to the slow elevator instead of the stairs. Opening the office door, some envelopes had come through the mail slot along with the junk circulars. Not surprisingly, the envelopes had canceled stamps or postage-meter markings on them.

All except one, that is.

I processed the regular mail and pitched the circulars, then turned the maverick around and over a few times. Just a plain white, business-sized envelope. No address—or return address—but sealed and very light in weight.

I opened it. There was a single sheet of photocopy paper, folded perfectly in threes, an image centered on one side when I smoothed the paper out. The image was of a xeroxed phone message from a pad like the one I'd seen at the reception desk of Epstein & Neely, the generic information printed, the specific in precise handwriting. It read:

TO: DML
FROM: Ms. Barber
TEL #: (617) 513-1944
DATE/TIME: September 3rd, 9:51 A.M.
MESSAGE: Please call her ASAP

Then, under the acronym for "as soon as possible," there was scrawled a second message, in different, seemingly hurried handwriting and at a forty-five-degree angle to the vertical. It read:

WWG,
Got a closing. Can you call her back?

DML

I went over the xeroxed image again. It was dated seven weeks before, or almost six weeks before Woodrow Gant died. "DML" had to be Deborah Ling's initials, and "WWG" Gant's. But the exchange was the same as the law firm's, and the name "Barber" came up again. The temp Patricia had used it when she interrupted Ling and me the first time I'd visited Epstein & Neely. And the same name was repeated by Imogene Burbage at the reception desk the prior Friday. In her office, Ling had said Barber was just one of Woodrow Gant's divorce clients anxious to sell a marital home. Which made sense at the time.

If Ling had been telling me the truth, that is. Which she hadn't always.

Then I looked at the photocopied message as a whole and thought about who might have slipped the envelope through my mail slot. I came up with a pretty good candidate, but I used the telephone first.

After dialing the number on the message, I heard two rings and then "Kim Baker."

"I'm sorry," I said. "I thought this was Ms. *Bar*-ber's number."

Some breathing on the other end before, "Who is this, please?"

"I'm returning Ms. Barber's call."

More breathing. "Call for whom?"

I said, "Woodrow Gant at Epstein & Neely."

More breathing still, then just a hang-up.

I dialed again, but nobody answered this time, and no tape machine or voice mail had kicked in after ten rings.

Opening the drawer of my desk that held the photo album, I took out my reverse phone directory and ran down the number.

The small office building on lower State Street was just a coin toss from Boston's elevated Central Artery that, once depressed, will no longer be a "pedestrian-flow barrier" between the Quincy Market area and our waterfront. I didn't have to look at the lobby directory for "Harborview Realty Company":

Its stenciled picture window constituted most of the visible ground floor.

I walked inside the door next to the window. A woman beaming a Pepsodent smile sat at the front desk to my left. It was removed from the dozen others in two rows behind her, at which three women and two men sat, several with telephones cradled at the shoulder while they scrolled information across computer screens. The reception desk seemed far less cluttered than the others. Just a pad and a telephone console.

"I'm Kelly O'Shea." The beaming woman beamed at me until I turned and she noticed my right eye. "Uh, welcome to Harborview Realty. Can I help you?"

"I'd like to speak to Ms. Baker, please." I enunciated the syllables carefully, just so O'Shea wouldn't think the punch-drunk in front of her had said "Barber."

"And your name, please?"

"John Cuddy."

"One moment." O'Shea lifted her receiver and hit two digits. I could see a fortyish woman who hadn't been on the phone pick up her extension.

The receptionist said, "Kim, a Mr. Cuddy is here to see you."

The woman at the rear desk smiled and beckoned to me while mouthing something into her line. O'Shea nodded, and they hung up in unison.

I said, "Do you drill together often?"

"Pardon me?" replied O'Shea.

"Never mind. I can find my way."

I moved down the aisle between the desks, Kim Baker rising from behind hers. She stood about five-one and wore a stylish, green wool dress with a scarf artfully draped over a shoulder and part of her chest.

When I got within greeting distance, she extended a hand, professionally oblivious to the damage my face showed. "Mr. Cuddy, Kim Baker. A pleasure."

"Same. But I do have kind of a threshold question."

A wariness crossed her features, as much from my voice, I think, as my words. She said, "A threshold question?"

"Yes. Is there a reason you go by 'Barber' as well?"

Wary graduated to stiff. "Who are you?"

"The man who called a while ago."

"Show me some identification, or I'm calling the police."

"If you'd like, I can give you the separate line for Homicide."

"Oh, God. On television, you people always come in pairs."

I didn't want to disabuse Baker of the notion I was a cop. "I'm afraid this is real life."

She looked around quickly, then said, "Let me get my coat."

"I like to eat lunch out here." Kim Baker's tone didn't suggest much of an appetite right then. "This bower effect and the water, it's really . . . soothing."

We were sitting on a bench in Christopher Columbus Park, about a three-block walk from her realty office if that area of town were measurable in blocks. The park is only a few acres of lawn and paths, but the sun shining through the latticework of the bower overhead created a pastoral pattern of shadows on the ground around us.

"Ms. Baker, could we go back to my threshold question?"

Both hands grappled nervously on her lap, feet flat on the ground, knees close together. Then Baker shivered a little, and I didn't think it was from the air temperature.

"I used the name 'Barber' for confidentiality. It's easy to remember because it's so close to the real one."

"Confidentiality because of your divorce case?"

A blinking look. "My what?"

"Woodrow Gant was a divorce attorney at Epstein & Neely. Somebody there said you were a client of his."

Baker squeezed her eyes shut briefly. "That makes sense, actually."

She'd lost me. "Maybe I should stop asking questions and have you just answer them."

"I don't understand."

"Okay, let's start with an easy one. What was your relationship with Mr. Gant?"

"Professional and client."

"And how was he representing you?"

277

"No," with a shake of the head. "No, you've got it backwards."

"Backwards?"

"Yes. Woodrow came to me—or called me, actually."

"Called you as a real estate broker?"

"Right."

I was getting deeper and deeper into the woods, so I just said, "Go on."

"Well, he wanted me to start scouting properties, but naturally Woodrow didn't want anyone to know, so I suggested we use the name 'Barber' with my direct-dial number at Harborview because I'd never used it before."

"Never used what before?"

"The name 'Barber.' As a cover. You know, like in the spy stories?"

Spy stories. "But why would you need any 'cover' at all?"

Baker looked at me, a little more relaxed now that she believed I was a dunce. "So nobody at the firm would recognize me."

"Because?"

"Because I was the one who'd helped the senior partners when they did the same thing."

"What same thing?"

"Left their old firm, of course."

That stopped me. "Woodrow Gant was leaving Epstein & Neely?"

Baker's turn to stop. Then, "You didn't know?"

The penny finally dropped. "He hired you to find him new space for his own office."

"Their own office, actually."

"Meaning?"

"Deborah Ling was leaving with him. They were going to be partners together."

"But Ms. Ling was barely out of law school."

"Yes, but Woodrow said she was contributing half the capital to get things started."

"Why would he tell you that?"

A disdainful expression. "Any commercial lessor worth its

278

salt would want a credit rating on a new tenant. The typical commercial lease is for five years, with an option to renew, and the lessor has to be sure the tenant is a good risk."

I turned it over. "So Ms. Ling was putting up good-faith money from her end."

"Yes."

Meaning from Nguyen Trinh's end, probably. Another way he'd have gotten to control Woodrow Gant, to "watch him from the kitchen" at a higher level.

The penny also dropped on the photocopied phone message I'd received. "So that's why you called both Mr. Gant and Ms. Ling at the firm."

"Yes." Baker looked toward the water, a couple of gulls wheeling and diving for something on the surface. "But when Woodrow got killed, I was in Europe, so when I returned last week and called the firm, naturally I asked for him." She gnawed on her lower lip. "God, it was such a shock, but Deborah assured me she was still interested."

"Interested?"

"In setting up her own practice." Baker looked back to me. "In fact, that's why we were going to have lunch when . . ."

She shook her head.

I said, "Do you mean last Friday?"

"Yes." Baker's eyes returned to the harbor. "When it got later and later without any word from Deborah, I called the law firm twice and left blind messages for her just to get back to me."

I'd heard one of them at Epstein & Neely's reception desk.

Now Baker closed her eyes again. "Then that night, on the news . . ."

After a moment, I said, "Even without Mr. Gant as a partner, Ms. Ling was still thinking about leaving the firm?"

"Not just 'thinking' about it, either. She'd made up her mind." Baker came back to me. "I guess Deborah had major doubts."

"About what?"

Baker shrugged. "About the viability of Epstein & Neely for the future."

279

"Why?"

"Well, with Woodrow gone—dead, I mean—and the other partner being made a judge, there—"

"A judge?"

"Yes. I guess it wasn't public information yet, because Deborah insisted I had to keep that in strictest confidence."

I remembered Nancy telling me about the new slots being approved by the legislature. "Do you know which partner Ms. Ling was talking about?"

Another shrug. "She never said."

I remembered seeing somebody at the firm I didn't expect to be there. Then I thanked Kim Baker for her time.

After she left me, I spent a good hour on that bench, but I didn't pay much attention to the seagulls any more. Or anything else, for that matter. I was pretty much lost in thought.

Then I got up to go see the person at Epstein & Neely who I figured pushed that photocopied message through the mail slot in my office door.

Chapter 22

I WAS ABOUT to press the button for the small elevator when I heard the car approaching the ground floor and saw the diamond window line up with the lobby door. Through the glass, Uta Radachowski was hiking the strap to a backpack higher on her shoulder. I stepped to the side before she looked up, letting her open the door.

When Radachowski came out, I said, "Knocking off early?"

She jumped, then turned around. "You scared me."

The eyes behind her distorting lenses confirmed the emotion. "Why?" I said. "Trinh and Huong are both dead."

A different look now. "I caught it on the news. And can see it on your face."

"Bloodied, but unbowed."

Another hike at the shoulder strap. "Then what do you want here?"

"Maybe to know where you're heading."

"Not that it's any of your business, Mr. Cuddy, but I have a charity event I'm already late for. Now, is that all?"

"Except for an invitation to your swearing-in."

Radachowski lips narrowed. "My what?"

"The ceremony when you put your hand on the Bible and promise to be a good judge."

"Mr. Cuddy, I don't know—"

"I do know, counselor, and bluffing's not going to work anymore."

Her eyes swam behind the distorting lenses. "Who?"

"Who told me, you mean?"

The eyes were steady now. And angry. "That's what I mean."

I couldn't see any reason not to protect Kim Baker. "Nobody. Not directly anyway."

"That's not possible."

"Sure it is. All those client files of yours being carried to Frank Neely's office. Transferred to him, really. The visit by Parris Jeppers to you last Friday."

"There was nothing inappropriate about that."

"Maybe not. A little odd, though, given that Jeppers had told me he wasn't investigating Woodrow Gant anymore."

Radachowski didn't say anything.

"But our man at the Board might have been keeping his ear to the ground for you. Making sure nothing came up to scotch your nomination."

She didn't bother to look around because the lobby was too small a place for someone to hide. "I'd be the first declared lesbian on the bench, Mr. Cuddy. It would be very embarrassing to the governor for this to leak before he's ready to make the formal announcement."

"It won't, at least not from me. I just needed to hear you confirm what I suspected."

Radachowski took a minute before saying, "I guess I have to take your word on that."

"I guess you do. Like you 'had' to recommend Woodrow Gant to Nicole Spaeth."

Radachowski blinked. "I don't . . . ?"

"You recommended Gant to her, even though you were aware of his 'reputation' with female clients."

"They were just rumors. Unsubstantiated allega—"

"You strike me as pretty street-savvy. I think you felt the rumors were more true than false, yet you still recommended your law partner to the woman. Why, Ms. Radachowski?"

"I already told—"

"Because you were a little worried about your old firm's 'future viability' without new business flowing into it?"

The jaw set. "Mr. Cuddy, it seems I'm doomed to be terminating conversations with you."

Despite that last line, Radachowski waited until I turned to open the elevator door before saying, "You're wasting your time."

"Sorry?"

"Frank wasn't in his office, and Elliot's been off at a meeting all afternoon."

"How about Ms. Burbage?"

"Imogene's still there," said Uta Radachowski, though even from the kindly judge-in-waiting, it came out more as, Imogene's always there.

"Me again."

Burbage hadn't been watching the elevator door, maybe assuming that Radachowski had forgotten something and was coming back to get it. My voice threw the woman behind the reception desk enough that she looked up with her mouth open.

"Mr. Cuddy, I'm . . . I'm afraid no one's available to see you."

"That's okay. You're the one I want to talk to."

Burbage looked back down at the message pad and began writing on it. "We have nothing to talk about."

"You should have used a carrier pigeon."

She raised her head again. "A what?"

"Carrier pigeon. Frank Neely told me that to send a message on one, you have to roll the paper and stick it into this little quiver on the bird's leg."

No response from Burbage.

I reached for the inside pocket of my suit jacket. "But since you sent this through the mail slot in an envelope," laying the photocopied phone message on her desk, "I could see how neatly creased it was. And when my name didn't appear on even the envelope itself, I realized that was probably because the handwriting would match yours on the slip, since the only other writing was Deborah Ling's, and she was well past being able to hand-deliver anything anymore."

Burbage gave up the game. "You're really a lot smarter than you like to show, aren't you?"

"If so, we're two of a kind."

"Flattery doesn't work with me, Mr. Cuddy."

"That's too bad. You've earned some."

A confused expression. "What do you mean?"

I moved my hand in a small arc. "Everything you do around here. Secretary, bookkeeper, functional office manager. I'm betting your IQ beats any lawyer's in the firm by twenty points."

A jaundiced look. "Now you're not just flattering me, you're buttering me up. For what?"

"I want to know why you brought this message slip to my office."

"That's pretty obvious. I didn't want you to know who left it there."

"Not what I meant. Why did you think someone connected with the investigation into Woodrow Gant's death should know about Ms. Barber's call to Deborah Ling?"

Burbage looked back down at the sheet I'd laid in front of her. "Because I was *his* secretary, too."

"Mr. Gant's, you mean?"

"Yes."

Vague, but I thought I saw it. "Frank Neely became aware of this message, didn't he?"

A nod without looking back up. "I was covering the switchboard here that day. The voice mail was down again, so I wrote out Ms. Barber's message, leaving the pink copy for Ms. Ling in her slot." Burbage motioned to the plastic holder on the reception desk. "When Ms. Ling came out from her office to go to a closing, she picked it up. After reading the message, however, she scribbled a note on it, saying I should give it to Mr. Gant personally."

Now I pointed to the message holder. "As opposed to just leaving that pink copy in his own slot."

"Exactly. But I thought Ms. Ling just meant he needed to see it quickly."

"Not that no one else was to see it at all."

Another nod. "So, when I was relieved by a temp here at the board, I carried Ms. Barber's message back to my desk in order to give it to Mr. Gant as soon as I saw him."

"Only Frank Neely came out of his office first."

"Yes. He was asking me about a file, and I had what he wanted on the floor beside my desk. When I looked back up, Mr. Neely had the pink copy in his hand, glaring at it like he was going to tear it up. Then he set the message very carefully on my desk, and asked me to have Mr. Gant see him as soon as he got back." Burbage grew quieter. "I could tell Mr. Neely was seething, so I made a photocopy of the message, in case he wanted one later for some reason. But I couldn't see why Mr. Neely was so upset. I mean, I didn't recognize the name 'Barber,' but he obviously did."

"No, he didn't."

Burbage shook her head. "What?"

"Your boss didn't recognize the name." I pointed to the line underneath on the photocopy, the one that read 513-1944. "He recognized the number."

"I'm afraid you're right, John," said Frank Neely's voice, the business end of his Colt forty-five preceding the sleeve of a chamois shirt and the leg of some khaki slacks around the corner of the corridor.

After frisking me for a weapon I wasn't carrying, he marched us very slowly toward his office, Burbage in front, me in the middle, him bringing up the rear. Once inside, Neely waved his secretary toward the interior door.

"Open it, Imogene, and climb the stairs. One at a time."

When she was three deliberate steps up, at the first curve of the spiral case, Neely said, "Stop," and then, "Now you, John."

Reaching the base of the stairs, I paused until he told both of us to start moving again. Burbage climbed stiffly in front of me, her hand shaking the metal bannister every time I touched the railing. Neely came on but kept at least one turn of the staircase between us at all times, giving me no chance to do anything while preserving a nearly clear field of fire for his gun. Something about the spiral nature of the climb made things harder on my ribs, and I was breaking a sweat by the time we reached the top.

"Step out into the garden," said Neely.

Burbage and I did. As the staircase door closed behind us, I looked over my shoulder, Neely using a key from his ring to lock up.

He said, "The contractor who did the renovations for me planned to put only a dead bolt on here, but I wanted a little more security." Neely made a ritual out of returning the ring to his pants pocket. "Glad now that I did. Okay, follow the path."

Burbage and I moved through the foliage to the marble cocktail table and wrought-iron chairs. When we turned around, my right hand inadvertently brushed the left side of her skirt at the waist. She surprised me by reaching for and holding that hand, her elbow digging into my rib cage just enough to make me flinch.

Neely noticed it. "I heard you got a little banged up dealing with that loan shark and his pal. Broken rib along with the eye?"

"I'll live."

Neely just smiled with a sense of something approaching accomplishment.

I said, "Uta Radachowski told me you weren't in your office."

"She was right. I'd come upstairs to do a little gardening, so I changed clothes." With his free hand, Neely tapped the chamois shirt and khaki slacks. "Then I remembered a phone call I hadn't returned, so I went back down to look for the message on my desk. I'd just found the number when I heard your voice, John, talking to Imogene in the reception area."

"About a number you didn't need to find."

Neely smiled, but this time without the air of accomplishment. "You picked up on it, too."

Burbage said, "Picked up on what?"

I glanced at her. "Woodrow Gant and Deborah Ling were planning to leave Epstein & Neely to open their own law office."

"No," said Burbage to me.

"I'm afraid so. The real estate broker they'd asked to help them rent space was one Frank here once used, to find this place when he was breaking off from the last of his old firms. The broker was smart enough, though, to use a different, if similar, name. 'Barber' instead of 'Baker.' "

" 'Barber.' " The secretary addressed her boss. "But then how would you know who she was?"

"The telephone number itself, Imogene. The exchange was the same as ours here, not surprising given the few blocks between Ms. Baker's office and this one."

Burbage seemed awed. "You remembered the last four digits for eight years?"

"More like fifty-some," I said.

Now she was confused. "What?"

Neely lost his smile. "The last four numbers are one-nine-four-four. The year of D-Day, Imogene."

"My God," she said.

I was pretty sure of the rest. "And seven weeks ago, when you saw that phone message for Gant via Ling on Ms. Burbage's desk, you knew what it meant."

"Betrayal, John," said Neely.

"Because Gant was bailing out and taking Ling with him."

"Of course." The senior partner seemed to go inside himself, reliving something. "Almost four years ago, when Woodrow approached me about joining the firm, I could tell he was a real go-getter, just what we needed, given Len's dying months before. We never had a written partnership agreement here, but I made it clear to Woodrow that we needed his loyalty, a commitment to stay and build and be a part of the team. He agreed, and I took him at his word." Neely came back to us. "But in the end, Woodrow betrayed me, John."

"Then why didn't you kill Uta Radachowski as well?"

Burbage drew in a breath, but Neely didn't seem to notice. He said, "Uta? Why?"

"She was leaving the firm, too, and from the files being transferred to you from her, you had to know about it."

"Uta told me, straight out." Neely shook his head. "At her interview for my first firm, in fact. She made no bones back then about wanting to be a judge someday. When we all broke off from the second firm to form Epstein & Neely, Uta expressly promised Len and me that she'd stay with us forever unless she got a judgeship. Not only wouldn't I stand in her way, I applauded the opportunity." Neely fixed me with a baleful look. "No, Uta was forthright. It was Woodrow played the Judas."

"Just following in your footsteps, Frank."

A cocking of the head, a lot like Vincennes Dufresne at the Chateau in Southie. "What kind of a crack is that?"

"You and Leonard Epstein jumped ship on your old firm, just the same way that Woodrow—"

"Not in the least! You never knew Len, but you know me. And we were both men of honor, then and now."

"A man of honor sets up an innocent stooge to take the fall for him?"

The accomplishment smile. "Your Mr. Alan Spaeth."

"That's who I was thinking of."

"Then you can hardly call him an 'innocent,' John. He abused his family, first by neglecting them, then by putting them through the mill in his divorce case. He was . . . perfect."

"You'd heard Alan Spaeth berating Gant that day a few months ago at the deposition downstairs, even threatening him. Easy enough to wait one night until everybody else had gone home, then get Spaeth's boardinghouse address in Southie from the divorce file."

"Woodrow even helped out there, telling us at lunch a few

weeks after the deposition about his client's being afraid of the gun Spaeth still had."

"I can see you knowing about the revolver. I haven't figured out how you got it from Spaeth's room at the boardinghouse."

"I didn't. Mr. Michael Mantle got it for me."

"Not based on what I've heard from the landlord there. He— and even Spaeth himself—said Mantle was loyal to his friends."

"And so he was, John. To a fault, you might even say. Once I realized what a perfect scapegoat Spaeth could be, I began to spend my evenings following him. I started by using a car, but I noticed he and Mantle went out from the boardinghouse at least three times a week to different bars within walking distance, so I just dressed the part and parked, waiting until one night when Mantle went out by himself. I left the car and tailed along to this dive, then sidled up to Mantle and began talking to him. Pretty soon I was standing for drinks, and soon after that he started opening up about this friend of his having such a terrible time with his divorce. So terrible that poor old Mick was afraid poor old Alan might do something really stupid with his gun."

Christ. "You persuaded Mantle to steal Spaeth's gun to protect his friend from himself."

"Very good, John. Can you work out the rest, now?"

I thought about Dufresne recounting the payment of the room tab. "You told Mantle he could save his friend and pick up a little money on the side by taking the gun and selling it to you."

"Go on," said Neely.

"That gets you the right gun, but you also have to make sure Spaeth doesn't have an alibi for the night in question."

"What night?" said Burbage.

Neely glanced at her. "Please, Imogene. Don't interrupt the man."

I thought about it some more. "So you tell Mantle that you're going to use the gun a week ago Wednesday, the night Gant was killed."

"Actually I told the little drunk that the guy I sold it to was going to carry the thing into a liquor store, maybe even fire it, because he was another hotheaded Irishman."

"So Mantle decided he'd better baby-sit his friend Spaeth."

"I decided for him. Even made sure he had enough cash to get Spaeth good and drunk."

"Before Mantle left him to meet you."

"Excellent, John." Neely went inside himself again. "I told him, 'Mick, you meet me late Wednesday night, over in this derelict shell by some warehouses. I'll let you know then if your friend has anything to worry about.' "

"But once you got Mantle in that shell, you strangled him."

Burbage said, "No."

Neely glanced at her again. "I'm afraid so, Imogene. After all my careful planning, I couldn't very well leave Spaeth with a real alibi, now could I?"

I said, "You left Mantle's body instead, to be eaten by the rats."

Burbage gagged.

Neely looked away from her. "Sweet Jesus, John. I hadn't expected it would take so long before he was found."

"Only when I came around last Wednesday, rattling your cage with my doubts on Spaeth's guilt, you decided his 'alibi' might need a little help in exploding."

"I called a hospital the next night, late."

"Why did you wait a day and a half?"

"So as not to have the 'news' seem obviously triggered by your visit to us."

"And the hospital number was one you knew wouldn't record your voice for later comparison purposes."

"Correct. I faked a 'street-black' accent to report Mantle's body, and Woodrow's a week earlier." Neely smiled some more. "Careful planning always pays off, John. I learned that from my trusts and estates practice."

I wanted to change the focus a little. "You said you followed Mantle and Spaeth. You must have followed Gant, too."

"I did. And he deserved what he got for just that reason."

"Fooling around with one of his clients."

"One of the *firm's* clients, the rutting pig. Woodrow was a fine-looking man. And, divorced as he was, he could have had his pick of the litter."

I felt Burbage's hand start to tremble inside mine.

"But no," said Neely. "He couldn't keep away from the forbidden fruit."

"And so you followed Gant, too. Enough to establish that he liked to take Nicole Spaeth to Viet Mam."

"A certain restaurant five miles from his love nest, one that was most conveniently accessed by a very dark and lonely road."

Squeezing my hand now, Burbage said to him, "You killed Mr. Gant?"

"Imogene, Imogene." Neely shook his head some more. "For such a bright woman, you are indeed a slow learner in some ways."

Burbage began to let go of my hand, me now holding hers more tightly.

I said, "Everybody has blind spots, Frank."

He came back to me. "Yes. Yes, I suppose they do. Woodrow's was that he thought he'd gone well past anyone from his prosecutor past who might want to kill him. I could tell by the way he left his car that night, after I'd shot out the tire."

I tried to picture the scene. "Gant thought he had just a flat?"

"Yes. My ricochet must have punctured the fuel tank, though, because I could see him get down on his bad knee to inspect under the rear bumper. And, once I was near enough to Woodrow, I could smell the gasoline myself."

"At which point, you shot him, too."

"Not immediately, John. No, first I had a little talk with the boy. Told him why he was going to die."

Burbage's hand trembled violently inside mine.

I said, "And then you went around to the passenger side of the car and dropped the gun into Nicole Spaeth's lap."

"Yes."

"Why didn't you kill her, too?"

"I'd thought about it, believe me. As a contingency plan, just like you allow for when drawing a client's complicated will. And I would have killed Mrs. Spaeth, too, if she'd been sober enough to see or hear anything incriminating."

"But since she was drunk, you didn't have to."

"And didn't want to, John. Even with the wig and sunglasses, I recognized the woman. But if possible, I didn't want to kill her. Can you guess why?"

"Because while you had a motive to kill Gant, only Alan Spaeth would have had a motive to kill him and *not* to kill a potential witness only Spaeth himself loved."

"And . . . ?"

It took me a minute. "And only Spaeth would have a revenge reason for a 'practical joke,' letting his wife know who killed her new lover by leaving 'his' gun as the murder weapon in her lap."

A fatherly smile. "You would have made a fine trusts and estates lawyer, John."

"Not if it'd mean turning out like you."

The smile flew off his face. "Woodrow Gant betrayed me!" Neely waved the gun around his greenhouse. "Just like those bastards in Army intelligence betrayed my Ranger outfit in 'forty-four. Not telling us the guns at Pointe-du-Hoc had been moved, letting half my friends be cut down by enemy fire climbing that goddamned rock that didn't mean a thing anymore. My first outfit was betrayed that day, and Woodrow betrayed my current outfit in his own way."

"Oh, be honest, Frank. It takes a lot of money to maintain your little version of 'the Pointe' up here. You're on the mortgage personally with no other tenants to help carry it. You needed the proceeds from the policy on Gant's life."

"The *firm* needed it."

"No, Frank. There wasn't going to be a firm anymore."

"There always—"

"Uta Radachowski was in line for her judgeship, and Deborah Ling intended to pull the ripcord, too, with or without Gant. The firm was going to lose most of its rainmakers, which would jeopardize your staying in this building as a home."

Neely seemed to soften for a moment, even relent. "I'd been through two partnership breakups, John. The only real asset I had was 'Epstein & Neely,' bringing in cash to carry the build-ing here. At my age, I couldn't start over again." A hardening. "And I shouldn't have to. I survived a war, goddamnit. It was supposed to be my turn to take it easy as a senior partner, not hustle for clients like some insurance salesman."

"Tell me, Frank, is bailing out really what Ling wanted to see you about the morning she died?"

Neely ground his jaw. "Deborah came into my office, said she had to talk with me. After Woodrow was gone, I was sure she'd stay, build her real estate practice inside the firm. But no, I seemed to be the only good lawyer around. Deborah confirmed that she was a traitor, too. Leaving us over her 'ro-mantic involvement' with that gangster, Trinh."

I closed my eyes for a second.

"Yes, John," said Neely. "I'd never heard the name until the afternoon before, when you'd mentioned him as a criminal connected to the Vietnamese restaurant Woodrow visited. Trinh and Deborah being a couple seemed a bit too convenient to be coincidental."

"So you saw a chance to punish Ling for her 'betrayal' and to cash another million-dollar policy, both in one fell swoop."

"Actually, killing Deborah worried me more than you can guess."

Burbage's hand squirmed in my own.

Neely made a tsking sound. "I had to follow her last Friday and do the deed in broad daylight, stuffing her handbag into that big old briefcase of mine, all without any real planning ahead of time."

The reason he'd used the same method of killing that had worked with Mantle. "But why couldn't you plan it, Frank?"

"Because that morning in my office, Deborah told me not just about quitting the firm, but also that she was going to the District Attorney with the fact of her representing the gangster/ boyfriend in purchasing that restaurant building."

Which meant I really had panicked Ling. "And her blowing that whistle would have widened the official investigation—"

"—like a floodgate—"

"—and tied Woodrow Gant's murder more closely to the firm."

"Exactly. I certainly didn't want the authorities thinking they had to reopen that whole can of worms. Sweet Jesus, John, you were bad enough."

"But then you thought of a way to kill two birds with one phone call."

The accomplishment smile again. "Trinh's number was in Deborah's handbag. I'd met Grover Gant often enough, and one street-black voice is very much like another. Not too difficult to fool Trinh, 'if you know what I'm saying, man.'"

That last in dialect. "So Trinh buys that it's Grover calling him to say I was the one who strangled his girlfriend, Ling."

"As I'd hoped. And it worked, almost perfectly."

"I killed Trinh and Huong, but they didn't quite kill me."

"No, but with them both unable to give their versions, they turn out to be quite nice remainder suspects, and even with you still alive, no reason to think any further investigation was needed to get Alan Spaeth—'innocent stooge'—off the Woodrow Gant hook."

Burbage said, "You killed Mr. Gant, and this poor man named Mantle, and Ms. Ling. And then you tried to get somebody else to kill Mr. Cuddy?"

"Let me guess, Imogene. With all this talk of betrayal, you somehow feel I've let you down, too."

Burbage now wrenched her hand away from mine, forcefully enough that the motion torqued my ribcage, and I had to let go of her.

She stepped toward Neely and in front of me. In a strong, even voice, Burbage said, "Woodrow Gant was my boss, too."

"I'm sorry you feel that way, Imogene. But even if you didn't, I'm afraid I have no—"

Whether Burbage realized Neely was going to kill both of us, or whether she simply snapped, I'll never know. But she ran at him just as the report of the Colt, even muffled by her body mass, thundered in the confines of the greenhouse. The exiting forty-five slug tore a grisly hole the size of a plum in the center of her back before whistling past my left arm and thumping into a tree behind me.

There was nothing I could do for Imogene Burbage, so I

turned and dove into the little forest myself, the ribs punishing me for the effort. One more shot from the rear, the unmuffled report even louder, its bullet making a zipping noise as it plowed through the leaves near my head and ricocheted off the brick kneewall.

My ribcage pounding, I crawled through the foliage and onto the narrow, bordering walkway around the glass windows of the greenhouse. Getting into a squatting position, I listened stock-still for which route Frank Neely would take toward me.

Absolute silence from him, too.

Then just his voice with, "John?" A short pause. "I don't expect you to answer me, of course. But I thought talking this through might make more sense than chasing you down."

Silence again, as though Neely really did expect me to answer him, before, "Here's the way I see it, John." His voice still came from near the table and chairs where he'd shot Burbage. "We can play hide-and-seek for a while, but I'm a little old for that, and honestly there's simply no place for you to go. The staircase door is locked, and my elevator in the apartment requires a key as well. Furthermore, it's kind of a long way down to ground level by air."

A small laugh. "Sorry. I shouldn't be joking about this. But I can't see either of us being stupid when the end of the game isn't in doubt."

I forced my mind to weigh the options. Why would Neely be offering me the chance to walk up to him for a functional suicide? I looked around. It was the glass, stretching from the ridgepoled peak down to the knee wall. He didn't want to fire another shot that might shatter a pane and draw attention from Commercial Street below us.

"John?"

On the other side of the trees and shrubs, Neely had shifted, toward my right and the front of the garden.

I looked around again, this time more specifically. No rakes or shovels or even buckets, nothing that could be a makeshift weapon.

"John, please. Let's be dignified about this, all right?"

More to my right now, and closer to turning a corner at the front of the roof. Where he'd spot me easily.

I tried to picture Neely where I'd last seen him. The Colt in his right hand as Burbage lunged forward, behind us the table and . . .

If not a weapon, maybe a shield?

A very slight crunching sound to my right, and I hopped like a frog back into the foliage as the forty-five boomed again, another round screaming off the brick kneewall as my cracked ribs screamed at me. This time I kept going, plunging through the leaves until I reached the patio furniture again.

I stepped over Imogene Burbage, her blood making the burgundy tiles slick. Bending down, I lifted the cocktail table on my left side. Heavier than its size suggested, I tilted it so the marble top was in front of me like a knight's jousting shield.

I heard a footstep just before the next shot made a noise somewhere between a thump and a whine as it struck the top of the table. Hunkered down, with the marble covering as much of me as possible, I started running forward. To close the gap between Neely and me, functionally making my shield bigger and hopefully throwing off his trigger timing.

Another shot and another still, the last ripping a chunk off the meaty outside of my right shoulder. A feeling like being branded. Then the impact of the tabletop on Neely's chest, a whoofing noise from the lungs as he went backward. I felt his heels catching on something, his hips coming up and—

The sound of breaking glass.

Shattering, actually. I'd driven him through one of the vertical panes of the greenhouse right at the knee wall. Neely bellowed as he went out into the air, his arms making whirlygig motions, futilely trying to regain his balance. Seconds later, a whumping sound rose from the street.

I dropped the table to the tiled floor and forced myself toward the jagged opening in the glass. As I looked down at the body sprawled across the righthand lane, pedestrians from the sidewalk rushed over to it, then turned away abruptly, probably appalled that a five-story drop in real life wasn't quite as stylized and sanitized as television dramas had led them to believe.

Clamping my left palm over the wound on my right shoulder, I watched the scene below until the wail of a siren began growing closer. That's when I realized my view likely was pretty similar to the one a German soldier would have had fifty-plus years ago, looking down on the casualties from that Ranger battalion heroically scaling the cliff of Pointe-du-Hoc.

Shock started setting in on me, making my legs rubbery. Before the shakes got too bad, I moved back toward the center of Frank Neely's greenhouse to say a little prayer over Imogene Burbage.

About the Author

Jeremiah Healy, a graduate of Rutgers College and Harvard Law School, was a professor at the New England School of Law for eighteen years. He is the creator of John Francis Cuddy, a Boston-based private investigator.

Healy's first novel, *Blunt Darts*, was selected by *The New York Times* as one of the seven best mysteries of 1984. His second work, *The Staked Goat*, received the Shamus award for the Best Private Eye Novel of 1986. Nominated for a Shamus a total of eleven times (six for books, five for short stories), Healy's later novels include *So Like Sleep*, *Swan Dive*, *Yesterday's News*, *Right to Die*, *Shallow Graves*, *Foursome*, and *Act of God*. His tenth novel, *Rescue*, was a Main Selection of the Mystery Guild, and his previous book, *Invasion of Privacy*, was a Shamus nominee for Best Novel of 1996.

Healy has served as a judge for both the Shamus and Edgar awards. His books have been translated into French, Japanese, Italian, Spanish, and German. Currently on the National Board of Directors for the Mystery Writers of America, he was president of the Private Eye Writers of America for two years. Healy has written and spoken about mystery writing extensively, including the Smithsonian Institution's Literature Series, *The Boston Globe* Book Festival, and international conferences of crime writers in New York, England, Spain, and Austria. A member or chair of panels at ten World Mystery Conventions ("BoucherCons"), Healy also served as the banquet toastmaster for the 1996 BoucherCon and as Guest of Honor at the 1997 Dallas mystery convention.